Praise for Jennifer Joyce

'I haven't laughed so much at a b

'Great read . . . I was delighted w

'Awesome . . . Brilliant.'

'Highly amusing . . . Consumed my every waking moment.'

'Hilarious . . . I could not stop giggling
my way through this book.'

'Fun and fantastic . . . Had me giggling.'

'Charmingly funny.'

'Brilliant! . . . This book had me in stitches!'

'Pure escapism . . . Exactly what you want
from a romantic comedy.'

'Fun, fresh, current, fabulous, funny and a joy to read . . .
So many funny moments. I loved reading this book.'

JENNIFER JOYCE is a writer of romantic comedies who lives in Manchester with her two daughters and their Jack Russell, Luna. She's been scribbling down bits of stories for as long as she can remember, graduating from a pen to a typewriter and then an electronic typewriter. And she felt like the bee's knees typing on THAT. She now writes her books on a laptop (which has a proper delete button and everything).

Also by Jennifer Joyce

The Christmas Cupid

JENNIFER JOYCE

ONE PLACE. MANY STORIES

HQ
An imprint of HarperCollins*Publishers* Ltd
1 London Bridge Street
London SE1 9GF

www.harpercollins.co.uk

HarperCollins*Publishers*
1st Floor, Watermarque Building, Ringsend Road
Dublin 4, Ireland

This paperback edition 2022

1
First published in Great Britain by
HQ, an imprint of HarperCollins*Publishers* Ltd 2022

Copyright © Jennifer Joyce 2022

Jennifer Joyce asserts the moral right to be
identified as the author of this work.
A catalogue record for this book is
available from the British Library.

ISBN: 9780008581213

Printed and bound in Great Britain by CPI Group (UK) Ltd, Croydon CR0 4YY

For my amazing girls, Rianne and Isobel

Chapter 1

Christmas Eve

It's far too early to be getting up for work but I can't sleep and there's so much to do before tomorrow's festivities, so I drag myself out of bed, wrapping myself in my fluffy frog dressing gown – hood up, because the heating hasn't kicked in yet – and head into the living room. The room is festooned with glitter and reindeers and jolly Santas and the whole place is given a warm, comforting glow from the Christmas tree when I plug the fairy lights in. I feel a shiver, but I'm not sure whether it's a Christmas-is-near tingle or because it's proper frosty at half-past four in the morning. Hot chocolate. That's what this morning needs to get going. A hot chocolate and one of my neighbour's festive biscuits, because if you can't have biscuits for breakfast on Christmas Eve, when can you?

I choose something to watch while the milk's warming in the microwave, opting for one of the cheesy made-for-TV films I've recorded. I adore them, with their gorgeous winter scenery, swoon-worthy heroes and, most importantly of all, the happily ever after. This one is a re-telling of *A Christmas Carol*, and I munch on the biscuits and sip my hot chocolate while the too-busy-to-see-her-loved-ones career bitch is replayed her past to show her the error of her ways so she can have the happiest, picture-perfect Christmas at the end. Batting the biscuit crumbs off the front of my dressing gown, I grab my knitting bag and clack away with the needles while I watch the rest of the story unfold. My current knitting project is a pair of reindeer socks, which are supposed to be a gift for my mum. I've been a bit distracted over the past few days so my fingers are having to work at lightning speed to get them finished on time. Handmade gifts are much more special than shop-bought, I think, and I can't wait to see Mum's face when she opens them, to feel my chest fill with love and pride, to know that my hard work has brought a smile to her face.

But there's no smile on my face right now, not even when Career Bitch is transformed into Mrs Christmas Joy, bestowing lavish gifts on her friends and family as they sit around the lit-up Christmas tree. I don't even crack a smile when they break out into a beautifully harmonious version of 'Let It Snow' and instead throw my knitting aside so I can snatch up the remote to turn the telly off. It's no use. I can't do it. I can't pretend this is a normal Christmas because it isn't, and trying to force some Christmas spirit into myself isn't working. I've tried it all: the festive films, the seasonal treats, and the Christmas music, which is *the worst* with the smug, 'we're so in love we can't help but shout it from the snow-topped rooftops' classics, or the bouncy, 'I'm so happy I could burst into a cloud of glitter and spread yet more Christmas sparkle' party tunes, and the mushy, 'let's snog under the mistletoe' ballads. All those cheery Christmas songs can piss right off. *All of them.* I don't want to step into Christmas, or hear about how many sleeps there are until your sickly-sweet perfect boyfriend walks through the door to spend the perfect Christmas with you. Because no number of sleeps will bring *my* perfect boyfriend through the door to spend the perfect Christmas with me. Because *he dumped me* two days ago. (Three, technically,

2

I suppose, since he walked out on me after the Terrible Row. But he didn't 'officially' dump me until the day after, when he packed up his things and vacated the flat for good). So I don't care what Mariah wants for Christmas. All *I* want for Christmas is Scott, and that isn't happening because he won't even pick up when I call, or return any of my WhatsApp or Facebook messages. He's blanking me completely, which doesn't bode well for a Christmas reunion. Scott and I won't be having a merry little Christmas together if he won't even speak to me.

Who does that though? Dumps somebody three days before Christmas? (Or four, depending on how you're measuring the dumping. Storming out of the flat post-row or actually moving out?) *Scott* did that. Dumped me, completely out of the blue, over a silly row that started over him throwing his coat over the back of the chair instead of hanging it up. Yes, I may have nagged him about it a bit, but it isn't something to end a three-year relationship over.

The flat's too quiet now the telly's off. Usually, Scott would be making a comforting racket at this time in the morning as he dashed about the place, hunting for lost shoes or the 'only tie' that goes with the shirt he was wearing, or clattering about the kitchen making far more noise than is necessary while making a piece of toast. I miss that noise. The noise that reminded me I wasn't alone. Now, there is only silence and the reminders that Scott isn't here; the cool, smooth duvet on his side of the bed, the empty hangers taunting me with their rattle every time I open the wardrobe, the lack of toothpaste clumps in the bathroom sink. The sink is gleaming now, but the sight of it doesn't fill me with joy. The sparkly enamel has sucked all the happiness from my body, leaving me feeling hollow, and if I'd known that the smears of Aquafresh would be the last remnants of our cohabitation, I wouldn't have rinsed them away.

I should probably bung myself in the shower. My hair is greasier than the frying pan in the café next door after a day of cooking bacon, and my eyes are puffy from a night of snot-crying into my pillow. I probably stink and while I couldn't care less about personal hygiene right now, I'm not sure my boss would approve of me driving customers away from the shop like a reverse Lynx effect. But there's yet more reminders of Scott's absence in the bathroom, and the space where his tatty old dressing gown usually hangs from the back of the door is like a fist to the gut that takes my breath away. That dressing gown was threadbare and a weird greyish/brown colour, but it was also as comforting as a hug from my long-dead gran. Now I'll never see either of them again.

I force myself into the shower and into clean clothes but my spirits remain low, even when I pull on a pair of socks with a chirpy-looking robin in a bobble hat that usually make me smile. In another bid to cheer myself up, I pop the last three chocolates out of my advent calendar and shove them into my mouth without even bothering to note their festive shape. I haven't been in the mood for enjoying the little daily treats since Scott walked out on me, and it turns out I'm still not in the mood for them now. I'm hate-chewing the chocolates as I head out of the flat and clump down the stairs, and when I hear the door slamming above and the thunderous feet of my upstairs neighbour hot on my heels, I don't even bother to move out of the way. If she bulldozes into me and sends me tumbling down to the foyer with a snapped neck, it would probably be a blessing right now. But she manages to squeeze past me and hurtles down the stairs without even slowing her pace.

'You *did not* tell me your mother has gone vegan. What are we going to feed her tomorrow?'

One of my downstairs neighbours is ranting on the phone as she pulls her front door shut behind her. She holds up a hand in greeting as she shoots her gaze up to the ceiling and shakes her head.

'I don't have time to pop into Tesco. You'll have to grab her something before they shut . . . I have to work too! And she's *your mother* . . . I don't know – a bag of mixed leaf salad? What the hell do vegans eat? Oh, bugger. I was going to roast the potatoes in goose fat. Do you think she'll notice?'

I'm about to slip past Miranda and head out of the main door, but she grabs my arm to stop me.

'I have to go now, but make sure you get her something. I will not have the same kind of drama we had last year with her.' Miranda rolls her eyes as she ends the call and tuts. 'Men. Bloody useless, the lot of them. Oh, God. I'm *so sorry*.' Her eyes widen and she bites her lip as she shoves her phone into her cavernous handbag. 'I wasn't thinking. I mean, I was . . . I was going to ask how you are, and then I go and put my foot in it like the big idiot Pete's always telling me I am.' She tilts her head to one side. 'How *are* you, my darling? Coping okay? Because Pete and I are always here for you. You know that, right? All you have to do is pop down here and we'll crack open a bottle of wine and have a good natter. You're not on your own, okay?'

'Thanks, Miranda. That's really sweet of you.'

I like Miranda, even if she can be a bit full-on at times and she *never* stops bickering with her husband.

'What are you doing for Christmas?' Miranda wrinkles her nose. 'You're not spending it on your own, are you? Because you are *more* than welcome to join us. Lord knows, everyone else is! We've got my mum and dad, Pete's mother, his sister and her brood, and an uncle who can't keep his hands to himself.' She wrinkles her nose again. 'I'm not selling Christmas at the Wolfenden's, am I? It'll be fun, I promise. Once you get used to Bernie's wandering hands and the headache from Kath's four kids running riot has subsided. I'm looking forward to having a full house, really I am, and there's definitely room for one more.'

'It sounds great, really it does.' It sounds *horrendous*, but working in retail has really honed my diplomacy skills. 'But Franziska's already invited me round to her place for the day. She was going to be alone too, so it's nice we have each other now.' This is the *only* silver lining I've found to being dumped so far.

'Well, you just let us know if there's anything we can do.' Miranda smiles as she gives my arm a squeeze.

'Well, actually . . .' This feels a bit awkward because it has nothing to do with Scott leaving me on my own at Christmas, but it's something I've been meaning to bring up for a while. 'It's not a major problem or anything.' I glance behind me, towards the narrow hallway that leads out to the communal yard at the back of the property. 'It's just Pete's bike . . . I wouldn't say it's in the way or anything, but . . .' But I scrape my legs on its pedal every time I empty the bins. And then again on my way back up to the flat. My calves are full of bruises. 'Franziska will be putting the Christmas tree up later, and there isn't much room . . .'

'I *knew* it was in the way. I *told him.*' Miranda's mouth is screwed up tight as she rummages in her handbag. 'Don't you worry, my darling, it'll be gone by the time you get home from work.' She produces her phone, pressing it to her ear as she lifts her free hand in farewell. 'Pete! What did I tell you about that bloody bike?'

Chapter 2

'*Frohe Feiertage!*'

Having given Miranda a couple of minutes to stalk away from the building, still sniping at Pete over the phone, I'm about to push the door open and head off to work, but Franziska is standing in the doorway to her flat with a plate of German cookies in hand, and there's no way I can refuse one of those babies. Heartbreak may have robbed me of the desire to eat advent calendar chocolates, but it hasn't diminished my appetite for my neighbour's baked goods.

'Merry Christmas Eve, Franziska.' I take one of the cookies – a little delicate-looking thing with a chocolate and walnut topping.

'You are coming round tonight, aren't you?' Franziska prods the plate at me until I take another biscuit. 'To start the festivities?'

Franziska grew up in Germany, where Christmas Eve is the main celebration so in effect we're going to be having two Christmases. Ordinarily, this would be *delightful*, but this year, for obvious reasons, I'm struggling to muster the enthusiasm for one day full of joy, never mind a double dose.

'Of course I'll be here.' In body if not in spirit. 'What time do you want me?'

'The sooner the better. You have the parade this afternoon, yes? Then you are free to come home?'

Oh, God. The parade. I don't know how I'm going to get through today, but I have to, and I have to do so with a smile plastered on my face.

'If you are back in time, you can help me decorate the tree in the hall. I bought some *beautiful* glass baubles at the Christmas market yesterday and I can't wait to add them to the collection.'

This will be my first Christmas here, as Scott and I only moved into the flat over the summer, but I've heard wonderful things from Miranda about the Christmas tree Franziska erects in the communal hall every year, filling it with glass baubles and homemade cookies and sweets. I'd been really looking forward to seeing it, and do you know what, I'm going to enjoy seeing it later and I'm going to show it, even if I have to hook my fingers into the corners of my mouth and stretch them up into a display of happiness. Christmas is my favourite time of the year and I can't let it pass by in a blur of misery. I will summon Christmas joy from somewhere, even if I have to fake it.

'How is your internet working now?' I shake my head when Franziska nudges the plate of biscuits towards me again. 'Any better?'

'Much better. Thank you for fixing it for me.'

'It was nothing.' I'm not being modest here, it really was nothing. Franziska's internet was playing up a couple of weeks ago, but only because her computer was connecting to the free Wi-Fi from the café next door. The connection was so weak, she could have made herself a brew – and probably baked a batch of these delicious cookies – in the time it took to refresh her inbox.

'Well, thank you anyway. I appreciate the help and I'm all caught up with my emails.'

'How is Klaus?' I try not to smirk as I ask the question, but it's extremely difficult. Franziska will deny it until her dying breath, but the reason she was so keen to get her internet back up and running properly was so she could chat to her old friend back in Germany.

'He is fine, thank you. Now, off you go before you miss your bus. And wrap up warm. It's cold enough to freeze your danglies off out there.' Franziska winks at me before she retreats into her flat. She wasn't kidding about the weather; I'm wearing a cardi over my dress and a thick woollen coat buttoned to the chin, but I'm still taken aback by the sharpness in the air as I step out onto the street, and my feet are like blocks of ice despite thick tights, the chirpy robin socks and lace-up boots. Pulling my bobble hat firmly over my ears and forehead and re-wrapping my yellow scarf to make sure there are no gaps to let the cold air in, I set off for the bus stop, munching away at Franziska's biscuits during the short journey. Franziska may be several decades older than I am, and I've only known her a few months, but she's quickly become one of my best friends (and that's only partly due to her knack for baking).

Eventually, the bus turns up and I shuffle my way along the packed seats until I find one near the back, but I wish I'd chosen to stand instead even before my bum cheek reaches the questionably-stained seat. Because right in front of me is a couple who are clearly in the early throes of a relationship, when you can't keep your hands (or lips) off each other. And while a week ago I probably wouldn't have even *noticed* the heavy-petting pair, today I want to wedge myself in between them just to stop the public display of affection.

I know I'm being a proper Grinch, and it isn't their fault that I've been dumped, but it makes my chest ache to see them snogging and pawing at each other. I remember when Scott and I were like that, when the world shrank to just the two of us, and it wouldn't have even occurred to us that someone might take offence at our teenager-like snogging on the bus, and I can't quite believe that it's gone. The passion, the love, the relationship. All of it vanished – poof! – just like that.

Scott and I met three years ago in the toy shop where I work, while Scott was browsing for a birthday gift for his niece. I helped him choose a doll with purple hair and a sparkly T-shirt, and we flirted a little bit because why not. He was incredibly handsome and charming with the right hint of cheekiness, and I fancied him *a lot*, but I never thought anything would come of it. With the doll in hand, he thanked me for my help and headed for the cash register and that should have been it. Except we ran into each other again a few weeks later, in a bar close to the shop. We were both in there for Friday night drinks with our colleagues and it was Scott who approached me.

'Hey, Shopgirl! I owe you a *massive* thank you, because my niece *loves* the doll you suggested. She takes it *everywhere*. Let me buy you a drink. It's the least I can do after all the brownie points you scored me. I'm the *best uncle ever*, apparently.'

We got chatting, flirted a bit more, and at the end of the night when he asked for my number, I gave it to him.

'It's Zoey,' I told him, when I noticed that he was saving my contact under 'Shopgirl'. 'It's with a Y. Z. O. E. Y. Zoey Beake. Like a bird, but with an E on the end.'

'I know.' Scott slipped his phone into his pocket without correcting it. 'Not about the Y or the beak. Not until now, anyway. But you'll always be Shopgirl to me.'

When did he stop using the nickname? Because he hasn't called me Shopgirl for a long time, and I hadn't even noticed. I look away from the pawing pair and stare out of the window. There are signs of Christmas everywhere, from the hats and scarves people have bundled themselves into, to the trees in the windows we're chugging past and the wreaths on the doors. The bus is filled with a weird mix of energy, a blend of anticipation (it's Christmas tomorrow!) and fear (will I get everything ready on time?) and it's making me feel a bit queasy. It's either the strange energy swirling around the bus or the fact I've eaten three advent chocolates and several German cookies for breakfast that's making me feel a bit sickly.

It appears I'm not the only one who's feeling a bit off, as there's a girl, late teens, I'd guess, sitting across the aisle who's looking a bit twitchy, as though she doesn't know whether to remain seated or to bolt down the aisle and throw herself off at the next stop. She has a book on her lap, with her thumb holding her page, but she doesn't appear to be interested in reading it. It's a battered hardback with a faded brown cover and gold lettering, and because I'm too nosy for my own good, I lean towards her, under the pretence of scratching my calf, to see what it is she's reading.

A Christmas Carol. How apt for Christmas Eve, though she'd better get a wriggle on if she wants to finish it during the festive period because she's only about a third of the way through according to her thumb bookmark.

The bus stops and she suddenly jolts upright, and I do the same, my heart beating wildly at the prospect of being caught mid-snoop. But she isn't interested in me. Her neck is stretched giraffe-like as she tries to see around the standing passengers to the front of the bus. The bus is already jammed, with all the seats taken and not much more room for standing, but passengers pile on board, squeezing into every inch of space available. Once everybody is packed in like sardines, the bus sets off again and the girl with the book slumps in her seat. She opens the book, but I don't think she reads a word of it as we make our way into town.

I forget all about the girl with the book as soon as the bus pulls into the station. The estate agency where Scott works is off to the left, and I wonder if I have enough time to dash over to see him before my shift at the shop. He can ignore my calls and texts, but what's he going to do if I'm standing there, right in front of him? But I'd be cutting it very fine even with the briefest of visits, and there's no way I can be late today. Christmas Eve is always hectic, especially with the parade taking place this afternoon.

Shooting the estate agents a mournful look, I plough on ahead, focusing instead on the fitness tracker Scott bought me for our anniversary six weeks ago. I'm nowhere near my daily steps goal, but I'll definitely have reached it by the time the parade is over. In fact, I'll probably have set a new record, which is something

I can tell Scott if he ever gets round to speaking to me again. He'll be pleased about the achievement. I know he will.

C&L's Toys isn't even open yet, but the air is thick with frantic energy as staff dash about, ensuring everything is in place in time for opening, knowing their efforts are fruitless because by the end of the day, every floor, from the lower ground floor café to the dolls and action figures section on the second floor, will resemble a jumble sale. And it'll all have to be put back in place again in time for the Boxing Day sale.

I chat to my co-workers on my way to the staffroom, pushing a smile onto my face and exchanging festive pleasantries. Most of them don't know about my break up with Scott, and I'd like to keep it that way. It's one thing being miserable in my own head, but I don't want to bring everybody else's mood down as well. While I'm at the shop, I'm my usual happy self. I'm Zoey-with-a-smile. I'm jolly and bright. I'm a flipping Christmas elf.

Literally, *I'm a Christmas elf.* Reaching into my locker, I pull out the red-and-white stripy leggings and the itchy green-belted dress that, along with a jingly green hat and ridiculous curly-toed shoes, has made up my uniform since the toy shop's grotto opened at the beginning of November and I was temporarily moved from my usual spot in dolls and accessories to the North Pole.

Decked out in my elf outfit and pushing my heartbreak aside, I head up to the second floor to spread the festive joy I'll have to summon from somewhere very deep inside.

Chapter 3

'I Want a Hippopotamus for Christmas' is being piped into the festive village that has taken over the entire seasonal department floor space, and I squash down the urge to yell about what *I* want for Christmas (Scott), because that isn't something jolly and bright Zoey-with-a-smile would do. Instead, I push my lips into a smile so wide you could count all of my teeth if you so wished, and follow the maze of Christmas trees around to the gingerbread house. A simple shed-converted-into-a-grotto isn't good enough for our toy shop – we have a whole wonderland of festive joy for the children to enjoy, because the managing director of C&L's Toys wants to create an 'experience the little ones will never forget' when they come to visit Santa in our shop. The grotto 'experience' begins with a gingerbread forest of Christmas trees, each decorated with its own theme: dolls and accessories, Lego, dinosaurs, iced gingerbread and homemade decorations made by the kids at our weekend craft sessions, and everything else you can imagine in-between. Once you emerge from the bedecked foliage, there's a gingerbread-style cottage where I find two of my fellow grotto helpers chatting underneath one of the apple trees.

'Is the gingerbread ready today?'

I'm still Zoey-with-a-smile, even if I do sound a bit peeved as I fire the question at Shannon. She definitely drew the longest straw when it came to grotto costumes; while Milo and I are trussed up in the red and green elf get-ups, Shannon looks elegant in a floor-length cloak made of red velvet with a white fluffy fake-fur trim. She looks like a snow queen, but a nice one who wouldn't dream of casting evil, frosty spells on her land.

'Oh. Sorry.' She pulls the corners of her mouth down and gives a half shrug. 'I forgot.'

She forgot yesterday. And the day before that. And all the days she's been on shift since the grotto opened.

'No worries.' I check my watch – there are still fifteen minutes until opening, plus I'm inching closer to my daily steps goal according to my tracker. 'I'll go and grab the first batch.'

'I can go if you'd like?' Milo starts to move away from the apple tree, but I hold up a hand.

'It's fine. Really. Can you make sure the candy canes are stocked up?'

'Already done, and I've put a spare box in the gift shop booth, just in case. I think it's going to be a busy day.'

'Yes, I think it probably will be quite busy.' I smile extra-wide at Milo before I head down to the café on the lower ground floor. This will be Milo's first Christmas Eve working at C&L's as he's a seasonal temp and he has *no idea* how manic things are about to get.

I head down to the café, looking out for my best friend en route, but it's one of the other members of staff who grabs the mini cellophane-wrapped gingerbread men (people?) from the kitchen. She's already looking frazzled, her curly red hair already escaping from the net underneath her jingling reindeer antlers, so I don't hang about to wait for a quick chat with Eloise. I doubt she has time, and I better get the gingerbread people – and myself – back up to the grotto. No doubt Shannon will need chivvying along and Cliff – aka Santa Claus – will need dragging in from

14

his cigarette break (if it can be classed as a break if you haven't even started the workday yet).

'Zoey?'

I'm about to step onto the escalator that will take me up to the second floor when I hear the unmistakable clip-clop of the managing director's heels making their way towards me.

'Can I have a quick word? It's about the parade?'

Oh, God. I usually look forward to the Winter Wonderland parade that the town holds every Christmas Eve, but being broken-hearted really dampens your festive spirits, and the thought of actually taking part in the parade is like a deadweight on my shoulders. How am I supposed to spread festive cheer when all I want to do is crawl back into bed with a plate of Franziska's German cookies?

Tucking the box of gingerbread people under one arm, I cross the fingers on my free hand, hoping it's the good kind of 'quick word'. The kind where Philippa says she doesn't need me to take part in the parade after all, so I'll be free to finish early and slope off home to get stupidly drunk on Franziska's lethal gluhwein. A Christmas miracle, if you will. I can feel my festive spirits starting to stir already. Maybe I'll even help to decorate the Christmas tree in the hallway.

'We have a teeny-weeny problem.' Philippa holds up her thumb and forefinger, just a sliver of air between them. I'm hoping the teeny-weeny problem is that there are too many people taking part in the parade and they need a volunteer to step down, in which case my hand will be firmly in the air.

'We're a man down.' Philippa bites her lip and pulls her eyebrows down low. 'Due to a tummy bug. Very nasty, apparently, but I'll spare you the details. Anyway.' Philippa claps her hands together and takes a deep breath. 'I'd like you to step in.'

'Me?' I hitch the box of gingerbread to rest on my hip. 'But I'm already part of the parade.'

'Yes, as a regular elf, but we have plenty of those.' Philippa gives a dismissive wave of her hand. 'I want you to take the place as the head elf.'

'Isn't Santa head elf?' And then it dawns on me. Every Christmas, C&L's has a different theme for its seasonal displays and entertainment, and this year we have a circus theme. I take a sharp intake of breath when I realise what Philippa is suggesting here.

'Now, I'm not asking you to juggle.' She leans in close. 'Unless you can? No? It was a long shot. Anyway, you won't have to juggle, so don't worry about that.'

'But the stilts?'

Philippa beams at me. 'Piece of cake, apparently. You'll pick it up in no time. You can have a little wander around the staffroom to find your feet before the parade. It'll be fun!' Philippa beams at me and then she's gone, stalking off to no doubt spread some more good cheer.

No Christmas miracle then.

No early finish.

No getting blind drunk on Franziska's heavy-handed gluhwein.

Ho oh no.

'I can't do it. I'm going to fall flat on my face and everyone will laugh.'

I'm in the staffroom, dressed in the special head elf's outfit, which has extra-long stripy trousers to accommodate the stilts that I'm just about standing upright on, but only because I'm clinging on to the bank of lockers lining the wall. My best friend is standing across the room, her arms stretched out in front of her, her knees bent and a look of determination on her face.

'You *can* do it. And you won't fall over. You've just got to be brave and let go of the lockers.'

It sounds so easy when she says it like that, but my stomach is churning and my heart is thumping away like Animal on the drums, and there's no way my fingers are loosening their grip on the edge of the locker.

'Come on, Zoey. You can do it.' Eloise waggles her hands, ushering me forward, her eyes wide and her mouth stretched wide. I feel like she should be recording me on her phone, ready to upload to Instagram Stories (Zoey took her first steps today! #ProudMummyMoment) but it's oddly motivating and I find myself sliding my hand down the locker, peeling my fingers away slowly, until I'm standing on my own two feet. Or rather, my own two stilts.

'That's it! Well done!' Eloise claps her hands and jigs about on the spot before she stops still, knees bent once again, and waggles her hands at me. 'Try and walk towards me. Slowly. One step at a time.'

'I won't fall over?'

'You won't fall over.'

'And you won't laugh if I do?'

Eloise straightens and plants her hands on her hips. 'Absolutely not.'

'Liar.' I catch her eye and we both giggle, which causes me to wobble. My hands are clinging to the locker again before I can even *think* about falling on my arse, but Eloise is having none of it and waggles her hands again, barking instructions at me until I comply and take my first tentative step. It's a bit shaky, but my elf-shoe-clad stilt lands solidly on the ground. I take another step, then another. My arms are outstretched for balance, but it's a start. I'm actually moving across the room.

'How long have we got until we have to leave for the parade?'

I check my watch with extra care so I don't topple with the movement. 'Ten minutes.' All this practice is adding to my steps for the day. After a morning in the grotto, handing out candy canes to the kids and guiding them to the end of the queue to see Santa, the steps have really clocked up. If I get this right, I'll easily reach my goal and have something positive to say to Scott rather than simply begging him to come home. I just have to not break a leg on these bloody stilts.

'I think we need to work on your face.' Eloise stretches her arms out and takes a lumbering step while screwing up her face. 'It looks like you're more constipated with every step.'

Great. So that's one more thing to worry about, after causing myself an injury and humiliating myself.

'You're so lucky to not have to take part in this stupid thing.' I take a cautious step, concentrating both on my footwork and my facial expression, which I'm trying to keep non-constipated.

'Lucky?' Eloise snorts. 'Sensible, more like. *You* put your name down for it back in October.'

'I didn't put my name down for *this*.' I lift a stilt, which is a mistake because I start to lose my balance. It takes two shuffles back and another shuffle forward to right myself, but I manage to remain standing. 'And I thought it'd be *fun*. I had no idea I'd be feeling so miserable this Christmas.'

'Scott still hasn't been in touch?'

I shake my head. 'Not heard a word from him. I've left messages with everyone – his mum, his sister, his mates, even the woman on reception at his work. I don't know what else to do.'

'He might just need some space. It might do you both good.'

'But I don't want space from Scott.' I want to be with him. I love him. 'I just wish I had the opportunity to put things right.'

'I know.' Eloise closes the gap between us and reaches up on tiptoe so she can give me a hug. It nearly topples me over, but it's worth it. There are many reasons why Eloise Farmer is my best friend, and being a champion hugger is one of them.

'Are we ready?'

Philippa pops her head round the staffroom door, eager smile in place. I should tell her that no, I'm not ready. That I can't do this after all, because I'm about as steady on my feet as a newborn foal, but I don't. I've never been one for confrontation, and I always strive to stick to my word and not let anyone down, so I return Philippa's eager smile with a constipated-like one of my own and nod my head (very, very gently so I don't knock my balance).

'I'm ready.'

I just hope I don't live to regret those words.

Chapter 4

The Winter Wonderland Parade has taken place every Christmas Eve for the past eight years, and it grows each time, with more local businesses and community groups taking part. This is my fifth parade as part of C&L's contribution, and definitely the most difficult. In the past, I've dressed as a maid-a-milking for our '12 Days of Christmas' theme and 'milked' a papier-mâché cow on a float (and yes, it did look rather suggestive for a family event) and the turkey costume for our 'Christmas Feast' was hot and cumbersome, but the stilts are proving rather tricky. I've managed to hobble to the town square, where the procession is due to start any minute now, and although I think I'm starting to get the knack of moving with extended limbs, the parade route around the town centre seems awfully long right now.

'Zoey!' Philippa pushes her way through the crush of parade participants, and my stomach lurches. What now? Does she want me to walk a tightrope along the rows of oversized fairy lights stretched across the buildings? Tame a lion? Because these stilts are the very limit of my circus skills.

'There you are. I didn't think I'd be able to find you.'

Under normal circumstances, I'd find that hard to believe since I'm towering above normal height, but there are so many of us crammed into the space behind the town hall and I'm not the tallest object here by far. There's the giant ringmaster puppet and oversized penguins and snowmen milling around, not to mention the double decker bus with the shopping centre's Santa at the wheel (our own Santa from C&L's was most put out that he wasn't asked to do the honour).

'I grabbed this for you.' Philippa thrusts a long, lurid green cylindrical object at me. 'To make up for the lack of juggling.'

The cylindrical object is a jumbo bubble mix and wand (2 for 1 in our stocking filler section). So not only am I expected to master stilt walking, I have to do so while blowing bubbles into the crowd.

'Everyone likes bubbles, don't they! They're fun!' Philippa starts to back away, almost knocking an acrobat over as she stretches in preparation for the tricks she's about to perform during the parade. 'Anyway, good luck, and if I don't see you after the parade, merry Christmas!' She turns and squeezes her way back out of the crush just as the distant sound of a brass band starts to play 'Good King Wenceslas', marking the start of the parade. C&L's circus acts and their elf helpers are at the back of the parade, sandwiched between a troupe of little girls in reindeer costumes and a group of drummers who are warming up with some lively beats, so it's a good few minutes before we set off.

The town centre's streets are crammed with families, all wrapped up warm in hats and scarves, gloved hands clutching the promotional material that's being handed out; leaflets reminding everyone that the local panto is still running until the first week of January, paper crowns advertising food venues, balloons promoting shoe shop sales. Just ahead of me, on either side of our cartwheeling acrobat, Shannon and Milo are handing out candy canes and mini gingerbread people along with leaflets shouting about our Boxing Day sale. Although I'm concentrating on blowing bubbles towards the grinning children in the crowds while trying to remain upright, my eyes are on the lookout for

Eloise, who said she'd give me a wave. I haven't seen her yet, but we're only a third of the way around the parade route. My watch buzzes as we pass Greggs, signalling I've reached my daily steps target, and the unexpected vibration is enough to make me stumble on my stilts. I manage to remain on my feet, though my pulse rivals the beat of the drummers behind me. It's just started to slow down to a normal rhythm again when a human cracker races towards me, singing a very bad karaoke version of 'Wonderful Christmastime'. The shiny green cracker tells the worst joke ever invented before racing off to inflict his singing and jokes on the next section of the crowd.

We pass Primark and Boots, but I still haven't spotted Eloise. The little girls dressed as reindeer in front of me have performed a dance routine to 'Rudolph the Red-Nosed Reindeer' on a loop countless times and I'm starting to get a headache from the enthusiastic drumming behind, but at least the town hall square is almost in sight again, meaning we've almost completed the circuit around the town centre. Blowing bubbles into the crowd first to the right and then to the left, I scour the crowd for my best friend. Being on stilts does have its advantages, it seems, because being so tall means I have a better view. Which is how I spot them outside McDonalds. Him, braving the cold in a hoodie and ripped jeans, his closely-cropped afro hatless and exposed to the elements. Her, wrapped up in a puffy white jacket that is somehow slimming and doesn't make her resemble the Stay Puft Marshmallow Man. She looks as though she's stepped out of the pages of a magazine feature of a winter wonderland with her honey-blonde hair cascading onto her shoulders from underneath a baby-pink bobble hat. Her hands are clad in matching mittens while a super-thick scarf is wound around her neck so only her eyes, nose and rosy cheeks are visible. Beneath the jacket, she's wearing a super-short white skirt with vertical black-and-grey stripes over thick tights that show off an amazing pair of legs that my stilts and I simply cannot compete with.

What is he doing here? Scott never attends the parade. He says it's for kids, and he's always too busy at work but, judging by the casual attire, he hasn't even been to the office today.

Also, *who is this goddess he is with*? Because she isn't a stranger to Scott; she's resting her pretty little head on his shoulder, for goodness' sake, and he's got his arm wrapped around her waist. I'm finding it difficult to drag myself out of bed each morning and *he's got himself a shiny new girlfriend*? And she is shiny, but not in a greasy-skinned kind of way. She's glowing and dewy and looks blissfully happy with the man who dumped me *three days* ago (two, officially).

How is this possible? How can he have forgotten about me so quickly and moved on? Didn't I mean *anything* to him?

'Watch out!' The drummer has to shout over the din of the music but it's too late and he collides with me. I hadn't realised I'd come to a standstill but the huge drum pushes into me and I lurch to the side, tripping over my stupid clunky elf shoes. But I'm okay – a bit wobbly, but upright. Like Elton John, I'm still standing, dignity (pretty much) intact. It's the collective gasp that alerts me to the impending doom. My inner celebrations come to an abrupt end as I twist my body and clock the double decker looming dangerously close. It's going at a snail's pace but the shopping centre Santa isn't paying attention as he drives, his focus instead on the crowds as he waves to the good girls and boys. My instinct is to leap out of the way but my movement is impeded by the stupid stilts and although the bus is barely moving, it clips me on the shoulder as I turn away and knocks me off my feet. The bubble mixture tube flies from my hand, sending an arc of liquid in the air, and I sort of twist as I stagger forwards, so when I fall to the ground, I land flat on my back, my head smacking against the tarmac.

It's a strange feeling as I lay there on the tarmac, looking up at the string of Christmas lights against the grey, overcast sky. My shoulder is throbbing from the impact with the Santa Express bus, and I feel like I could throw up, but I don't feel embarrassed or afraid. I feel . . . light. I don't even appear to be bothered about Scott and the new girlfriend anymore, which is very strange indeed and I'd laugh if I wasn't so winded.

I try to sit up, but my head smarts from its impromptu meeting with the tarmac, so I stay very still and instead close my eyes, because a nice deep sleep seems like a very good idea right about now.

Chapter 5

I don't know how long I sleep for. It should be hours, since I awake feeling refreshed, the pain in my shoulder and head now completely gone, but it can't have been more than a few minutes because the crowds are still gathered on the pavement, their collective chatter creating a loud hum as I pick myself up from the ground with ungainly effort. Each footstep feels spongy, as though I'm sinking into dry sand on the beach, which isn't helped by the unwieldy stilts.

'Zoey!'

I hear somebody calling my name, but I ignore it. What if it's Philippa, instructing me to hurry up and finish off the parade? Or worse, what if it's Scott with the new girlfriend in tow?

'Zoey!'

I turn around on the sand-like tarmac, frowning at the scene in front of me. There's an ambulance, with a paramedic crew trying to revive some poor soul. A poor soul with unnaturally long legs clad in stripy trousers. Her glasses are wonky on her face, but nobody seems to have noticed, and her green elf hat is lying abandoned on the road. The shopping centre Santa is sitting on the pavement, his hat and beard by his feet and his head in his hands, while policemen try to keep the gawping crowds back. I

24

can no longer hear the hum of the crowd, only my name being called with increasing volume.

'Zoey?'

It isn't Philippa, or Scott, or even Eloise. I'm not sure who this woman walking towards me is. She's wearing a long, white dress and a golden crown and looks a bit like a picture of the *Christkind* in one of Franziska's books. She must be part of the parade.

'It's so lovely to see you again.'

She smiles at me, and I know then that she isn't part of the parade. That she isn't the *Christkind*. She's an old woman in a white nightie and an orange paper crown from a Christmas cracker on her head.

'Gran?' My voice is hoarse, my throat dry and scratchy as though I haven't spoken for weeks, and the backs of my eyes burn intensely. 'What are you . . .? You're . . .' I swallow against the grainy feeling in my throat, unable to finish my sentences, physically or emotionally.

'I'm dead.' Gran nods and sighs. 'Happens to us all, I'm afraid. Even you.'

She turns, and I follow her gaze to the poor soul on the ground. I want to crouch down and nudge her glasses back into place. Why hasn't anybody noticed her glasses are so lopsided? Of all the things that should bother me, it's this. Not the look of determination as the paramedic pumps away at my chest. Not the horror on the faces of the kids in the crowd who will remember this Christmas Eve forever for all the wrong reasons. Not even the delight of the drama of it all from some of the adults. No, it's the glasses that get to me.

'It was the knock to the head that did it. Trauma to the brain.' Gran turns back to me, the lines in her forehead deepening. 'You didn't suffer, did you?'

I shake my head. 'It hurt, but not enough to kill me.' I take a step towards my body. The paramedic is still trying to resuscitate me, putting every last bit of energy into saving me. *Keep going.*

Save me. Bring me back. I want to scream the words at her, but nothing will come out.

'She wouldn't be able to hear you even if you screamed until your lungs popped.' Gran says this as though I said the words out loud. 'She can't see you. None of them can. We're not really here, you see.'

'Then where are we?'

Gran tilts her head to one side and rubs her cheek with a wrinkled hand. 'I'm not sure. A sort of in-between place. Neither here nor there.' Gran reaches out and touches my cheek, smiling at me. My eyes sting again at the contact. I haven't felt Gran's touch since I was a kid. She died when I was nine or ten – a decade and a half ago. 'You're not ready to go yet. It shouldn't be your time.'

'So I'm going to live?' I turn back to the paramedic. The poor woman must be exhausted, but she has to carry on.

'Sort of.' I tear my eyes away from the paramedic as Gran takes my hand in hers. Her skin feels cool and fragile, as though it could tear without a delicate touch. 'You're lucky. You're being given a second chance.'

'I'm going to live?' I turn back to the paramedic, but she's no longer performing chest compressions. She looks defeated but resigned to the fact that she did her best but hasn't been able to revive me.

Don't stop! Carry on! I'm allowed to live!

'It's okay.' With her hand on my cheek, Gran turns my face away from the scene of the accident. 'That's not important.'

Not important? I'm *dead*.

'You're being given a second chance at life, Zoey. You're very lucky – not many people are given the opportunity. But it doesn't come for free.'

Well, that's just great. Because Christmas is the time I'm most flush, especially when my boyfriend has left me with sole responsibility for the rent and bills of our flat.

'I'm not talking about money, you silly sausage.' Gran tinkles out a laugh, and suddenly I'm four years old, searching for Gran as we play hide and seek. She giggles as I pass the pantry, so I open the door and there she is. *Found you!* 'You're being given a task, and if you fulfil it, you won't be hit by the Santa Express on Christmas Eve.'

'And if I don't?'

I jump as Gran claps her hands together, the noise jarring against the silence. 'Then you're taking the Santa Express to the next life.'

Harsh, but to the point.

'What do I have to do?'

Gran smiles, the lines at the corners of her eyes crinkling into deep crevices. 'You must spread some festive joy.'

Easy! I can do that. I've been an elf since November – it's literally my job to spread Christmas joy. Admittedly, I haven't been much good at it over the past few days, but it hadn't been a matter of life and death then.

'You'll go back to 1st December, and it's your job to bring together six couples before the Santa Express hits you on Christmas Eve. They have to be proper love matches, mind you. No extramarital affairs, or one-night stands.'

'Like a Christmas Cupid?'

Gran's face lights up. 'Exactly that! Bring together six couples and you get to live. What do you say?'

'I say yes, obviously. Let's do it. Six couples before the bus hits me on Christmas Eve.' I can do that. Right?

Gran leans in and kisses me on the cheek. 'Good luck.'

I open my mouth to thank her, but the words won't come. The letters are a jumble in my brain as the hum of the crowd starts again.

'Just remember one thing: don't waste your time on relationships that are never going to work. Sometimes it's better all round to call it quits and move on.'

The hum of the crowd gets louder and louder until it feels like my brain will explode. Shoving my hands over my ears to block out the din, I squeeze my eyes shut as a wave of dizziness descends. My legs feel weak and I find myself on my knees, sinking into the soft, grainy tarmac. A strangled cry erupts from my mouth as fear bubbles up from my gut. I don't like this. I've changed my mind. I don't want to do this. But it's too late. The noise grows even louder and I slump on the ground in the foetal position, tucking myself up as small as possible.

And then the noise ceases. There is nothing but silence and blackness. I blink and it's far too bright. I squeeze my eyes shut before easing one open again, very slowly. Street lighting is beaming into the room through too-thin curtains but I manage to open my eyes fully. I'm no longer on the tarmac watching my lifeless body being transferred into the ambulance. I'm in bed, and I'm not alone.

What the hell!

It can't be true, can it? What Gran said?

Being careful not to wake Scott, I slip out of bed and tiptoe into the living room. The tree is no longer standing in the corner and all the festive knick-knacks I put out on the mantlepiece have vanished. My little family of nutcrackers aren't lined up on the shelf and there isn't the hint of cinnamon and spiced orange in the air from my candles. The only sign of Christmas is my advent calendar, propped up on the breakfast bar. When I creep towards it for a closer inspection, I find all the windows are sealed shut and my watch tells me it's 1st December, 7:16 a.m.

What the actual hell?

I pad back into the living room area and turn the telly on, sinking onto the sofa as my knees turn to jelly when I see the news report. A goat escaped a petting zoo and ended up in someone's back garden, where it chomped its way through the winter veg she was growing to eat on Christmas Day. I'd thought it was funny when I heard the report almost a month ago, because the woman had mistaken the goat for her dog for almost half an hour before she clocked it wasn't her beloved Dougie.

'I kept calling Dougie in for his breakfast, but he wasn't interested, which is very unusual.' The woman, Patricia from Bolton, frowns at the camera while she rubs Dougie's ears. 'And it was confusing, how Dougie had let himself out into the garden. Because he can't open doors, you see, never mind unlock them.'

I'd burst out laughing first-time round, because Patricia from Bolton looked genuinely confused at the dog-versus-locked-door situation, but the humour is buried deep beneath my own incomprehension this time round. I should be dead, but I'm sitting on my sofa, in my living room, very much alive.

'Daft old cow.' Scott scratches himself as he wanders across the living area to the kitchen, where he wiggles the kettle to check its contents. 'How can you mistake a goat for a dog? Especially one the size of a rat? That goat probably has bigger turds than Dougie.' He plonks the kettle down and flicks it on. 'Make us a brew while I jump in the shower, will you? I've got a breakfast meeting and I'm running late.'

I'm not dead. But even stranger, I've somehow been transported back in time and have been given the chance to change things so I don't end up being hit by that bus on Christmas Eve.

Chapter 6

'Zo?'

Patricia from Bolton and Yorkshire Terrier Dougie have disappeared from the TV screen and have been replaced by a 'news' story about a minor celebrity being 'caught' buying a trolley full of booze from a *discount supermarket*, but I don't notice the transition until Scott nudges me out of my reverie.

'Sorry, what did you say?' I fake yawn and stretch my arms above my head. 'Still half asleep.'

How is this even possible? How can a person get mowed down by a crawling bus one minute, resulting in their tragic death, and then be sitting in their living room, very much alive, the next? It doesn't make sense, because I *know* it isn't possible. Am I actually dead and this is my heaven? Because there's nobody I'd rather spend eternity with than Scott. But Scott is still alive, cosying up to that other woman in the pink bobble hat, so how could he be here with me?

Maybe I didn't die at all. Maybe I hit my head and slipped into a coma and I imagined all that stuff with Gran. Which would mean I'm still unconscious and dreaming up this very moment. I'm not in my living room with Scott. I'm . . . where? The hospital, most likely.

'Zo? Hello?' Scott throws his eyes up to the ceiling when I focus on him again. 'Can you make me a brew while I jump in the shower? Kettle's on.'

'Yeah, of course.'

'Thanks.' Scott plants a kiss on my head. 'You're an angel.'

A cup of tea is the least I can do, really, since the last time I woke up Scott wasn't even living in the flat anymore. I'd make him all the cups of tea in the world if it meant he'd stay.

I sit ramrod straight on the sofa, and a light bulb would be pinging above my head if I were a cartoon character. *I'd make him all the cups of tea in the world if it meant he'd stay.* Now, it would probably take more than a few cups of tea, but I *could* make him stay, if I really put my mind to it. Preventing the Terrible Row would be a good idea, and, in the meantime, I could present myself as the perfect girlfriend. Show Scott that I'm worth sticking around for. That he couldn't find a better replacement, and especially not that shiny, catalogue-cute girl I saw him with earlier (or later, in the future. Whatever). If it's the 1st December now and the Terrible Row happened on the 21st, that gives me just shy of three weeks to save my relationship. I have no idea if any of this is real, but I have to give it a go, just in case.

Springing up from the sofa, I skuttle across the open-plan room to the kitchen, grabbing the Man U mug from the cupboard and popping a teabag inside. Toast! I'll make toast to go with the tea so I can send Scott off to work with a full tummy. The tea and toast is waiting on the breakfast bar by the time Scott wanders back into the room with just a towel slung around his waist. It may be December, but it's suddenly very hot in the flat. I have to do *whatever it takes* to fix our broken relationship, because I can't lose him all over again.

'Thanks, babe.' Scott scoops the mug from the breakfast bar and takes a noisy slurp as he heads for the door again.

'I made you some toast.' I hold the plate out towards Scott, but he doesn't even slow his stride, never mind stop and turn around.

'I told you I have a breakfast meeting. There'll be pastries and stuff so I don't want to fill up before I get there.'

At least that's what I think he says, as he's already left the room and his voice grows quieter as he heads down the hall to the bedroom.

I get myself showered and changed once Scott has left for work, and I'm horrified when I clock my fringe in the bathroom mirror. It was still a bit wonky by the time I was hit by the Santa Express bus, but at least it was starting to inch its way back down towards my eyebrows. Now it's wonky *and* far too short, but then of course it is because it was only a couple of days ago that I hacked at it with the kitchen scissors to try to rectify the butchered job the trainee hairdresser had performed (that I was too polite to point out and demand it was fixed there and then, and subsequently made worse once at home). I try to pull it down to a more reasonable level, but it refuses to stay anywhere but a few inches away from my hairline (as it did the first-time round, and no amount of straightening or hairspray would change the fact that my fringe was hideous, so I don't bother this time). Still, at least I can cover it with my elf hat at work, and it's certainly bobble hat weather for the journey there and back.

I can't find my favourite mustard-yellow scarf with the over-sized pompom trim as I'm getting ready to leave the flat, so I have to make do with the blue and white pompom-less one I find tucked into the sleeve of my old black parka. The pale blue clashes with the emerald-green of my woollen coat, but then my clothes are always a mishmash of shades. My mum says I look like I've stumbled blindfolded into a charity shop, grabbed hold of the first six items I've fallen upon and thrown them on (but in a cute, quirky way, apparently). Today, for example, I'm wearing an orange pleated skirt and a royal-blue knitted jumper with cable-knit grey tights and my favourite brown brogues, which sounds like a dreadful combo but I think it works, in a cute, quirky way. Besides, I'm alive, which matters far more than my wardrobe selection.

Making sure my hat – which is burnt orange with pointy fox ears that matches neither my scarf nor my gloves – covers my dodgy-looking fringe, I set off for the bus stop, marvelling at the lack of festive touches on the way. The simple but majestic-looking potted fir tree outside my upstairs neighbour's flat is missing, as is Miranda and Pete's 'Santa, Please Stop Here' sign from their front door and Franziska's oversized wreath isn't filling the hallway with the Christmassy smells of pine and cinnamon. There's a set of multicoloured fairy lights in the window of the café next door, but the glittery snowflake stickers are missing, along (thankfully) with the creepy-looking Santa Claus figure who has been eyeing me from the ledge every morning and evening.

There are a few hints of the season during the bus ride into town, with the odd Christmas tree standing in the windows of houses, but the abundance of festive spirit I've become accustomed to over the past couple of weeks is missing, making the streets look barren. This all changes as soon as C&L's Toys comes into view. The imposing four-storey Victorian building is lit up with twinkling garlands above the doors and windows, and the huge floor-to-ceiling windows of the ground floor are dressed with this year's circus theme. The first window I come to is backdropped with a red glitter curtain while a giant snow globe sits in the centre. Inside, a mechanical clown juggles Christmas puddings while mechanical trapeze artists swoop down to pass a gift-wrapped parcel between them above. It's mesmerising, but I have to get inside. Passing the other window displays, I head for the alley to the side of the shop and duck into the staff entrance, waving hello to Cliff, who's puffing on his e-cig by the industrial-sized bins. I really, really want to head down to the lower ground floor café in search of Eloise so I can offload the craziness that has rained down on me (and to also inhale a mince pie or three. My appetite has returned with a vengeance now Scott is back where he belongs) but there are a couple of hurdles in the way:

1) Eloise will think I've gone absolutely potty if I tell her I was hit by a Santa-driven bus, died, spoke to my gran who's been dead for fifteen years, before coming back to life and

2) The shop is opening in less than ten minutes and I haven't even changed into my elf costume yet.

The shop is nowhere near as busy as it was yesterday (or three-and-a-half weeks in the future. Honestly, this time-hop thing is giving me more of a headache than cracking my skull on the tarmac did). The grotto is so quiet, I'm relieved of my candy-cane-distributing duties in the North Pole area and seconded to the gift-wrapping station on the ground floor. There's enough of a gap between customers that I can take my time over the presentation, ensuring the bows are placed just so and the ribbon is at maximum curl, but not so much that I'm left hanging around with nothing to do. The trickier-to-wrap toys are usually the ones that end up at the gift-wrapping station, but I've perfected the art of making even the most oddly-shaped objects look beautifully presented after watching many, many YouTube videos and I'm in the middle of wrapping an arctic fox stuffed toy when my watch pings. Which is odd because there's no way I've managed to reach my daily steps goal already.

Six? That can't be right. It's more than six steps from my bed to the bathroom. But there's a six flashing on my watch, alternating with a heart with a crack down the middle. I shake my wrist, to see if it fixes the glitch, but the flashing heart and number continues. Broken heart, six. Broken heart, six. Broken heart, six. What the . . .?

And then it dawns on me. The mission Gran gave me before I was brought back to life. The Christmas Cupid mission, to matchmake six couples before the end of the parade on Christmas Eve. I'd forgotten all about my agreement to carry out the task in all the excitement of possibly being alive and seeing Scott again (especially in that little towel) but I have to do this, because what's the point in keeping hold of Scott and avoiding the Terrible Row if I'm going to end up dead as a doornail a few days later?

But where to start? I've never matchmade in my life, have never even set any of my friends up on dates (pre-Scott, I'd had trouble securing dates of my own, never mind successfully pairing up other people) and I'm hardly inundated with queries of the romantic kind. I am not the person people turn to when they're unlucky in love, so without prior experience or the opportunity to try out a new matchmaking skill, what's a girl supposed to do? Drag people together off the street, *Streetmate*-style?

'Bobby, put that down. *Now*.' The woman who's waiting for the gift-wrapped arctic fox wrenches her son away from the circular display of stuffed rabbit toys based on the shop's mascots and tosses the mini bunny plush back into the pile. 'You chose the fox. The lady is wrapping it up for Santa.' She wrestles her son into his buggy while I finish up the gift-wrapping as quickly as possible, waving them off as the boy squeals and fumbles with the clasp keeping him strapped in place. Poor woman. We see this often at this time of year; parents trying their best to get everything ready for Christmas while the excitement bubbles in their offspring, spilling over when it all becomes too much. Granted, it usually takes a little bit longer than the first day in December and it doesn't really boil over until the final few days before Santa's scheduled chimney-drop, but we all react differently when put under pressure. I, for example, seem to be taking this whole back-from-the-dead thing in my stride when I'm sure I should be a gibbering wreck. Instead of freaking out, I'm plucking the bunny plush from the pile of monkey plush toys and returning it to its rightful place as though this is a normal day at work.

'Zoey?' Milo rests his hands on the counter as I return to the gift-wrap station, his cheeks flushed beyond the artificial rosy-red circles of his elf persona. 'You're needed in the grotto. A parent and toddler group have just arrived and it's got a little bit busy up there.'

I don't know Milo very well – he only started working in the grotto midway through November, after the last photographer was sacked for harassing the mums for their phone numbers and sending unsolicited dick pics to the unfortunate ones he wore down – but I do know that Milo is so laidback, he may as well be horizontal, and if he says it's 'busy', it must be frantic up there.

'Dominic's going to cover the wrapping station.' Milo pushes himself away from the counter and starts to walk backwards. 'He's just unpacking a new delivery of crayons and then he'll be over. I need to go and grab another box of gingerbread men – Shannon forgot to stock up this morning. I'll see you up in the grotto.' He turns and legs it towards the escalators, his fast footwork skillfully dodging a remote control car that comes flying his way.

I pop the 'Back in 5 Minutes' sign up on the counter and head for the escalators, cautious of wayward cars. The last thing I want to do is end up falling over again. I'm not sure I'd be given a third chance at life if I smashed my skull on another floor.

Chapter 7

I'm frazzled by the time we wave goodbye to the last toddler and his mum, drained of all energy so that I can't even muster a whimper of relief as they disappear from view. That boy was a devil-child who decided the mechanical reindeer in the North Pole section was a bucking broncho and almost wrenched its antlers off as he rode it while screeching his little head off as his mum and two of her friends attempted to drag him off the very expensive piece of festive equipment. His mini gingerbread person has been deposited in soggy little clumps around the Santa's workshop set, and Cliff has had to take himself off outside for a quick puff on his e-cig to recover after the little turd fish-hooked him with his moist, sticky, gingerbready fingers as he attempted to cling on to Santa when it was time to leave the grotto, almost detaching Cliff's bottom lip from his face. Still, Milo managed to snap a photo of the ghastly moment, which is giving us all a giggle as we gather at the photo gift station.

'We should print it on a mug and give it to Cliff for Christmas.' Shannon's eyes light up. 'Or a cushion! This would look *hilarious* blown-up on a cushion.'

'For us, maybe, but I'm not quite sure Cliff would see the humour.' Milo switches his camera off. 'I'm going to see if he's okay out there. Give us a shout if any more delightful tots show up.'

With Milo and Cliff out the back and Shannon . . . wherever she's wandered off to, I grab a broom and give the North Pole a quick tidy up, musing over my Christmas Cupid predicament as I sweep up gingerbread crumbs and stray bits of glitter and fake snow. I had a bit of a brainwave earlier: what if I set up a single parents' dating agency? I have a steady stream of parents at my fingertips – some of them must be single, and what better time to find your soulmate than Christmas? But when I did a bit of impromptu market research in the North Pole, the results weren't as encouraging as I'd have liked.

'If only,' one of the mums answered when I enquired whether she was a single parent ('I'm taking a quick survey for marketing purposes,' I'd fibbed). 'Having a husband is like having a fourth child, except I can't ground him when he misbehaves.'

'So you wouldn't be interested in joining a dating agency aimed specifically at single parents?'

The woman had snorted her derision. 'Believe me, if I was single, I'd do everything in my power to stay that way. Harper, can you *please* stop eating the snow. That stuff isn't toxic, is it?'

I didn't bother continuing my enquiries, mostly because I felt like I was intruding on these women's lives as they attempted to get through the Santa visit with their child – and their sanity – intact. I may as well have been creepy Ewan with his dick pics (which were definitely not the kind of photos he was paid to take and distribute to our customers).

So now I'm back at square one, with six couples to matchmake and not a clue how to do it. I'm hoping Eloise can be of assistance when I pop down to the café for a mince pie break mid-morning. Maureen, who's in charge of the shop's café, bakes the mince pies herself and they're delicious, with a buttery, melt-in-the-mouth pastry and just the right amount of spiced fruit filling and a generous dusting of icing sugar on top. My tea breaks with Eloise are my favourite part of the day, and they're made extra special when there are festive treats on offer.

'Do you know any single people who are looking for a date?'

I only have fifteen minutes for my morning break, and I've already used up five of them by nipping to the loo and queuing for my tea and mince pie, so I get straight to the point, even before Eloise has plonked her bum on the chair opposite mine.

'Why? Have you dumped Scott?' Eloise drops into the chair and leans across the table towards me, her eyes all wide and eager. 'Have you finally had enough of his lazy, selfish ways? God, you're keen. When Annie finished with me, it took me six months to get over her, and we weren't even living together or anything.'

There's a lot to unpick here. Firstly, Scott isn't lazy or selfish. He's very hardworking and very sweet. He may not be a fan of big gestures, but he always brings me a treat from the bakery across the road from the estate agents on a Friday evening, which is a delicious way to start the weekend, and he bought me the fitness tracker for our anniversary because he wants me to be healthy, despite my obsession with sugar-laden snacks. And secondly, I'm not sure Eloise *is* over Annie, even now, a year after the relationship – if you can call it that – finally limped to an end. In fact, Eloise thought they'd got back together a few months ago, but it turned out Annie was 'a bit bored and nostalgic' and the 'getting back together' turned out to be a one-night stand. Which finally dawned on Eloise after a week of ignored calls and texts.

But I don't have time to go into all this. I have less than ten minutes now and I haven't even touched my mince pie.

'The dates aren't for me.' I break off a chunk of pastry and the filling oozes out onto my plate. 'I want to spread some festive joy by bringing couples together in time for Christmas.'

'You mean the elf shoes aren't enough to spread festive joy? Or the big ears and rosy cheeks? What about the jingly hat?' Eloise flicks the bell on the end of my green elf hat, smirking to herself. It's okay for Eloise, working down here in the café. Her festive costume consists of a holly-filled tabard instead of her usual pink gingham one, and she won't even start to wear her antler headband until mid-December.

'Shut up.' I nudge her foot with mine under the table as I swipe the hat off my head. But this only makes Eloise burst into laughter when she clocks my dodgy fringe. She smothers her mirth with her hand and tells me that my hair is fine – *absolutely fine, it was just a bit of a shock, that's all* – but it's too late. I plonk the hat back on and shove the mince pie crust into my mouth. Why couldn't I have hopped back a few days earlier so I had the chance to cancel that bloody hairdressing appointment?

The mince pie cheers me slightly, but the effects have well and truly worn off by the time I trudge home after the longest bus journey known to man. Usually a ten-to-fifteen-minute ride, the constant stopping and starting extended the time to infinity, and I'm left with a swirly, queasy tummy by the time I'm released onto the pavement. The blast of cold air as I step off the bus is a blessed relief, and I'm feeling a bit more refreshed by the time I spot Franziska wrestling a bazillion carrier bags out of the boot of a taxi. She's attempting to hook the lot onto her wrists while the driver sits in the car, oblivious – or not – to her struggle. Hurrying over, I relieve my neighbour of half the burden and we make our way inside.

'I hope you didn't tip him.' I glare behind me at the taxi as it pulls away before following Franziska into the hallway, trying to juggle the weight of the bags while she unlocks her front door. 'Did you leave anything on the supermarket shelves for everyone else?'

Franziska uses her elbow to push the door open. 'It's December. My Christmas baking starts in earnest first thing tomorrow.'

My mood starts to lift again. With these few weeks to replay, I get to eat Franziska's sweet treats all over again: *spitzbuben* – raspberry or chocolate sandwich biscuits, both as delicious as the other –plum and almond tart, apple cake, and *lebkuchen,* all baked using recipes passed down to Franziska from her grandmother.

'Tobias, Debbie and the little ones are visiting at the weekend, so I'm making their favourites.' Franziska uses her elbow again, this time to switch on the hallway light. 'I've already made stollen. You'll have a slice with me, won't you? And a nice cup of tea?'

How could I refuse a slice of authentic German stollen, packed with spiced, rum-soaked fruit and marzipan? Besides, do calories even count if you know you're going to be offed by a double decker bus in less than three weeks? Because my hopes for winning this Christmas Cupid game aren't terribly high. How am I supposed to play matchmaker when my own love life is about to hit the self-destruct button and I'll end up on the singleton scrapheap myself?

'Make yourself comfortable.' The lamp has been left on in Franziska's living room, and it's casting a warm glow around the room. 'I'll pop the kettle on and throw this lot in the kitchen and you can tell me why you're looking so glum.'

I open my mouth to protest, but what's the point? I'm *feeling* glum and I've never been very good at masking my emotions, so my dejection will be on display for all to see.

'It isn't still about the fringe, is it?' Like my own flat upstairs, the living area and the kitchen are open plan, and Franziska is busy opening cupboards and throwing bags of flour, dried fruits and nuts into them. 'Because like I've said before, it'll grow back in no time.'

Dumping the carrier bags I'm holding to my feet, I reach up and touch my hair. My hat! I was so hot and stressed on the bus, I took it off, and then I was so eager to disembark I left it behind on the seat. I made that hat myself, knitting an owl version for Eloise so we could sport woodland creature hats together (in a cute and quirky way) and now my fox hat is making its way to Manchester city centre without me.

'I left my hat on the bus.' I pick the bags up and carry them to the kitchen, where Franziska takes them from me before shooing me back towards the seating area.

'I'm sure somebody will hand it in to the driver, or it will end up in the lost and found at the depot. We will telephone them first thing in the morning.' Franziska smiles kindly at me from the kitchen, and I feel better with just that small gesture, but Franziska has that effect on people. She's a very calming influence when she needs to be, and she took me under her wing when Scott and I moved into the building over the summer. She offered tea and cake to me and Scott and the movers, and she introduced us to Miranda and Pete and our upstairs neighbour, Isla, and that evening, when the flat was a chaotic mess of boxes and bags, she insisted I join her out in the courtyard for a glass of wine. The concrete yard at the back of the property has been transformed into a little oasis of calm and beauty, with potted trees and shrubs, blooming, scented flowers and a little set of bistro-style table and chairs. Franziska and I sat out in the sunshine until the bottle of wine was empty and Scott came to find me because I'd forgotten all about the casserole Mum had made for us, which I'd left in the oven and was now burnt to a crisp.

Having Franziska downstairs is a godsend, and not just because she's a feeder. Franziska is like a bonus Mum, someone always on hand to dispense advice and unwind with after a stressful day at work. But the relationship isn't all one way; Franziska often says I'm like another daughter, and I help her as much as I can with technical stuff – showing her how to use Netflix, setting her up on Facebook so she can keep up to date with her grandchildren, and 'fixing' her internet. Without me, she'd be waiting for weeks for Klaus' email to open.

A light bulb pings above my head. Franziska. Klaus. The emails they've been exchanging for the past couple of months. I know the story of Klaus, Franziska's first love: they were together for six years, back when Franziska was still in Germany, until Franziska decided she wanted to travel, to see the world before settling down. Klaus wanted something entirely different; he wanted to remain in Germany and take over the family tailoring business, so they broke up and Franziska set off on an adventure, eventually settling down in England and marrying Derek, the second love of her life. And Franziska lived happily ever after with Derek and their two children, until ten years ago when her husband passed away.

And Klaus has had a happy life too. He married, had children of his own, which Franziska found out when Klaus stumbled found her on Facebook and sent her a friendly, 'how are you doing after all these years' type of message, which kick-started the email exchanges. Klaus is divorced now. Has been for nearly eight years.

The light bulb above my head brightens as I wonder if this Christmas Cupid thing would work over email . . .

Chapter 8

I'm so invested in the Franziska/Klaus match that I'm daydreaming about what my bridesmaid dress will look like by the time Franziska sets the tea tray down on her walnut coffee table. I'm thinking something cut just below the knee, with a netted underskirt to make it sticky-out and twirly. Fifties-style, in a bold colour or print. Royal blue with oversized polka dots, or mint green with bright pink flamingos. Not classic bridesmaid wear, granted, but I think it could work. Franziska's granddaughter will obviously be a bridesmaid too, and the grandsons can be pageboys, if a twelve and nine-year-old would be up for that.

'Does Klaus have grandchildren?'

Franziska passes me a dainty China plate holding a huge slab of stollen. 'He does. Five, I believe. He is besotted. Posts photos of them on his Facebook all the time. It's very sweet, but Klaus was always a good man.' She perches on the armchair so she can fuss about with the tea. 'Why do you ask?'

'I was just wondering.' I wonder what the ratio of girls to boys is, and what the maximum number of pageboys is deemed acceptable? I don't think there's a limit on bridesmaids, but you never seem to see the same rule applied to pageboys.

'He doesn't get to see the youngest very often, which I know bothers him. His mother, Beatrice, and her husband moved to Switzerland a few years ago, before Daniel was born. Beatrice's work, I think. Klaus is very proud of his daughter, but it must be hard, not seeing them so often. My Tobias and his family only live an hour or so away, and that is hard enough. I'm really looking forward to their visit tomorrow. I'm going to take Georgia to see Santa Claus at your grotto – Toby is too old now, and Bradley is like a shadow to his brother, so he will not want to go either, but we will find something fun to do. And, of course, I am going to feed them all my cakes and cookies.'

On that note, I tuck into the stollen, which is *amazing* and so much better than the mass-produced stuff from the supermarket. I wonder who the lucky person will be who moves into my flat with the added bonus of Franziska's baking after I'm slain by the tarmac on Christmas Eve . . .

But no. No negative thoughts. It's only Day One of this Christmas Cupid thing and I already have my first couple lined up. They were in love once before and the fondness for one another doesn't seem to have faded, so hopefully they'll need only the smallest of nudges to reignite the flame.

'So. You and Klaus. Do you have any plans to meet up?'

Franziska holds out a cup of tea, and I balance the plate of stollen on my lap so I can take it.

'Goodness, no. It's been far too long for anything like that. It is nice to catch up though. Like a little visit to memory lane.' Franziska takes a sip of her tea. 'Klaus has mentioned the video calling thing a couple of times, like I do with Georgia and the boys, but I am not keen. I keep putting him off.'

'Why?'

Franziska places her teacup down on her saucer and clasps her hands together, a small smile playing at her lips. 'It has been fifty years since I saw Klaus. I was in my early twenties, not the wrinkled old lady I am now.'

'First of all, you are not old and wrinkly.' I don't know if it's excellent genes, or all the Zumba and kickboxing Franziska does, or whether she uses a bloody good night cream, but there's barely a crease on the woman's face. She has more energy than anybody I know, and she is usually fearless. For her seventieth birthday, the woman threw herself out of a plane for a charity sky-dive, for goodness' sake. 'And second of all, aren't you interested in what Klaus looks like now?'

Franziska rolls her eyes as she reaches for her plate of stollen. 'Oh, I know what Klaus looks like now. He is so very vain. Always posting photographs of himself on Facebook.' She chuckles and breaks off a piece of marzipan-enriched cake.

'I think you should go for it. You only live once.' At least, most people do. 'Seeing someone's photo and swapping emails isn't the same as seeing someone live and having an actual conversation. I can help you, if you'd like?'

Franziska lifts one shoulder in a shrug as she chews. 'I will think about it.'

Pete's hanging the 'Santa, Please Stop Here' sign on his front door when I leave Franziska's flat, full of stollen and tea and hope that I can get Franziska on board and fulfil part one of my task. He rolls his eyes as he points at the sign, but he's smiling.

'I have no idea why Miranda insists we put this up every year. We don't even have kids.' He lifts a fist with his thumb sticking up, which he bends down. 'Firmly under the thumb, I am.' He chuckles as he returns to his task while I fling myself up the stairs. Scott's lounging on the sofa when I step into the living room, and I have to pinch myself to prove that this is real, that he's back home and I've been given a second chance to put things right. He's still wearing his office wear, but his tie is snaked across the back of the sofa and he's untucked his shirt and undone the top couple of buttons. He wears a shirt and tie for work, but he's far more comfortable in a pair of jeans and a hoodie. Which is a real

46

shame because he looks *hot* in a suit. He was wearing one the first couple of times we met, first in the toy shop and then the bar.

'How was your day?' I kiss Scott on the cheek. His hair is longer again and I run my hand over the top of it, marvelling that I can do this. These simple actions that I'd taken for granted were lost to me yesterday, but I won't let that happen again.

'It was all right.' Scott shrugs. 'There's a rumour going round that they're going to replace the knackered old kettle in the staffroom, so fingers crossed.' He lifts his hand to display his entwined middle and forefinger, smirking at me before turning his attention back to the quiz show on the telly.

'We had a bit of a nightmare this morning. Twenty babies and toddlers, all at once.' I head into the kitchen so I can browse the fridge for mealtime inspiration, but I spot the tomato-sauce-smeared plate on the side which signals Scott has already eaten, which is a shame because this was a good opportunity to showcase my Perfect Girlfriend skills. Instead, I wrestle the overstuffed bag from the kitchen bin and head down to the bank of bins in the courtyard because I know how much Scott hates this job. The bin bag catches on the pedal of Pete's bike in the hall, but I keep calm, even when tea bags (which should be in the kitchen waste caddy, really) spill onto the carpet. I am serene. The very picture of tranquility, unlike my upstairs neighbour, who barges her way through the main doors like a bailiff, all thundery steps and barely repressed anger in her voice as she hisses into her mobile. The woman always seems to resemble an *Apprentice* candidate in her slim-fit trouser suits, silk blouses and statement dangly earrings, but I've yet to hear her utter a twattish slogan ('if you sliced me open, you'd find success written through my body like a stick of Blackpool rock'). Today, however, she isn't projecting power and confidence. She looks rattled, with her forehead etched with lines and the travel mug in her hand about to be crushed between her fingers. Spotting me crouched by Pete's bike, plucking soggy teabags from the carpet, Isla's features soften, the lines receding as she mouths the word 'sorry' at me and glances at the door, which, miraculously, is still hanging from its hinges. And then she's off again, hissing into the phone about forecasts and budgets as she thumps her way up the stairs. I have no idea what my neighbour does for a living, but it sounds even more stressful than dealing with twenty babies and toddlers en masse. I don't know much about Isla at all, which is a shame because I know Miranda and Pete pretty well and Franziska is my bonus mum. I should make more of an effort to get to know her. Who knows, maybe she's single and on the lookout for romance?

Scott's still on the sofa when I step back into the living room, shouting out answers to the quick-fire round of the TV quiz.

'What do you think about having the others in the building over for Christmas drinks?' If we invite the others over, my sudden interest in Isla won't seem so weird. We can have cocktails and prosecco while Michael Bublé plays softly in the background. 'Maybe next weekend, before everyone's calendars start to really fill up?'

Scott tears his eyes off the TV screen to scrunch his nose up at me. 'You mean like Miranda and Pete?'

'And Isla and Franziska.' I head into the kitchen and slide the dirty plate from the side into the dishwasher. 'Franziska's always inviting me over for tea and cake.' Not to mention the wine and the pot roasts and potato pancakes. 'It'll be nice to return the favour. We can get some nibbles in. Pretend we're fancy for a change.'

Scott scrunches his nose again. 'I don't know. Sounds like a ball-ache of an effort, and I don't even really know these people. Pete's all right, I guess, but Miranda reminds me of my old school headmistress.' He shudders dramatically, and turns back towards the telly. 'And Franziska's ancient. Why don't we get our actual mates round instead? Dan's got the new Xbox. He can bring it over so I can see if it's as good as the reviews say it is.'

'That sounds good.' It sounds appalling. Despite Scott and I being together for three years, I barely know his best friend. And what I do know about Dan, I'm not all that enamoured with. But pointing this out will only cause a rift, and that's the last thing I need right now. I have to keep everything smooth between us. 'Maybe we could combine the two? Drinks, nibbles and Xbox?'

'Whatever makes you happy, babe.'

I clap my hands together, excited about the prospect of inviting people over to the flat. I contemplate cooking something for myself but there's not much use in cooking for one and I'm still full from the second slice of stollen Franziska insisted I put away before leaving her flat. Scott shuffles up to make room for me on the sofa, holding out his arm so I can tuck myself into his body. It's my favourite place to be. This is going to work. I'm going to fulfil my Christmas Cupid mission, and I'm going to keep Scott and I together.

Chapter 9

2nd December

Scott doesn't have a breakfast meeting today so we head for the bus stop together, running into Isla on the way down the stairs as she scuttles past us, already stressed out with the phone call she's having. With my fox hat still away on its bus-ride adventure, I'm forced to put my hood up in a bid to hide my hideous fringe as we step out of the building. I still can't find my favourite mustard-coloured pompom scarf, so I've had to make do with the blue one again.

'I'm hoping my hat's been handed in to the lost and found.' Scott sits next to the window on the bus and I plonk myself down next to him at the aisle, conscious that my hood's still up. I don't know what's worse – looking like a teenager hanging out on the streets or showing off my wonky, too-short fringe. 'I'm going to ring the depot when I get to work. I tried them earlier, but nobody answered.'

'Yeah, good idea.' Scott's head is down as he slides his thumb across the screen of his phone, over and over again, probably checking out the online housing listings. He works too hard sometimes.

'I think I'll put the Christmas tree up tonight. Make the flat look festive. And we'll need to go Christmas shopping at some point. Sooner rather than later, before everyone starts panic buying at the last minute. I know I say this every year, but I mean it this time.' I grin at Scott's profile, to share the in-joke of my Christmas shopping flakiness, but he's too busy scrolling through the listings. 'I need to get something for my mum and dad, and we need to sort out your side of the family. Did you ask Kristen what Maya and Sophia would like?' I know he hasn't: I'd been worried about having to have a last-minute dash around town after the parade on Christmas Eve as Scott had left it so late to ask his sister about his niece's gifts, but then we'd broken up and it wasn't my issue anymore. But this time we *will* still be together on Christmas Eve and I don't want to be joining the crush in the shops.

I watch Scott for any sign that he heard my question, but if he did he certainly isn't showing it. I could nudge him and repeat what I just said, but that usually ends up with Scott getting irritated, which in turn leaves me in a huff. Instead, I park the enquiry for later and leave him to his work. Not everyone is lucky enough to clock out and leave work behind until clocking in time rolls around again like I am.

The girl with the book is sitting across the aisle from me. *A Christmas Carol* is on her lap, a crumpled bus ticket poking out from the first few pages. I remember seeing her on Christmas Eve with the same book, not much further in than she is now, which is a bit odd. Maybe she's a particularly slow reader. I try to look out of the window so I can spot the beginnings of the season cropping up, but although it's freezing outside, it's hot on the bus and the windows have started to fog up. My scalp is starting to itch with the added warmth of having my hood up and although I try to power through, I'm forced to remove it in the end, exposing the dreaded fringe to the bus full of passengers. Not that anyone's paying attention to me and my hair blunder. Like Scott, most people are focused on their phones, or, heads lolled against the fogged-up windows, are using the commute as an extra naptime. A couple of people are reading, though *A Christmas Carol* is still lying closed on the girl's lap across the aisle. Still, I can't help feeling self-conscious and try to push the fringe towards my eyebrows with the palm of my hand. I bet the woman I saw Scott with on Christmas Eve doesn't have these sort of hair malfunctions. *Her* honey-blonde locks looked perfect, sitting just so on her shoulders, not a strand out of place, never mind a full-on fringe disaster for people to snigger over.

The bus hisses to a stop and the doors swish open, bringing in a welcome blast of cool air. It isn't enough to allow me to shove my hood back up, but I'm grateful and somewhat refreshed nonetheless. The girl with the book sits up straighter and fumbles with the book, opening it up to the bus ticket-marked page. Her eyes flick from the page to the front of the bus, obviously on the lookout for somebody, but the seat next to her is still empty when the bus sets off again, so whoever she was hoping to meet up with isn't here. The book remains on her lap, unread for the rest of the journey.

Scott and I part ways at the bus station, with Scott heading left towards the estate agents while I pass through the town centre to C&L's on the outskirts of the main thoroughfare. I've worked at C&L's Toys for the past six years and although it can be stressful at times, I do love the bustle and high energy that this time of year brings. It's exhausting but there's never a dull moment during the run up to Christmas when you're in retail.

After changing into my elf ensemble, I find a quiet corner down in the storeroom, sandwiched between boxes of art supplies, and phone the bus depot again. This time someone answers, but it isn't good news: the hat hasn't made its way to lost property, and if it isn't there by now, it's highly unlikely that it'll turn up. I can try again in a couple of days, but . . .

I can't help feeling glum as I make my way up to the grotto. I loved that hat, and I was so proud when I finished it back in September. It was cosy and made me smile with its little fox face, even if Scott did say I looked like an oversized toddler while wearing it. Pausing by a bird-filled tree in the grotto's Christmas tree maze, I reach up and stroke the soft feathers of a little robin. I could knit another fox hat, I suppose, but I could also use this opportunity for a bit of a change. Make myself something a bit less 'quirky and cute' and a bit more sophisticated. Perhaps something in a softer tone. Baby pink, maybe, with a regular-sized bobble. Oversized pompoms are fun, but maybe something a bit more sensible would suit me better.

Hearing laughter reverberating out from beyond the Christmas trees, I continue on my way, emerging into the clearing where the gingerbread house stands. Here, the children stop their journey through Santa's village for a story inside the cottage, followed by a gingerbread person treat, supposedly fresh from the little oven within the cottage. There are no children here yet, only Milo and Shannon, who is covering her mouth as she giggles at something the photographer has said. She bats him on the arm with her other hand and shakes her head when he says something I can't hear from where I am.

Perhaps these two could be my first match (or second, if things work out between Franziska and Klaus)? They're both single as far as I know, and they clearly get on well. Shannon is very pretty, with long, wavy black hair, and she looks utterly stunning in her red velvet cloak. Milo doesn't look quite so stunning in his stripy leggings and elf hat, but he is pretty cute with his boyish, slightly too long hair that wouldn't have looked out of place on a member of a Britpop band back in the nineties. They'd make a good match I muse as I sneak past them and make my way to the North Pole. And they may not be the only grotto staff I could matchmake. What about Cliff? Everybody loves Santa, so it shouldn't be too hard to find him a date.

A not unpleasant prickly sensation starts up in the pit of my stomach, growing and spreading until it makes my fingertips tingle. Suddenly, this Christmas Cupid thing doesn't seem impossible and, dare I say it, it could turn out to be fun.

'What do you think about Shannon and Milo as a couple?'

It's my tea break and I'm enjoying one of Maureen's mince pies and a cup of tea down in the café with Eloise. She gasps, covering her mouth with her hand to prevent a shower of pastry crumbs.

'Why? What have you seen? Did you catch them going at it in the gingerbread house?'

'Eww, no. Nothing like that. I just think they'd make a cute couple.'

Eloise looks up towards the brightly-lit ceiling, with its squillions of sunshine yellow, domed light fixtures that have been installed to compensate for the lack of windows down here in the basement. Despite the absence of natural light, the café is bright and airy, with the stark white walls decorated with artwork from the children's weekend craft sessions, and a sparkly white floor that reflects the light back up into the space. The tabletops are also white, with contrasting yellow chairs, and there's a cordoned-off soft play area with equipment in vivid primary colours that offsets all the white and gives the place a cheerful look.

'I'm not sure about that.' Eloise shrugs. 'I mean, Milo's nice enough. *Too* nice, probably, because Shannon's a bit . . .' She looks up at the ceiling again as she picks her words carefully. 'Not nice.'

'I think she's all right.' Okay, so I have to make sure her gingerbread people are stocked up so we don't end up with a bunch of miffed kids on our hands when they find the tray in the little wooden oven is void of baked goods, and her fifteen-minute breaks often stretch into half-an-hour breaks, but she's perfectly pleasant and she seems pretty good at storytelling in the gingerbread house.

'Don't you remember why Thomas from the storeroom quit over the summer?'

I shake my head. I don't remember Thomas from the store-room, but then Eloise has the advantage of chatting to most of the workforce when they pop down to the café for their breaks.

'They went out for a bit. Thomas fell madly in love with Shannon, *proposed*, and she said no. He couldn't face seeing her every day after that so he quit.'

'That's hardly Shannon's fault. She can't control how the guy feels, and she shouldn't marry someone she isn't in love with.'

'What about Dominic from arts and crafts?'

I frown. 'He still works here.' I saw him this morning as I made my way to the grotto.

'But Shannon dated and ditched him as well, just before he got together with that girl from Boots. And Marvin from soft toys, Wayne from pre-school, Troy from Bookworm Corner. Even Ted the doorman has bought her dinner, and he's in his sixties. She's only been here since June – that's six guys in six months.'

'So what? She's young. She can play the field as much as she wants to.'

'But that's my point. Milo doesn't seem a playing-the-field kind of guy to me.'

'I disagree.' I have no basis for this evaluation, but I have six couples to match and not very much time to do it in. I thought matching up Cliff was going to be a doddle and even had a potential match in mind earlier – a sweet-looking granny pushing a buggy – but I spotted a wedding band on closer inspection and my complacency started to dip. It didn't help when my watch flashed up the broken hearted six again, reminding me of the task set out for me in order to live. I need to put everything into matching up these couples before it's too late.

'I'm going to try to get them together.' I take a sip of my too-hot tea and wince. 'I just need to figure out how to do it.'

'What about the work's Christmas night out tomorrow? A few drinks, a sprig of mistletoe. I don't think it takes much more with Shannon, to be honest.'

I almost choke on the chunk of mince pie I've just shoved in my mouth. Of all the events I'd like to repeat, the work's Christmas night out at Rhumble is at the bottom of my list, second only to the Terrible Row. I got pretty tipsy at the nineties-themed club and ended up waking Scott when I stumbled into the flat at three in the morning. He was fuming and refused to speak to me for the remainder of the weekend. And, to make matters worse, I was on shift the next day and had to deal with over-excited kids with a raging hangover while we were understaffed because Shannon had called in sick. (To be fair to Shannon, she *had* ended the work night out with a trip to A&E, so I couldn't accuse her of not being a team player.)

But that doesn't have to happen this time. I have the power to change events. I simply won't allow a drop of alcohol to pass my lips tomorrow night and I'll head home earlier – and without making a sound in case Scott is asleep – and hopefully match-make my first couple. And who knows, with the aid of a sprig of mistletoe and a room full of merry people, I may be able to match all six couples and save myself from a Santa Express death in one fell swoop.

Chapter 10

Isla looks far less stressed out than the last couple of times I've seen her as she heads towards me, quickening her pace when she clocks me holding the main door of the building open for her. She's wearing her usual sky-high heels and a pale grey trouser suit but rather than having her phone pressed to her ear, she's lugging a three-foot potted fir tree. It's simple yet elegant and I know that it'll look beautiful placed outside Isla's flat, brightening the space with the clear lights she'll entwine through the branches later.

'Thank you so much.' Isla puffs a stray bit of hair from her face as she squeezes past me into the entrance hall. 'I'm not sure I'd have managed the door by myself. This is much bigger than it looked on the market stall.'

'It's very pretty though.'

Isla smiles, wide and sincere. Her whole face lifts, her eyes shining, and she's like a completely different woman to the stressed-out neighbour I'm used to seeing. 'Isn't she? I couldn't resist when I saw her sitting on that stall. I only popped onto the market for a celebratory mulled wine and a little browse and I ended up with a mini Christmas tree.'

'What are you celebrating?' I check her hand for an engagement ring but her finger is bare. Job promotion?

'Surviving the week.' Isla turns to flash me a wry smile as we start to climb up the stairs. 'I don't even like mulled wine, and I only had a couple of sips, but it was just such a relief to get out of the office and leave my work behind for the weekend.'

'You're lucky. I work in retail, so my working week isn't even over.'

'Oh no, and with Christmas coming up it must be manic. How do you cope?'

'Alcohol helps.' Isla turns to meet my eye again and we laugh. 'But I actually don't mind it. I quite like how crazy it gets at this time of year.' Isla lifts her eyebrows, as though she doesn't quite believe me, but it's true. I had a little blip with the Christmas spirit thing when Scott dumped me, but I'm back on track now he's home and I'm looking forward to decorating the tree tonight with a glass of wine and a cheesy festive film playing in the background. 'What is it that you do?'

Isla shifts the weight of the fir tree. 'I'm a senior finance officer for an academy trust, which basically means I'm constantly trying to stretch the stupidly small budget we have between three quite large schools. And we're looking at taking on another school from September.'

'That sounds . . . fun.'

Isla shifts the weight of the tree again. 'It does not. And if it does, you're not hearing it right.' She gives me the wry smile again. 'I do enjoy my work really, but I can't say I'm not looking forward to the Christmas break. Do you even get one, working in retail?'

'Christmas Day, and that's it unless you win the rota lottery for Boxing Day.' We pause as we reach the top of the stairs. Isla's flat is to the left, mine to the right. Scott isn't home yet; I can tell by the lack of video game noises leaking out into the hallway. 'We were thinking about having people over for Christmas drinks soon. You should pop over.'

'I'd like that. Let me know a date and time.' Isla hefts the tree under one arm so she can give a quick wave before we part ways.

As suspected, the flat is empty and deathly quiet. I didn't use to mind a moment of peace and quiet, but since those awful few days of being alone in the flat, the silence is almost suffocating so I move about the living area, switching on lamps and turning the TV on to create a bit of background noise. I'm not in the mood for a cup of tea but I flick the kettle on anyway, the tension easing from my shoulders as the faint rumble begins. There's no way I want to end up living alone ever again. I couldn't bear it.

There's a festive feel-good movie that's almost finished, but I watch the happily ever after bit at the end as I make a start on decking our little hall. The couple meet under their small town's Christmas tree on Christmas morning and snowflakes start to flutter down as they kiss, the distant sound of carollers in the background. A few days ago, before the Santa Express incident, I'd have chucked the remote at the TV screen in protest at the sickly-sweet scene, but I find it quite heart-warming right now and I wish I'd been around to see the story unfold from the beginning. I'm still smiling when Scott arrives home, and my happiness grows when he presents me with a cupcake from the bakery across the road from his office. This Friday sweet treat tradition began when we first moved into the flat and Scott brought home a cupcake topped with a cute little marzipan frog to mark our new cohabitating status, and it's continued ever since, with Scott taking the time to choose a different treat to surprise me with. Today's offering is a gingerbread cupcake with a cinnamon cream cheese frosting, topped with fondant holly berries and leaves and a light dusting of icing sugar to give it a truly festive feel. It's so delicious, I don't even mind when Scott scrunches up the paper bag it came in and tosses it onto the kitchen worktop, mere inches from the bin.

We have a lovely evening, the kind we used to have when we first moved into the flat, which was only a few months ago but feels like forever ago. Scott jumps into the shower while I throw the last few decorations on the tree and give the kitchen a quick tidy-up, dumping the collection of used teabags from the corner of the sink into the kitchen caddy and rearranging the dishwasher before setting it going. The paper bag from The Bake House is dropped into the bin and I pop a frozen pizza in the oven. One of the magnets has been knocked off the fridge, bringing down the photo souvenir from Alton Towers. I stoop to pick them up, smiling at the memory of that day. It was only a few weeks into our relationship and pride hadn't let me admit how terrified I was of big rides. The photo revealed my feelings pretty clearly – as had my screams of terror as we plummeted to the ground. Scott had doubled over laughing when we went to pick up the souvenir photo and he'd clocked my face, with my eyes almost popping out of my skull, my mouth gaping wider than nature should allow, and my hair flying everywhere. It's been almost three years so I can laugh about it too now.

I place the photo on the fridge door, securing it with the frog magnet. His big googly eyes wobble, mimicking mine in the Alton Towers photo. There's another photo on the fridge, taken during our first holiday together. We're beside the hotel pool, squinting against the sun, tanned and glowing, the image totally capturing how happy I felt that day. About thirty seconds after the photo was taken, Scott had scooped me up in his arms and tossed me in the pool before dive-bombing in himself.

'We should book a holiday in the new year.' The pizza's ready and we're eating it together on the sofa with a glass of wine for me and a can of lager for Scott. It's hardly date night at a fancy restaurant but I wouldn't want it any other way. 'Somewhere hot and sunny.' And pretty cheap, because money hasn't exactly been flowing since we moved into the flat. But we need to get back to being that happy couple in the holiday snap, before the stresses of adulting took over.

'I'm hoping to get a big commission soon, so yeah, definitely.' Scott grabs the remote and starts to flick through the TV channels.

'I invited Isla from across the hall over for Christmas drinks. You know when we invite Dan and the others over. You don't mind, do you?' He hadn't been over keen on inviting the neighbours over but I think it'll be fun. The more the merrier.

'Why would I mind? She can keep Dan company.' He winks at me and grins before returning to his channel hopping.

'Won't Jess be with him?'

'Who?' Luckily, Scott doesn't take his eyes off the TV screen otherwise he'd see my face drop at the slip-up I've just made. Dan won't get together with Jess until later in the month. Who was it he cheated on with Jess?

'I meant Niamh.' I think. It's hard to keep up with Dan's rapidly revolving door of girlfriends.

'They broke up.' Scott jiggles his can of lager before tipping the last few drops into his mouth. 'She saw some texts from his ex and went ballistic.'

'What kind of texts?'

Scott slides the empty can onto the coffee table before reaching into the mini fridge beside the sofa. I hadn't wanted the mini fridge – what's the point when you live in a little flat, with the kitchen mere footsteps away? – but he'd worn me down and he got one in the end.

'The kind you don't want your girlfriend reading.' He settles back down into the sofa and pulls the tab on his fresh can of lager.

'Were they old texts from when they were together?'

'Nope.' Scott places the back of his hand against his mouth as he belches. I have no idea why Scott is friends with this horrid little man. Okay, they've known each other since primary school, but Dan's behaviour towards women is abhorrent and if I wasn't so averse to confrontation, I'd tell him as much. 'Anyway, enough about that bellend.' 'Bellend' is said with affection and not the way I would use it while describing Scott's slimy pal. 'Have you decided what you want for Christmas yet?'

Decided? I've been hinting for *months* about a charm bracelet from Tiffany's. I'm not sure how Scott hasn't picked up on the clues, but then men are notoriously bad at things like that, aren't they? I could tell him outright about the bracelet right now, but I push the thought away. It's pretty expensive and if I've learnt anything from this extremely weird Christmas, it's that material things don't matter. Besides, I'd rather the money went towards our summer getaway, which will be much more fun.

'Just you.' I kiss Scott on the cheek and snuggle into him. He shifts his arm, draping it around my shoulders so I can burrow further into his body. 'Spending the day with you will be the best gift ever.'

'So you don't want the new Xbox then?' Scott grins at me as I twist my neck painfully to look up at him. And because I am not a man, I feel the full weight of that Christmas wish list hint.

'Believe me, if I unwrap any kind of games console on Christmas morning, you'll end up wearing it.' I poke Scott playfully in the ribs before lunging for the remote so I can put the soaps on. Scott wriggles free from my hug and stretches his arms above his head.

'If you're watching that rubbish, I'm off to the pub.'

'I could come with you?' I'm not *that* interested in the goings on of Walford, and I can always catch up later. I'd much rather spend time with my boyfriend.

'Nah, it's all right. I said I might meet up with Dan and Liam. You don't mind, do you?'

'No, of course not.' I am a Perfect Girlfriend, and Perfect Girlfriends don't mind sacrificing Friday evening sofa snuggles with their boyfriends. 'Have fun. But not the kind of fun Dan has.'

Scott rolls his eyes. 'As if.' He stoops down to kiss me and I resist the urge to cling on to him. It's okay to let go, because I know he'll be back.

I pour myself another glass of wine and settle down in the corner of the sofa, hugging a cushion in lieu of Scott. I didn't used to mind spending time on my own before the Terrible Row – in fact, I quite liked my own company – but now it's torture and I need something other than *Eastenders* to keep me occupied. I decide to make a start on my fox replacement hat (because I can't keep going out with this dodgy fringe on display) and settle on a pattern for a chunky ribbed bobble hat. It's when I open my knitting bag in search of a pair of suitable needles that I find my favourite mustard-coloured scarf. Half-finished and giant pompom-less. So *that's* why I couldn't find it – I was still knitting it at this point in the first December. I probably have enough mustard yarn to make the hat as well, especially if I omit the giant pompoms. For once, I'll have matching, grown-up knitwear.

It's past midnight when I admit to myself that it's time for bed. My eyes are so squinty I can barely see the stitches on my needles and I've got work in the morning. Scott isn't home yet, so when my phone pings with a message as I'm crawling into bed, I assume it's him letting me know he's on his way home via the kebab shop. But it's Eloise and my stomach fills with dread when I read her message.

Annie's just texted me. She wants to hang out. What do I do?

I remember this message from the first time I lived this December, and it turned out that 'hang out' was Annie-speak for 'I'm bored and want no-strings sex'. She'll then blank Eloise until she's at a loose end again, leaving my best friend feeling worthless. Again.

You should stay clear. You know how this will end. How it always ends xx

I keep an eye on my phone, waiting for a reply, which obviously comes just as I'm drifting off to sleep and jolts me awake.

You're right. Thanks xx

I know she'll go over to Annie's anyway, even if this wasn't a repeat of what happened last time. We've been here way too many times before, but Eloise can't seem to resist. I wish there was more

I could do than be there to pick up the pieces when Eloise gets her heart broken again, but no matter what I say, she can't seem to see that being single is better than being in a bad relationship.

Chapter 11

3rd December

I sneak around the flat, tiptoeing across rooms and closing doors with the upmost care so that I don't wake Scott, which is made doubly hard because I'm actually running late for work and it would be quicker to charge about the place without a care about noise. The lateness is my own fault, but I couldn't resist snuggling into Scott's warm body for five more minutes. And then five minutes more. And then just one more snooze of the alarm . . .

Safe in the knowledge that he wouldn't have to get up early today, Scott was out with Dan and Liam until nearly three and had clearly put away quite a few drinks as he could barely walk straight (it was him crashing into the dressing table and sending everything scattering that alerted me to his arrival back at the flat) and he's left his clothes in a pile on the bedroom floor. I don't have time to pick them up, so I leave them for Scott to sort out and rush out to catch the bus. I'm in such a rush, I think I even beat Isla in a dash down the stairs, and I don't even have time to chat to Franziska when we meet in the hall.

The girl with the book is on the bus, though she doesn't appear to have advanced much further through the pages. Christmas is starting to creep back in, with more decorated trees dotted about and there's been an influx of festive lights that will be merry and bright during my journey home. But I don't have to wait until the evening for a bit of cheer as Eloise is practically buzzing with merriment, as though she too is plugged into the mains, when I pop down to the café for my mince pie break. It's the first Saturday of December, when people are jolted by the approach of Christmas and pile into the shops to get a head start on their shopping, so the grotto has been jammed. I sink down into my seat with a groan, lifting up my feet to take the weight off them for a minute.

'Ho ho ho.' Eloise pulls the chair opposite out and performs a twirl before she drops down into the seat. 'Only twenty-one shopping days until Christmas.'

While Eloise beams across the table at me, my stomach churns. If there are only twenty-one shopping days until Christmas, that means there are only twenty-one days until the Winter Wonderland parade. I can practically hear the engine of the Santa Express revving in preparation of my demise. I need to get matching some couples, and quickly.

I pop out to the Christmas market on my lunchbreak, picking up a sprig of mistletoe for tonight's matchmaking. I have just enough time to enjoy a hot chocolate while I wander around the stalls before I have to head back to the grotto.

'Shannon!' I spot my colleague as I'm winding through the maze of Christmas trees. 'What size shoe are you?'

Shannon pokes a foot out from beneath her cloak and looks down at the red bejewelled ballet flat. 'A five. Why? Philippa isn't sticking me in the North Pole with a pair of those minging elf shoes, is she?' She whips her foot back beneath her cloak and wrinkles her nose as she inspects my curly-toed footwear.

'No, don't worry. I was just reading an article that said the average shoe size for women in the UK is a six and I was wondering how true it is.' The fib slips easily out of my mouth, which is surprising as it's completely off the cuff. 'I'm a five as well.' Which may not fit in with the article's assessment but is perfect for my plan tonight.

The rhythmic intro to Culture Beat's 'Mr Vain' starts as we step into Rhumble, the nineties-themed club we've arranged to meet at for our work's Christmas night out. Squealing, Eloise grasps hold of my arm and starts to bounce up and down, her free arm waving in the air until she's nudged out of the way by an impatient patron wanting to get to the bar. We push our way through the crowds until we spot a few familiar faces over by a set of booths in the corner. My skin prickles with apprehension as we approach our workmates. I enjoyed myself so much the first time this night out happened, until I got home and it all went horribly wrong, and I don't want history to repeat itself. But things are going to turn out differently this time. I've already set the two occasions apart by choosing a completely different outfit than last time, opting for an emerald-green off-the-shoulder top with matching tights and a red-and-charcoal tartan skirt, which is still quite festive (and nineties leaning in style, which was a happy accident) but not as full-on as the vintage-style, full-skirted dress with a Santa and snowman print I wore last time. It was definitely what Mum would describe as 'cute and quirky' but I decided to tone down my attire as well as my drinking. I need to keep my head in the game tonight, and that game is of the matchmaking kind.

I scan my workmates as we approach the set of booths. Dominic from arts and crafts is here, but he's no good to me as he's already very much in love with the girl from Boots, along with Shannon (who looks *stunning* in a sequined, gold, fitted dress with a plunging neckline) and Cliff (who, like last time, has claimed he's 'only staying for a quick drink to show my face'. I wonder if he'll have to be folded into a taxi at the end of the night like last time . . .). The music's blaring, but we shout our greetings as Dominic and Cliff budge over in the booth so Eloise and I can sit down. I'm worried about Eloise after she met up with Annie because although she seems upbeat right now, she'll soon transform into the distraught shell her ex-girlfriend always leaves behind.

'Is there anyone here you fancy?' I reach into my handbag, shoving the spare pair of shoes out of the way so I can pull out the sprig of mistletoe and give it a jiggle in front of Eloise's face. If I can distract Eloise from Annie's imminent ghosting, I'll be happy. And if I find her a love match – a proper one, not the kind of toxic thing she's got going on with Annie – then that'll be a big fat bonus.

'She's pretty cute.' Eloise nods towards a woman with wild red curls who's braving the dance floor early on. 'But I'm not getting any queer vibes.' She scrunches up her nose and shrugs. 'Shall we go and get a drink?'

We de-wedge ourselves from the booth and join the crush surrounding the bar as Culture Beat makes way for R.E.M.'s 'Shiny Happy People'. There's a man and a woman next to me who I can't help noticing are rather flirty. She keeps breaking eye contact before looking at him coyly while toying with her low-hanging necklace and drawing attention to her cleavage, and she's going to end up with chapped lips if she keeps licking them like that. He can't keep his eyes off her, and I know it's pretty busy in here but I'm not sure he needs to be standing *that close* to her. I don't get the sense that they're actually dating, and this is confirmed when I lean in close to try to catch their conversation.

'I increased the sales of garden canes by twenty-three percent in the first quarter.' He gives a lazy one-shouldered shrug, as though it's inconsequential and he isn't trying to big himself up, and she widens her eyes, mouthing the word 'wow' while fiddling with the necklace. There's no way these two people are in a relation-ship. Not if he's trying to impress her with garden cane sales and she's pretending to be fascinated by the conversation and not the bulging biceps stretching his tight T-shirt.

I don't know if it's cheating or not (they're clearly going to end up snogging of their own volition if she didn't walk away at the mere mention of garden cane sales) but I decide to give them a nudge anyway and whip out the mistletoe. I've barely shaken the sprig above their heads when he lunges, and she's quite happy with the situation judging by the way her hands are grasping the back of his head, pinning his face in place.

Job done: one couple down, five more to go! We're only a few minutes into the night out, so this matchmaking thing could turn out to be a breeze.

I get a bit mistletoe-happy after that first successful attempt, and while some people look at me as though I'm mad (perhaps I am, with this whole back-from-the-dead thing) others are more than happy for the excuse to make their move. Milo arrives as I'm dangling the mistletoe over a couple inexplicably grinding to the rap bit of a 2 Unlimited song, and I make a beeline for him so I can direct him towards Shannon. Unfortunately, she's currently dancing with somebody else, but I pounce at them with the mistletoe anyway (a match is a match, right?) and scour the room for someone Milo may take a shine to. The club's really starting to fill up now, which makes the job both easier (lots of people equals lots of potential matches) but also harder (as in, it is becoming increasingly more difficult to move around and I find myself wedged between a wall of plaid shirts and a shelf lined with lava lamps).

'There you are.' Milo reaches around a blue plaid shirt, smiling an apology as the bloke is forced to step out of the way. He takes hold of my hand and guides me out of my plaid-shirted prison. 'Eloise has been looking everywhere for you. She's requested "Cotton Eye Joe" and says you have to dance with her when it comes on.'

I groan. Dancing to 'Cotton Eye Joe' was bad enough the first time we did this, but at least I'd had numerous mojitos to soften the cringe. Being sober isn't quite the genius plan I'd thought it'd be.

'If I'm doing this, you are too.'

Milo opens his mouth to rightly protest, but I'm not interested in any words that translate to 'hell, no' and I drag him towards the dance floor with a determination I wasn't aware I was in possession of. Eloise finds us just as the song begins, and though I will never admit this out loud, it's actually quite fun as we slap our thighs, stamp our feet and twirl around with arms linked until we're dizzy. Milo in particular throws himself into it as he frolics around the dance floor, linking arms with anyone he comes into contact with. He looks like he's having the time of his life, and his enthusiasm is infectious. I'm exhausted by the time we shuffle off the dance floor, leaning on one another for support as we make our way back to the booth, giggling at our antics despite being breathless. Cliff's sitting in the booth, drunkenly chewing Dominic's ear off, his 'one drink' policy long broken.

'Dominic?' I plonk myself onto the bench opposite and shuffle along until I'm facing Cliff. 'I think Philippa's looking for you. Wants a word about . . . something.' My brain doesn't work on the lie swiftly enough to manage more than that, but Dominic seizes my pitiful effort with both hands, jumping out of his seat and flashing me a look of pure gratitude before he darts away.

'Hey, Cliff.' I pat the space next to me on the bench and Eloise plonks herself down while Milo sits next to our Santa. 'Are you enjoying our C&L's Christmas night out?' I'm used to seeing Cliff decked out in his red suit and fluffy beard by now, and I'd forgotten how handsome he is, like an older David Beckham. I wonder if there are any women here who'd like a moment under the mistletoe with him. Most of the clientele are in their late thirties and forties and beyond, here to enjoy the music of their youth, so it isn't an impossible mission to match him up.

'It's been great.' Cliff lifts his pint, which is almost empty. 'I'll just finish this though, and then I'll get going.'

'Why don't you come and have a dance with us first?' There's a trio of women on the dance floor, and one definitely keeps looking over at Cliff. Although I've already helped at least ten couples find some festive joy this evening, one more won't hurt.

'Nah.' Cliff shakes his head and wafts his free hand. 'I'm no dancer.'

'Neither is Milo, but that didn't stop him.' I grin at my co-worker, to show I'm only kidding. 'Come on, it'll be fun. You only live once.' At least, most of us do. 'Finish your pint and we'll go and have a boogie.'

Cliff looks as though he's about to protest, but he shrugs, downs the last dregs of his drink and follows us to the dance floor, where he proves his assessment really was true. I think it'd take more than a bit of mistletoe to matchmake Cliff after his bout of dad dancing, but we have a laugh dancing to PJ & Duncan, The Spice Girls and Gina G. He throws the towel in when 911's 'Bodyshakin'' starts, however, and slopes off to the bar. It proves too much even for Milo, and we follow in Cliff's footsteps, only to return to the dance floor before we've been served when 'Macarena' comes on. We somehow still know the moves, and my face is aching from smiling so much by the time we stagger towards the bar for refreshments. If it's possible, I'm having even more fun this time and I'm not even drunk.

After our drinks, we head back to the dance floor, but I have to peel away as midnight approaches. I need to get home early enough not to cause a rift between me and Scott, but there's one more thing I need to do before I jump in a taxi. I spot Shannon through the crowd, making her way to the bar. It happens quickly: one moment she's standing, the next she's buckled and is clinging on to the arm of the guy standing next to her, which is the only thing that keeps her upright. I dash over, helping her to limp to a quieter spot to assess the damage.

'Oh no.' Shannon has whipped off her shoe and she's holding it up by the strap. The needle-thin heel has snapped and is dangling from the shoe. 'What am I going to do? I can't go home – it's way too early and that guy hasn't asked for my number yet.' She nods across the club, towards the bar where the guy she almost brought down with her is queuing for drinks. He didn't come with us to make sure Shannon was okay after her stumble, so he's hardly Prince Charming. 'I'm going to have to go barefoot.'

'You can't do that.' I shudder at the memory of Shannon's bloodied foot after she'd stepped on broken glass outside the club. Milo had kindly offered to take her to A&E where she'd been cleaned up and bandaged but thankfully hadn't needed stitches. Still, it can't have been pleasant having to hobble about on a cut-up foot; and being understaffed in the grotto hadn't been fun either.

'Here.' I pull the spare shoes from my bag – black ballet flats with gold chain detailing. The closest shoe match I had for her outfit. 'You can wear these.' Shannon looks down at the shoes. She looks far from impressed. 'It's better than being barefoot. You could step on anything, especially when you need to go to the loo.' That cinches it. Shannon grabs the flats and shoves her feet into them before she heads back to the bar and Prince Uncharming. I follow because although I need to get home and I don't think he's worthy, I want to make sure I've got all my matches done and dusted.

Despite being completely sober, I take extra special care to creep up the stairs to the flat just after midnight, and I ease the front door open without making a sound. It turns out my caution wasn't needed, however, because there's nobody in the flat. The lamp and the fairy lights have been left on, but all the rooms are empty and the bed hasn't been slept in. It isn't until just before 3 a.m. that Scott wanders into the flat, looking surprised to see me curled up on the sofa.

'I didn't expect you back so soon.' He shrugs off his jacket and throws it onto the armchair. 'Crap night out?'

'No, it was fun.' Cold air hits me as I wriggle free from the knitted patchwork blanket I draped over myself while trying not to fall asleep in front of the telly. 'I didn't know you were going out.'

'I just popped down to Pete's. I'd have come back up earlier if I'd have known you were home.' Stretching up into the air, he yawns loudly, mouth cavernous. 'I'm knackered. I'm off to bed.'

'Me too.' I fold the blanket into a neat rectangle and arrange it over the back of the sofa, trying to calculate how many hours it'll be before my alarm goes off to get me up for work. I yawn myself as I follow Scott down the hallway towards the bedroom. Snuggling into the warmth of his body is lovely, but I can't help thinking about this night the first-time round. How had I managed to wake Scott and cause the row if he'd only just got back from Pete's a few moments before I'd arrived home? Had he really been asleep when I'd got back from the club – and if not, why had he been so angry with me? I'm too tired to figure it out, and I've managed to swerve the argument this time, so that's all that matters. I'm feeling good – about Scott *and* the Christmas Cupid task – as I quickly drift off to sleep.

Chapter 12

4th December

Of all the days not to show up for work, Shannon chooses the first Sunday of December, when the grotto will be heaving and when we're all knackered and some of us hungover from the night out at Rhumble. And none of us are fooled; Shannon isn't ill – she's got a raging hangover, like an awful lot of the other staff at the toy shop. Even Cliff – who apparently had to be propped up by Dominic and 'head of gift-wrap' Carlos and manhandled into a taxi while singing 'Wannabe' at the top of his lungs – has managed to drag himself to the grotto. I mean, he'll probably give the poor kids who enter the grotto a fright with his craggy, grey skin and bloodshot eyes, but at least he's here, being a team player. Part of me wishes I hadn't bothered to save Shannon from the broken glass now.

I'm not in the best mood this morning, which is mostly due to the late night I had last night and a teeny-weeny bit because of the clothes strewn about the bedroom floor. I'd been in a rush yesterday, so I'd left the discarded clothes for Scott to deal with, but instead of shoving them in the washing basket, he'd doubled their number with yesterday's jeans and hoodie added to the pile.

And even though he'd had the whole day to himself, he didn't bother to tidy up the mess he'd made on the dressing table or pop to the shop to buy a fresh loaf of bread or a pint of milk. Breakfast this morning had been a bowl of dry cereal and a glass of water. Still, I'd gritted my teeth and kept my grievances to myself, because Perfect Girlfriends don't let their cranky moods cause squabbles first thing in the morning.

With Shannon MIA (or HIA – Hungover in Action) I'm put in charge of the gingerbread house, which means I get to sit down for most of the day, and I'm not going to complain too loudly about *that*. It's Milo I feel sorry for, as he has to double up as the photographer for the grotto *and* a North Pole greeter and candy cane distributor, meaning he has to run around all day between the two jobs. The circus acts, who have been brought in to draw shoppers to C&L's at the weekends, are 'borrowed' from the entrance and placed in the North Pole to keep the children entertained as they wait. Juggler Jez is here, and I try not to glare at him every time our paths cross because although I blame him for the predicament I'm in (because I wouldn't be in this weird Christmas Cupid quandary if it wasn't for him and his stupid stilts) I also feel the biggest bout of gratitude towards the man, because I also wouldn't be back with Scott without him.

Life at the gingerbread house turns out to be rather fun, gathering the kids around me in the little cosy living room of the cottage for story time, swaying gently in the rocking chair as I read to them before pulling the gingerbread people from the little wooden oven and giving them out to the delighted kids. But only for the first hour or so. There are three stories on the shelf in the cottage – *The Night Before Christmas*, *The Gingerbread Man* and *Hansel and Gretel*, which I alternate so many times over the morning, I practically know them off by heart. As fun and as comfortable as it's been sitting reading stories to the children, I can't help feeling a surge of gratefulness when Shannon finally pokes her head around the cottage door and relieves me of my duties. She doesn't look well, despite the thick layers of make-up attempting to mask the problem, but she's here and seemingly up for duty and I'm more than happy to hand over the reins. We were so busy, I missed my morning break, so I'm gasping for a cup of tea by lunchtime and pelt it down to the café for refreshments. As well as an all-day breakfast and a mug of tea, I order a mince pie, even though I've been nibbling on gingerbread people throughout the morning (perk of the job, especially when you're foregoing your break).

'Do you think I should dye my hair?'

Eloise raises her eyebrows. 'Do you think it'll shift the focus from your fringe?' She waits a beat before she grins at me. I stick my tongue out at her and pretend to be all huffy, but I can take the teasing about my hairdressing bungle from Eloise because she's my best mate, and what are friends for if not to poke fun at your misadventures?

'I just fancy a change.' I pull my elf hat off and have a little futile tug at my fringe. 'Maybe blonde?'

My hair is and always has been brown, usually somewhere between jaw- and shoulder-length (and usually with a normal-looking fringe) so I think taking the plunge and going blonde will make a huge impact.

'No, not blonde. You'll end up like this.' Eloise bows her head, to show off the dark, two-inch wide path of dark brown running down the middle of her white-blonde hair.

'Not if I actually, I don't know . . .' I tap my finger against my chin and narrow my eyes as I pretend to think deeply about it. 'Made regular trips to the hairdressers?' Eloise may have been bleaching her hair since she was fourteen, but she's never mastered its regular upkeep. 'Anyway, I was thinking about something softer, like Holly Willoughby's.'

Eloise nods slowly while she chews. 'Holly has gorgeous hair. Sort of golden blonde. I bet it'd suit you.'

'Do you think?' I stretch out a strand of hair and inspect it between forefinger and thumb.

'Yeah, but then I like your hair the way it is.'

'So you don't think I should dye it?'

Eloise shrugs before she scrapes her chair back. 'It's your hair. The only opinion that matters is yours.' She reaches down and gathers up her empty plate and cup. 'Call me later, yeah?'

'Do you want to have a quick wander around the Christmas market after work, before it closes?'

'I would *love* to, but Annie said she'd text me about meeting up so . . .' She does a little bouncy thing on the spot without her feet leaving the ground, her whole face lighting up with a beatific smile. I don't want to burst her bubble, I really don't, but I know for a fact that Annie isn't going to get in touch. I've lived through this scenario before, back during the original December, and I'm about to nudge my way into the topic but my watch starts to vibrate against my wrist. When I look down, a familiar broken heart flashes up, followed by a six. Which can't be right because I was an amazing Christmas Cupid last night, and that sprig of mistletoe saw more illicit action than a married premier league footballer.

I flick the watch, my brow furrowing with annoyance, and eventually it stops flashing. But when I look up, Eloise has disappeared back into the kitchen.

The grotto calms down by around two o'clock, so much so that Jez and the other circus acts return to the entertainment space at the entrance and I manage to have a catch-up with Milo in between ankle-biting customers. As suspected, Shannon *did* go home with the guy she snogged under my mistletoe, which proves my watch is on the blink. But it's when I'm nipping to the loo during my afternoon break and spot an old man helping his wife onto the escalator that I remember my gran saying something about true love matches, and that one-night stands wouldn't count. Which sort of buggers up my Cupid Count when they *all* came from couples snogging in a club on a Saturday night, which isn't the most romantic of settings and doesn't usually end in a long-term relationship.

In a nutshell, none of the matches from last night counted and I'm screwed.

I spend the next couple of hours pondering my task while herding children from the North Pole area towards Santa's grotto. I'm back at square one, with six couples to matchmake and still no idea who these people should be. I'm still thinking about it the next day as I return to work, bleary-eyed because it turns out it's quite hard to drop off to sleep when you're worrying about being bulldozed to the ground by a double decker bus driven by a crowd-loving Santa Claus.

'Do you know if Maureen's single?' As always, Eloise is my sounding board as we sit together for our break, and inspiration strikes when I spot the manager of the toy shop's café across the room.

'Maureen?' Eloise turns towards her boss. 'Yep. Has been for years. Divorced about twenty years ago, I think, and hasn't really seen much action since.'

'Is she looking, do you think?'

I crane my neck so I can get a better look at the woman. She's attractive, in her early sixties, and has a lovely swishy reddish/ brown bob underneath her hair net and she's always friendly to the customers, even the horrible ones.

'I really have no idea, but Zoey . . .' Eloise reaches across the table and places a hand on my arm. 'She's really not my type.'

I shrug Eloise's hand off my arm and roll my eyes. 'I'm not talking about for you, you banana. I was thinking about Cliff.' They're both about the same age, and getting them both in the same room shouldn't be too much of a problem since they both work in the same building. Right?

'Ah, yes. You're on that Christmas joy spreading kick. Any chance you could sprinkle a bit my way?' She sinks lower in her seat and puffs out a sigh. 'Annie never called yesterday. I don't know why I thought she would.'

This time it's me who reaches across the table and places a hand on Eloise's arm. 'Because you still have feelings for her, and you hope that you can work things out. Believe me, I know what that's like. It hurts and it's frustrating, but one day you'll look back and be thankful that Annie isn't in your life anymore.'

'But right now I *want* her in my life. More than anything. I'm willing to put up with her shitty behaviour on the off chance she'll find a flicker of interest towards me.' She pulls the sleeves of her stripy cardigan over her hands and tucks them underneath her armpits. The cardigan is at least a couple of sizes too big so the sleeves are constantly hanging over her hands, and it's so old the wool has started to bobble. She only wears this cardigan when she's feeling blue, because she finds comfort in its bulk and familiarity. 'How sad is that?'

'It isn't sad at all.'

I wish I didn't have to rush back upstairs, or that I could find a quick fix for my friend because I hate seeing her in so much pain. But there's nothing I can say that will erase her feelings towards Annie. I've said all the words I can think of and nothing has worked.

'I'm really sorry but I have to get back up to the grotto.' Shannon hasn't showed up again – a delayed reaction to the hangover, we figure – and although the shop isn't nearly as busy as yesterday on a termtime Monday morning, there's only me, Milo, Cliff and one of the seasonal temps manning Santa's village, flitting between the gingerbread house, the North Pole area, the grotto and both the ticket and photo gift shop booths. 'We can meet up after work. Go to the Christmas market for hot chocolate and one of those giant chocolate-covered marshmallows.'

Eloise smiles, and it isn't completely forced. 'I'd like that. But forget the marshmallows – I'm going for cake and lots of it.'

I head back up to the grotto, my finger brushing against the soft feathers of a robin as I pass the bird-filled tree. I need to cheer Eloise up, and properly, not just a papering-over-the-cracks slice of cake, and I also need to find a way to bring Maureen and Cliff together. The simple solution is the café, but Cliff doesn't usually head downstairs during his breaks for a brew and a sweet treat like the rest of us. He prefers a few puffs on his e-cig out by the bins.

'Cliff?' The North Pole area is empty, and Milo tells me there aren't any kids in the grotto, so I head inside, my mouth dropping open when I'm greeted by Cliff puffing away. 'Cliff. You can't do that in here.'

'It's only an e-cig. And it's Christmas pudding flavour, so the smell only adds to the ambience.' Despite his defence, Cliff slips the e-cig into the inside pocket of his red jacket. 'Everything all right out there?' He nods towards the North Pole, refusing to meet my eye.

'Everything's fine.' I open the door wider, hoping to dispel any lingering scent. 'I just came to tell you that there's a special offer on mince pies down in the café. Two for one.'

'Bleurgh. Horrid little things.' Cliff pats his jacket, where the e-cig is nestled. 'I'll stick to my Christmas pudding.'

'You don't like mince pies? But you're Santa. Next, you'll be telling me that Rudolph doesn't like carrots.'

Cliff is easing himself up from his tinsel-entwined chair, but he settles back down and beckons me over, continuing to twitch his fingers at me until I stoop down and he can whisper in my ear.

'Can you keep a secret?' The overly fluffy white eyebrows stuck above Cliff's own normal eyebrows raise. 'I'm not the *real deal*. Look.' He unhooks his beard and taps his nose. 'Keep it to yourself.' He groans loudly as he levers himself up to his feet. 'Now, I'm off for a sneaky cig break before more of the little blighters turn up. Haven't we got a school booked in today?'

'That isn't until two o'clock.' Unicorn Class from Boyd Mill Primary School. Thirty six- and seven-year-olds all at once.

Fun. 'But you couldn't pop down to the café, could you? Ask Maureen for a couple more boxes of gingerbread people so we don't run out?'

'I can, but it'll have to wait five minutes.' Cliff hooks his beard back into place and takes his e-cig from his pocket before he strides out of the grotto. Fingers crossed, he'll get chatting to Maureen while he's down there. Maybe I should pop down with my mistletoe, just in case they need a much bigger nudge, because Cliff doesn't strike me as the kind of bloke who enjoys a bit of spontaneous flirting. Or any kind of flirting at all.

Chapter 13

5th December

I don't go down to the café with my mistletoe; the others take Santa's absence as an opportunity to temporarily close the grotto (because what is a grotto without the Big Man?) and go off on their own sneaky breaks, neglecting the fact that the North Pole looks like a tornado has swept through it and the stocks of gingerbread people and candy canes are dangerously low. I do a quick sweep and a tidy-up, restocking the goodies using the reserves stored in the photo gift shop, and Cliff is back on his tinselly chair by the time I've finished. I've been mulling over the Christmas Cupid task while I've been busy sorting out the North Pole, and I suspect a sprig of mistletoe won't cut it when it comes to a Cliff/Maureen romantic alliance. I need to forge a plan to bring them together in a non-work setting, where they can get to know each other not as Santa and café manager, but as the wonderful people they are.

As arranged, I meet Eloise after work and we hurry over to the Christmas market that's set up in the square beside the town hall, making a beeline for the hot chocolate stand before it closes. It's dark now but the square is lit up with a bazillion fairy lights that are strung up between the streetlamps, woven through the branches of the market's Christmas tree centrepiece, and twinkling from the garlands framing the wooden hut stalls. Even the bare branches of trees lining the square are brought back to life with tiny multicoloured lights.

'Don't you love the Christmas market?' With my hands wrapped around my mug of hot chocolate, I take in a deep breath, closing my eyes to really savour the smells of Christmas surrounding me; cinnamon, ginger, nutmeg and spiced apple from the festive bakes and handmade candles and soaps, roasting chestnuts, the leather from the handcrafted gifts stall. Even fried onions, which shouldn't summon any sort of Christmassy feeling at all but somehow does when combined with the spices and other smells.

'It's one of my favourite places to be.' Eloise takes a sip of her drink, wiping her nose with a gloved hand to get rid of the whipped cream on the tip of her nose. 'I come here with Rosemary, Lexi and Danielle every year. Rosemary *always* buys us a bar of handmade soap each – has done since we were little – and we pick out a new decoration for the tree.'

Eloise's parents divorced when she was a toddler, and she lived with her Mum at first, staying over at her dad's at the weekend until her mum moved to Malta following a holiday romance when Eloise was ten. Eloise and her older sister, Lexi moved in with their dad, stepmum Rosemary and stepsister Danielle and remained there even when their mum returned to Britain eight months later with a broken heart and an empty bank account.

'I brought Mum once, but it wasn't the same.' Eloise links her arm through mine as we head towards one of the cake stalls. 'She complained about the cold and said the brass band was bringing on a migraine. We stick to indoor venues for our Christmas activities now. Usually places where Mum can get hammered on gin.' Eloise grimaces before taking another sip of her hot chocolate.

'All the cakes are half price now, ladies.' The woman manning the stall we're approaching doesn't have to tell us twice. We dash to the hut and choose a selection of cakes to take home before we finish our drinks and return the mugs to the hot chocolate stand. We're heading towards our break away point – Eloise will need to go right towards her tram stop, while I'll be heading left for the bus station – when I spot the poster in the window of a pub.

'Hey, how do you fancy taking part in this?' I stop outside the pub and nod towards the poster advertising a weekly quiz. If I can get together a team from work, including Cliff and Maureen, it will give me a real chance at matchmaking the pair, especially if there's alcohol involved.

Eloise brushes pastry crumbs from the front of her coat. 'Sounds fun. And the two hundred quid prize for first place would be nice. I still haven't started my Christmas shopping yet.'

That's settled then. Starting tomorrow, it will be my mission to put together a C&L's pub quiz team.

I can't help starting on the apple strudel I bought from the market as the bus pulls away from the station, and when the first piece is finished, I accidentally inhale the other one that was supposed to be Scott's. He's right; I really do eat too many cakes, but then he feeds my habit with his Friday night treats from The Bake House so it can't bother him that much. Still, I make sure all traces of crumbs are brushed away from my coat as soon as I'm off the bus, and instead of going straight up to the flat I make a quick detour to the courtyard so I can dispose of the paper bag evidence in the wheelie bin. I'm darting along the narrow hallway when I collide with Pete's bike, laddering my tights and causing quite a few swears to erupt as I hobble away. Pete catches me between words rhyming with 'brother mucking dastard' and 'batting car-sole'.

'Whoa.' He holds his hands up as he backs away. 'Someone's not having a good day.'

'I was, until your bike assaulted me.' I hold my leg out, and Pete pulls a sheepish face. 'You're a nuisance, Pete Wolfenden. Not only has your bike taken a layer of skin off my shin, you also kept my boyfriend out *very* late on Saturday night.'

'I'm sorry about the bike. I'll shift it . . .' He looks around the small space in the hall. 'Somewhere. And I'll buy you some new tights. Or at least give you the money for some new ones. But I don't know anything about Saturday night.'

'Don't worry about the tights.' I have far bigger fish to fry than a ruined pair of tights right now. 'But what do you mean, you don't know anything about Saturday night? I'm talking about Scott. At your place until nearly three o'clock in the morning.'

Pete shakes his head. 'Scott must have been talking about a different Pete. He wasn't at ours on Saturday night.'

Oh. Maybe he *was* talking about a different Pete. I'm not aware of another Pete in Scott's life, but that doesn't mean he doesn't exist. He could be someone from work I haven't met yet or someone from the pub.

'You're still a nuisance.' I cock an eyebrow and nod towards the bike. 'I bet Miranda's told you to move it already, hasn't she?'

Pete snorts. 'Multiple times. At least once a week, actually.'

'You should listen to your wife more, and maybe let her know about your mum being a vegan *before* Christmas Eve.'

Pete's making his way towards the bike, but he stops so he can gape at me. 'How did you . . .?' He shakes his head, completely befuddled. Not that I can blame him.

'Just make sure you tell her, okay?'

Still gaping, Pete nods his agreement and I start to climb the stairs, my shin smarting with each step. Scott's home, currently parked on the sofa, leaning forward with the Xbox controller between his knees as he bashes away at the buttons. He doesn't even acknowledge my arrival as I head for the kitchen to check on the chicken curry I set going in the slow cooker this morning (that I'm no longer in the mood for after the double helping of strudel on the bus) but he gets like this when he's completely immersed in a game.

'I thought you were with Pete from downstairs on Saturday night.' I grab a can of lager from the mini fridge for some extra Perfect Girlfriend points. 'But I just ran into him in the hall and he said you weren't with him.'

'Are you checking up on me or something?' Scott is no longer engaged with the game playing out on the screen and is instead frowning at me, deep crevices lining his usually smooth forehead.

'No, of course not.' I pass the can to Scott, but rather than being pleased with my Perfect Girlfriend act of thoughtfulness, he glares at it as he plonks it down on the coffee table. 'We were just chatting and I mentioned you being out late on Saturday night . . .'

'I *am* allowed out, you know. You're not my jailer.'

'I never said I was, and I didn't mean to sound like I was annoyed at you being out.' I tiptoe towards the armchair, sinking down slowly onto it as though I can smooth away the brewing argument with micro movements, as though any sudden change will ignite the flame.

'I suppose you *didn't mean* to check up on me either.' Scott sneers as he says it, throwing the controller into the corner of the sofa. 'What next? Checking my texts and emails? Go ahead.' He grabs his mobile from his pocket and thrusts it towards me. 'Go on, check for incriminating evidence. Catch me out in whatever it is you think I'm up to. *Go on.*' He stands up so he can thrust the phone closer to me. 'It's unlocked. Snoop all you like, because you won't find anything.'

'I don't want to snoop.' I tuck my hands underneath my thighs, not wanting to even *touch* the phone, let alone snoop for information on it. Information on what, I have no idea. I don't even understand what's going on here. I didn't intend for any of this to happen, and I'm not sure how it has. I was simply making conversation and suddenly Scott is glowering down at me, accusing me of things I haven't done.

'Have a good look, Zo. Get it out of your system.' Scott drops the phone on the sofa and storms off. I hear the bedroom door slam a moment later, followed by the sound of Stormzy pounding through the wall.

It takes me ages to coax him out of the bedroom, and I try not to feel offended that it's the offer of salted popcorn and *Die Hard* that lures him back into the living room and not my chicken curry. He's out of the bedroom and has accepted my apology, and that's all that matters. I try to relax as we watch the film, but my stomach is churning (and it has nothing to do with the salted popcorn, which always leaves me feeling bloated). That tiff came from nowhere, but it could have quite easily escalated into a premature Terrible Row. I have to tread so carefully from now on, because there's no way I can squander this second chance with him.

Chapter 14

6th December

After last night's argument, it's a relief to hear Scott clattering about the bedroom when I wake up. He's still here. I haven't wrecked our relationship all over again.

'Have you seen my blue tie with the white spots?' When I peer out from underneath the covers, squinting against the light pouring in through the too-thin curtains (we really do need to replace those) I see Scott rifling through my underwear drawer. Quite why his tie would be in there is beyond me but I'm not awake enough to question my boyfriend's logic.

'Have you looked in the wardrobe, on your tie rack?' It's my day off, so I snuggle back down under the covers and close my eyes. I don't see the derision on Scott's face, but it's clear in his voice.

'Duh. It was the first place I looked.' I hear the underwear drawer slide shut and another one opening. 'Have you moved it?'

'I haven't seen or touched it.' I can feel the fuzziness of sleep wearing off but I'm determined to drop back off to sleep. I take deep, relaxing breaths to invite slumber, but it's incredibly diffi-cult to coax your body to sleep when your boyfriend's slamming drawers closed and yanking others open in the same room, all while muttering obscenities under his breath when his search proves fruitless.

'Can't you wear a different tie?' My eyes are squeezed shut, as though I can force myself into unconsciousness through sheer stubbornness.

'The blue one with spots goes perfectly with this jacket.' The bed jolts as Scott flops onto it, and I prop myself up onto my elbows to peer curiously at him. That last sentence came out incredibly whiny, but Scott Le Tissier doesn't *do* whiny. He banters. He swaggers. He gets loud when he's annoyed or frustrated, but he never whines. 'I'm showing that massive house near Boyd Park so I need to look sharp. My massive commission depends on it, and no commission, no holiday.'

No wonder he's stressed out. The house on Boyd Park is important to the company, but it's also super important to Scott. To us. We need that break away and I'm touched that Scott realises it too.

'Have you checked the laundry basket? Maybe it got mixed up with your shirt last time you wore it?'

Scott takes in a huge lungful of air before releasing it in one big puff as he pushes up from the bed, and I feel an inexplicable stab of guilt, as though I'm responsible for the wayward tie. He stomps out of the bedroom and I peel off the covers, giving up on the idea of a lie-in. I'd need to get up soon anyway as I've arranged to meet up with Mum for lunch. The cold air bites at my warm skin, and I remember we had trouble with the boiler earlier in the month, which meant there was a 50/50 chance of the radiators heating up. Scott said he'd call the landlord about it but he was too preoccupied with work and I ended up doing it. If I recall, there was a bit of a tiff when I brought it up, so I won't mention it this time and instead simply call the landlord once Scott has set off for work.

Shuddering against the cold, I wrap myself in Scott's tatty dressing gown and tie it tightly around my middle. On the off chance, I have a quick peek in the wardrobe, and there it is. The blue tie with the white spots that goes perfectly with the suit Scott's wearing, sitting on the tie rack, only slightly obscured by a plain red tie.

'Found it.' I dangle the tie triumphantly in the air as I step into the living room, expecting to find Scott elbow-deep in the laundry basket. Instead, I find him sitting on the sofa, scrolling on his phone.

'Brilliant.' Eyes still on the screen, he reaches out a hand for me to place the tie in. I hover for a moment, waiting for a hint of gratitude or an enquiry of where the tie had been 'hiding', but I give up and head into the kitchen to put the kettle on when neither is forthcoming.

'Did you ask Kristen what the girls would like for Christmas?' I'm meeting Mum in town for lunch, so I may as well have a nosy around the shops while I've got the chance.

'I'll do it later.' Scott slips his phone into his pocket and flicks his collar up as he strides across the living room. 'I might go over to Dan's after work. That's Dan O'Brien, my best mate, if you want to check up on it later.'

I thought we'd smoothed everything over after our argument last night but clearly not. I open my mouth to apologise again, but Scott has already left the room. He returns a moment later, his tie draped around his neck, waiting to be knotted. He holds out a little red box, fastened with fine white ribbon finished off with a delicate little bow. My heart flutters and a huge smile spreads across my face. Scott *has* forgiven me, and he has a gift to prove it.

'This was on the doorstep.' He places the box on the breakfast bar and pushes it towards me.

'I wonder what it is.' I grin at Scott as I pick it up. The little cardboard box fits in my palm and has clearly been crafted by hand. It's rustic-looking, which only makes it more special, with a handwritten tag attached to the ribbon:

Sankt Nikolaus Tag! (Happy St Nicholas Day!) xxx

It isn't from Scott after all. It's from Franziska, and inside there are three homemade chocolates nestled on silver tissue paper. It's such a beautiful gesture that I'm only a tiny bit disappointed the gift isn't from Scott.

Still in my pyjamas and Scott's dressing gown, I head downstairs so I can thank my neighbour. Franziska invites me inside, and I stay for a quick cup of tea before heading back upstairs to get ready to meet Mum. The little red box is still on the breakfast bar, but the lid has been removed and the silver tissue paper is dumped on the side. The box is devoid of its little chocolates. Scott must have eaten them before he left for work.

I know it's silly to get upset over a handful of chocolates, but an overwhelming surge of hurt and anger rises within me. Why would he *do* that? Okay, my name wasn't on the tag, but Franziska is *my* friend (how was it Scott described her a couple of days ago? Ancient?) and what gave him the right to eat them all himself?

My hands are trembling as I pick up the tissue paper and press it gently into the box, but I need to keep calm. To swallow down the rage and dejection before it spills out into something I can't control. My relationship with Scott is already on thin ice – if I add any more weight to our problems, it could cause irreparable damage. An image of Scott stuffing clothes into his gym bag pops into my mind and it's enough to quell the fury and panic coursing through my body. I can't – won't – let that happen again, and certainly not over something as petty as a handful of chocolates.

Mum waves at me through the window as I reach the restaurant, and I'm glad she's managed to bag a seat overlooking the Christmas market. The market is pretty quiet, but there are a few people milling around with mugs of mulled wine and hot chocolate, stooping over the stalls to look at handmade gifts and treats. The smell of a hog roast as I passed through on my way to the restaurant has made my stomach rumble, so I can't wait to get inside and grab a menu.

'Hello, love. You're looking lovely.' Mum stands so she can kiss my cheek before I start to unwind the pompom-less mustard scarf and the matching hat I managed to finish while Scott and I were watching *Die Hard* last night. 'Oh.' She eyes my fringe, which I attempt to smooth down, even though I know it'll make no difference to the atrocity sitting high on my forehead. 'That's an . . . interesting new look. Very quirky. Very *you*.'

I'm not sure whether to be offended by that last bit (a terrible haircut is very 'me'?) but I know Mum is only trying to make me feel better so I let it go. Besides, I'm way too hungry to worry about my fringe.

'I'm thinking of going for a new look, actually.' I drape my coat over the back of the chair and sit down opposite Mum. 'Maybe blonde?'

'Really? But I love your hair.' Mum's eyes flick to my fringe and although she doesn't add 'except that bit', she doesn't have to. But then we're on the same page on that one. 'It's so lovely and natural. Why would you want to dump a load of chemicals on it?'

'You dye your hair.' There are already a couple of menus on the table, so I open one, flicking to the lunchtime section.

'That's because I'm riddled with grey, which I'm far, *far* too young to have. If I left it to how nature intended, I'd end up looking like my mum which, I'm sure you'll agree, is not a look you aim for.'

'I don't know about that.' I lower my menu and look across at Mum. 'You're a very attractive woman, plus you don't have this great big hooter.' I point at my nose, which I've always felt is far too big for my face. It enters a room five minutes before I do. Beake by name, beak by nature.

'Rubbish. You have a beautiful nose, inherited from your gran.'

'So it's okay for me to have Gran's nose, but you disguise her hair?' I'm about to raise my eyebrows at Mum, but change my mind when I realise it'll only draw attention to where my fringe is supposed to be sitting, rather than an inch or two further up.

'That's different. I'm just trying to halt the ageing process. I'm in my early fifties – I don't want to look like a little, frail old lady.'

'Gran wasn't that little or frail.' Granted, she didn't seem to loom over me when I saw her the other day like she did when I was little, but she was a robust-looking woman.

'No, I don't suppose she was.' Mum smiles wistfully. 'I suppose that's why it was such a surprise when she passed like that. So suddenly, out of nowhere. We thought she was still sleeping off her Christmas lunch, and it was only when your Uncle Jack went to wake her up so we could help her up to bed that we realised . . .'

'I forgot she'd died at Christmas.'

Mum nods, the corners of her mouth turned down. 'Christmas Day, in fact. You and Ashleigh had gone up to bed by then, thankfully.' My cousin and I hadn't wanted to go to bed – it was Christmas Day and there were still toys we hadn't got round to playing with yet – but we must have fallen asleep quickly because neither of us knew about Gran's passing until the morning after. 'So it was just me and your dad, and Uncle Jack and Aunty Lynne downstairs when it happened. She was in her nightie and slippers.' Mum smiles fondly at this sudden memory. 'And she still had the hat from her cracker on her head. Refused to take it off because it was "jolly".'

'Was it orange?' My stomach is doing funny things, and it isn't because I'm hungry and can't wait to order the macaroni cheese with streaky bacon bits. At the scene of my accident, Gran had been wearing a floor-length nightie and an orange paper hat from a cracker. I never knew this detail from the day she died – Mum was too distraught at the time to bring up anything so trivial, and I'm sure it has never been discussed since.

'I have no idea.' Mum shrugs. 'Could have been, I suppose. But then it could have been any other colour.'

It was orange. I know it was. And for some strange reason, this knowledge makes me feel light and almost giddy. Gran visited me. It wasn't a dream or a hallucination. She actually visited me, and she gave me a second chance at life – and at love.

Chapter 15

I have a wander around the shops after lunch with Mum and pick up a few bits for Christmas (mainly tubs of sweets and chocolates that won't last until the 25th) and, despite wolfing down a chocolate orange torte after my pasta, I do a little detour to the bakery across the road from Scott's office on my way to the bus station. The window of The Bake House always looks appealing with its display of cakes and biscuits, but it looks extra special now with its sprinkling of Christmas magic. The window has a frosted look, with a large, slapdash circle cleared in the middle, as though a gloved hand has wiped it clear to peer at the goodies on show. The centrepiece is a gingerbread house, iced in pastel shades with Christmas trees and a couple of reindeer standing outside, while marzipan snowmen proudly present festive-themed cupcakes and iced biscuits. I'm eyeing up the reindeer cupcakes and the Christmas-tree-topped chocolate sandwich biscuits, and debating which to go for, when the door to the bakery opens and Scott steps outside. He shuffles to a stop when he sees me, his eyes wide and startled.

'Is my fringe that bad?' I was too hot walking around the shopping centre so I'd removed my newly knitted hat, but I drag it out of my bag now and plonk it on my head.

'I just wasn't expecting to see you here, that's all.' Scott manages a shaky sort of smile, clearly still traumatised by my ghastly fringe even though it's now out of sight. 'What *are* you doing here?'

I point at the treats in the window. 'I think I'm going to go for the reindeer cupcake.'

'No, don't.' Placing his arm around my shoulders, he starts to guide me away from the bakery. 'I've already bought you one.'

'On a Tuesday?'

Scott shrugs. 'It's my little way of saying sorry, for going off on one last night. I shouldn't have done that. I don't know why I did. I think I'm just a bit stressed with work and stuff. I need to get that house near Boyd Park off my books before Christmas. I really, *really* want to take you away, somewhere nice. You deserve it.'

'*We* deserve it, and I'm sure you'll do it, because you're amazing at your job. And I'm sorry if it sounded like I was accusing you of anything, because I really wasn't.'

'I know.' Scott stoops to kiss my cheek. 'I'm an idiot.'

'I'm not going to argue with that.' I nudge him playfully with my elbow. 'So, where is it?'

'Where's what?'

He really is an idiot at times. 'The cupcake.' I stop and look him up and down. He's carrying a take-out cup of coffee but nothing else, and there's no way a cupcake would fit in his suit jacket pocket. Not unless he's transformed it from a cupcake into a pancake.

'Oh. That.' Scott aims his coffee cup across the road, towards the estate agents. 'It's in my desk drawer. I bought it earlier.'

'You've been to the bakery twice in one day?' The boy is getting as bad as I am when it comes to sweet treats.

'The kettle's still on the blink and I needed coffee before I strangled somebody.' He takes a sip of his coffee, wincing at the heat. 'Anyway, I'd better get back in there, before somebody strangles *me* for skiving.'

96

'I'll come in with you.' Taking hold of Scott's hand, I start to pull him towards the kerb, looking in both directions to check for traffic.

'What? Why?' Scott digs his heels in before I can cross, despite there being a clear gap for us to go.

'Don't worry, I'm not going to stay. In fact, I'll wait down in reception and you can nip upstairs and grab my cupcake.' There's still a big enough gap, so I try again and this time Scott moves with me. 'You don't expect me to wait until you get home to have it, do you? Not now I know it's there, begging to be eaten.'

'No. I guess not.' We head over to the estate agents and Scott opens the door for me. 'I won't be a minute. Why don't you say hello to Elaine while you wait?'

I've met Elaine a few times over the years, and she's always been nice enough, so I head over to the reception desk. I explain the situation, and Elaine sighs dreamily.

'He's such a sweet boy, isn't he? You're a very lucky girl.'

I don't need Elaine to tell me this. I'm well aware of how lucky I am to have Scott back in my life.

She smiles at me, and I smile back, neither knowing what to say now. It's all starting to get a bit awkward and I'm willing Scott to return with my cupcake so I can leave. The seconds that pass stretch on for what feels like hours.

'That's, erm, a lovely wreath.' I look over my shoulder, towards the door I've just passed through and which I'd quite like to run back out of right now.

'Really?' Elaine places a hand on her chest as she beams at me from behind the reception desk. 'I made it. Do you really think it's lovely?'

'I do.' Which is true. It's very festive with its greenery and red berries, and the hint of cinnamon and orange as we passed through was a nice touch.

'I'm running a wreath-making workshop at the library on the thirteenth. You should come!' Elaine yanks open her desk drawer and rummages around for a moment before producing a slightly crumpled business card. 'There's no need to book. You can just turn up. Hopefully people will this time.' Elaine gives such a sad-looking smile, I have no choice but to take the card and murmur a vague sort of commitment. 'It's only twenty pounds per person. Half what it was last year. I'm sure that's what put people off and not me.' Her top lip flickers as she delivers an unconvincing laugh. I'm so grateful when Scott returns to the reception area, but his face is creased with angry lines.

'You're never going to believe it, but somebody's nicked the cupcake. They've gone into my desk drawer and taken it. Who does that?' He shakes his head, the lines deepening. 'I swear, if it isn't nailed down, it gets lifted in this place. Do you know how many staplers I've gone through this year? Seven! That's more than one every couple of months. And don't get me started on pens . . .'

'It's fine.' I drop the business card in my handbag and place a hand on Scott's arm, hoping the small gesture will calm him down. 'I'll just pop over and buy another one on my way to the bus station. It's no big deal.'

'No.' Scott grabs my arm as I start to turn away. '*I* wanted to get the cupcake. You know, for that thing last night . . .' His eyes flick towards Elaine, even though he's lowered his voice. 'You go home and I'll buy you another one. I'm afraid you're going to have to be patient for once in your life.' He nudges me and we both smile. I'm so glad to see the lines smoothed away from his face that I would have agreed to anything, and waiting a few more hours for a cupcake seems reasonable.

'Okay. I'll see you in a bit.' I kiss his cheek and head for the door, but I stop before I reach it. 'But didn't you say you were going to Dan's after work?'

'I'll come straight home.' Scott cocks an eyebrow. 'I wouldn't want to keep the lady waiting any longer than necessary for her cupcake.'

I have a stupid, goofy grin on my face as I pass by the cinnamon- and orange-scented wreath, because that gesture – that sacrifice from Scott, of him putting me first – is sweeter than any cupcake.

Chapter 16

7th December

I can't help singing along to Mariah Carey playing on the radio as I prise open the window on my advent calendar. Door number seven reveals a little chocolate teddy bear. Yum. I pop it into my mouth, humming along with the queen of Christmas as I prop the calendar back up on the breakfast bar.

I'm in extremely good spirits this morning, and it has everything to do with the reindeer cupcake Scott presented me with when he got home from work yesterday (and also a little bit to do with what happened afterwards. Is it weird that I can't remember the last time we had sex before last night? Probably, but I'm in too good a mood to delve too deep into the question). We even watched *Love Actually* together, and Scott didn't gag or roll his eyes once, not even when Andrew Lincoln's character held up the cards on Keira Knightley's doorstep, and I was particularly impressed when he didn't declare that the little kid 'deserved a hand-job at the least after all that effort' after he caught up with the American girl at the airport and she pecked him on the cheek.

I turn up the radio and belt out the lyrics along with Mariah as I make my way into the kitchen. The paper bag from the reindeer cupcake is still on the side, and I get a weird niggly feeling in the pit of my stomach as I pick it up. There's something about it, something I can't quite grasp, that's bothering me, but I'm distracted by someone banging on the wall. It's Scott, who's still in bed because he's booked the day off work to let the plumber in to fix the boiler mid-morning. Shoving the paper bag in the bin, I dash across the room and turn the radio down. I make him a cup of coffee and leave it on the bedside table as an apology for waking him up before I leave for work. On my way out, I find Franziska hanging a wreath on her front door. It's even more impressive than the one Elaine made; bigger, with jingly silver bells, shiny red baubles and a fragrance that is filling the whole entrance hall with the smell of Christmas. If I close my eyes, I could be standing in Gran's kitchen, helping to make a boozy Christmas pudding.

'Did you enjoy your Christmas truffles?'

I'd completely forgotten about the chocolate incident yesterday, but I don't want to admit to Franziska that Scott ate them all himself so I simply smile and fudge the truth. 'They were delicious. Thank you.' I mean, it isn't a lie – the truffles probably were delicious if Franziska's other baking triumphs are anything to go by.

'I'm so glad! Georgia and Bradley helped me to make them at the weekend. Such good helpers, even if they did sneak half the chocolate as we made them.' Franziska winks at me, and I'm hit with another memory of baking with Gran, of her slipping me a handful of leftover chocolate chips after we'd popped a batch of cookies in the oven with a whispered 'don't tell your mum'.

'Are you ready for your video call with Klaus tonight?'

The mischievous glint vanishes from Franziska's eyes as she turns away to straighten the already perfectly-aligned wreath. 'I'm not sure it's going to be possible. My internet is playing up. It's so slow, I can't even check my emails.'

'Oh, that's nothing.' I dismiss the 'problem' with a wave of my hand. 'It's connecting to the café next door, that's all. I'll just set it to connect to your Wi-Fi and it'll be perfect.'

'How do you know that's the problem?'

Yikes. I *shouldn't* know about that yet. Not until I've had a look at her settings. 'Because it happens to mine all the time.' It's only a teeny harmless fib. 'I'll sort it when I get home from work.' Lifting a hand in farewell, I make a dash for the door before Franziska can probe any further and I end up tripping myself up again.

The bus takes forever to arrive, and I'm halfway to becoming a human snowman by the time I drop into the only available seat. I'm so preoccupied by trying to keep my teeth from audibly chattering that it's a few minutes before I realise I'm sitting next to the girl with the book. It's the gilded title of *A Christmas Carol* that catches my attention. As usual, the book is closed on her lap and the shabby bus ticket bookmark has barely made it up a quarter of the pages.

The bus stops and the girl is suddenly alert. Back straight, her eyes are trained ahead to the front of the bus as passengers squeeze on board and try to find a space to stand. I see the moment she clocks him; her eyes light up and she sits up even straighter, her cheeks taking on a pink tinge as she tracks his journey. He looks about her age – seventeen, eighteen, I'd guess – with shaggy dark blond hair poking out of a beanie hat. He apologises as he maneuvers his way through the throng, trying not to bash people with his backpack. He stops beside my seat so he can cling on to the rail, and when I sneak a peek at the girl next to me, her cheeks have turned an alarming crimson shade. *This* is who she's been looking out for. I noticed it on Christmas Eve, so she'll continue her daily ritual of seeking him out on the bus without saying a word to him for weeks to come. Unless I do something about it. Which is what I'm here to do after all, as part of my official Christmas Cupid duties.

'Excuse me?' I shuffle to the very edge of the seat and stand up. 'Would you like to sit here? I'm getting off in a minute.'

'Are you sure?' He looks like he would very much like to sit down but is too polite to simply plonk himself in the seat.

'I'm sure.' We both shuffle in the small space so we can trade places. He sits down and wedges his backpack between his feet.

'Hi. We're in the same English lit class, right?'

It seems I don't have to do anything more. The kid has turned straight to the girl to engage in conversation.

'I sit a couple of seats behind you. I'm Stephanie-Jayne Grindley.' She closes her eyes briefly and scrunches up her nose. 'Steffi-Jayne, really, or just Steffi. Whatever.' She closes her eyes again, looking like she'd very much like to slide down in her seat until she's on the floor of the bus, where she can crawl under the seat in front to hide out for the rest of the journey. I can't help smiling to myself though, despite her embarrassment, as I remember how awkward I was around Scott to begin with. The way words spilled out of my mouth, one after the other, beyond my control. I even told him that I loved frogs for some reason, so when he presented me with a stuffed toy version during our next date, I had to pretend to adore it. It didn't take much acting skills, because it *is* pretty cute, and I adore the sentiment around it, and I did such a good job that Scott is still under the impression that frogs are my favourite animal and our flat is full of them. Scott even bought me a little frog keyring to go onto my set when we got the keys for the flat, which was very sweet.

'That's a lot of names for one person.' There's a hint of humour in his voice, but I don't think he's laughing *at* the book girl. 'What do your mates call you?'

'Steffi-Jayne.'

He nods and holds out a hand. 'Hi Steffi-Jayne. I'm Owain.'

'I know.' She cringes, but then she manages to laugh at herself. 'Hello, Owain.'

'*A Christmas Carol*, eh?' He nods down at the book. 'Are you enjoying it?'

Steffi-Jayne opens her mouth, considers what's she's about to say . . . and then shakes her head as her shoulders drop. 'Not really. I thought I would. It's a classic, and it's Christmas but . . .'

'It's a bit boring?'

'More than a bit.'

Owain nods. 'I prefer The Muppets' version.'

She laughs, her eyes widening at the sudden noise, and she clamps a hand over her mouth. But her new friend grins, clearly very pleased that he's made her laugh. My watch vibrates, and though I'd like nothing more than to continue watching the pair, I tear my eyes away.

There's a heart on my watch, this time whole without the crack down the middle, and there's a flashing number one inside, which I'm pretty sure means I've just matched up my first couple. I want to jump up and down on the bus and wave my arms about in celebration, but I resist and have a mental happy dance instead. I did it! I actually fulfilled the first part of my Christmas Cupid task. And if I do that five more times, I'll survive the Winter Wonderland parade and live happily ever after with Scott.

'All I Want for Christmas is a Smurf Hat' is playing as I enter the gingerbread forest of Christmas trees, ready for when the shop opens in a few minutes, and I find myself humming along. I'm feeling pretty good after officially matching up my first couple and there's been a pleasant buzz in my stomach ever since my watch signalled the successful pairing. I don't know what's going to happen with Steffi-Jayne and Owain in the future, but I hope it's happy and filled with love and laughter.

'You always stop at this tree.'

I hadn't even realised I'd come to a stop, but here I am, standing in front of the bird-filled tree, my fingers stroking the silky soft feathers of the little robin.

'Do I?'

Milo nods and points at my hand. 'And you always stroke that robin. Is it for luck or something?'

'No, nothing like that.' It isn't even a conscious thing, but I guess I do gravitate towards the little red-breasted bird. 'I think it just reminds me of my gran. She loved robins, whether it was Christmas or not. She had a family of them who used to feed in her garden. She'd put food out for them every morning and she'd sit and watch them with a cup of tea, like they were the most fascinating thing she'd ever seen. She died, my gran, with an orange Christmas cracker hat on her head.' I don't know why I'm telling Milo about the cracker crown, but it's stuck with me ever since Mum revealed that little detail. She died with that paper hat on her head and she's still wearing it now, and that thought makes me feel a bit funny inside. Because I don't want to spend eternity hobbling about on a pair of stilts.

'She must have been happy, though, when she died. Or just before, at least.'

'Why do you say that?' We've started to move along the row of Christmas trees now, passing the Barbie tree with her sparkly accessories.

'She was wearing a Christmas cracker hat. You can't be anything but happy when you're wearing a paper crown. You might be miserable when you put it on – my stepdad grumbles about it every year and he whips it off as soon as Mum's back is turned – but only happy people keep the crowns on for any length of time.'

I'm not sure how scientifically true Milo's assessment is, but I'd like to think Gran was happy that evening, surrounded by the people she loved. And slipping away in your sleep is a much better way to go than being knocked to the ground by a double decker bus in front of a load of gawping strangers.

'There's a pub quiz tomorrow at The Spindles.' We pass the Thomas and Friends tree, with its smiley train faces and plastic track snaking around the branches like tinsel. 'I'm putting a

C&L's team together if you're interested?' I've already got Eloise on board, and I'm planning to talk Cliff and Maureen into it, and if I could push Milo and Shannon together again, something might happen this time . . .

'Yeah, sounds fun. Count me in.'

I don't even have to try to convince him with the two hundred quid prize.

'Great. Why don't you ask Shannon if she wants to join us? I need to go and . . .' I wave a vague hand back through the Christmas trees and dash away before any further explanation is needed. I hang out by the dinosaur tree for a few minutes before taking a peek through the trees at the gingerbread house. Shannon is leaning against one of the apple trees outside, scrolling through the phone that should be switched off and stored in her locker, and Milo is nowhere to be seen. But there's good news as I pass through on my way to the North Pole.

'Milo says there's a quiz tomorrow?' Shannon has put her phone away and is checking the fake fur trim around the cuffs of her cloak for foreign bits of gingerbread crumbs and glitter that are rife in Santa's village.

'There is. Eight o'clock at The Spindles. Everybody welcome.'

'Is there a prize?'

'Two hundred quid for first place.'

Shannon pauses her fur-check and looks up at me, her lips pursed. She gives a curt nod before returning to her inspection. 'I'll be there.'

So that's four so far. Now I just have to convince Cliff and Maureen to come along, and who knows, maybe I'll clock up a couple more matches.

Cliff and Maureen need a bit more persuasion than Milo and Shannon, but I eventually win them round by stroking their egos: I tell Cliff we don't stand a chance without his expert general knowledge, while Maureen is suitably flattered when I tell her we're in dire need of her admirable culinary know-how (plus, the cash prize would come in handy at this time of year . . .).

So the buzzy feeling is still going strong in my tummy as I head home, and it only increases when Franziska's face pops up on her computer screen after I've 'fixed' her Wi-Fi issue, even if it does look a little worried.

'Relax a bit. You look like you're about to fight to the death with a tiger, not speak to an old friend.'

Franziska nods but the stricken look doesn't leave her face. We have a few minutes until the call has been scheduled to take place, so I decide to take her mind off it, so she can unwind before she faces Klaus.

'Not long until Christmas now. Are you looking forward to spending the day with your son?'

Franziska loves talking about her family. Her whole face lights up and she exudes warmth and love, and that's the look we want Klaus to see.

'Tobias and Debbie are taking the kids to Florida for Christmas.'

Bugger. I *knew* this – it's why Franziska and I were going to spend the day together. Rather than giving Franziska a warm glow, I'm going to bum her out, just in time for her call. I am an idiot.

'They invited me along, but I didn't fancy it.' Franziska scrunches up her nose. 'I can't think of anything worse than standing around in massive queues all day, pretending to be merry while you're sweating like a pig in the heat. Christmas should be cold enough to freeze your danglies off. It should be bitterly cold, with blankets and roaring fires, not bikinis and sun cream.'

'And you definitely can't go to your daughter's for the day?' I feel horribly guilty now, as though I'm abandoning my friend after our pact to spend Christmas Day together, even though the pact hasn't been made yet because Scott and I are still together.

Franziska looks at herself on the computer screen and fluffs up her hair. 'I don't want to travel all that way.'

'Don't they live in Bolton?' Which is only on the other side of Greater Manchester.

'All right, all right.' Franziska turns away from the computer and folds her arms across her chest. 'It's Malcolm. My son-in-law. He's a mummy's boy, and if there's one thing I cannot stand, it is men who act like children. He is forty-eight years old and the man is still clinging on to those apron strings.' She makes a severe scissor-cutting gesture with two fingers. 'They need snipping, and until they are severed, I shall do my best to avoid the pair, because she'll be there too, the overbearing mother. Picking up after him like he is still five years old. Do you know, the last time I was there, she dragged the ironing board out and ironed his work shirts for him. What kind of grown man cannot operate an iron?' She rolls her eyes and is about to go on when Klaus' call comes through.

'Are you ready for this?' The mouse pointer hovers over the connect button on the screen, and when Franziska gives a firmish nod of the head, I click it and dive out of the way so I'm not caught on screen.

And then there's Klaus, Franziska's first love from fifty years ago. He's quite handsome, with tanned skin glowing against his silvery hair and stubble, and his eyes look kind with their crinkled corners, the lines bleeding into his cheeks as he smiles at my neighbour. They speak in German, and although I don't know what they're saying, the exchange seems chatty and not at all awkward or stilted. Franziska's shoulders have relaxed into their natural position and she's no longer gripping the edge of the desk as her hands fly about, as much a part of the conversation as her words.

I creep out of the room, tiptoeing down the hallway and easing the front door open. I wait until I'm halfway up the stairs before I check my watch. No heart symbol to indicate a match, but the conversation has only just started. Maybe they need time to rediscover the flame that once engulfed them as teenagers before it counts as an official match? Because the match on the bus didn't register as soon as Owain sat down next to Steffi-Jayne – it took a bit of time for them to chat, to connect before my watch pinged, so hopefully the same will be true of Franziska and Klaus.

Crossing my fingers, I make my way up the rest of the stairs. I really hope this matchmaking thing works over the internet, because Steffi-Jayne and Owain's pairing won't be enough to save me from the Santa Express and an afterlife attached to a pair of stilts.

Chapter 17

8th December

According to Franziska, the conversation with Klaus went very well last night, and they reminisced about their younger days until almost midnight. So I'm a bit put out that my watch doesn't reflect that and is still stubbornly set at one couple. Maybe Franziska and Klaus aren't a true love match after all and their time has been and gone? Or maybe I'm a terrible Christmas Cupid and I should resign myself to the fact that I'm going to fail my mission and end up on the tarmac on Christmas Eve, destined to forever wobble on silly stilts and even sillier oversized elf shoes.

I'm feeling pretty glum as I leave Franziska in the hallway, even with a piece of leftover stollen to enjoy as a second breakfast as I wait for the bus. My neighbour is in good spirits after her catch-up with Klaus, but then she doesn't know what is at stake here.

Scott is with me, physically if not in spirit, and I give up trying to compete with whatever's on his phone long before the bus pulls up. He barely pauses in his scrolling as he steps on board, aims his phone at the reader to register his fare, and shuffles along the length of the aisle to find an empty seat towards the back. I fall into the seat next to him, glad that he's picked this seat because we're slightly raised up, giving me a good view of Steffi-Jayne a couple of seats ahead on the opposite side of the aisle. As usual, she has a book with her, but it isn't *A Christmas Carol* and she's actually reading it this time. As I passed, it looked like a well-thumbed romantic comedy.

Outside, hints of the season are growing; there are more Christmas trees standing proudly in windows, there's a fairy-lit hedgerow and lots of 'Santa Stop Here' signs, and more and more people are donning their winter gear, upgrading thick jackets with hats, scarves and gloves, and switching shoes for boots.

The bus stops and Steffi-Jayne closes her book. With her neck craned so she can look towards the front of the bus, she grabs hold of her bag that's sitting on the seat next to her, timing it just right so that the seat is free for when Owain passes. He plonks himself down and although I can't hear what they're saying, they chat throughout the entire journey and Steffi-Jayne is giggling at something he's said as we disembark at the bus station. I definitely haven't failed with this pairing, and it puts a spring back in my step as I head towards the toy shop. My confidence isn't fully restored but it's at least topped up enough to make me determined that I'll do my absolute best to bring together two more couples at the pub quiz tonight.

I race home after work so I can get something quick to eat and change into something a bit fancier than the flower-printed shirt dress and slouchy cardigan I wore to work, and it's me who almost collides into Isla in my haste to get down the stairs this time.

'Sorry.' I cling on to the bannister to steady myself after my sudden halt. It took longer than I thought it would to find something in my wardrobe that actually matches both in colour and style, and now I have less than twenty minutes to get to the pub.

'No worries.' Isla smiles, but it barely reaches her mouth, never mind her eyes.

'Is everything okay?' Isla is usually not much more than a blur as she rushes in and out of the building, but you can tell that she's a jovial person, even when she's weighed down by a load of stress. The Isla before me looks as though she's had all the joy sucked from her body, leaving nothing behind but a dejected husk.

'Yeah.' Isla tries to smile again but decides it isn't worth the effort halfway through. 'Just had a date cancel on me at the very last minute, that's all. I wasn't even that into them, so I'm annoyed more than anything.'

'How do you fancy taking part in a pub quiz instead? I'm just on my way there now.'

I know I'm attempting to set Milo up with Shannon, but it doesn't hurt to have a back-up plan. And Isla is *gorgeous*. There's no way Milo won't be interested, and I can certainly see the appeal of my grotto companion. My type is stockier and rougher round the edges, but Milo has an adorable boy-next-door vibe that I hope Isla will be interested in. It's worth a shot, at least.

'I mean, I have no plans other than sitting in front of the telly by myself now.' Isla glances up the stairs, towards her flat. 'Are you sure nobody will mind me tagging along?'

'Of course not. And it'd be a shame to put that dress to waste.' Isla said she wasn't that interested in her date, but she's certainly made an effort. The halter-neck with a short, swishy skirt is a cute and flirty take on the little black dress, especially when teamed with a pair of snakeskin ankle boots, and the smoky eye make-up she's applied really brings out the green tones in her hazel eyes.

'You know what? You're right.' Smiling genuinely this time, Isla leads the way down the stairs. We have to leg it to the bus stop as there's one visible up the road, but we make it in time, panting and giggling as we collapse into our seats.

The others are already sitting in the pub with drinks, apart from Shannon who's flirting with the barman, so I make some quick introductions before Isla and I head to the bar.

'Zoey, come and meet Xavier.' Shannon grabs my arm as I approach and drags me to her side. 'He. Is. *Hilarious*.' She reaches across the bar with her free hand to tap the barman on the chest to emphasise each word. 'We were just talking about that kid that came into the grotto last week. You know the one who tried to stick his head up my cloak, and instead of telling him off, his dad asked if he could have a go next? Do you remember?' Shannon throws her head back and laughs her little socks off while I attempt to turn my grimace into a playing-along smile. To be fair to Xavier the barman, he doesn't look impressed by the tale either.

'Yes, I remember. Quite vividly.' I clear my throat before plastering on a much more convincing smile. 'Can I get a glass of white wine and . . .' I turn to Isla.

'I'll have a glass of white as well, please.'

Shannon picks up a half-empty glass from the bar and gives it a jiggle, the ice cubes jangling against the sides. 'And I'll have another of these if you're getting a round in.'

'Double vodka and Coke?'

Shannon's eyes light up when the barman remembers her order. 'That's exactly it! Isn't he amazing, Zoey?'

Xavier places our drinks on the bar and I have to drag Shannon away as the quizmaster announces the start of Round One.

'We had to come up with a team name.' Eloise leans in close to whisper as Milo scribbles down our answer to the first question. 'We went with Santa's Helpers, what with us all working in a toy shop. Sorry, Isla, we would have picked something else if we'd known you were coming.'

Isla bats the issue away with her hand. 'Don't worry about it. I quite like the idea of being an honorary elf for the evening.'

'Ssh.' Maureen glares at us, the corners of her mouth turned down as she covers her lips with her finger, and we try not to giggle like naughty schoolgirls as we mutter apologies before pressing our mouths tightly shut. We listen intently to the next question, and I do my best not to meet Eloise's eye because I know that if I do, a floodgate of mirth will open up and I'll get another telling-off from Maureen for disrupting the quiz.

'Is it The Rolling Stones?'

We're huddled together, properly into the quiz by Round Three: Pop Music, our voices lowered so the teams around us can't steal our suggestions. The second round focusing on horticulture was particularly bad for us, so we have some catching up to do over the next few rounds.

'Of course it isn't the bloody Rolling Stones.' Cliff forgets to lower his voice as he scoffs at Maureen's suggestion. 'That's Mick Jagger. *Everybody* knows that. Even Shannon.'

If Shannon is offended by this, she doesn't show it and simply knocks back her vodka-coke as though she's playing Pub Quiz Bingo and is crossing off 'Teammate Spat' with a rather large sip.

'Which band is it then, you pompous tit?' Maureen leans across the table and hisses at Cliff. This matchmaking thing isn't going well at all.

'Hey, hey. No name-calling.' I give Maureen a stern look, ignoring Eloise's trembling shoulders as she covers her mouth with her hand because it'll set me off giggling too.

'Then tell him to stop belittling me. Especially when he doesn't know the answer himself.' Maureen glares across the table at Cliff, challenging him to prove her wrong by providing the correct answer. She folds her arms across her chest and adopts a smug look when he remains silent, staring down into his pint.

'It's The Kinks.' Milo points to the answer he's already written down on our sheet of paper. 'Ray Davies is the frontman of The Kinks.'

'See?' Cliff leans forward, aiming his taunt at Maureen. 'Told you it wasn't the bloody Rolling Stones.' He grabs his e-cig from his pocket when the quizmaster announces the end of the round. 'I'm going for a cig break.'

'Disgusting habit.' Maureen tuts as he passes. 'I could never be with a smoker. The smell. Ugh.'

'It's an e-cig, you daft bat.' Cliff wafts it in her face. 'Offended by the smell of Christmas pudding, are you? Jealous because it doesn't smell charred like your mince pies?'

He chuckles to himself as he walks away while Maureen's face turns a worrying purple shade.

No, I don't think this pairing is going to work at all. Luckily, I have my Plan B in the form of Milo and Shannon, which seems to be going well judging by the way Shannon keeps leaning towards Milo as she whispers her answers, making sure her boobs are pressed practically under his nose. I started counting how many times she touched his arm, her fingers lingering on his jumper, but stopped once I reached twenty. This has to be a good sign, and I'm feeling so positive about this match tonight that I'm practically glowing. Very soon, my watch will ping and Milo and Shannon will join my bus lovebirds on my list of Christmas Cupid matches.

Chapter 18

'What's been the worst job you've ever had?'

We're halfway through the quiz and a short break has been called. We've all nipped to the loo and refreshed our drinks, and we're sitting around waiting for the next round when Milo asks the question to the group.

'Working in the grotto, right now.' Shannon fiddles with the straw poking out of her glass. 'All those kids covered in snot. Bleurgh. I can't wait until it's over and I can start my proper career.'

'I've worked at C&L's since I was sixteen, back when it was still Cinnamon & Leah's Toys, way before the rebrand in the nineties. And I love it now.' Maureen places a hand over her heart. 'But back then the café was run by Mrs Thacker. Now, she wasn't a woman to be messed with, and she didn't have a joyful bone in her body.'

'Sounds familiar.'

I nudge Cliff with my foot under the table and shoot him a warning look before making my own contribution to move things away from his snide remark. 'Mine was working on my uncle's fruit and veg market stall. Super-early mornings – no thank you. And the cold! I'm surprised I ever thawed out.'

'What was yours, Cliff?' I'm momentarily cheered when Maureen includes him in the conversation. 'Cleaning chimneys when you were a lad?'

'I'm not that old, you cheeky bugger.' I nudge him under the table again. 'If you must know, it was bricklaying. Back-breaking work, that was.' He holds the small of his back and winces. 'Still gives me trouble now.'

'Mine was working in the café on the inside market.' Eloise shudders and pulls a face. 'Rank doesn't even come close. The grease lining every surface was an inch thick, and the owner used to wash the dishes and ashtrays together. If you can call swishing dishes in filthy, lukewarm water washing them.'

I remember that café. I used to pop in for a brew to try to warm up when I was working on Uncle Jack's fruit and veg stall, until one of the waitresses (who turned out to be Eloise) warned me about the hygiene standards of the place. Or the lack of them.

'I only warned you because I had a bit of a crush on you,' Eloise says when I tell the group about her good Samaritan act. 'Obviously you didn't have that half-fringe going on back then, otherwise I'd have left you to your rank tea and toast.' We all laugh, including me even as I cover the daft fringe cock-up with my hand. 'What about you, Isla? Can you top the greasy-spoon experience?'

'Absolutely.' My neighbour folds her arms slowly across her chest. 'I worked as a cleaner when I was at uni, and you won't believe how disgusting some people are. Skid marks left in the toilet, crusty undies stuffed down the side of the sofa cushions, week-old dirty dishes languishing in the sink. I needed a hazmat suit to enter some of the properties.'

'That is grim.' Eloise lifts her glass and clinks it against Isla's in grotty-work solidarity.

'What about you, Milo?' I give him a nudge because although he asked the question, he hasn't answered it himself yet. 'What was the worst job you ever had?'

'Nothing as traumatic as skid marks in the bogs.' He turns to Isla to fake-gag and she nods along, grim-faced at the memory. 'But my worst job was working in a call centre. It was soul-destroying.'

'Oh, God, you were one of those annoying people who call about accidents and stuff, weren't you?' Shannon makes a fist with her thumb and pinky sticking out, pressing it to her ear like a landline phone that she probably never uses these days. 'According to our records, you've been involved in a car accident within the last two years. Well, that's funny mate, because I haven't even passed my test yet.'

'I'm afraid I was one of those guys.' Milo groans and covers his cheeks with his hands. 'In my defence, I had bills to pay and I only stuck it out for a couple of months. And now I think we should move on . . .'

'Okay, I've got one.' It's Isla who comes to his rescue with a new question. 'What do you pretend to like but actually hate? Mine's mulled wine. Horrible stuff, but you have to drink it at Christmas, don't you?'

'God, no.' Milo and I have the same response, at the exact same moment, and the precision timing of it makes us laugh.

'It's disgusting, isn't it?'

Milo fake-gags again. 'Like paint stripper. I can't even pretend to like it.'

'Me neither. I'd much rather have a drink I actually enjoy.'

'Like hot chocolate.'

'Yes!' I'm far too animated, almost jumping out of my seat, but it's like discovering a kindred spirit. 'Have you tried the gourmet hot chocolate on the Christmas market?'

Milo rolls his eyes up to the ceiling and emits a low groan. 'Oh, yes. They're *amazing*. I can't decide which is my favourite – the raspberry ripple white chocolate or the crème brûlée.'

'You obviously haven't tried the sticky toffee pudding.'

'I have – and it's definitely in my top five – but the raspberry ripple is the best. No, crème brûlée. No . . .' He shakes his head. 'I can't decide. They're tied.'

'It's a pity the market's only there for the festive period.' Although I *am* in the blessed position of repeating December, which I should make full use of. 'We should go for a hot chocolate tomorrow after work and try each other's favourite. See if we can change each other's minds.'

'You're on.' Milo holds out his hand, and I give it a firm shake.

'It means you'll have to decide on raspberry ripple or crème brûlée though. I'll be sick if I drink both at once with all the whipped cream and marshmallows they load them up with.'

Milo's face falls. 'Damn it. There's always a catch.'

I suddenly realise that our group conversation has splintered off, and that the hot chocolate debate has been between only me and Milo while the others are discussing Brussels sprouts, with a ratio of 3:2 not in favour of the little green veggies. Milo, however, doesn't seem to have noticed and has moved on to his next question.

'Would you rather have to drink mulled wine once a day during December, or never be allowed to drink hot chocolate ever again?'

I gasp. 'That's an evil question.'

Milo grins. 'I know. Do you give up a delicious, comforting drink forever or have a daily December dose of the devil's piss? Which one are you going for?'

It's a tough one, because I really do love a hot chocolate, and Milo's description of mulled wine is spot on. 'I guess I'd have to stomach mulled wine for a month.' I pull a face at the mere thought. 'Now it's your turn to answer a question.' I tap my chin as I think of something probing. 'Would you rather be the smartest or the funniest person in the room?'

'Er, I think you'll find I'm both.' Milo looks around the pub and gives a satisfied nod. 'Most handsome too, it seems.'

'With that assessment, you're definitely the funniest.'

Milo clutches his chest, his mouth gaping at me. 'Ouch. Way to chop someone's ego down to the tiniest nub. It'll take me minutes to build it back up again.' His lips are twitching as he grabs his pint, and there's a definite smile being hidden as he takes a sip. 'My turn for a question . . .' He places his pint back down on the table and narrows his eyes at me. 'Tell me two truths and one lie.'

I consider the task for a moment, before settling on three facts to bamboozle Milo with. 'Number one: I've travelled back in time with a mission to matchmake six couples by Christmas Eve. Number two: I can do the splits, and number three: I can fit two digestive biscuits in my mouth at once. Whole.'

Milo settles back in his seat, his eyebrows raising as he takes in my admissions. 'Well, the first one is obviously bogus, so that means you can do the splits. Wow. That's . . . wow. Can you show me?'

'Not in this skirt.' The purple velvet pencil skirt wouldn't accommodate such a move, even if I could actually perform the splits. Which I can't. Not without doing myself a great injury that meant I'd never be able to pick myself up off the floor again.

'You could always go home and change into something with a bit more stretch.' Milo leans in towards me and juts his eyebrows up and down.

I whack him on the arm. 'You could always forget about the splits and tell *me* two truths and one lie.'

Milo tilts his head so he can look at my skirt again. 'I'd rather sit here and think about you doing the splits, if that's okay?'

I whack him on the arm again, but I have to hide my own smile by taking a sip of my wine.

'Sorry about that.' The quizmaster hoists himself up onto his tall stool and rubs his belly with the hand not holding his microphone. 'That break went on for longer than I expected. I had a curry for my tea and, well, it's not really agreeing with me.' He grimaces as he signals to the bar staff to pass him the set of questions being stored by the till. 'Next round: Sport.'

There's a collective groan from our table, apart from Milo who clenches his hands into triumphant little fists that he jiggles rapidly in front of his chest. With Milo's knowledge, we don't do as appallingly as I suspected we would during the round, although we do come seventh overall. Out of eight teams.

'Well, that was a bit of a flop.'

The quiz has ended and Shannon and I are in the loos. Shannon's touching up her lippie while I'm simply hanging around the sink area to try to gauge where she's at with the Milo thing. She was definitely flirting with him during the first few rounds of the quiz so I'm hoping the whole night wasn't wasted.

'I don't think it was a flop.' I pluck an abandoned – and soggy – mass of paper towels from one of the sinks and dump it in the bin. 'We had a laugh, didn't we? And you and Milo seem to be getting along nicely.'

Shannon lifts one shoulder in a shrug as she clicks the lid back onto her lipstick. 'I get on with most people. It's just the kind of person I am.'

'But you seemed particularly friendly with Milo.'

Shannon catches my eye in the mirror and scrunches up her nose. 'Did I?' She shrugs again and drops her lipstick into her miniature handbag. 'He's a nice enough lad. Sweet. But not my type.'

'So you're not interested in him?' My stomach feels like it's dropped to the floor, and my heart starts to flutter in mild panic. I've spent the whole night hoping to match up two couples and failed on both counts. I've been too distracted by actually having a good time. I need to concentrate and get it right.

'I am interested,' Shannon pouts at her reflection and dabs at the corner of her mouth with the tip of her little finger. 'But only in his photography skills. Did you know he's studying part-time to become a photographer? I'm hoping he'll take some shots of me – mates' rates, i.e. for free – so I can put together a modelling portfolio. I reckon I've got what it takes, don't you?' She doesn't wait for an answer before she sashays out of the loos, her hips in overdrive as they sway from side to side.

Great. So definitely no match there, but the night isn't over and I have my Plan C.

'Where's Isla?' Panic makes my pulse all fluttery again as my eyes roam the pub. Milo's still sitting with Cliff at our table, chatting as they finish their pints, and Shannon's made a beeline for a bloke with arms like tree trunks thrusting out of the tightest T-shirt known to man, while Eloise is standing next to the Christmas tree tucked in the corner of the pub near the jukebox. Maureen left as soon as the quiz results were announced and I hope my neighbour hasn't followed suit.

'She's at the bar.' Eloise points her out. She's mostly hidden by a bloke in a knee-length leather jacket that must be baking him in the pub's heat. 'She's getting you another wine. We thought we'd have one more before we head off.'

'Good idea.' I sneak another peek at Milo. He doesn't look like he's eager to get going. Maybe I should buy him another pint, just to make sure he stays put for a bit longer. 'What do you think about Milo and Isla?'

Eloise nods. 'I like them. They absolutely suck at general knowledge, but then we all do, it seems.'

'No, I mean as a couple.' My gaze flicks towards Isla, who seems to be placing her order with Xavier now, but it shoots back to Eloise as she snorts loudly.

'Sorry.' She covers her mouth with her hand, removing it once she can keep a straight face. 'I don't think Milo's Isla's type.'

'What is it with "types" all of a sudden.' I make quick, angry quotation marks with my fingers, ignoring the fact I have a 'type' myself. 'So somebody smokes like a chimney – so what? And what exactly is wrong with Milo? He's cute and sweet and attentive. He actually listens when you talk to him instead of constantly looking at his phone. Is that so bad?'

'It's not bad at all, but *he's* not Isla's type.' Eloise widens her eyes at me, as though she's trying to convey some hidden meaning.

'You already said that, and I'm saying that although he's *nice* rather than being the sort of bad boy some women go for, people should give him a chance.'

'No.' Eloise grabs my arm. 'You're not getting what I'm saying. Milo isn't Isla's type in the way *he* isn't *my* type.' She does the wide eye thing again before tutting and shaking her head, as though I'm a huge disappointment. 'I'm saying *I* have more of a chance with Isla than Milo does.'

'Nah.' I look towards the bar, where Isla's trying to edge her way around the leather-jacket guy without spilling the drinks. 'She isn't gay.'

'Believe me, she absolutely is.' Eloise pats me on the arm before going to relieve Isla of a couple of glasses. I watch them carry them back to the table, watch as they set them down and drop easily into whatever conversation is happening between Milo and Cliff.

If Eloise is right about Isla, and Shannon only wanted Milo for freebie photos, *and* Maureen has her red lines about smoking, I didn't stand a chance tonight. There was no way this quiz was going to be a Christmas Cupid success and the realisation makes me want to bash my head against the wall. Repeatedly.

Or get very, very drunk.

I go with the latter, and I'm on my way to the bar when I spot a wallet on the floor.

'Excuse me. Is this yours?' I hold the wallet out to the bloke standing practically above where it had been lying a moment ago. He takes the proffered item on autopilot but shakes his head once he realises what he's holding in his hand.

'It's not mine. I'll go and hand it in at the bar.'

It's not that I'm mistrusting or anything, but I watch as he crosses the pub and hands it to Xavier, who pops it beside the till. The bloke is still hanging around the bar even after I've ordered a round of drinks, and I can't help but take another peek as I sit down. He's at the bar, chatting to Xavier and, if I'm not mistaken, flirting a little bit. We're getting ready to leave when I spot the wallet bloke tapping his number into Xavier's phone. My watch pings and a heart flashes up, displaying a two, indicating I've matched up another couple. I can't believe I've inadvertently matched up a pair of strangers but I want to perform a celebratory jig anyway, because a match is a match, accidental or otherwise. I'm drinking wine, but surely it should be something with a bit more fizz after this?

It's now two down, four to go. If only all the matches were this easy!

Chapter 19

9th December

It's my day off from the shop but I'm up and dressed by the time Scott leaves for work. I walk downstairs with him, popping into the café next door for a couple of bacon butties. Having the café next door is both a blessing (yay, bacon butties are a matter of steps away!) and a curse (uh-oh, bacon butties are a matter of steps away) and I'm pretty sure that while I fell in love with the light and airy open plan living room and kitchen, I was equally influenced by the adjoining café when it came to deciding that this was the flat for us.

'Breakfast?' I hold up the delicious-smelling paper bags when Franziska answers her door. My neighbour is constantly feeding me, so it's about time I repay the favour, even if I didn't prep the food myself.

'I've already had my muesli, but I never turn down a second breakfast.' Franziska winks as she steps aside so I can duck into her hallway. 'I'll put the kettle on.'

We sit in Franziska's living room and catch up over tea and the bacon sandwiches. I tell Franziska about last night's quiz, which it turns out is a weekly event and we've all agreed to try

125

our luck again next time, apart from Maureen, who I suspect will never willingly share a space with Cliff again. There's also a Christmas karaoke planned in just over a week, but I'm not sure that's quite up our street.

'How are things going with you and Klaus?' I ask the question casually, even though it's the main reason I'm here. 'Still chatting?' I may have clocked up my second Christmas Cupid match last night but there's more work to do and the wallet match made me realise all may not be lost with my neighbour and her FaceTime buddy. My watch didn't ping straight away last night – Xavier and the wallet guy were chatting for a while, but nothing happened until they exchanged numbers. So just because my watch hasn't pinged for Franziska and Klaus, it doesn't mean it won't happen. The match hasn't necessarily failed, they may just need a bit more time.

'We chat every evening.' I'm sure I see Franziska's cheeks start to take on a pinkish hue before she dips her head to take a sip of tea. 'It's like no time has passed at all. It's quite extraordinary, really. If it wasn't for my creaking joints, I'd feel like a teenager all over again.'

This is Very Good News. I've been given a second chance with Scott and maybe this is Franziska's second chance with Klaus. They were in love before and there doesn't seem to be a reason – other than geography – for those feelings not to resurface.

'I thought I'd feel guilty about chatting to Klaus again. As though I were betraying Derek. But . . .' Franziska smiles wistfully. 'I will never let go of my husband. He is here.' She places a hand over her heart. 'But I know he would want me to be happy, and Klaus makes me happy, even after all this time.' She places her cup on a coaster, the smile easing off until the corners of her mouth are almost downturned. 'Though I am not sure how Tobias and Aggie will feel about their mother talking to another man. Especially an old boyfriend.'

'I'm sure they'd want you to be happy too.'

'We will have to see about that, but it is something to worry about in the future. Right now, I am enjoying catching up with an old friend.' Franziska gathers up the cups and plates, batting away my offer of help. 'Do you have to rush off or do you have time for another cup of tea?'

I have no plans until this evening – other than a pile of ironing to tackle and a few presents to wrap – so we have another cup of tea. Franziska insists I take a leftover slab of apple cake (*Oma's apfelkuchen*) back up to the flat with me and while I vow to reward myself with the cake once I've worked my way through the ironing pile, I end up scoffing it while watching a segment on homemade office Christmas party accessories on *This Morning*, and the clothes are still awaiting a pressing when I head out to meet Milo outside C&L's. He looks confused to see me outside the staff entrance at the back of the shop at closing time, his brow wrinkling as he struggles to comprehend my presence.

'We had a date with a gourmet hot chocolate, remember? I can't believe you forgot. I'm offended.' I stick out my bottom lip and turn my head away while watching him out of the corner of my eye in mock umbrage.

'I didn't forget.' Milo looks mortified, and I feel a bit bad for hamming it up just now. 'I just assumed with it being your day off that we'd do it another day. Tomorrow, maybe. I didn't think you'd go out of your way for it.'

'For a sticky toffee pudding hot chocolate?' I make a pfft sound. 'There's no such thing as out of my way.'

'A raspberry ripple white hot chocolate, actually.' We set off, making our way towards the town square. 'We're giving each other's favourite a go, remember?'

'And you made a decision between the raspberry ripple and the crème brûlée? I'm impressed.'

'Sort of.' Milo links his arm through mine to guide me out of the way as a teen on an electric scooter whizzes by. 'I flipped a coin for it.'

A bubble of laughter escapes at the thought of Milo taking his hot chocolate ruling so seriously.

'Hey, it was a tough decision.' Milo sticks out his chin and puffs up his chest, but I can see his lips are twitching despite the indignant stance.

'No, I get it. Last year, I had a scoring system for the German sausages at the market.' I've never told anybody this – not Scott or even Eloise – but I kept a tally in a little notebook and everything, with points awarded for aroma, taste, texture and presentation.

'Which one was the winner? It has to be the bacon frankfurter, right?'

'That one did score highly, but I'm a purist. It has to be a good old bratwurst served on a crusty roll for me.'

Milo nods. 'Fair enough.'

The bright, multicoloured lights from the market's Christmas tree and mini Ferris wheel are visible through the gaps between the buildings ahead, luring passers-by to take a detour and surround themselves with the child-like magic and wonder, and even from this distance I can hear the murmur of Paul McCartney singing about a wonderful Christmastime through the sound system. Milo stops and unthreads his arm from mine, where it's remained even though the electric scooter is long gone, and he takes his phone out of his pocket, holding it up and taking his time to grab the perfect shot of the Christmas market peeking out at us. Leaning over, I have a glimpse before he puts his phone away. It's a fantastic shot that really captures the enchantment of the season.

'Shannon says you're studying photography.'

'Yep, but this one's just for Instagram.' Milo slips his phone back into his pocket and we set off again. 'Photography's always been a passion of mine, but I made some wrong choices along the way.'

'Like working in a call centre?'

'Exactly. But I feel like I'm back on track now. Sort of.' He looks at me, his brow lightly furrowed. 'Can you be back on track while dressing as an elf five days a week?'

I snort. 'You're asking the wrong person. Mind you, some might say the elf costume is more stylish than my everyday outfits.'

For the second day in a row, I've made a conscious effort to match my clothes, and I'm wearing a black pleated skirt with an oversized silver leaf pattern teamed with a creamy-pink knitted jumper and thick black tights. The red buckled shoes stick out from the rest of the outfit, but I really couldn't help myself.

'I like your style.' Milo shrugs. 'It's quirky and vibrant, and if everybody dressed the same, it'd be a very boring, cookie-cutter world.'

I bump my arm against Milo's. 'I like your viewpoint.'

'But will you like my hot chocolate?' We've reached the top entrance to the market, the lights even brighter and even more inviting now.

I give Milo's arm another little bump. 'Let's find out.'

The gourmet hot chocolate is served from one of the wooden huts near the carousel. There's a vast menu to choose from, and each is served in a midnight-blue mug with a bright and festive Christmas market print. Every cup of hot chocolate is loaded up with a snowy mountain of whipped cream, gooey polar-bear-shaped marshmallows and a mini Flake. There are probably a week's worth of calories in one sip, but it's totally worth it.

'That. Is. Delicious.' Milo and I have been wandering around the market, blowing occasionally on our hot chocolates until they're cool enough to drink, and I almost pass out with joy at my first taste. The white hot chocolate has a light creaminess to it, while the raspberry gives a surprising little tangy kick.

'More delicious than the sticky toffee pudding?' Milo holds his mug up, spotting a blob of melting cream that is about to plop off the side. He licks the cream before it descends any further, and the unexpected sight of his tongue running along the mug does funny things to my insides and I have to look away.

'Not quite.' I take a sip of my drink, swiping at my top lip in case I've left a creamy moustache behind. 'But it's a close second.' I take another sip. 'Very close.'

'I think I'll put the sticky toffee pudding in joint first place with the raspberry ripple and crème brûlée.'

'But how will you decide which one to drink?' I hide a grin behind my mug as I tease him. 'There are only two sides on a coin.'

'Funny.' Milo sticks his tongue out at me, and I'm reminded of the way it slid along the mug, picturing it in slow motion, porno-style. What the hell is wrong with me? 'Do you mind if we stop off at the bath bomb stall? I want to get one of the create-your-own hampers for my mum and my sisters, but I'm absolutely useless at this stuff. I could really use your help, if you don't mind?'

'Of course not.' Anything to get my mind out of the gutter. 'How many sisters have you got?'

'Two. Holly-Mae and Ruby. One older, one younger, so I'm in the middle. But don't worry – I don't have Middle Child Syndrome. I was very loved growing up. Obviously, Ruby being the baby means she was – *is* – spoilt rotten, but we're all guilty of it. I was eleven when she was born and I've always felt over-protective of her.'

'That's sweet.' I give him a playful nudge with my elbow. 'And you're lucky having siblings. I'm an only child, which means I get to deal with all the parental rubbish on my own.'

'Are you close to your parents?'

We follow the huts along to the manger scene and turn right towards the giant Christmas tree. 'I'm close to my mum, but not my dad so much. He's pretty selfish. He always puts himself first, with both me and Mum, and he expects her to run around after him like it's still the 1950s. I don't know why she puts up with him.'

'Could be any number of reasons, I suppose. Fear of change or being alone, low self-esteem. And it's sometimes easier to see how rubbish a relationship is from the outside.'

'How can she not see it?'

Milo gives the tiniest of shrugs and offers a half-smile. 'Perhaps she's blinded by love?'

'You seem to know a lot about this stuff.'

'I grew up in a toxic household, until I was about eight and my dad left. I didn't understand at the time why Mum was so upset – I felt nothing but relief that he'd gone. Then it was just Mum, Holly-Mae and I, and we were happy for a couple of years. When she met Jeff, I thought that was it – back to a world of arguments and slammed doors and walking around on eggshells, but it was the complete opposite. We were still happy, but there were more of us, and then Ruby came along and it felt like we were a real, proper family.'

'It sounds lovely.'

'I mean, it's not perfect, but what family is?'

Not mine, that's for sure. 'Do you still see your dad?'

'He died when I was seventeen. I hadn't seen him more than a handful of times after he left us, but it was still pretty tough. I think I mourned the loss of the relationship we *could* have had, rather than the one we did have, which wasn't much of one at all.'

'I'm sorry.' What must he think of me, whingeing about my feckless father when his is dead?

'Don't be.' Milo picks up the pace, grabbing my hand so he can guide me around a group of people. 'Be happy and festive.'

As well as the bath bombs, the stall has an array of homemade soaps, candles and wax melts. We put together three hampers for Milo's female family members: a floral medley of rose, lavender and jasmine for his mum, a citrussy blast of clementine, lemon and lime for his older sister, and a sweet selection of vanilla, marshmallow and chocolate for his 'baby' sister ('She's eighteen now, but to me she'll always be the podgy little toddler who followed me around the house like a shadow . . .').

'Are we taking these back? Or taking them home?' Milo lifts his long-empty mug, which you can take back to the stall for a refund of your small deposit, or keep as a memento.

'I'm going to take mine home. You can never have too many festive mugs.'

'That's true. Home it is then.'

We leave the market behind as it's starting to shut down for the night. I'm about to head for the bus station, but Milo insists on giving me a lift, even though it's completely out of his way.

'You made the extra effort to come and meet me this evening, and you helped me with my Christmas shopping, so it's the least I can do.'

I don't put up much more of a fight. It's pretty cold by now and the idea of standing in the draughty bus station this late isn't something I'm particularly keen on, so I follow Milo back towards C&L's, where there's a car park around the corner. Milo carefully places his paper bags of goodies on the backseat before climbing into the driver's seat.

'Do you live with your Mum and family?'

He snorts as he starts the engine. 'God, no. I love them to death, honestly, but there's only one bathroom in that house and three women. I moved out as soon as I could afford it. And by afford it, I mean house-share with two of my mates and a cat that's sort of adopted us.'

'The cat adopted *you*?'

Milo switches on the radio, turning it down when Mariah blasts her Christmas wish at us. 'Yep. Turned up one day in the kitchen. Went away, came back the next day and settled herself down on the sofa. She left again but kept coming back until one day she decided not to leave. We tried to find out who she belonged to – checked if she was chipped, put posts up on local Facebook groups, Jordan even bought a collar so he could attach a note to it – but we never did find out where she came from and it's been three years.'

'It definitely sounds like she's yours now.' I click my seatbelt into place and try to check that my fringe is still covered by my hat in the wing mirror. 'What's she called?'

'Faith.'

'That's cute.'

Milo gives me a wry smile before he pulls out of the parking space. 'Jordan named her after a woman he fancied at work. Luckily, nothing ever came of it. Can you imagine how awkward *that* conversation would have been if they'd got together?'

'Faith, meet Faith the cat. I named her after you. No, no, it isn't creepy. It's *romantic*.'

Milo laughs. 'That's exactly how I imagined it going, followed by Faith the human's swift exit. Bless him. It's no wonder Jordan was single for so long.'

I twist in my seat so I'm facing Milo. 'Is he still single?' I'd forgotten all about my Christmas Cupid mission during the fun of the Christmas market, but I still have four couples to match and time is ticking away.

'Amazingly not. He met a girl over the summer. Really lovely girl – no idea what she sees in Jordan, but horses for courses and all that. Why? You on the lookout?' Milo glances at me as he stops at a junction. 'I thought you had a boyfriend?'

'I do, but it's not for me. It's for a friend. She wants me to set her up on a blind date.'

Milo pulls a face. 'I can't think of anything worse than being set up on a date.'

Which is obviously music to my ears when I've spent the past few days trying to find his true love match.

Chapter 20

I see my first successfully matched couple on the bus on the way to work, their heads pressed together as they share a set of earphones to listen to whatever is playing on Owain's phone. Scott is sitting next to me, and it strikes me that we can't even share a conversation during our joint commute, never mind a pair of earphones. And what would we listen to anyway? There's only so much Stormzy I can stand first thing in the morning (or even well into the afternoon or evening) and there's no way Scott would entertain listening to The Pretenders or Fleetwood Mac or anybody else on my playlists. But this is what happens in relationships, isn't it? You can't get enough of each other to begin with, absorbing everything about them. Their passions become your passions, and you give each other cutesy nicknames that get lost along the way, but it doesn't mean anything. You're simply at a different stage of your relationship and although I'm a bit sad that Scott and I are no longer in that frenzied first flush of love, I'm more grateful than I'll ever be able to express that we're together. *That* means far more to me than a set of earphones split between two.

Still, I'm in need of a cheering mince pie by the time I've dashed from the bus station to C&L's in the rain, so I pop down to the café once I've changed out of my damp skirt and into my elf costume. The café always seems a bit odd without the usual background noise of children dashing about in the soft play area or the nattering of parents over coffee, almost as though the room is too large, the yellow fixtures too bright, everything *too much*, and I find myself tiptoeing across the floor, afraid to break the silence of the empty café. Which is probably how I end up scaring the life out of Eloise as she emerges from the kitchen and almost throws a box of ketchup sachets up in the air like confetti.

'Jeez, Zoey.' She dumps the box down on the nearest surface and places a hand on her chest. 'You nearly gave me a heart attack. What are you creeping around for?'

'I'm not creeping around. At least not on purpose.' I drop down onto a too-yellow chair. 'Any chance the mince pies are ready yet? I'm in dire need.'

'It isn't even nine o'clock yet.' Eloise picks up the box of ketchup and carries it to the other end of the counter, where she starts to transfer the sachets into a wicker basket. 'What's happened? Scott lost one of his shoes and blamed you? Burnt his toast and blamed you? Missed his bus and . . .'

I hold a hand up to stop her. 'Blamed me? No, none of those things happened. And why would you say that? As though Scott holds me responsible for everything bad that happens to him?'

Eloise raises an eyebrow. She holds my gaze for a few seconds before she returns to her task without saying a word. I could push it, but I don't like confrontation at the best of times, and certainly not with my best friend.

'Where are we on the mince pies?'

'Still in the oven.' Eloise shrugs an apology. 'Can I interest you in a gingerbread man? We've got those coming out of our ears.'

'Eww, no thanks. Not if they've come out of your ears. I don't fancy earwax-glazed biscuits.' I grin at Eloise, whatever she was insinuating a moment ago forgotten. 'I'll just have a cup of tea.' I check the time on the oversized clock above the till. 'A small one. I'll need to get up to the grotto in a few minutes. It's Shannon's day off and I don't want to leave the setting up to Milo.'

Eloise joins me at the table a couple of minutes later with two cups of tea, but she seems a bit fidgety, and it isn't because she's nervous about Maureen catching her skiving ('She's a pussycat, really. All meow but no bite'). I know for sure there's something going on when she tugs the sleeves of her stripy cardigan down over her hands and starts to nibble gently on one of the cuffs.

'Is everything okay?' We assessed my mood earlier, but we should have been focusing on Eloise.

'Why wouldn't it be?' Eloise knows as well as I do that chewing on her sleeves is a stress-induced gesture, so she whips the garment away from her mouth, shoving her hands under her thighs so that they're out of the way.

'You seem a bit jumpy.' There was the almost-tossing-the-ketchup-in-the-air incident, the ants-in-the-pants and chewing-on-her-sleeve nervous energy, and now she can't meet my eye. I even dip down to catch her lowered gaze, but she flicks her eyes towards the clock above the till. I know what's coming, even before she says it.

'I should be getting back to work. I still need to do some kitchen prep and Maureen's asked me to clean the bottom shelf of the fridge. Milk spillage.' She stands up, colliding with a chair as she backs away. She flails but manages to keep both herself and the chair upright.

'Eloise, what's going on?'

The sleeve is back between her teeth, but she edges forward, lowering herself into the chair opposite mine. 'Do you promise not to get all judge-y and worried and . . . Zoey-like.'

'I don't know.' I reach across the table and gently pull on her sleeve until it's no longer in her mouth. It's muffling her voice, and she's going to end up ruining a lovely, cosy-looking cardigan. 'I can't commit to any promises until you've told me what it is. For example, if you're about to tell me that you're planning to run naked through the Christmas market this lunchtime, then I obviously can't promise to be un-judge-y. Or worried, for that matter.' I'm joking to lighten the mood, but Eloise isn't taking the bait. She's looking down at the table, only braving the briefest of glances at me.

'It's Annie.'

I can tell Eloise wants nothing more than to shove her sleeve back in her gob, and sure enough, her hand starts to move towards her face. I pull it away pre-emptively.

'What about Annie?'

Eloise gives the tiniest, barely-there smile. 'She called me last night.' Internally, I groan, even as I try to keep my features neutral and non-judge-y. 'And she invited me over, and I went, but it wasn't like it usually is. We talked, like all night, and we laughed and it felt like old times, like when we first got together.'

I can't help picturing the couple from the bus this morning, with their heads touching as the set of shared earphones connected them. But Eloise and Annie aren't that couple. To be honest, I don't think they ever have been. Annie has always had the upper hand and she's exploited the power she has over Eloise. She clicks her fingers and Eloise comes running, never once considering the misery that inevitably lies ahead.

'We're going out for dinner.' Eloise finally looks me in the eye for more than a nanosecond, her chin rising in defiance of the judgement she knows I'm clutching tightly so it doesn't spill out. 'Tonight. On an actual date, outside of Annie's flat. It's going to be different this time, I know it.'

The problem is, I know it isn't, because we've literally been here before, and it leaves me with a horrible uneasy feeling in the pit of my stomach. I want to support my friend, I really do, but I know for a fact that she's going to get hurt, only there's no way I can convey that without confessing my December do-over and sounding like I need professional help.

In the end, I don't say anything but a murmured 'I hope it goes well', which convinces neither of us but at least it doesn't cause a rift. I neck my tea down in a couple of gulps before heading up to the grotto, subconsciously finding myself at the bird tree, my fingers stroking the robin's feathers as I worry about my best friend. 'All I Want for Christmas Is My Two Front Teeth' suddenly starts up over the sound system, and if I'd have had a box of ketchup sachets in hand, they'd be raining down on me right now. Jolted out of my moment of contemplation, I head through to the North Pole, where Milo is giving the mechanical reindeer the once-over to check they're all still in working order.

'Everything okay?' His eyebrows pull down as he dusts the bits of fake snow and silver glitter from his hands. I hadn't realised I had such a glum expression on my face, but I pull my lips upwards into a smile and drag my shoulders back.

'Everything's great. Just Friday mornings, you know?' I scrunch up my nose and stick my tongue out of the corner of my mouth. 'The weekend's almost here, but not quite. Always makes me feel blah.' I pull the face again, even though it'd place highly in a gurning competition.

'We work in retail, Zoey. There's no such thing as a weekend.'

The boy has a point, but I can't backtrack now. 'I have the day off tomorrow, actually.' I'm back in again on Sunday, but whatever.

'Any exciting plans?'

I start to count my Saturday itinerary off on my fingers. 'A lengthy lie-in. Probably a bacon butty for a late breakfast while I catch up on my soaps. I'm going to start a new knitting project – a pair of the cutest reindeer socks for my mum – while watching a cheesy Hallmark Christmas movie.' My shoulders slump as I get to the end of my list. 'That sounds really naff, doesn't it?' I'm twenty-five but I have the weekend plans of a pensioner. Where is the dancing and the drinking and the singing really badly as you stagger home from the pub?

'It sounds good to me. If I could knit, obviously.' Milo looks me dead in the eye, his face serious as he tells me, 'Any socks I attempted to make would be a disaster. I couldn't even manage a scarf. It's why I'm always cold. And speaking of being cold . . .' He lowers his gaze and nods at my stripy elf leggings. 'You're wearing stretchy pants today. They're perfect for demonstrating your ability to do the splits.'

'Er, what has that got to do with being cold?'

Milo grins. 'Absolutely nothing. I'm just keen for you to show off your talent.'

'No can do, I'm afraid. Even with my stretchy pants.' I jut my hip out and place a hand over it. 'I hurt my hip a couple of years ago, and the doctor said that doing the splits just one more time could result in serious, permanent damage.'

'Have you thought about getting a second opinion about that?'

I roll my eyes as I head for Santa's workshop to check the candy cane levels. 'Have you thought about not being a pervert and forgetting about the splits?'

'Pervert?' Milo splutters as he follows me into the long wooden hut. 'I'm interested from a purely artistic angle.'

I roll my eyes again. 'Yeah, right.' But I have to press my lips together to stop myself from giggling – this kind of behaviour shouldn't be encouraged – and it isn't until much later that I remember Eloise's infatuation with her ex-girlfriend and the worry starts to worm its way back in again.

Chapter 21

Eloise doesn't mention Annie as we meet up outside the shop's staff entrance, but I catch the beam on her face before she obscures it with the chunky scarf I made for her last Christmas. And although the worry has evolved into a tight knot in my stomach, I don't want to be the reason her happiness is wiped away so I don't mention her either. Besides, what if it has the potential to work out this time and by airing my doubts I'm becoming the anti-Christmas Cupid? Maybe Annie's changed. Maybe she's become less self-centred? Maybe pigs will fly.

'It's *freezing* tonight.' Eloise slips her gloves on, wriggling her fingers into place as we head across the yard at the back of the shop and emerge onto the side road. 'Do you think it'll snow?'

I look up at the inky-black sky and shiver. 'Maybe, but I hope it waits until we're home.' I love snow, but it's always best enjoyed when you have the option to duck inside and warm up with a hot chocolate. Being stuck quivering with cold on the bus – or feeling as though you're being roasted alive because the heating's cranked up to the max, there's no in-between on public transport – isn't ideal.

'Do you remember that time when we had the really bad snow and it froze the doors shut?' Eloise threads her arm through mine as we move along the pavement.

'And Cliff tried to chisel his way through the ice with his debit card?'

Eloise giggles into her scarf at the memory. 'And the corner chipped off.'

'But not one bit of ice.' I catch Eloise's eye and we both snigger, remembering the rage that emitted from the store's Santa Claus as he held the broken debit card in one hand and the snapped-off plastic shard in the other. 'The steam coming out of his ears should have melted the ice away.'

It feels good to giggle with Eloise again. To side-step the subject of Annie, even if she's still here with us, lurking behind us and trying to nudge her way in.

'I probably won't see you until Monday now.' We've reached the corner, where Eloise breaks off to head towards the tram stop and I have to go in the opposite direction for the bus station. She bangs her gloved hands together in a muted clap. 'I'm off on Sunday and . . .' She stops herself, her mouth hanging open awkwardly. She has plans with Annie. I'd know this from the awkwardness, even if this wasn't a December do-over.

'Well, have fun.' I kiss her on the cheek and start to back away, eager to get going in case Annie manages to burst through. 'Call or text me whenever.' *Whenever Annie lets you down* is the subtext here, so I turn and scurry away before I cause even more tension with my big gob.

Eloise wasn't wrong about it being cold – it seems to have dropped a couple of degrees since this morning – and I wrap my scarf tighter and dig my gloved hands deep into my pockets. It's a relief when I step into a toasty warm flat and the kettle starts to rumble reassuringly as I grab Scott's Man U mug and my froggy one from the cupboard. Scott is already home – there are signs of it everywhere, from the telly murmuring to itself to the abandoned jacket on the back of the sofa and the kicked-off shoes poking out from underneath the coffee table. Stormzy's blaring from the bathroom, drowning out the sound of the running water of the shower.

With a couple of teabags in the mugs and the kettle still boiling, I head through to the bedroom, where I ease my shoes off and replace them with the fluffiest frog slippers that make it feel as though I'm walking on clouds, which is most welcome after a full day on my feet at the shop. The pile of clothes from a few days ago is still languishing on the floor and I feel a spike of irritation as I bundle them into my arms. I'm tired, and anxious about the effect seeing Annie again is going to have on Eloise and it's making me cranky. I'm looking forward to curling up on the sofa with Scott and switching off for the evening.

The kettle's boiled by the time I've dumped the laundry in the washing basket. I finish off the tea, taking Scott's through to the bedroom so he'll find a nice little surprise when he gets out of the shower, before settling down on the sofa with full control of the remote. *Hollyoaks* is just starting and although I haven't watched it for a couple of years and have *no idea* what any of the storylines are, I don't have the energy to keep flicking through the channels.

'Babe?' Scott is out in the hallway and can't wait a few more seconds to communicate and instead yells through the walls. 'Where's my long-sleeved black shirt?' I wait a few more seconds and he appears in the doorway, dressed only in a pair of skinny jeans. 'Babe? My shirt? I need it for tonight.'

'Tonight?' There's a cat fight playing out on the screen, but it can't compete with my topless boyfriend.

'I'm going out.' Scott speaks slowly, a ridge slowly deepening on his forehead. 'The office Christmas party. We're getting something to eat in the Northern Quarter then going for drinks. You said you'd iron my black shirt with the long sleeves.' He stretches his arms out, as though to demonstrate what sleeves are. 'I've looked in the wardrobe and it isn't in there.'

No, it isn't. It's in the middle of the pile of yet-to-be-ironed clothes in the bedroom. I meant to tackle the pile yesterday, but

I got distracted and I totally forgot about Scott's planned night out with his workmates.

'I'm so sorry.' I find a pot of energy from somewhere deep inside and scrabble up to my feet. 'I forgot to iron it, but I'll do it now. It won't take me a minute.'

'Zo.' He throws his head back and groans, but I'm already dashing across to the kitchen so I can drag the ironing board out. 'I'm supposed to be in town for eight.'

'And you will be.' I check the time on my watch, swallowing the panic that rises and force humour into my voice. 'Cinderella, you will go to the ball!'

Scott doesn't find it even mildly amusing.

I iron the shirt and practically throw it onto Scott's frame, and he has to bat my hands away as I start to button him up like a child.

'I'm sorry.' I apologised a million times as I ran the iron over the shirt, but I say it again, to hammer home the point. I don't want to lose any of the Perfect Girlfriend points I've accumulated since I was thrown back to 1st December.

'Don't worry about it.' Scott stops fastening the shirt at the third-from-last button and stoops to kiss me on the cheek. 'I'd better run now though. Oh, don't forget your cupcake.' Scott lifts his jacket from the back of the sofa, grabbing the paper bag from underneath it. And then he's off as soon as the bag makes contact with my hand.

'Have fun!' I call after him, but the only response is the rattle of the front door closing behind him.

I should probably make myself something proper to eat, but my energy reserves are completely sapped and I sink onto the sofa, already peeking into the paper bag. Inside is a white-icing-topped bun that shimmers with edible glitter. It's decorated to look like a snowman, with chocolate chips for eyes and a wide, dotted smile, and a fondant carrot nose, which has been slightly knocked out of place in transit from bakery to home.

Sliding the cake out, I dump the paper bag on my lap and peel back the case. I'm about to take a huge bite when the paper bag catches my eye. It's printed with The Bake House's branding of a white background with vertical black and grey stripes, and, as it lays across my lap, it sparks a memory of Scott and that girl on Christmas Eve. Of the super-short white skirt with the vertical black-and-grey stripes over thick tights. Which wasn't a super-short skirt at all, I realise now. It was a Bake House apron worn over leggings.

Scott must have met her in The Bake House. He may have *already* met her. She may be the one serving him my Friday treat cupcakes. *This* Friday treat cupcake.

I place the cupcake down on the coffee table and whip the paper bag off my lap, balling it up tightly before pushing it as far down the bin as I can. I've been worrying about Eloise's relationship with Annie today, but really I should have been worrying about my own relationship with Scott.

Chapter 22

11th December

The bus is late, jam-packed, and at a temperature nearing that of the sun. The windows are completely fogged up, but they're not much use to me anyway when I'm standing in the middle of the aisle, crushed between a very tall, extremely broad-shouldered bloke and a woman in a fake fur coat that doubles her width, and my only views are armpits, coat lapels and the brown synthetic fur that keeps tickling my nose every time the bus sends me lurching forward. There's a kid screaming somewhere towards the back of the bus, which would be annoying if I wasn't desperate to throw my head back and join in the howling.

It's Saturday morning, around fifteen hours since I made the connection between The Bake House branding and the stunning girl I saw Scott with on Christmas Eve – and I've thought of nothing else since. Scott probably already knows the girl he's going to replace me with in nanoseconds of our break up, and I can see – in sickening technicolour – how it will all play out: Scott will lumber into The Bake House, looking suitably miserable after the termination of his three-year relationship. Red-eyed, shoulders slouched, chin down. Maybe even on the verge of tears.

'OMG, Scott.' (The girl looked the sort who would actually say 'OMG'.) 'You look *terrible*. What's happened?'

And he'll tell her everything; how I'm such a rubbish girlfriend I can't even remember to iron his shirt for his work night out, how I nag him about silly little things – teabags being left on the worktop, his collection of mugs on the bedside table that are starting to grow new life forms, that kind of thing – and she'll listen intently, her face solemn, her hand resting lightly on his knee as the sorry tale comes spilling out. They've moved out of the shop by now, and are sitting in some sort of room at the back, where there are chairs placed conveniently close together. The Bake House Girl has brought cakes through with her to cheer Scott up even though his appetite has completely vanished and he can't imagine putting the red velvet cupcake anywhere near his mouth. She'll inch forward, the pressure of her hand on his knee increasing just enough, and she'll sigh and say, 'Oh, Scott. You poor baby.' (She looked like the kind of person who could say 'poor baby' without sounding like a complete dork.) 'Is there *anything* I can do to make you feel better?'

And if that isn't an invitation for some really, really dirty sex, I don't know what is.

The bus turns sharply and I stumble (as much as I can in the tiny amount of space I have) and end up with my nose stuffed into the fake animal pelt.

'Sorry.' I mumble my apology while trying to ward off a sneeze with the back of my hand. I didn't sleep at all last night. Firstly, because I was waiting for Scott to come home, convinced he would leave me immediately now that I knew about The Bake House Girl, and then because I couldn't get the image of the two of them together at the parade out of my head. I lay next to his snoring form until I gave up at around five and dragged myself into the kitchen to make a cup of tea, which I didn't even bother to drink. My legs feel weak and my brain fuzzy, but I somehow manage to keep upright as the bus lurches its way into the town centre.

I'm not working today but I couldn't stand the thought of sitting in the flat, waiting for a hungover Scott to wake up, so I've decided to do a bit of Christmas shopping. And if I happen to get a bit peckish and need a sweet pick-me-up from The Bake House . . .

I don't head straight to the bakery, even though it's only a short walk from the bus station. I really do need to do some Christmas shopping, and also I'm a coward. I want to scope out the bakery and confirm my suspicions, but I also want to run as far away from the bakery as my fatigued body will allow. So I compromise – I'll do a bit of Christmas shopping first and bakery-snoop later.

The Christmas market has a different energy at this time of the day. It's buzzing with people, but the atmosphere is missing in full daylight and I miss the romantic element of a dusky sky lit up with colourful fairy lights. Still, I join the throng and manage to squeeze and shuffle my way to the bath bomb stall, where I buy hampers for Mum, Eloise and Scott's sister. A little voice in my head pipes up as I'm choosing the perfect combination of scents for Kristen, asking why I'm bothering shopping for Scott's sister when we might not even be together by the time Christmas Day comes along. Shouldn't it be The Bake House Girl shopping for Scott's family? Or Scott himself, though that would require a smidgen of thoughtfulness and organisation, which he is severely lacking in.

I'm shocked by the negativity of the voice in my head and push it away. Scott and I *will* be together at Christmas. I've been given this second chance with him and I'm not going to give him up without a fight.

I'm laden down with bags by the time I reach The Bake House. It seems shopping is a tonic for anxiety and exhaustion, and wandering around the market and the shopping centre has helped to clear my mind of negativity. Maybe I'm wrong about The Bake House Girl, putting two and two together and coming up with a brazen hussy in an apron. That original Christmas Eve was almost two weeks ago and I suffered a massive head injury after I saw them together so I could be completely wrong about the branding thing. The girl at the parade could have been wearing something completely different but I've stumbled upon this theory and run with it. Maybe I spent last night worrying about nothing?

I've ended up buying most of the gifts I needed, including the new (eye-wateringly expensive) games console Scott has been hinting at, which has eaten up most of my savings. I wanted to put that money towards our summer holiday, but this will definitely earn me major Perfect Girlfriend points. The rolls of festive wrapping paper are doing their best to gouge their way up my nostrils as I battle my way through the door, twisting this way and that as I try to stuff the shopping bags through the doorway. The Bake House is small but ultramodern, with slate-grey walls, wooden flooring and huge light fixtures that dangle above the L-shaped counter. There's a queue running alongside the counter, and everyone turns to look as I finally de-wedge the last shopping bag and stumble into the shop, spilling two rolls of festive wrap onto the ground.

'Are you okay there? Let me give you a hand.'

I'm crouching down, trying to keep hold of carrier bag handles while grasping at the slippery, cellophane-wrapped rolls of gift wrap, so I don't see who the kind citizen offering assistance is. I spot a pair of Chelsea boots stop in front of me just before a hand scoops up the rolls, but then I'm too busy concentrating on getting myself upright again without losing my grip on any of the bags to clock who she is until the rolls of gift wrap are tucked back into their bags.

'Thank . . .' I falter as I take in the honey-blonde hair – this time gathered in a topknot rather than cascading down onto her shoulders in soft curls – and the wide, gleaming-white-toothed smile. '. . . you.'

It's her. The girl from the parade. She's wearing a pair of jeggings with the Chelsea boots – along with a white apron with black and grey stripes. I was right. Oh, God. *I was right.* This is where Scott meets her – has *already* met her, because he's in here every Friday, buying my Friday treats. He's a regular here. They probably have a friendly little chat while she places my cupcake into a paper bag. *Any plans for the weekend? I hope your girlfriend enjoys the cake* (if he's even mentioned me at all). *See you next week!* Maybe they're even on first-name terms.

'No problem.' Her smile widens and she places a hand on my arm. She's younger than I am, I realise. Not by much, because that would be obscene, but she's definitely in her very early twenties, and she's even prettier up close. Fresh-faced with pink-tinged cheeks and perfectly-arched eyebrows framing big brown eyes. No wonder Scott moved on with the speed of Usain Bolt if this is what was on offer.

The Bake House Girl heads back behind the counter while I join the back of the queue. I'm not in the mood for cake (which means my spirits are dangerously low) but I can't leave empty-handed (so to speak, since my hands are extremely full right now). I pick the first treat my eye falls on as I reach the front of the queue, not even caring that it's getting crushed as I cram it into one of my bags. As I leave the shop and head for the bus station, I know what I have to do. I have to keep Scott as far away from The Bake House Girl as I can, because if I fail in my mission to keep us together, I need to know that he's not going to fall straight into the arms of the beautiful girl who's just served me. I need the security of knowing that if we do break up during the festive period, that I have a chance of winning him back. Because if he gets together with her, why on earth would he ever come back to me?

Chapter 23

12th December

The cute couple from the bus are holding hands as we shuffle along the aisle and step out into the bus station on Monday morning, and he stoops to kiss her temple as they amble away towards the college. It must be extra romantic falling in love during the festive period, with all the twinkly lights giving off a fairytale vibe, and going for walks always feels better when you're wrapped up warm, holding the hand of someone you love (or at least fancy the pants off). Not that I remember what going for a romantic walk feels like, because dashing from the bus station to the toy shop in the drizzle doesn't count. Still, at least I'm out of the flat, which felt rather oppressive over the weekend. I didn't want to put a foot wrong and it's strangely gruelling tiptoeing around on eggshells in your own home.

I'm still thinking about the cute bus couple as I arrive at work and change into my elf gear. I watched them for the entire journey as they giggled and flirted and kissed while Scott and I sat side by side, the only form of conversation from flat to bus station a muttered farewell as we started to go our separate ways. No wonder he was able to move on to The Bake House Girl so quickly; it must have been incredibly thrilling to have someone new and exciting to talk to, someone who doesn't already know all your stories inside out and almost knows you better than you know yourself. The attention must have been flattering, a real ego boost after the monotonous relationship we've allowed ourselves to become embroiled in. I need to inject a bit more life into our relationship. A bit more excitement, like in the beginning when I used to meet Scott in bars after work instead of trudging home to change into comfy, cutesy slippers and spending the evening vegging out in front of the telly. We used to talk for *hours*, as though we'd never run out of new things to say to each other, and we'd laugh and flirt and kiss, just like the couple on the bus.

I can't actually remember the last time Scott and I made each other laugh.

We should go out more. Get dressed up and make an effort. We should talk and giggle and flirt again, because I miss that and I'm sure Scott does too. I need to show him that he doesn't need to go off with someone new to enjoy that buzz of a relationship.

'I knew you'd be here.' Milo appears from behind the Lego Christmas tree and joins me at the bird-filled tree, which appears to be my go-to place to muse. 'I brought you a little present.' He holds out a hand, where a tiny little foil package lies. I look from the foil package to Milo, a frown creasing my forehead.

'You brought me some weed?' I hiss the question, my eyes darting around us to make sure there's nobody in hearing distance.

'Of course not, you banana.' Milo's tone is wobbly with glee as he tries to suppress a smile.

'Then what is it?'

Milo pushes the foil package closer to me, but I don't dare touch it. 'It's something really lame if you were expecting weed. Actually, it's really lame no matter what.' He's about to close his fingers over the package, but I move in quickly, snatching it away before he can take it back. I peel back the corners of the foil and find a little chocolate sitting inside.

'It's from my advent calendar.' Milo scratches the back of his neck. 'It's a robin, and you said robins remind you of your gran.' He shrugs, his gaze dropping to his curly-toed elf shoes. 'And now they remind me of you.'

It's such a sweet gesture, it brings a lump to my throat and I find I can't speak as I stare down at the tiny chocolate robin. I really need to find him a girlfriend, and not just because it'll help to save my life. Milo's one of the good guys and whoever he ends up with will be very lucky.

'Told you it was lame.' Milo fiddles with one of the branches from the bird tree.

'It isn't lame. It's lovely that it made you think of me and my gran. Thank you.' I'm about to re-wrap the little bird in the foil but Milo puts his hand on mine to stop me.

'You don't have to keep it. You're supposed to eat it, otherwise it won't be fulfilling its advent mission to spread festive joy.'

'Its mission to spread festive joy?' That sounds very familiar. Luckily, the robin has an easier task than I do, and I pop it into my mouth, balling up the bit of foil and shoving it in my pocket. 'I can't believe you have an advent calendar.'

'Er, yeah.' Milo looks at me as though I've sprouted antlers. 'Advent calendars are *awesome*. Who doesn't want to wake up to a little piece of guilt-free chocolate?'

'All chocolate is guilt-free if you have the right mindset, but I get what you mean. They *are* awesome.'

'My mum buys me one every year, the more childlike the better in her opinion. This year it was a Peppa Pig one. Jordan and Lewis used to take the piss, but they buy their own now and line them up with mine on the mantlepiece. It's even become a bit of a competition to see who'll have the dorkiest one. I thought Mum's Peppa Pig one was a sure thing, until Jordan accidentally bought himself one meant for cats, crowning himself the Calendar Dork for this year. He claims it's for Faith, but that doesn't explain why he tried eating the first one and had to spit it out.'

I groan. 'He didn't.'

'I'm afraid so. I thought he was going to chuck up when he realised the chocolate wasn't for human consumption.' Milo grins at the memory of his housemate's discomfort and I can't help giggling myself.

'Mi-*lo*?'

Shannon's cry comes from deep within the grotto, and Milo and I both glance at each other before we set off, finding her fretting outside the workshop, Milo's camera in hand.

'I was trying to take a selfie with Papa Polar Bear.' She holds the camera up in one hand to demonstrate. 'But I must have accidentally pressed one of the other buttons, because the screen's blank and nothing I press is making it work.' She thrusts the camera at Milo. 'I'm *so sorry*. Don't tell Philippa. *Please*. I bought this *gorgeous* pair of shoes and put it on my mum's credit card, and they cost an absolute fortune so I can't lose another job. My mum would *kill* me.'

'Let me have a look.' Milo presses a couple of buttons before turning the camera so Shannon can see the screen. 'Don't worry, all fixed.'

Shannon puffs out a huge sigh of relief. 'Great. Thank God. Can you take my photo?' She stands beside the giant mechanical bear and pouts at Milo. I leave them to it and head down to the café to grab the gingerbread people before the shop opens. Eloise is setting out the crayons and colouring pages in the play area, and although she smiles and waves, it looks as though it takes great effort and she quickly turns back to her task before I have the chance to respond.

'Hey, you.' With the box of gingerbread people tucked under my arm, I head over to the play area, zig-zagging around chunky-wheeled tricycles and red-and-yellow ride-in cars. 'Tough morning?' The shop isn't even open yet, but rumour has it that Maureen can be tyrannical when she's had a bad night's sleep. She seemed fine and even-tempered when she handed over the gingerbread people, but I might have simply caught her during a more soothed period.

'Nah, it's been fine.' Eloise plucks the nub of a red crayon from one of the pots she's setting out on the miniature tables and replaces it with a full-sized one before robotically moving on to the next one.

'Really? Because you don't seem your usual chirpy self.' Plus, she's wearing her old, stripy cardigan again.

'I'm just tired.'

Which we all know is code for 'I'm feeling miserable but am playing it down' or 'I've spent the entire night crying into my pillow'. Her eyes don't look puffy, but there are some miracle-working make-up products these days.

'You know you can talk to me about anything?'

Eloise pauses, the crayon pot in her hand paused a couple of inches from the tabletop. 'So you can say I told you so?'

'Why would I say . . .' And then it dawns on me. Of course. 'Annie.'

'Yes, Annie.' Eloise plonks the pot down on the table and chucks herself onto the nearest miniature plastic chair, which can't be very comfortable with her knees now sitting up near her chin. 'We were supposed to have that date on Friday night, remember?'

It had completely slipped my mind in The Bake House Girl drama. I should have checked in with Eloise over the weekend, knowing what Annie would do, but I didn't even send a cursory text. I am a Very Bad Friend, and the realisation makes my stomach squirm.

'What happened?' I pull out a little chair and lower myself onto it. It's shockingly close to the ground and there's a moment of panic that I'm going to end up on the floor just before my bum meets solid plastic.

'*Nothing* happened.' Eloise balls her fists so she's clutching the overhanging sleeves of her cardigan and tucks her hands under her armpits. 'She didn't even show up at the restaurant, so I sat there on my own like a lemon until I finally gave up and went home.' She's been staring down at her knees, but she peeks up at me, her face drawn in pure misery. 'She didn't even reply to any of my messages – and I sent a lot over the weekend – until an hour ago. And all it said was "something came up". No apology. No real explanation. No suggestion that we rearrange the date.'

Why would Eloise *want* to rearrange the date? I know that no relationship is perfect, but some are more doomed than others. But I don't say this to Eloise. She doesn't need my judgement, or any hint of I-told-you-so. She needs empathy and comfort. She needs a friend.

'I'm so sorry. Is there anything I can do to make you feel better?'

Eloise shakes her head, but I'm not giving up that easily.

'How about an elf tap dance?'

Eloise raises her eyebrows. 'You can't tap dance. You have the coordination of a newborn giraffe.'

'Which will make it even more entertaining. Duh.' Getting up off the tiny chair proves a difficult task, but I manage to lever myself up to my feet. 'Ready? And one, two, three, four.' And off I go, prancing about the play area of the Lower Ground Floor Café, my arms and legs flailing about all over the place. Eloise strives to keep a straight face, but it proves too much when I accidentally kick a tricycle, swearing loudly as I hop around as my big toe throbs with pain. She covers her mouth with the sleeve of her cardigan, but even that isn't enough to muffle her giggles.

'I think you need to work on your tap dancing skills.'

I plonk myself down on a tiny chair, my stomach flipping with fear as I plummet dangerously close to the ground again, and grab my foot, rubbing vigorously to try to ease the discomfort. It hurts like hell, but it's nice to see a smile back on my friend's face.

'There are lots of skills I need to work on right now.' And tap dancing is at the very bottom of the pile. I really need to work on my Perfect Girlfriend skills before Scott runs into the arms of the first sympathetic listener, and I really, *really* need to work on my Christmas Cupid matchmaking skills, because we're almost halfway through December and I've only paired up two couples so far. If I don't pull my finger out, I won't only be alone this Christmas, I'll be dead. And there's nothing merry about that.

Chapter 24

There's no time to waste, so I use my lunch hour to pop across to the estate agents to surprise Scott with a romantic lunch. It's only a meal deal from Boots, but it's something we used to do during the early days of our relationship. We couldn't wait a whole working day to see each other, so we'd meet up in the town centre, finding a bench or a wall to perch on, even if it was raining, because it meant we could snatch that bit of time together. It's one of those things that we've misplaced along the way – like talking late into the night or Scott calling me Shopgirl – but I'm determined to rediscover those little gems that made our relationship shine.

I don't have time to change out of my elf costume (and back into it again later) but I have swapped my green, curly-toed shoes for my brogues and removed my elf hat and pointy silicone ears and scrubbed the large red spots off my cheeks. There was a bit of a queue in Boots but I still have over half an hour of my break left by the time I reach the estate agents.

'Hello, Elaine.' I lean against the reception desk and clutch my side. I've legged it all the way from Boots and I've got a stitch. All those sweet treats I keep shoving in my gob and the lack of exercise isn't doing me any favours in the fitness stakes (but I'm still going to eat the brownie I've just bought, because I have zero willpower when it comes to food and the likelihood of me being ploughed down by a double decker bus in less than two weeks is increasing by the second, so sod it). 'Can you let Scott know I'm here?' I lift up the Boots carrier bag. 'I've brought us some lunch.'

'Oh.' Elaine eyes the carrier bag as she catches her bottom lip between her teeth. 'Oh dear. I think Scott's across the road, at the bakery. The man's obsessed with their pork and cranberry sausage rolls!' She laughs heartily, even though she looks mortified at having to deliver the news that my surprise lunch is trashed.

This is not good news, and not just because I'll feel inclined to scoff both of the brownies in the carrier bag now. How frequently would one have to visit a bakery to be classed as 'obsessed'? Once a week? Twice? *More*?

'Did he know you were bringing lunch?' Elaine nods at the carrier bag, which I'm still foolishly holding in mid-air. 'Because maybe he's just popped over there for a coffee?' She smiles encouragingly at me. 'He does that a lot.'

Bugger. 'Obsessed' with The Bake House's pork and cranberry sausage rolls *and* a regular visitor for a caffeine fix is Very Bad News. This isn't a once-a-week habit.

'How much is a lot?'

Elaine's eyes widen and she opens and closes her mouth like a fish. 'Oh. I'm not sure. Maybe a lot is pushing it.' She tugs at the collar of her blouse, flustered as she imagines she's just dropped Scott in it by revealing he's been frittering away his wages on fancy takeaway coffees. She obviously has no idea how many mince pies I put away from C&L's café, not to mention hot chocolates from the market and other goodies. Scott and I have never interfered in how we each spend our money – we split the bills and whatever is left is ours to spend as we see fit.

'Did you have a think about the wreath-making workshop tomorrow?' Elaine is still fiddling with her collar, even as she changes the subject. 'You should tell your friends. Bring as many as you'd like. There's plenty of room.' She doesn't add 'please' to the end verbally, but the puppy eyes shout it loud and clear. 'It's at the library. Eight o'clock.'

'I'll see what I can do.' I back away from the desk before I commit to more and head back outside. The Bake House is across the road, full of treats and blonde beauties. I cross over the road and I'm deciding whether to pop my head in to look for Scott when the door opens and he appears right in front of me.

'There you are.' I hold up the Boots carrier bag. 'I brought you a surprise lunch, but Elaine said you might be here, already stocking up.'

'Afraid so.' Scott holds up a paper bag and takeaway coffee cup. 'Sorry.'

'No, it's my fault. I should have called you or texted, but it was just an impulse thing. Never mind. We can still eat together?' My tone goes up at the end, turning what was supposed to be a statement into a question. *Can* we still eat lunch together on a work day? Is that still a thing we can do? The doubt creeping in leaves me feeling cold, and it has nothing to do with the frosty temperature, because of course we can still eat lunch together. We're still very much a couple and I'm being daft with my worries.

'Yeah. Sure.' Scott looks up at the grey sky. 'Looks like it might rain though.'

'How about the bus station?' It's draughty in there, but at least it's sheltered and there are loads of benches to choose from at this time of day. 'It'll be like old times. Chilly but romantic.'

It doesn't feel as romantic as it used to do as we shiver our way through lunch, trying to chat as our teeth chatter uncontrollably. In the end, we give up the conversation and eat as quickly as we can to get it over with. *This* is probably why we stopped our lunchtime dates.

'That was delicious.' Scott scrunches up the paper bag and licks a flake of pastry from his thumb. Elaine was right about the pork and cranberry sausage roll.

'I don't think you should go to The Bake House anymore.' The words are out of my mouth before I've even thought them through, so when Scott gives me a quizzical look over his coffee cup, I have no explanation other than the truth, which I can't tell him. I need to keep Scott away from the bakery, or more specifically, The Bake House Girl. 'They, er, have rats. In the kitchen. Big ones. It's put me right off their cupcakes, so don't buy them anymore, okay? In fact, just stay away completely.'

Scott takes a sip of his coffee and wipes his mouth with the back of his hand. 'They don't have rats.'

'They do. Really big ones.' I hold my hands out to demonstrate the cat-sized proportions. 'It was in the papers.'

'So why haven't they been shut down?' Scott finishes his coffee while I struggle to come up with a response. I still haven't uttered a word by the time he tosses the empty cup and paper bag in the bin. *Why can't he do this at home?* The thought pops into my head, uninvited, unwelcome, and I push it away, ignoring the image of balled-up paper bags and used teabags littering the kitchen worktop.

'Well, I believe it, and I don't think we should shop there anymore, just in case. What if the chocolate chips aren't chocolate chips at all? What if they're *rat droppings*? Rat-dropping cookies – ugh.'

'They don't have rats.' Scott starts to walk away and I gather up my things, shoving my half-eaten brownie back into its wrapper as I scuttle after him.

'This was nice though, wasn't it?' I thread my arm through Scott's, skipping along to keep up with his long strides as we head towards the bus station's exit. 'We should do more stuff together. Like we used to. We could go out tonight. Nothing too fancy for a work night. The pub or the cinema?'

'I can't tonight.' Scott kisses the top of my head before breaking free from my grip. 'I've got this online gaming event with Dan and some others.' He raises his hand in farewell, already a few paces away. 'I'll see you at home.'

'Okay.' I'm trying not to feel too deflated that I've been rejected in favour of Dan and their shared interest in gaming, but my spirits are spiralling towards the ground like a punctured balloon. 'See you at home.'

I head back to the toy shop, nibbling at the brownie as I try to push away thoughts of Scott and The Bake House Girl on Christmas Eve. He looked cosy and loved up, as though no online gaming event could drag him away from the Hallmark festive movie moment. I feel helpless and frustrated, but what can I do? I can't ban Scott from The Bake House, and he doesn't seem deterred by the prospect of rat-dropping cookies. How am I supposed to play Christmas Cupid when I can't even sort my own relationship out?

But, wait. Is that it? Is that the answer to my problem – to *both* of my problems? Could I combine my Christmas Cupid duties with my need to keep Scott and The Bake House Girl apart? Because if I can match The Bake House Temptress with someone else, if I can ensure she's cosying up with someone else during the parade, that will leave Scott free and ready to be reunited with his true love on Christmas Eve.

I'll need to choose the match carefully, to ensure it's a foolproof venture. It'll need to be someone extra special. Someone who will capture her heart so that Scott can't find his way in there. Someone . . . I pause in the entrance of C&L's Toys, watching as Milo crouches down in front of a shy-looking little boy and whispers something that makes him giggle so hard his cheeks turn pink.

Someone like Milo.

Of course! He's sweet and kind and funny and thoughtful, and he's cute in that offbeat, dorky kind of way. He could be the perfect match. My saviour, sent to rescue my mess of a relation-ship without even realising it. I just have to find a way to bring the pair together . . .

Chapter 25

I have a plan. It's extremely basic and flimsy, but it's a plan all the same and happy little butterflies are fluttering in my tummy as I head into work, giddy with my plotting and full of hope that it'll come to fruition. I'm humming a merry festive tune as I pass the bird-filled tree on my way to the North Pole, running my fingers along the robin's feathers for luck and thinking about how this little bird is the perfect example of how kind and thoughtful my colleague is. Not only did Milo pick up on the fact that I stop at this particular tree, he remembered why and sacrificed his chocolate treat for me. He is a very special young man and The Bake House Girl doesn't know how lucky she is that the Christmas Cupid is going to bring him into her life.

I sow the seeds of my plan as soon as I spot Milo outside Santa's workshop, sighing long and loud enough to draw attention to it before declaring how hungry and in need of a sweet treat I am.

'Here. Catch.' Milo is filling the red-and-white striped bucket we store the candy canes in by the workshop's front door, and he tosses one my way. It cartwheels its way towards me and I hold out my hands, ready to whoop with joy when it lands neatly between my fingers.

Of course it doesn't. It pings off my little finger and drops to the floor, cracking in two within its plastic packaging.

'Bravo.' Milo applauds enthusiastically while I stoop to retrieve the candy cane before performing a curtsey.

'Thanks, but this isn't what I had in mind.' I sigh again as I pocket the candy cane (I may not want it *now*, but I'm sure I'll be in the mood for a peppermint treat later and we can't give it to one of the kids now it's damaged). 'I've had this massive craving for cake all morning.'

'They've got sticky toffee pudding on the specials menu downstairs?' Milo grabs a handful of candy canes and adds them to the bucket.

'No, I'm not in the mood for that either. I want a chocolate cupcake, covered with a shiny chocolate ganache and dripping with white icing and with a little marzipan holly and ivy on top to make it look like a Christmas pudding.'

'That's quite specific.' Milo squeezes a couple more candy canes in the bucket. 'I'm not sure that's on Maureen's menu.'

No, it isn't. And that's the point.

'They make them at that bakery near the bus station. I've had a craving for them all morning. We should go over at lunchtime.'

'We?'

'Yes, we. You and me.' And this is the extent of my plan to bring Milo and The Bake House Temptress together. I don't even know if she'll be working there this afternoon, but this is all I have. Feeble plans are better than no plans, right?

'I have a packed lunch up in my locker. Why don't you go with Shannon?'

'Because Shannon doesn't waste her daily calorie intake on cake. She saves them up for wine and vodka-coke binges.'

'Eloise then?' Milo picks up the box of remaining candy canes and heads off to store them in the photo gift booth. I follow, determined to have Milo follow The Plan.

'Lunchtime is Eloise's busiest period. There's no way she'd be able to leave when we shut the grotto for our lunch break. Please?'

Milo slots the box of candy canes on the shelf next to the blank mugs. 'You really need somebody to go with you?'

'Yes, I really need somebody to go with me, otherwise I'll end up buying all the cakes and stuffing them in my gob on the way back to the shop. You know me – I have no off switch when it comes to food. And then I'll be sick all over the grotto, and there's no way Shannon will clean it up and I'll be too ill to do it, so you'll end up having to mop up vomit. And if the kids see an elf chundering all over the North Pole, they'll be traumatised. Or maybe I'll even be sick *on* a child, who will *definitely* be traumatised. Or maybe . . .'

Milo holds his hands up in surrender. 'All right, all right, I'll come with you. Jeez, you paint a pretty picture.'

The morning passes slowly, even with three mass bookings to keep us busy, but finally the grotto is temporarily closed and Milo and I head to The Bake House.

'This cake had better be worth it.' Milo has brought his packed lunch with him, and he offers me half a ham and cheese sandwich. I decline; I've been desperate to try a pork and cranberry sausage roll since my lunchtime 'date' with Scott yesterday, to see what all the fuss is about. 'I was going to spend my lunch break reading the next chapter of my book. I'm so close to the end and I'm desperate to know whodunnit.'

'What are you reading?'

Milo clips the lid of his Tupperware box closed while somehow keeping hold of his triangle of sandwich. 'Agatha Christie. *Hercule Poirot's Christmas*. If you've read it, please don't tell me who the killer is.' He tucks the box under his arm and takes a huge bite out of his sandwich.

'Don't worry, I've never read an Agatha Christie novel.' I narrow my eyes as I wrack my brain. 'In fact, I don't think I've ever watched *Poirot* on the telly.'

'Oh, you should. Both the books and the TV show are excellent. I love a good whodunnit. I should be finished with it tonight if you fancy a read?'

'Yeah, why not?' It isn't as though I haven't got enough on my plate at the moment, what with trying to keep my relationship intact while attempting to matchmake four more couples so I don't end up being a tragic Christmas headline. Squeezing a whole novel in as well will be fine.

We round the corner, with The Bake House just ahead. Milo finishes his triangle of sandwich in three more quick bites before we step inside. We've managed to miss the bulk of the lunchtime crush, so there are only three customers ahead of us. One of which is Scott, who is leaning against the counter, chatting to The Bake House Temptress while she bags up his sausage roll (which sounds like a euphemism but isn't. Not yet anyway).

'Hey, you.' I mask the panic gurgling in my stomach with a bright smile. 'Fancy seeing you here. Elaine was right about your addiction.' I nod towards the paper bag that has just been placed on the counter.

'I wouldn't call it an addiction. Just lunch.' He pays for the sausage roll and the coffee on the counter and joins Milo and I at the back of the queue. I introduce him to Milo and they share a brief and awkward-looking hand shake. 'I thought you didn't like this place. You know, because of the . . .' He leans forward and whispers, 'Rats.' Milo's eyes widen, but Scott shakes his head. 'Don't worry, mate. There aren't any outside of Zo's vivid imagination.'

Milo looks at me, and I have to concede Scott's statement with a shrug/nod combo. I want to keep Scott away from the honey-blonde bombshell currently serving customers, but I don't want to start any rumours that could potentially harm the business.

'You don't have to stay with us.' Milo and I shuffle forward in the queue and Scott follows. 'You're probably really busy, and your sausage roll and coffee will be getting cold.' Plus, we're inching nearer to the honey-blonde bombshell, which is going against the plan to keep them apart.

'It's okay.' Scott gives a lazy one-shouldered shrug. 'We don't get to see each other during the day usually.'

My heart drums a happy little beat, glad that my desire to reboot our relationship isn't one-sided. If Scott and I are on the same page, it means we stand a good chance of succeeding.

'Back again so soon? We don't usually see you again until you finish work.' We've reached the counter, and the honey-blonde bombshell is giving Scott a bemused look. 'Unless I forgot something?' She bites her bottom lip, and dammit she looks adorable.

'No, nothing like that.' Scott slings his arm around me, accidentally swinging the sausage roll bag at me. 'I ran into Zoey. My girlfriend.'

'Oh. Hello, Zoey.' The honey-blonde bombshell beams at me, flashing a gleaming set of perfectly straight teeth as though she's part of a toothpaste advert. 'I think I've seen you before?' A slight frown dims the beam.

'The rolls of wrapping paper.' I turn towards the door, where I spilled my shopping at the weekend. 'I chucked them over your floor and you helped me to pick them up.'

'Yes!' The beam is back. 'I never forget a face. Or a favourite order, which comes in handy in this job.' She tinkles out a laugh and though I'm trying to hate her, the sound is infectious and I find the corners of my lips involuntarily pulling upwards. 'Scott, for example, likes a pork and cranberry sausage roll with a gingerbread latte for his lunch, and a hazelnut coffee after work, and on Fridays he always buys a cupcake.'

'That last one's for me.' I look up at Scott and beam a not quite toothpaste-advert-worthy smile at him. 'It's our "thing". He brings a treat home for me every Friday.'

'How sweet. I hope you've liked my choices.'

'*Your* choices?' I look from Scott to Honey-Blonde. 'What do you mean?'

'I pick one out for you every Friday. I try to make sure it's something different each week.' Her voice tails off towards the end and she looks slowly up at Scott to gauge his reaction, but he doesn't look put out.

'You know what I'm like, babe.' He shrugs. 'I'm useless at picking stuff out for you. That's why I'm glad you love frogs so much. Makes it much easier for me. Anything with a frog on it will do, right?'

Anything with a frog on it will do. Wow, that sounds romantic. And thoughtful. Scott doesn't see my face fall as he's turned to Milo and is nudging him with his elbow.

'She'd even be happy with a multipack of Freddos. Hey, there's an idea for Christmas.' He grins, as though he's joking, and he'd better be. I think of the games console hidden underneath a pile of bedding on the bottom of the wardrobe.

'Thank you. Your choices are always very good.' I turn to The Bake House Girl and push a smile onto my face. 'I particularly liked the Christmas pudding cupcake . . .' I glance back at the display unit, glad to see a row of the chocolate cupcakes there. 'Could I get one of those now, please?'

I ask Milo what he'd like – my treat – while she pops one of the cakes into a paper bag, but Milo declines, saying he's only there to stop me from gorging the entire stock. Scott snorts, and I'm sure he mutters 'good luck with that, mate' under his breath, but Milo's reminded me of the real reason we're here and I can't afford to get distracted again.

'This is my friend, Milo, by the way.' I gently push him forward towards the counter. 'He doesn't usually have pointy ears and red cheeks. We're elves at C&L's grotto.'

'How cute.' I was worried when Milo batted away my suggestion that he remove the silicone ears and wipe off the rosy cheeks before we left the shop, but it seems to be going in his favour, judging by the way The Bake House Girl is smiling sweetly at him. 'I keep meaning to bring my nephew to see Santa.'

'You should. It's a really lovely grotto, with story time and everything. Milo's the photographer.'

'So you're no ordinary elf?' She raises her eyebrows at Milo and I feel a frisson of triumph at the hint of flirting. If she starts to giggle and play with her hair, we're in. Unfortunately, the door opens and a couple of shopping-bag-laden women burst into the shop. The shop assistant is back in professional mode, taking the money for the Christmas pudding cupcake before turning her attention to the new customers. Scott, Milo and I head out of the shop and although my watch doesn't ping with a new match, it's okay because I have a good feeling about this little meeting. It's the start of something, I'm sure. I just have to work out a way to engineer another more meaningful meeting and I think I'll have another match in the bag.

Chapter 26

Milo eats the remaining triangle of his sandwich as we make our way back through the town centre while I let my cupcake dangle limply in its paper bag, the initial euphoria as we left the shop having quickly dissolved.

She knew his name. The girl from The Bake House knew his name. *Scott, for example, likes a pork and cranberry sausage roll with a gingerbread latte for his lunch.* This means they're not simply customer and bakery assistant. They're customer and bakery assistant *who chat.* They share details about themselves. Which would be fine if it wasn't for the fact that I know there's an attraction there, a connection, and they could end up together again if I'm not careful.

There's also something else niggling at me. Something that's probably incredibly petty but it keeps playing on my mind.

She chooses my Friday treat.

All this time, I've assumed it was Scott making the choice, poring over the selection of cakes and biscuits, wondering which one to surprise me with that week. The red velvet cupcake or the heart-shaped shortbread with pink icing swirls? I thought he'd taken the time to consider what I'd like, which one would make me smile the widest as I looked inside the paper bag. But all this time it's been her, a stranger (to me, at least) putting in the effort. The sweet, romantic gesture has lost a bit of its shine, no matter how much I tell myself that it doesn't matter *who* chose the cake. The gesture was still there. Scott was still thinking of me as he stepped into the bakery every Friday evening after work.

Or was he?

The question pops into my head and refuses to budge. In fact, it brings another, even more sinister one with it.

Am I just an excuse for him to pop into the bakery? A ruse to spend a few more minutes with this girl?

'Zoey?' A hand waving in front of my face breaks off my internal interrogation. Milo has been chatting to me, and although I could hear the murmur of words, I haven't deciphered a single one.

'Sorry. I was miles away.' Or rather a few yards away, back at the bakery. 'What were you saying?'

Milo aims his half-eaten sandwich ahead, towards the entrance to the Christmas market. 'Don't you love a brass band at Christmas?'

The band is playing 'Once in Royal David's City' and I find myself coming to a standstill as we approach them. Milo doesn't complain and we stand and listen – Milo munching the rest of his sandwich – and for a couple of minutes all thoughts of Scott and The Bake House Girl and Friday cupcakes disappear. The sun is shining, the air is crisp, and the sounds of Christmas are wafting over me. All feels right and I don't want the spell to break, but the song comes to an end and Milo brushes the crumbs from his coat.

'Best get back.' He looks up at the church clock opposite the market. The time is depressingly close to the end of our lunch break. 'The First Noel' starts to play as we move away from the brass band and Milo rummages in his coat pocket, pulling out a few bits of change which he slots into the collection tin that one of the instrument-free members of the band is holding out. I rummage in my handbag for the pound coin I usually use in supermarket trolleys, but it's the sharp edge of a business card I find instead.

'Oh, bugger.' The business card is cream with a green, leafy wreath in its centre. 'Handmade with Love' is printed in the middle of the wreath, with Elaine's contact details underneath.

'What is it?' Milo peers at the business card, which I shove back in my bag and continue the hunt for the pound coin.

'There's a wreath-making workshop tonight, and I said I'd go. And bring some friends.' I pause the quid hunt to pull a face. 'And I totally forgot and haven't organised anybody to go.'

'I'll come.'

'Don't be silly.' I resume the hunt, pulling aside old receipts and bus tickets. 'It's twenty quid each.'

Milo shrugs. 'Sounds like a bargain to me.'

'It's half-price or something.' Aha! Victory! My fingers grasp the pound coin, which I slip into the collection tin.

'Told you it was a bargain.' We start to move away from the market, the strains of 'The First Noel' fading as we near the toy shop. 'Where is it?'

'You don't have to come. I'm sure you have better things to do. Like finishing your Poirot and finding out whodunnit.'

'I only have a handful of chapters to go. I'll have time to do both, and I'll give the wreath to my mum. She'll love it. It's been years since I gave her something homemade. When and where is it?'

'Are you sure about this?' I can't believe Milo's willing to give wreath making a go. There's no way Scott will come along, but maybe Eloise and Franziska?

'Absolutely. I'm looking forward to it.'

I shoot Milo a skeptical look, but I pass on the details.

'Great. Sounds fun.'

I look at Milo, expecting him to be pulling a silly face to show that he's taking the piss, but he looks genuinely excited at the prospect of spending an hour or two creating a festive wreath with Elaine.

I was only going to attend the workshop reluctantly because I felt a bit sorry for Elaine, but Milo's enthusiasm must be contagious, because maybe it *will* be fun.

Eloise turns down my plea to join us at the wreath-making workshop ('Twenty quid? I'm skint and I still have my Christmas shopping to do'), as does Cliff ('Not my thing, love') and Shannon just laughs in my face, which I take as a no. Predictably, Scott also passes, as does Miranda, Pete, and even Franziska.

'I would have loved to have come.' We're sitting in her living room with a pot of tea and a plate of chocolate *spitzbuben* in front of us. 'But I'm having dinner with Tobias and his family. It's the last chance we'll get before Christmas. They're going to Florida and . . .' Franziska smiles coyly, her gaze dropping to the chocolate sandwich biscuit in her hand. 'Well, it probably won't happen because it's madness, but . . .' She sneaks a peek up at me. 'Klaus has asked me to go and spend Christmas with him.'

'In Germany?' I've picked up another biscuit, but it pauses midway between the plate and my mouth.

'I told you it was madness.' Franziska starts to fiddle with the teapot, lifting the lid to check on the brew. 'I haven't been to Germany since my father's funeral, and I haven't seen Klaus since I was not much more than a girl, and we have only been conversing for a few months – face to face only a matter of days. No.' She puts the teapot's lid back in place and shakes her head. 'It was a silly idea.'

'No, it isn't a silly idea at all. I think it's a great idea.'

Franziska's eyebrows shoot up her forehead. 'You do?'

'Absolutely, and this Christmas is the perfect time. Tobias and his family won't be here, so you won't miss out on seeing them by going to Germany, and it's the perfect excuse to get out of spending the day with Malcolm and his mum.'

'But who will decorate the tree in the hall on Christmas Eve?' She twists to look towards her front door. 'I do it every year, hanging up my beautiful glass baubles and homemade cookies and treats.'

'I'll do it. Just give me the decs before you go and I'll make sure they go up on Christmas Eve. I'll even send you a photo, or FaceTime you so you can see it.'

'You'd do that?'

'Of course.' It seems like a fair price to pay for another heart on my Christmas Cupid tracker. 'Shall we book your plane ticket now, before you change your mind?'

Franziska takes a couple of seconds to mull it over, then she nods once, firmly. 'Yes. Let's do it right now.'

I take a triumphant bite of my biscuit as we head to her computer. Couple number three, here we come!

The prospect of Franziska and Klaus edging closer to a reunion puts a definite skip back in my step after The Bake House thing this afternoon, so I'm feeling pretty chirpy by the time I step into the library and head for the wreath-making workshop in the room at the back. Milo is right – this should be fun, especially as I think of myself as a pretty creative person.

Milo's already in the workshop room, sitting at a table with crafty-looking bits and pieces in front of him. The only other attendees are two silver-haired women and a bloke wearing a library pass lanyard (and who looks like he'd rather be anywhere else than in this room) so I'm glad we came, to support Elaine if nothing else, because the class size would have been a bit woeful before the December do-over. I head straight for Milo, tucking my bag under the table and hanging my coat over the back of the chair next to his.

'I haven't missed anything, have I?' I didn't mean to be late but the bus didn't show up for ages and it got stuck at a set of temporary traffic lights forever.

'We haven't started yet.' Milo leans in and lowers his voice. 'Elaine's waiting to see if anybody else turns up. I'm not sure it's going to happen.'

Elaine is hovering by the door, her eyes flicking between the library space and her watch. Eventually, she claps her hands together.

'It looks like we're having a cosy session today, but that just means more mince pies and mulled wine for us.'

I catch Milo's eye and pull a face. Mulled wine? Yuck.

'Don't worry.' Milo reaches under the table and pulls out a battered rucksack. 'I've brought a flask of hot chocolate.'

'How resourceful.'

Milo shrugs. 'They always have mulled wine at these sorts of thing at Christmas. Mum and Holly-Mae do all this festive crafty stuff – card making, lino-printed wrapping paper, crochet-your-own-fairy-lights – and I swear they only do it to get tipsy on the mulled wine.'

Elaine claps her hands together again. 'Now, in front of you on the table you should have the basics for your wreath: a wreath ring, scissors, twine and florist wire. On this table over here . . .' she indicates the two tables pushed together at the front of the class, '. . . we have moss and a selection of foliage for you to use, along with natural decorations – pinecones, cinnamon sticks, dried orange slices – and some fun and festive trimmings, like bells, ribbons, tinsel, baubles, stars . . . Feel free to use as much or as little as you like. But first, let's start with a base for you to build up from.'

Elaine demonstrates how to create a sturdy base, securing moss to the wreath ring using the twine before attaching the foliage to produce the wreath form we're all familiar with. She talks to us about the foliage as she goes along, encouraging us to feel the different textures of the leaves and imparting her wisdom about each of them, and by the time she's finished I feel like I've had a one-to-one with Monty Don.

'You know a lot about plants, don't you?' The library worker puffs out his cheeks and collapses against his table, as though learning about spruce and evergreen oak has taken a physical toll.

'I guess I do.' Elaine drops the handful of eucalyptus leaves in the wicker basket in front of her. 'Sorry if I bored you. I get a bit carried away.'

'It wasn't boring.' I feel a rush of affection as Milo's words cause a smile to light up Elaine's face. 'In fact, we could have used somebody like you on our pub quiz team last week. We were *terrible* at the gardening stuff.'

'I *do* know a lot about gardening.' Elaine picks up the eucalyptus again and brings it to her nose, inhaling deeply. 'My mum was very green-fingered, as was my grandfather. They taught me everything I know.'

'There's another quiz on Thursday. You should join our team.' Milo looks at me for backing, and I nod. The more the merrier.

'Really?' Elaine bites her bottom lip. 'You'd want *me* on your team?'

'Absolutely.' Milo finishes attaching his final piece of foliage and holds it up for inspection. 'What do you think?'

I think he's a genius, because he's just given me an idea of how to get him and the girl from the bakery together.

Chapter 27

14th December

My hand is a bit jittery as it reaches for the door handle, and I almost chicken out and leg it back to the toy shop but somebody appears behind me, waiting to get into the bakery too so I'm forced to give the door a push and step inside. I indicate that the customer who follows me inside should go first and hang back while she's being served. I don't have a lot of time to dither as I've dashed over on my morning tea break, but I'm a bit anxious about how to go about this.

Scott's Bake House Girl is behind the counter, smiling that toothpaste smile as she chats away to the customer, her honey-blonde hair piled up in a messy but stylish topknot. I watch her as she moves around her workspace, grabbing tongs and plucking treats from the display counter without seeming to break eye contact with the shopper, chatting away as though they're old friends. I can see why Scott is attracted to this girl, and it isn't just because she's girl-band pretty. She oozes confidence. It radiates from her and fills the room, and when she smiles, I want to smile right back at her. She should be a rival but I feel strangely drawn to her, as though I want to be enveloped in her world. Maybe it's because of that saying: keep your friends close and your enemies closer.

'Zoey! Hello again.'

I'm caught off guard by her friendly greeting and the fact that she remembers my name when I don't know hers.

'Hi.' I take a couple of tiny steps towards her as the shop door closes behind the retreating customer. It's just me and her now. 'I'm sorry, I don't even know your name.'

'It's Kelsey.' She holds a hand out and as I shuffle forward to shake it, I notice her fingertips are painted a frosted pink shade with silver glittery specks. 'It's so lovely to see you again. Scott's told me all about you, so it's great to finally put a face to a name.' She tinkles a laugh, her little nose scrunching up like a bunny, and I find my lips lift up into a smile as I'm given a little burst of hope. Scott has told her about me, has made sure she knows he's in a relationship. Off limits. 'What can I get you today? I know you're a fan of our cupcakes, but I can highly recommend the tiramisu pavlova. It's Mum's speciality.'

'Your mum's?'

'This is Mum and Dad's baby.' Kelsey holds her hands palm up and glances around the shop. 'They do all the baking themselves. I think they were hoping I'd follow in their footsteps, but I can barely bake fairy cakes. I'm fine with serving, but I'm definitely not a behind-the-scenes person here.'

'So you don't know anything about food and cooking then?' My shoulders drop as my get-Milo-and-The-Bake-House-Girl-together plan starts to crumble.

'I'm more an eater than a creator.' Kelsey shrugs, and I feel a new reason to be drawn to her. *I'm* more of an eater than a creator too – I can bung a few ingredients in the slow cooker, but beyond that I'm all about frozen pizzas and jars of pasta sauce. 'Why, did you have something specific you needed to know? Because I can ask Mum . . .' She twists so she's facing a door that leads to an area at the back of the shop. 'She knows everything when it comes to food and baking.'

'No, no, it's okay.' I put a hand up to stop her rushing off to disturb her mum. 'It's just there's a pub quiz tomorrow night and we could do with more people. I thought if you were free and you wanted to, you could help us out.'

'I would *love* that.' Kelsey places her hands down on the counter and leans towards me, the silver specks on her nails glinting in the light from the low-hanging fixtures above. 'I love a quiz! Count me in.'

'Fantastic!' If I were alone, at home, I would do a little jig. But I'm not, and I'd probably end up kicking over the little Christmas tree decorated with iced biscuits if I attempted it here. 'It's at The Spindles, eight o'clock.'

'I'll be there.' Kelsey grins at me and hope starts to balloon in my chest. This could actually work. Okay, it didn't work out for Cliff and Maureen, but I'm sure Kelsey and Milo will get along marvellously. They both seem like pretty easy-going people so I don't think there'll be a personality clash this time. The urge to jig is strong but I contain myself and walk calmly towards the door.

'Erm, Zoey?'

'Yes?' The hope-filled balloon starts to slowly deflate. She's remembered she already has plans, or she's realised I'm a bit weird asking a stranger to join my pub quiz team and has changed her mind.

'Did you want something?' She nods towards the display counter stuffed with sweet treats.

'Oh! Yes! Of course.' I slam a hand against my forehead. Duh. 'I'll take a piece of the tiramisu pavlova please.'

Well, it does come highly recommended and I can't leave the shop empty-handed.

Slipping onto a bus seat the next evening, I unwind my scarf and take off my gloves, tucking them into my coat pockets before grabbing the paperback from my bag. Milo brought the Agatha Christie novel into work yesterday and although I'm only a couple of chapters in and I'm more of a romcom girl, I'm intrigued by the dark plot. I'm so intrigued, I don't notice we're approaching the bus station until the last second and have to throw myself to the front of the bus while still clutching the book.

The town centre is deserted at this time of night, with all the shoppers dispersed to their homes, and not even the bright festive lights strung up between the buildings can rid it of its eerie feel. My brogues clomp against the pavement, each footstep marked loud and clear, and I can't help listening out for another set of footsteps as I hurry through the barren high street. Perhaps reading a murder mystery before trekking through the town centre at night on my own wasn't such a good idea . . .

I'm breathless by the time I reach The Spindles after almost galloping my way to the pub while imagining all sorts of grisly outcomes, and I'm glad to see my friends are already inside. Eloise and Cliff have bagged a table near the fire, while Milo's waiting to be served at the bar.

'Didn't you bring Isla?' Eloise leans to the side so she can look past me as I unravel the scarf I was sure was going to end up as a murder weapon a few seconds ago. 'I thought she was part of the Santa's Helpers team?'

'She was at a loose end last week.' I unbutton my coat and shrug it off. 'I didn't think to invite her along tonight. Do you think I should have?'

'Hell, yes.' Eloise grins wickedly at me, her eyebrows lifting as she takes a sip of her Coke.

'I'll invite her to next week's quiz, as long as you promise not to drool all over her.'

Eloise shakes her head. 'I can make no such promise.'

'I thought you were desperate to make things work with Annie?' Not that I should be complaining – I'd much rather Eloise was interested in Isla than the ex who has broken her heart more times than I've scoffed mince pies during my double helping of December.

'A girl can look.' Eloise finishes off her Coke and stands up.

'Shall we go to the bar? Milo's already getting a round in but I fancy some crisps.'

Milo's already heading back to the table when we reach the bar. I keep my eye on the door as we wait to be served, looking out for Elaine and Kelsey.

'It was really sweet of Milo to invite Elaine tonight. I get the impression she doesn't have much self-confidence, so hopefully this will give her a boost.'

Eloise leans against the bar and raises herself up on tiptoe so she can see where the bar staff are. 'He's a really sweet guy in general.'

And he is. I didn't pay him much attention the first-time round; he was just the elf who took the photos in the grotto and occasionally flirted with Shannon. But I've loved getting to know him, so I'm grateful yet again for being given this opportunity to replay the month.

'Oh, Kelsey's here.' I've never seen her out of her apron, but she looks photoshoot-ready in a pair of skinny jeans Rylan Clark would deem 'a bit too tight' under over-the-knee brown suede boots. A camel-coloured cape and a superlong monochrome scarf ward off the cold while a coordinating handbag hangs from the crook of her elbow. Her hair is no longer wound up on top of her head and is now loose around her shoulders, creating a mane of soft waves. She looks absolutely stunning and I really, *really* need things to go well between her and Milo because there's no way I can compete with her for Scott's affection.

Lifting a hand, I manage to grab her attention and she heads over, kissing me on both cheeks as though we've known each other forever rather than having chatted briefly a couple of times with a shop counter between us.

'I'm so glad you could make it.' I turn to Eloise and make the introductions. 'We'll be sitting over there, with Cliff and Milo, who you met the other day.' I point them out at the table by the fire. 'We're just waiting for Elaine and Shannon and then our team is complete.'

'Scott isn't here?' Kelsey's brow wrinkles as she looks around the pub.

I'm relieved to hear her say that, because it means she doesn't know Scott *too* well right now, because if she did, she'd know that Scott would place pub quizzes on his list of least fun things to do (pubs are for drinking and pool and fruit machines, not taking a general knowledge test) and he isn't a great fan of surprises that don't involve unexpected football victories.

'This isn't really Scott's thing, but we're a friendly bunch. I'll grab us some drinks and I'll introduce you to the others.'

Elaine arrives as I'm making the introductions, and her face lights up when she sees Cliff.

'I know you! You're the Father Christmas from C&L's grotto. I recognise you from when I took my grandson a couple of weeks ago.'

'Ssh.' Cliff places a finger against his lips and winks at her. 'I'm incognito this evening.'

'Oops.' Elaine covers her mouth as she giggles. 'Don't worry, your secret's safe with me.'

'How do you even recognise him without the Santa get-up? Especially the beard?' Milo strokes his chin. 'It covers half his face.'

'It's the eyes.' Elaine sinks into the seat next to Cliff and rests her elbow on the table so she can prop her head on her hand as she gazes at him. 'They're so blue. So . . . expressive.'

I turn to Eloise, whose eyes widen as she mouths 'Oh my *God*' at me. This is an unexpected surprise, but not an unwelcome one. Here I was, hoping to match Milo and Kelsey up tonight and another potential pairing has cropped up. Bonus!

Chapter 28

We were still ridiculously hopeless at the quiz, even with our new members. Elaine excelled at the horticulture round, and Kelsey and Shannon could have aced the reality TV questions in their sleep, but our downfall was pretty much every other category in the quiz. Still, we had fun and I couldn't help feeling smug as Milo and Kelsey chatted all evening, even missing a couple of the questions as they were too busy giggling about something. And then there was the surprise potential pairing of Cliff and Elaine. My watch hasn't pinged for either of them yet, but it's early days and we've arranged to meet up again.

I'm telling Scott about this as we sit down on the bus the following morning (not the Christmas Cupid bits, obviously, because he'd think I was having a funny turn). I'm not expecting him to be actually paying attention – he's staring down at his phone, as per usual – but the excitement bubbling inside causes it to spill out. So imagine my surprise when he responds.

'Kelsey was at the quiz last night? The girl from the bakery? Small world.'

'Not really.' I unzip my bag and grab Milo's Poirot novel, resting it on my lap. The action makes me think of Steffi-Jayne and her copy of *A Christmas Carol*. I take a quick look around but I can't see her. 'I invited Kelsey to join our team. I thought she and Milo might hit it off – and they did!' A wave of self-satisfaction washes over me, and I can't help the corners of my mouth lifting into a smile.

'Milo?' Scott snorts. 'The dorky one you were with the other day? The one with the ears?' He pulls at the tips of his own ears to demonstrate Milo's pointy silicone set.

'Hey, I wear elf ears too.' I pull at his arm so he lets go of his ear. 'And Milo isn't dorky. He's a really nice guy – dead kind and caring – and Kelsey seemed to think so too. In fact, we're all meeting up again tonight for Christmas karaoke.' And hopefully my watch will ping with a new match or two this time.

'Christmas karaoke?' The corners of Scott's lips pull down and he nods his head slowly. 'Sounds fun. Count me in.'

I pull my head back to gape at my boyfriend. 'You want to come to the karaoke session with us? But you hate organised joy.'

Scott shrugs. 'You say we don't do enough stuff together, so let's do this.' I'm still gaping at Scott as he says this, but he's already reaching for his phone, closing the discussion. But he's right: I *do* want us to do more things together, to have fun like we used to, otherwise how are we ever going to save our relationship?

I watch Scott for a few more seconds, making sure a gotcha! grin isn't about to creep onto his face before he tells me he's only kidding and that he wouldn't be caught dead at a karaoke session, especially a festive edition. But he doesn't so much as flinch as he scrolls through his phone and my focus is pulled away from him when the bus stops and Owain steps aboard – with Steffi-Jayne. Interesting development. The wave of smugness returns as I open the Poirot novel.

I find myself humming along to Mariah and Justin Bieber's 'All I Want for Christmas Is You' as I hang around the North Pole, ready to escort the next child and their adult through Santa's workshop and into the grotto so they can tell Cliff what *they* want for Christmas. Seeing the cute bus couple's relationship blossom *and* having Scott volunteer to forego his gaming and spend some quality time with me tonight has filled me to the brim with Christmas spirit. My smiles as I greet the children are even wider than usual, and my mood even remained buoyant when one kid kicked me on the shin as a way of thanking me for his candy cane earlier.

'Season's greetings, and welcome to the North Pole.' My well-practiced reception is already out before I realise who is heading towards me, but my cheerful mood is further bolstered as Elaine takes one hand off the buggy she's pushing so she can give a little wave.

'Hello again! Fridays are nanny's day with the little man, and he's *desperate* for another visit to see Father Christmas.'

We both look down at 'the little man', who's fast asleep in his buggy. Either the excitement has exhausted Elaine's grandson or it isn't *him* who's desperate to visit Father Christmas again.

'Bad night's sleep, I think. Teething, poor thing.' Elaine pulls a sad face. 'But I'm sure he'll wake up once we're in there.'

'I'm sure he will. Or, if not, it'll make a funny photo for when he's older.' I reach into my bucket and pull out a candy cane. 'I'll let you give this to him later. We can go straight through, if you'd like?' The children usually have a wander around the North Pole, gaping at the mechanical animals and staring up at the canopy of stars above us, but there doesn't seem much point in hanging around this time. We head into the workshop, bypassing the mechanical elves as they work on the conveyor belt of toys, and head straight to the grotto.

'Hello, Santa. We have a good boy here to see you.' Sort of. I catch Milo's eye and try to keep the smirk from spreading across my face as he clocks Elaine.

'Ho ho ho, come on in.' Cliff beckons with his white-gloved hand, and this is usually the point where I retreat and return to the North Pole, but I find myself hovering by the door.

'I'm afraid Arthur's having a nap right now.' Elaine pushes the buggy fully into the room. 'He was up all night, apparently. Teething trouble, not naughtiness.'

Cliff winks at her. 'Noted. Why don't *you* sit on Santa's lap instead?'

Milo turns a splutter into a faux coughing fit behind me while I cover a gasp with my hand. I think I need to step in here before this turns into *Carry On Christmas*.

'I don't think that's a good idea. Health and safety and all that.'

'Or *elf* and safety.' Milo grins at his own joke while the rest of us groan. Even little Arthur – had he been awake – would have facepalmed.

'Perhaps Santa could give the lady a present to take with her for when Arthur wakes up?'

'Yes, good idea.' Cliff reaches into the bag by his side (and luckily doesn't make any lewd references to 'Santa's sack') and hands Elaine a package wrapped in nutcracker-printed paper. He doesn't release it straight away, and there's a moment of high tension when they simply stare into each other's eyes. 'I'll see you at the pub tonight, won't I? For the karaoke?'

'I'm in if you are.'

Cliff winks again. 'I'm definitely in. We should do a duet. "Fairytale of New York"? My Kirsty MacColl is legendary.'

Elaine erupts with laughter, startling little Arthur. He jerks upwards, but he doesn't wake and settles back down again.

'I'll see you later then, Father Christmas.' She places the present in the basket under the buggy, wriggling her fingers in farewell at Cliff before she pushes it towards the door Milo is holding open.

Duets aren't a bad idea for tonight. Perhaps I should put Milo and Kelsey down to sing 'Baby, It's Cold Outside' . . .

I nip down to the café for my tea break so I can pass on the goss to Eloise. The café staff have upped their festive game and Eloise joins me at my table wearing a pair of felt antlers attached to a red sparkly headband. She nooooo's and gasps and fake-gags in the right places as I tell her about Elaine's visit.

'So I think we should do duets tonight. Elaine and Cliff have bagged "Fairytale of New York", and I think Milo and Kelsey should do "Baby, It's Cold Outside". What other Christmas duets are there? "Rockin' Around the Christmas Tree"? I could be Kim Wilde and Scott could be Mel Smith.'

'Wait, what?' Eloise pauses, her mug of tea halfway between the table and her mouth. 'Scott's going to the karaoke tonight? How did you manage to convince him to do that?' She wrinkles her nose. 'Although, if it's something really mucky, keep it to yourself. Straight sex makes me want to gag.'

'It wasn't anything really mucky. Or anything at all. I mentioned it and he said he'd like to join us.'

'Wow.' Eloise raises her eyebrows before she takes a sip of her tea. 'That's . . . wow.'

'What do you mean, wow? I know karaoke isn't Scott's thing, but isn't it nice that he's willing to come along anyway?'

'It is nice.' Eloise places her mug carefully on the table. 'And that's why it's so surprising.'

I want to feel outraged, but I sort of get where she's coming from. Still, it stings and I try to numb the bite by going on the defensive.

'Scott does nice things all the time. I may not shout and brag about them, but he does them. He's lovely, actually. Really kind and caring.' I squirm in my seat and drop my gaze to the table so I don't have to meet my friend's eye. 'He may act aloof sometimes, but that isn't what he's like when it's just the two of us.'

'Okay. Sorry.' Eloise holds her hands up. 'I didn't mean anything by it.'

'I know, and I'm sorry.' I decide to move the conversation along, away from Scott. 'What do you think you'll sing tonight? You can duet with Shannon.' I grin across the table at Eloise, but she doesn't respond with humour.

'I can't make it tonight.' She adjusts the antler headband, making it shimmer in the light. 'I'm meeting up with a friend.' She's pretending to look at me as she says this, but her gaze is off by millimetres, so she's looking to my right.

'You mean Annie?'

She shrugs, still pretending to meet my eye. 'Yeah, I mean Annie. We're meeting up later. Keep me updated though. About Cliff and Elaine.'

I nod and smile tightly. I want to be pleased for my friend, but how can I be when I know it's going to end up like it always does, with my best friend getting hurt?

Chapter 29

Part of me is expecting Scott to have changed his mind about the karaoke session by the time I get home from work, but he's true to his word and comes along, even putting on a smart shirt for the occasion. I'm almost giddy with excitement as we catch the bus into town because it's been *so long* since we went out on a Friday night together. Separately, this isn't a strange occurrence, with Scott often meeting Dan in the pub, or me getting together with Eloise, but a night out together as a couple is something we've forgotten to do, and a takeaway pizza in front of the telly is about as exciting as our relationship has been since we moved in together.

'This is nice.' I snuggle up against Scott's shoulder as we trundle past festively lit-up houses. 'We should go out on dates more often.'

'Yeah.' Scott shifts and I think he's about to whip his phone out of his pocket, but I'm pleasantly surprised when he doesn't. 'We should.'

'How about the Carols by Candlelight event at the Christmas market?' I'd suggested it the first time I lived through this December, and Scott had scrunched up his face as though I'd asked him to sniff my armpit. But then he's making the effort tonight, so it's worth a shot.

'Carols by Candlelight? That sounds a bit . . .'

Romantic? Super-festive? Dreamy?

'Crap.'

Luckily, with my head resting on his chest, Scott can't see my face fall at his evaluation. 'You don't think it'll be cosy and romantic?'

'Nah, it'll be freezing and ball-achingly boring. You know how I feel about choirs.' He shudders over-dramatically, jostling my head. I sit up and rub my ear where it bashed against his chest. 'They're so cheesy, especially the ones with kids. They think they're cute and everything, but they sound like a bunch of cats having their nuts twisted off. They make me cringe.'

'So that's a firm no then?'

Scott slides his phone from his pocket. 'The firmest.'

I have Milo's book with me, so I lose myself in the pages of Poirot's Christmas murder mystery until Scott nudges me with his elbow as we approach the bus station.

Shannon's already in the pub, chatting to one of the barmen and doing her flirty, touchy-feely routine, but none of the others are here yet. The table by the fire has been bagged by a group of women who look as though they've already downed a small vineyard's worth of wine. They cackle so loudly, we can hear them from across the room, and when I turn at the sudden sound, they're nearly falling off their stools as they grasp at each other in their mirth. It's the kind of table that's fun at first but soon becomes draining. Scott and I move along, finding a free table sandwiched between a frenziedly flashing fruit machine and an over-tinselled Christmas tree. It's a bit far away from the karaoke area, but that isn't necessarily a bad thing.

'I'll go and get us some drinks. Keep an eye out for the others.' I point towards the door as I turn and head for the bar. Shannon is mid-hair flick when I reach her and I'm kicking myself that I didn't bring my mistletoe with me tonight. I'm no longer sure Shannon is at the stage of her life where she's looking for a true love match, but you never know when one lands at your feet and takes you by surprise. I certainly wasn't expecting to meet the love of my life at the toy shop.

My phone buzzes in my handbag while I'm waiting to be served. It's a message from Cliff, letting me know that he isn't coming to the karaoke session tonight. And neither is Elaine, because they're going out for dinner together.

I clamp a hand over my mouth as an unexpected squeal slips out. Shannon gives me an odd look as she crunches noisily on an ice cube from her glass.

'Sorry about that.' But I'm not sorry at all. I'm *ecstatic*. My watch hasn't pinged – I check as I drop my phone back into my handbag – but this is promising. Not only are they spending the evening together, they've taken on the role of organising the date themselves. I'm no longer the driving force of this potential relationship and that *has* to be a good sign.

I pay for the drinks and crisps and head back to the table and Scott rubs his hands together with glee when he spots the packet of Monster Munch. He dives straight in, nodding along as I tell him about Cliff and Elaine, though he's clearly showing more enthusiasm for the snack than my Cupid skills. Still, Milo soon arrives and is much more receptive to the development.

'I bet that's why he had to dash off for a loo break when she left the grotto. He really ran after her to get her number, the sly old dog. How else could they have arranged to meet for dinner instead?'

'It's quite sweet though, don't you think?'

'Absolutely. But only in a I-never-want-to-imagine-them-snogging kind of way.' Milo pulls a face before he picks up his pint and takes a swig.

'That's a given.' I look up as I hear the door opening, as I have every few minutes since Scott and I arrived, and this time it's Kelsey stepping inside. She's arrived looking photo-shoot ready again, this time in a long, cowl-necked sweater with chunky over-the-knee socks pulled over black leggings, the tops just visible over long boots.

'Kelsey!' I stand up and wave my hand to draw her attention as she glances around the pub in search of a familiar face. Her face lights up with her beatific toothpaste-ad smile and she heads over, her smile somehow growing wider as she reaches our table. She knows Milo and Shannon from the quiz, and Scott from the bakery so there's no need to make any introductions today.

'I'm not late, am I?' She plonks her handbag down on the ground and toes it under the table. 'Dad gave me a lift into town but I had to wait ages for him to finish tinkering with his dolly. Not a euphemism.' She tinkles out a laugh as she shrugs off her leather jacket and drapes it over the back of the chair we've saved for her. 'He's got this really old Citroen from the eighties. Minging thing it is, but he loves it and is restoring it in the garage. Mum says it keeps him happy so . . .' She shrugs and plonks herself down on her chair. 'Have I missed anything?'

'You almost missed my round.' Scott rubs his hands together. 'Shall we get this night started properly with some shots?'

'Some of us have to get up for work in the morning.' I give Scott a pointed look, but he gives a lazy shrug.

'I don't, and it's Friday night. I'm getting some shots in. Milo? Kelsey? I don't think I have to ask you, Shannon.'

Shannon giggles while Milo lifts his pint. 'I'm fine with this, thanks, mate.'

'I'm in.' Kelsey springs out of her seat. 'I'll come and give you a hand.'

I wait until they're out of earshot before I turn to Milo. 'She's lovely, isn't she?'

'Who? Kelsey?' He glances behind us, towards the bar where Kelsey and Scott are trying to edge their way closer to the bar staff. The karaoke is starting in a few minutes so there's been a mass migration for drinks. 'Yeah, she seems nice. Very friendly.

Usually.' Milo's frowning, and I twist in my seat so I can follow his gaze. Kelsey's arms are folded across her chest and her features are scrunched up, causing lines to cross her forehead as she leans towards Scott. Whatever she's saying, it doesn't appear to be a happy conversation.

'What's going on there?' Milo's twisted around fully so he can watch without craning his neck.

'No idea.' We both whip back round as Scott looks in our direction and almost certainly clocks our nosiness. 'Anyway, what do you fancy singing tonight? Still up for a duet with Kelsey?'

Milo shrugs. 'I'm up for that. Or the five of us could do a group number. "2 Become 1" by the Spice Girls?'

'Er, I don't think so.' I pull my chin back and snort with derision. 'That is *not* a Christmas song.'

Milo mimics my snort. 'I think you'll find it is. Christmas number one in . . . '96?'

'Being Christmas number one doesn't make it a Christmas song. There are loads of non-Christmassy Christmas number ones. Bob the Builder. The X-Factor winners' singles. Rage Against the Machine.' I lean forward, presenting my non-Christmassy Christmas number one trump card, but Milo doesn't seem fazed.

'Next you'll be telling me that East 17's "Stay Another Day" isn't a Christmas song.' He shakes his head and lifts his pint, catching my eye and making a pfft noise before he takes a sip.

'Of course it isn't a Christmas song. It doesn't mention Christmas once. It doesn't talk about winter or snow or anything festive.'

'They have big coats on in the video.'

I give Milo my best hard stare. 'And that makes it a Christmas song?'

He shrugs and takes another sip of his pint, this one longer while retaining eye contact. 'To me it does.' He wipes his mouth with his hand, but I see the flash of a smirk before it gets covered up. He's deliberately pushing my buttons.

'Then that's what you should sing. On your own. No need for a duet. In fact.' I stand up, smirking myself now. 'I'm going to put your name down for it right now.'

A guy dressed as Elvis, complete with oily quiff and white jump-suit embellished with gold sequins, gets up first to sing 'Blue Christmas', followed by the group of tinselled, tipsy women from the fireside table who belt out Kelly Clarkson's 'Underneath the Tree'. What they lack in vocal talent is more than compensated for with enthusiasm. There are versions of 'Last Christmas', 'Jingle Bell Rock' and 'Walking in a Winter Wonderland' before Shannon and Kelsey get up to sing Ariana Grande's 'Santa Tell Me' together.

'What were you and Kelsey arguing about earlier?' Milo's gone to the bar and this is the first time Scott and I have been alone since we got here.

Scott tips the last few peanuts from the packet we've been sharing into the palm of his hand. 'We weren't arguing.'

'It looked pretty heated.'

He shrugs and throws the peanuts into his mouth, chewing slowly before washing them down with a swig of his drink. 'We were just debating which is the best Christmas song. I said Wizzard, because it's a classic, while Kels said it was some John Legend crap.'

'Duh.' I elbow him playfully on the arm. 'It's obviously Shakin' Stevens' "Merry Christmas Everyone".' I clap my hands together. 'We should sing that later. And then you can find this girl under the mistletoe and snog her by candlelight.' I lean in for a kiss, but Scott hasn't noticed and has leaned forward to grab his pint at the same time, so my lips land heavily on his ear. Milo has arrived with a tray of drinks anyway, and if there's one thing Scott hates, it's public displays of affection. At least he has since we left the can't-keep-our-hands-off-each-other stage behind.

'No shots?' Empty glasses litter the table, but Scott swipes them to one end to make room for the new set of drinks.

'Afraid not.' Milo transfers the new drinks to the table and fills the tray up with the empties.

'Never mind. Here, I'll take that.' Scott lumbers to his feet and takes the tray from Milo. 'Back in a sec.'

Milo sits in the seat opposite mine. 'He's going to buy more shots, isn't he?'

'Yep.' I groan, imagining the scene later as I have to wedge his drunken form into a taxi. 'But anyway, what do you think about Kelsey's performance?' I nod towards the karaoke area, where Kelsey is performing a slut-drop. Milo's eyebrows jump up his forehead while he nods appreciatively. 'I bet she can do the splits as well.'

'I was only winding you up about that. I'm not that sleazy.'

'I know you're not a sleaze, but you have to admit she has talents.' I turn back to the karaoke area, where Kelsey is grinding against Shannon. 'And I think she likes you.'

'Me?' Milo points to himself and snorts. 'I doubt it.'

'No, she does. And why wouldn't she?'

'Because I look like a twelve-year-old boy with this stupid floppy hair? Because I have the strength of a weary gnat?' He stretches out an arm before flexing it while squeezing his bicep. 'Nope, nothing.'

'Not everybody is into big muscles.'

'You are.' Milo twists round and nods towards Scott, who's making his way back with a tray of shots.

'*I'm* not Kelsey.' I look pointedly at the karaoke area. The song is coming to an end to rapturous applause. The girls milk the attention for as long as they can before making their way back to the table. Shannon grabs a shot and tips it straight down her throat.

'I'm going to be so hungover in the morning.' Kelsey picks a shot up gingerly. 'And I'm supposed to be helping to set up the shop first thing.' She eyes the amber liquid before shrugging and downing it. 'How are you not even slightly pissed yet?' She ruffles

Milo's floppy hair (which is neither stupid nor twelve-year-old-boy-like) and sinks into the seat next to him.

'Because I've got to deal with a load of overexcited kids in the morning, so I'm pacing myself.'

Kelsey sucks in a lungful of air before releasing it in a sigh that sees her physically deflating as she slumps against the tabletop. 'I need a sensible boyfriend like you. Someone responsible and uncomplicated.'

'You make me sound so thrilling.' Milo raises an eyebrow.

'No, no, you're great.' Kelsey straightens so she can place a hand on Milo's chest. 'You're brilliant and funny and . . .' She covers her mouth with her other hand and swallows hard. 'And I think I'm going to be sick.' She dashes off towards the loos, with Shannon tottering after her to offer assistance.

'No more shots for Kelsey.' Milo pushes the tray of shots further along the table.

'On it.' Scott grabs the two tiny glasses that still contain fluid and drops the drinks into his mouth in quick succession. I hope he doesn't throw up too, but I'm more concerned about Kelsey and Milo. There's no way they're going to hook up with Kelsey being this drunk and vomitty, which is a shame because things were going so well. I need to get them together again – preferably in a setting without alcohol to ruin the mood.

'Do you know what we should do?' I look at Scott and Milo, my grin growing wider as the genius idea germinates. 'We should all get together and do one of those escape rooms. There's a Christmas-themed one in Manchester, and I bet Kelsey and Shannon will be up for it.'

'Nah.' Scott shakes his head, burping against the back of his hand. 'It'll be fully booked by now. There's no chance we'll get in.'

'You never know.' Grabbing my phone, I search for the escape room I had in mind and find the booking form. 'See? There's space tomorrow, just after the grotto closes. It'll be tight but we should make it. Shall I book it?' I don't even wait for Scott's reply before I fill in the form and submit, booking tickets for the five of us plus Eloise.

By the time Kelsey emerges from the toilets ('I didn't spew after all') Milo has been called up for his turn at the mic. Grabbing his parka from the back of his chair, he slips his arms through the sleeves and pulls the hood up for his East 17 performance. He puts his all into it, grabbing the air with his fist and pointing out at the audience while his face is set with an earnest expression as he sings the love song.

'Well played.' I hold my hand out as he re-joins us at the table and he shakes it. 'I think I owe you a drink after that performance.'

'I won't say no to that.' Milo shrugs off his coat while I head for the bar. When I turn back to check on my group of friends, Milo and Kelsey are heads-together deep in conversation. I check my watch. Nothing. But I'm not worried. I've got this one in the bag.

Chapter 30

17th December

Operation Naughty or Nice List is housed in an ordinary-looking building just off Deansgate. Milo, Eloise and I head over together as soon as the shop shuts and we meet the others in a bar a few doors down. Isla, a replacement for Shannon who 'had better things to do' (the cheek!), is already at the bar when we get there, while Scott and Kelsey arrive soon after. I've been looking forward to taking part in the festive-themed escape room all day and I can barely conceal my enthusiasm as we huddle in the tiny foyer to wait for our turn. I'm jiggling from side to side so much both Scott and Eloise tell me to stop.

'If there was a zombie apocalypse, which three fictional characters would you want on your team and why?'

I'm pretty sure Milo's only asking the question to keep me occupied during our wait – like a toddler with a colouring sheet and crayons at a restaurant – but it's a fun question so I decide to play along.

'Katniss Everdeen, because she's proper kick-ass, Sabrina the Teenage Witch . . .' I hold a hand up so I can clarify. 'But only the Melissa Joan Hart version, and only if she can bring Salem with her.' I put my hand down and am about to pick my final choice when Milo interrupts.

'So that's three then.'

'No, Salem is a bonus. He comes *with* Sabrina. Like Ant and Dec. You wouldn't class them as *two*, would you?'

'Er, yeah.' Milo looks at me as though I'm mad. 'That's cheating. You've picked your three.'

'All right then. Who would you pick?' I try not to allow any sulkiness to infiltrate my tone. But I fail big time. I really am that toddler, now bored with her colouring sheet and crayons and about to cause a fuss.

'I'd pick Kevin McCallister, because he's ace at booby traps and that would definitely come in handy while trying to escape the zombies.'

'I love *Home Alone!*' My sulkiness vanishes as I bounce up and down. 'It's one of my favourite Christmas films. Who else would you pick? Not Harry and Marv, obviously, because they'd get you killed like that.' I click my fingers and Milo nods.

'No, definitely not those guys. I'd go for Mr Miyagi because he'd whoop some zombie butt, and Johnny 5, just because I've always wanted to meet him. Best. Robot. Ever.'

'Better than the Terminator?' Scott screws up his face and shakes his head. 'Nah, mate. The Terminator is the best robot to have on your side during a zombie apocalypse.'

'Who else would you pick?' I'm so pleased Scott's joining in our little game I do the little bouncy thing again. Eloise and Isla certainly aren't going to chime in with their choices; they're too busy chatting on the edge of our little group to pay any attention to us. It was Eloise's idea to invite my neighbour after Shannon pulled out and I was happy to go along with it. Anything to steer her mind away from Annie for the evening.

'Along with the Terminator, I'd pick . . .' Scott looks up at the ceiling as he considers his options. 'John McClane and Rambo, for obvious reasons.'

'What about you, Kelsey?' Milo asks. 'Who would you want to help you out during a zombie apocalypse?'

Kelsey shrugs. She's a bit pale, her hair still gathered up in the topknot she wears for work, and she's wearing a pair of ripped jeans and Converse instead of one of her photo-shoot ensembles. She's piled the make-up on, but she still looks rough after last night.

'I don't know . . . Can I pick the entire cast of Geordie Shore? Or just the girls? Because they can be pretty feisty.'

That's got to be cheating, surely – it's more than three and not fictional but Milo doesn't tell her so and we're called up to start our escape room mission anyway. We're led through the tiny, dark reception area into what appears to be a rather large office. There's a huge mahogany desk to one side while a treadmill and exercise bike take up a chunk of space opposite. There's a Christmas tree with wrapped gifts underneath in the corner and the back wall is lined with bookshelves. Scott is handed a note and then the door is shut behind us.

'It's Christmas Eve and Santa's naughty or nice list has been stolen.' Scott pauses his reading of the note to glance at us, creating a bit of tension. 'You've tracked it down to a shady toy shop owner . . .'

'Is it Philippa?' Milo jokes, and Eloise and I laugh along before Scott continues.

'. . . who wants parents to buy their kids their presents instead of getting them for *free* from Santa.'

Milo gasps dramatically, his hands covering his cheeks, Kevin McCallister-style. 'That *is* shady.'

'The toy shop owner is hosting a posh party and you've sneaked in posing as waiting staff. You've slipped away upstairs to the toy shop owner's office . . .' Scott indicates the room we're standing in. 'And you have just thirty minutes to solve the clues and find the list before it's time to serve the Christmas pudding.'

There's a timer above the desk, and it's already starting to count down our allotted thirty minutes. We spring into action, running around like idiots until Isla discovers a key. Unfortunately, the key is attached to an iron ring with a series of complicated knots.

'I was in the Cubs when I was a kid.' Milo takes the knotted rope and gets to work while the rest of us search the office for something that needs unlocking. Milo has worked his way through the knots and has released the key by the time Kelsey discovers a safe hidden behind a mirror on the wall, and inside we find a note. But as soon as we pull the note from the safe, the lights go out and we're plunged into darkness. The only thing we can see clearly is a message scrawled in special paint that glows from the wall: the generator is powered by the pedals.

'Pedals?' I can't see Kelsey's face as she says this, but the confusion is clear in her voice. 'What pedals?'

'The exercise bike!' Scott feels his way to the exercise bike and starts to pedal furiously. Within a few seconds, the lights are flickering back on.

'Keep going.' Milo opens the note, but it's only a partial and another key falls out onto the carpet. 'We need to find another safe.'

We do find a safe, secreted in the desk drawer, but it has a keypad rather than a keyhole to gain access, and while the drawer below is locked, the key doesn't fit. We keep looking until Eloise discovers one of the gifts under the tree has a tag saying 'unlock me' on it. She tears into the paper and finds a small metal box with a padlock.

'I'm knackered.' The lights have started to flicker on and off as Scott's pedalling slows down. 'Someone swap with me.'

Milo takes over the pedalling while Eloise unlocks the box. Inside is another key, and this time the key fits the desk drawer. Isla swaps with Milo on the bike ('I'm sorry. I have no stamina. I'm a disgrace') and we find a newspaper tucked in the drawer, along with another piece of the note we found earlier. The date on the front of the newspaper is ringed in thick red pen.

'The 24th December.' Scott spreads the newspaper out on the desk. 'That's Christmas Eve.'

200

My stomach turns at the thought. Christmas Eve. The day I died. The day I *will* die if I don't fulfil my Christmas Cupid mission. And it's approaching fast.

'What does that mean? What does it tell us?' Eloise turns in a circle, her face becoming even more puzzled somewhere during the rotation. 'Are there any more clues in the newspaper?'

Scott flicks through the newspaper while the rest of us stand around feeling useless.

'Nothing.' He chucks the newspaper back down, and that's when I notice it. The little advert for a bookshop in the corner.

'Christmas Eve is *the night before Christmas.*' I jab a finger at the bookcase, and we all rush towards it, eyes scouring the books for the festive tale. But it isn't there. Like Santa with his list, we check the bookcase twice.

'Can somebody take over?' The lights dim for a moment before Isla finds a bit of renewed energy to pedal some more. 'My thighs are killing me.'

'I'll do it.' Eloise hops on the bike while Isla hobbles towards the desk. She taps the advert we've all just looked at.

'You guys. Look.' She points at the little advert, at the copy we didn't bother to read.

Books Make the Perfect Gift!

There's a moment of hesitation before we all dive towards the tree, each grabbing a present and tearing at the paper. It's Milo who's triumphant, holding the copy of the book above his head. Inside the pages is the final piece of the note we need, and once they're put together, we have a puzzle to solve:

Number of reindeer x gold rings x the number of candy canes in the room x geese-a-laying.

We all race around the room in search of candy canes – apart from Eloise, who is still pedalling like a trooper – and, using the calculator on the desk, end up with a four-digit number. Scott inputs the number in the keypad to the safe and there it is – Santa's naughty or nice list! We did it!

'That was so much fun.' Eloise is walking like John Wayne as we leave the escape room, but she's grinning from ear to ear. 'I didn't think we were going to do it when we couldn't find the book on the shelf.'

'I didn't think I was going to get through those knots right at the beginning.'

I nudge Milo playfully. 'Not even with your cub scouts training?' I look down at my watch. It *has* been a fun evening but my watch hasn't pinged for a Milo/Kelsey match. I need to keep trying. Perhaps something more romantic, to really encourage a match. But how can you do romantic as a group?

'Shall we go for a celebratory drink?' Isla indicates the bar we met in earlier.

'Yes please.' Eloise threads her arm through Isla's and leans her head on her shoulder. 'I need to sit down. Badly.'

We head into the bar, where there's a lovely piano version of 'O Come, All Ye Faithful' playing softly over the sound system. It makes me go all warm and fuzzy inside. All feels right when there are Christmas carols playing.

And that's when it hits me. I know how I can get Milo and Kelsey on the perfect romantic date while still being part of a group.

Chapter 31

18th December

'You really don't have to come if you don't want to. I know it's not your thing, and it isn't like I'll be on my own if you stay at home. Eloise and Isla are going to be there, and Milo and Kelsey.'

My whole body buzzes with anticipation of the day ahead. There's a week until Christmas and my Cupid count is still at two. Today *has* to go well if I want to stand a chance of surviving the Santa Express in six days' time.

'I want to come.'

I raise my eyebrows at Scott. 'Really? Because you hate choirs, remember?' It was only a couple of days ago that he'd told me choirs sounded like cats having their nuts ripped off or something, and now he's volunteering to spend the evening at the Christmas market for the Carols by Candlelight event.

'It'll be cosy and romantic and we can snuggle up with mulled wine.'

'I hate mulled wine.' I pull a face. 'It tastes like paint stripper.'

'Hot chocolate then. Whatever. You were right when you said we don't spend enough time doing stuff together.' Scott shrugs. 'So I'm trying to change that.'

My misgivings evaporate and a grin replaces the frown lines as I wrap my arms around my boyfriend. I knew we could save our relationship, and Scott making the effort too fills me up to the brim with hope for Christmas and the future beyond.

'Thank you.' I kiss him long and noisily on the cheek while he rolls his eyes. 'I need to go and say goodbye to Franziska and then we can get ready to go. Won't be long.' Pecking him on the cheek, I head downstairs to Franziska's flat. She welcomes me in with the offer of tea and cake.

'It needs eating. It'll only go stale while I'm away otherwise.'

How could I refuse? Food waste is terrible, especially when it's homemade by my very talented neighbour.

'Are you all ready for your trip?' Franziska is setting off for her memory-lane adventure this afternoon, hence the need to empty her cupboards of baked goods.

'All packed and ready to go.' Franziska carries a tray laden with tea things and sweet treats, with a selection of spiced biscuits, slices of apple cake and raspberry custard tart, and crackers ready to be loaded up with homemade raspberry conserve. 'I'm a bit nervous, to be honest. A lot of years have passed since I saw Klaus, and I'll be spending Christmas with his family. I'm afraid it will feel odd, as though I'm intruding.'

'They wouldn't have invited you if that was the case.' I reach for one of the little china plates on the tray and help myself to a slice of the apple cake.

'Perhaps, but I can't help feeling apprehensive. Still, I shall try to enjoy my time in Germany. It has been so long since I've had a proper Christmas. Speaking of which.' Franziska crosses the room, grabbing the cardboard box on the breakfast bar. 'The decorations for the tree. It is being delivered the day before but you mustn't decorate it until Christmas Eve.'

'I promise.' I pop a forkful of the apple cake in my mouth. It's soft and moist and delicious.

'Be very careful with the decorations. Some of the baubles belonged to my grandmother.'

'I'll be *extremely* careful.'

Franziska pats me on the knee. 'I know you will. You're a good girl.'

We eat the cake and biscuits until we absolutely can't stuff anymore in, and Franziska piles the rest into a plastic tub for me to take up to the flat.

'Let me know when you've landed safely.' I pull her into a tight hug as we say goodbye at her front door. 'And have a lovely time.'

I head upstairs with my box of goodies and Eloise rings while I'm making sure I've got everything ready for our evening at the market: purse, hat, scarf and gloves, Milo's Agatha Christie book for the bus ride . . .

'I don't think I'm going to make it to the carol service.'

I stop rifling through my handbag in search of my tube of lip balm. 'Why? Are you ill? Because my throat's been a bit scratchy today. I thought it might have been a delayed after-effect of the karaoke the other night, but if you're not well . . .'

'I'm fine. Really good, actually.' Eloise giggles before lowering her voice. 'I haven't even got out of bed yet, other than to make tea and toast.'

'So you *are* ill?' I place my fingers against my throat and swallow to test the scratchiness.

'Nope.' Eloise giggles again, and dread washes over me as it dawns on me why she hasn't bothered to drag herself out of bed. Annie. Of course. They 'hung out' on Friday night and now they're 'hanging out' a bit more.

'You're at Annie's, aren't you?' I continue the search of my bag and find two tubes of lip balm. Bonus.

'Nope. I'm at home.' Eloise lowers her voice again. 'With Isla.'

'What?' Wedging my phone between my ear and shoulder, I check my watch. It hasn't pinged, and when I tap it to bring up the Christmas Cupid count, it still says two: the cute bus couple and the wallet guy and barman Xavier. I'm definitely responsible for bringing Eloise and Isla together, so what the hell? I've been cheated out of a match!

'I told you she was gay.' There's an air of smugness to Eloise's tone, and I wonder if that's why my watch hasn't pinged. This isn't a true love match but rather a bit of fun with a bit of point-proving thrown in the mix. But at least she isn't with Annie and she sounds genuinely happy.

'Well, have fun. I'll see you tomorrow.'

'Bye. Love you.' And then she's gone. I check my watch again, just to make sure, but the counter is still stubbornly stuck at two.

There's a sharpness in the air as the sun starts to dip, making my nose tingle as we head towards the nativity scene where we've arranged to meet up with Milo and Kelsey. A snow machine has been set up to create a flurry of flakes around the Christmas tree area, and fake snowdrifts have been placed between the market stalls to give an extra wintery feel to the space. The carol service isn't due to begin for half an hour or so, but a brass band is adding to the festive atmosphere as people gather around the Christmas tree in readiness for the event. The Christmas market isn't just a place to buy gifts, it's a place to meet up with friends and family, to create memories and that warm, fuzzy feeling you get while watching Hallmark movies.

I give Scott's hand a squeeze as we make our way through the sea of bulky winter coats towards the nativity scene. Even Scott is taken in by the festive atmosphere and he wriggles his hand free so he can take a couple of photos of the manger. Kelsey's already there, wrapped up in a burnt-red-and-black shawl and a glittery black bobble hat. She looks much better than she did yesterday without the cloud of a raging hangover hovering over her, and her cheeks and the tip of her nose are adorably pink.

'Milo's already here too.' She aims a glittery black mitten across the market. 'He's gone to get me a hot chocolate because I was cold. He's *so* sweet, isn't he?'

'The sweetest.' I'm desperate to check my watch, because *surely* this is a match. Steffi-Jayne and Owain didn't even kiss on the bus and my watch pinged, so what's taking Milo and Kelsey so long to register? They're a good match. Kelsey seems like a nice girl and she seems to like Milo, who *is* sweet. What more do I have to do? Smoosh their faces together myself, like a Barbie and Ken doll?

'Here he is now.' Kelsey waves as Milo approaches with a mug of cream and marshmallow-topped hot chocolate in each hand. 'Thank you so much. You're the best!' Kelsey kisses his cheek as she reaches for one of the mugs, and I peel back the cuff of my coat to check my watch. Nada.

'I didn't know when you'd get here, so I only got two.' Milo thrusts his thumb behind him. 'But I can go and grab a couple more now you're here.'

'No, it's fine. We'll go.' Grabbing Scott's hand, I start to tow him away from Kelsey and Milo. 'You guys stay here. We won't be long.' Chat, kiss, whatever it takes to make my watch ping. We head for the gourmet hot chocolate stand where I give the crème brûlée a go while Scott opts for a Turkish delight flavoured drink. Milo and Kelsey are giggling about something as we return, though there's not a peep from my watch.

'Shall we go and stand by the tree?' The corners of Milo's lips are still twitching over whatever it was they'd found so amusing. 'Before we end up right at the back?'

The sun has well and truly disappeared by now, and the multicoloured fairy lights threaded through the trees and their warm golden counterparts twinkling from the market stalls ups the festive, fuzzy feels as we collect our battery-powered lanterns and song sheets before joining the crowd gathered in front of the giant, lit-up Christmas tree. The carol service begins with the cutest little choir of small children from one of the local primary schools, who are dressed in long white dresses with silver tinsel halos. They begin with 'Away in a Manger' and it's such a sweet, endearing sound that I find I've got a lump in my throat, and I'm reaching for a tissue by the time they get to 'Silent Night'. Returning the pack of tissues to my bag, I reach for my phone so I can take a photo of the little ones in front of the tree, but my phone isn't in my bag. I check my coat pockets, but it isn't in there either. I had my phone earlier, while I was speaking to Eloise and then . . . I put it down on the breakfast bar, meaning to charge it for a few minutes before we left because I noticed it was running low. It's annoying not having my phone with me, but I borrow Scott's to take the photos, which I'll send to myself later.

'What did you think?'

The carol service was beautiful, with numerous choirs taking centre stage, from the primary school kids, to a breast cancer survivor group, various church contributions and a consort of care home residents whose voices rang out with joy. The song sheets and lanterns have been returned and the crowds have dispersed but we've hung around the market for another hot chocolate and a browse.

'It was okay.' Scott shrugs and takes a sip of his hot chocolate, but I take his words as high praise. He didn't complain once, or fidget, and his phone only came out of his pocket to take photos.

'Thank you for coming.' I reach up on tiptoe to give him a marshmallow-scented kiss. 'It means a lot.' Milo and Kelsey are a couple of stalls ahead looking at wooden Christmas tree decorations. Milo's holding up a star by its string and Kelsey's face lights up as it spins in front of her nose. 'Do you think we should creep away home and leave them to it?'

'Not yet.' Scott lifts his mug. 'I haven't finished my drink.'

I haven't either, but I'm willing to sacrifice my sticky toffee pudding hot chocolate if it means love will start to blossom between the pair. But I'm not going to turn down spending time with Scott either, so if he wants to stay a bit longer, we'll hang around until he's ready to leave.

'Oh, look. Mistletoe.' I stop by the stall displaying natural festive trimmings. I didn't think to bring my sprig with me to give Milo and Kelsey a nudge, so I buy another, heading straight for the pair who are now poring over wooden toys. 'Merry Christmas!' I hold the mistletoe above them, and Milo rolls his eyes good naturedly before leaning in to kiss Kelsey on the cheek, who pretends to swoon.

I check my watch.

Nothing.

Damn it!

Kelsey sees me looking down at my watch and checks the time on her phone. 'This has been really lovely, but I should get going.'

'Me too.' Milo places the ladybird-shaped xylophone back on the stall. 'Do you want a lift?'

'You wouldn't mind?' Kelsey beams at him. 'That'd be great.'

'Do you guys need a lift?'

Scott opens his mouth to respond to Milo's offer, but I get in there first. 'We're going to stay for a bit longer.' I lift my mug. 'Haven't finished my drink and I want to have a little wander around. Soak up the atmosphere a bit more. Take this with you though.' I hand him the sprig of mistletoe and lean my head against Scott's arm. 'We don't need it.'

We wave them off, waiting until they've disappeared around the corner before we head for the bus station. Scott complains about waiting around in the cold when Milo could have dropped us off, but he doesn't understand what's at stake.

We're trundling our way home on the bus, me with my nose in Milo's Agatha Christie book and Scott scouring his phone screen, when my watch pings. Match number three! My plan to bring Milo and Kelsey together must have worked and I'm now halfway through my mission.

For some reason, however, the jolt of joy I experience when I see the tally is short-lived, and I find my mood quickly plummets and I can no longer concentrate on Poirot's investigation. Maybe I'm feeling off kilter because there's less than a week to go and I'm still only halfway to reaching the goal that's going to keep me alive.

Yes. That's it. I'm sure of it.

Chapter 32

19th December

It's my last day off before Christmas (and even then, I'll only have Christmas Day off before I'm back in for the Boxing Day sale) and I was hoping for a leisurely lie-in to recharge my batteries before the real onslaught of Christmas begins. Because the next few days are going to be hectic with panic buying, last-minute shoppers and grotto visits, plus the parade, which I'm trying very hard not to think about for obvious reasons.

But the lie-in doesn't happen. Scott snoozes his alarm too many times, meaning he's in a fluster when he eventually drags himself out of bed, knocking everything over in his rush to get ready for work and slamming the drawers shut as he's in too much of a hurry to close them gently. I'm wide awake by the time he's giving a running commentary on the process of dressing himself ('Where have my socks gone? What're they doing under the bleeding bed? How did they get under there?') and I'm buttering him a piece of toast by the time he emerges from the bedroom.

'Thanks, babe.' He bites the corner off the toast, continuing to speak even as he chews. 'Have you seen my keys?'

I look away so I don't have to be subjected to the mushed-up toast in his mouth, eyeing his coat on the back of the sofa. My shoulders feel bunched up with tension when I turn back to Scott but I don't say anything about the coat. Or the perfectly functioning coat hooks out in the hallway. It's a tiny thing, and what actual harm is his coat doing, in the grand scheme of things?

I take a deep, calming breath. 'Have you checked your coat pocket?'

'No, not yet.'

Seriously, when did he start displaying the chewing process for all to see? Has he always chewed with his mouth open, or is this a new habit he's formed overnight?

'Found them.' Scott brandishes his set of keys with a look of triumph on his face. It's as though he's uncovered some long-lost treasure rather than his bunch of keys from the most obvious place they would be. I really did need that bit of extra sleep this morning because I'm feeling extremely prickly, as though anything Scott does right now will make my jaw tighten with annoyance. I can't wait for him to head out to work but he seems to be hanging around the flat even though he's running late.

'Shouldn't you be going?' I tap my watch, looking pointedly away when the action causes a heart to appear on the little screen with a number three in the middle. That would explain why I'm feeling so grouchy; I have three more couples to match and only five days before the Santa Express is due to catapult me across the tarmac.

'Just need my wallet.' Scott turns slowly in a circle, as though the wallet will magically leap up from its hiding spot and fly across the room into his hands.

'Jeans pocket?'

Scott clicks his fingers before striding off to the bedroom, where the jeans he was wearing yesterday are sprawled on the floor instead of in the laundry basket.

'Found it! See you later!' The words are yelled from the hallway, and I let out a massive sigh and sink onto the sofa as the front door slams shut a moment later. I need to get a grip, because it's only a couple of days until we had the Terrible Row during the original run of this December, and if I air my grievances now, I may set the ball rolling for a repeat performance.

Relieving the tension with a few more deep breaths, I take stock of the situation. It's five days until Christmas Eve and the deadline for my Christmas Cupid mission. I've matched three couples so far (the cute bus couple, the wallet guy and the barman in the pub, and Milo and Kelsey) and I still have the possibility of a Franziska/ Klaus match. They're in Germany, where it's much harder for me to intervene and I haven't even heard from Franziska yet to see how it's all going, but I'm still optimistic. Then there's the Cliff and Elaine pairing that still has potential after their dinner date, so that leaves one more couple. Who do I know who's single?

Shannon isn't in a relationship with anything other than her own reflection, but she seems to be enjoying the single life. Which is fair enough, but incredibly inconvenient for me and my matchmaking mission. There's Maureen, who will need to be matched with a non-smoker (is Juggler Jez single? And does he smoke? And is he into women old enough to be his mum?) and I'm not entirely sure where Eloise stands relationship-wise. Is she still seeing Annie even though she's started something with Isla? Whatever the answer is, it isn't a match otherwise my watch would have pinged to let me know by now.

My social circle, I'm beginning to realise, is quite small. But then we usually hang out with Scott's friends, and there's no point in trying to match them. They're all more committed to their games consoles than they are women, and they seem to purchase new models every five minutes. Scott himself only bought a new console back in September (the month is etched in my mind because he used the money that was supposed to pay his half of our first set of bills and I had to dip into my savings to cover it) and yet there's already an even newer model that I've hidden under a pile of blankets at the bottom of the wardrobe that I'm going to give him for Christmas.

I put on one of the festive movies I recorded over the weekend while I wrap some presents. I'm pretty much sorted now on the Christmas gift front, apart from Scott's nieces because he still hasn't told me what they'd like. Pushing aside the rolls of gift wrap and Sellotape, I hunt down my phone so I can send him a reminder to ask Kristen what they're into. The phone's on the breakfast bar, still plugged into the charger. There's a couple of missed text messages from yesterday on there:

Eloise
18 Nov, 17:52

Sorry (not sorry) about missing the carols. Have fun! I know I will ;) xx

Franziska
18 Nov, 21:07

Landed safely. Waiting for my luggage. Why does it always take forever? Speak soon!

I reply to both messages, apologising to Franziska for the late reply and asking how things are going, before sending the text to Scott. Franziska phones as I'm packing away the Christmas wrapping paraphernalia, and it's so lovely to hear her voice, especially as she sounds so happy.

'It's wonderful seeing Klaus again. If it wasn't for the wrinkles and grey hair, it'd be like fifty years hadn't passed. And I didn't need to worry about his children – I've already met his sons and they're lovely, and Beatrice says she can't wait to meet me in a couple of days.'

It sounds promising, so I'm feeling a bit lighter and less prickly when I hang up, but all that evaporates when Scott arrives home in the evening. Not only has he failed to answer my question about his nieces' Christmas presents, he's brandishing a Bake House paper bag. All the fear and panic I've been feeling about the Christmas Cupid mission manifests as rage when I spot that white bag with the black-and-grey lines, and a strange trembling sensation starts in the pit of my stomach.

'It isn't even Friday, and I thought we talked about not eating from The Bake House anymore.' The trembling has travelled up through my body and along my limbs and digits, so my finger is shaking as I point it towards the bag. 'Because of the rats.' Milo and Kelsey may have triggered my watch last night, but I can't take any chances. The glow from Kelsey's face as she looked at my boyfriend on Christmas Eve (or rather, *her* boyfriend, because we'd split up and she'd taken my place) is still imprinted on my brain.

'And I thought we'd agreed there weren't any rats.' Scott tosses the bag on the breakfast bar and shrugs off his coat. 'But you're welcome.' He dumps his coat on the back of the sofa and stalks off into the hall, with the bedroom door slamming a few seconds later. I want to stomp after him and vent until the trembling stops, but I force myself to stay put. To take deep, calming breaths. Because I need to prevent this little spat from escalating. The Terrible Row happened in a couple of days during my original timeline so I need to be really careful not to let history repeat itself. I've been given this second chance with Scott and I can't mess it up now.

With the paper bag – cupcake and all – stuffed into the kitchen bin and the trembling at a minimum, I creep towards the bedroom, pushing gently on the door as though any sudden movement could cause my whole world to crumble in front of my eyes.

'I was trying to do a nice thing.' Scott's lying on the bed with his back to me, scrolling through his phone.

'I know you were, and I'm sorry.' I push the door fully open and step inside. 'I didn't mean to sound ungrateful or snippy. I think I just had a bad night's sleep or something.'

Scott continues to scroll through his phone, making no attempt to look at me or speak. So I head for the wardrobe and take out the wrapped box from underneath the pile of blankets.

'I know it isn't Christmas yet.' I place the box on the bed and perch next to it. 'But a few days won't make much difference.'

Scott glances over his shoulder, scrambling into a sitting position when he spots the sizable gift.

'I can open it now?'

I nod and push the box closer. Scott tears at the paper, whooping with child-like joy when he spots the logo.

'I can't believe you got me this!' Leaning across the bed, he wraps an arm around me and pulls me in for a kiss. 'You're the best! I'm going to set it up now.' Bounding off the bed, he scoops up the games console and scurries off to the living room. Gathering up the torn wrapping paper, I give a huge sigh of relief, thankful I've been able to smooth things over again.

Chapter 33

20th December

Despite managing to sidestep a full-on row last night, I wake up with a weighty dread pinning me to the bed. We're just one day away from when the Terrible Row occurred the first time round and I have a sense of foreboding of what is to come. And the ominous feeling only intensifies when I get to work and see Milo in the North Pole. He's sweeping up bits of stray fake snow and glittery strands in preparation for the grotto's opening, and I stand and watch him for a moment. An image of Kelsey's face alight with joy as the wooden decoration twirled in front of her nose at the Christmas market on Sunday fills my head and my stomach churns. It's the way she looked when she was with Scott on that alternate Christmas Eve, and the fear that events will repeat themselves squeezes at my chest until I feel breathless. I can't let it happen again.

'Are you going to stand there and watch all morning?' I hadn't realised Milo had stopped sweeping, but he's looking across the North Pole as I hover on the edge of the gingerbread forest, half-hidden by the fake foliage. 'Or are you going to help set up?'

There's a teasing note to Milo's questioning, but I feel a jolt of guilt. 'Sorry. I was miles away. How are we for candy canes?'

'The bucket's full and there are five boxes in the gift shop.' With only a matter of days until the big day, we're expecting chaos in the grotto, especially as the local schools have now broken up for the festive break. 'But we could do with some gingerbread men for the cottage. I sent Shannon to get some, but that was twenty minutes ago. I think she's wandered over to soft toys again. Dominic's been moved over from arts and crafts and you know how flirty they are.'

My spirits rise as I think about how I could encourage the flirtation into something more, until I remember Dominic is dating the girl from Boots.

'Speaking of flirty . . .' Stepping out of the foliage, I adopt a coy tone as I make my way closer to Milo. 'How are things going with you and Kelsey?'

I already know the answer, thanks to my watch, but I want to hear it from Milo. I haven't seen him since he left the market on Sunday so I want all the goss. Well, the family-friendly version anyway.

'How do you mean?' If Milo is playing dumb, he's very good at it as he aims a bemused look my way.

'You and Kelsey. You were looking very cosy at the Carols by Candlelight, and I thought that maybe . . .' I make a heart shape with my hands. 'You know?' From the look on Milo's face, he doesn't know. 'You kissed?'

'We didn't kiss.' Milo resumes his sweeping. 'I dropped her off at home and that's it.'

'That's it?' I look down at my watch, which claims otherwise. But then the couple on the bus didn't even need to kiss to activate the match. Sitting next to each other and striking up a conversation was enough, so maybe it's the same with Milo and Kelsey. Still, I need to be sure the match is secure, because without it, I'm getting Santa Expressed in a few days' time and Kelsey will be free to swoop in on Scott.

'Have you seen her since?'

Milo wedges the brush into an awkward corner. 'Why would I?'

'Spoken to her then?'

'Without seeing her? What, like this?' Milo props the brush against the candy cane fence so he can cover his eyes with his hands. 'Hi, Kelsey. How are you?'

'There's this new invention called *the telephone*.'

'But they involve these new-fangled things called *telephone numbers*.' Milo uncovers his eyes and picks up the brush again, but he clocks my drop-jawed expression before he starts sweeping again. 'What? Why are you gawping at me like that?'

'You. Don't. Have. Her. *Number*?'

I don't believe this! How on earth can they have made a true love match if he doesn't even have her phone number? That's the very basics when it comes to a relationship, surely? Even people who hook up in clubs swap numbers, even if neither party has any intention of ever using it.

'I don't have your number either.' Milo shrugs before he stoops over the brush and continues his sweeping.

'But that's different. We're just friends.'

'So are Kelsey and I.' Milo doesn't break his sweeping stride, and he doesn't look over to see the anguish his words have caused. They didn't kiss. They haven't exchanged numbers. He sees her as just a friend. How can any of that add up to a match? It doesn't make any kind of sense.

'Grab two boxes,' Milo calls after me as I make a dash back through the gingerbread forest, but I'm not heading for the café. I'm heading for my locker, where I switch my phone on so I can check my messages. Franziska sent her message letting me know she'd landed safely and was waiting for her luggage at 21:07. It wasn't much longer until my watch pinged with what I assumed was a Milo/Kelsey match, but what if the notification was nothing to do with them at all? What if the moment Franziska and Klaus reconnected at arrivals was enough to trigger a match? That would mean match number three has nothing at all to do with Milo and Kelsey. And that means

Franziska and Klaus are no longer potential match number four, and that even if Cliff and Elaine *do* match, I'll still need *two more* couples before the parade. But, worse than all of that, it also means Kelsey's still very much free and single – and Scott's still making his daily visits to the shop.

Eloise pounces on me as soon as I step foot in the café. It's less than a minute until opening and Milo almost flipped out in a panic when both Shannon and I returned to the grotto empty-handed, so I've made a dash down to the lower ground floor to grab the gingerbread people.

'You're here.' The little bells on Eloise's antler headband jangle as she throws her arms around me. 'I need your advice.' I open my mouth to protest – Milo's going to lose his shit if I don't make it back up to the gingerbread cottage with a supply of spiced people-shaped biscuits in approximately thirty-nine seconds – but Eloise is already towing me towards the nearest table. 'It's Annie.' She plonks herself down on one of the yellow chairs and indicates I should do the same. I do, hesitantly because of both my time constraints and the subject matter. 'She's asked me to meet her after work.' She flicks her eyes left and right before reaching into her apron pocket and pulling out her phone. She shows me the message. It's concise and to the point, with the request, time and place in less than fifty characters – exactly Annie's style. 'Her colleagues are going to be there. She's *never* asked me to meet her workmates. Ever. Not even when we were in a proper relationship and she'd met Dad and Rosemary a bunch of times.' She shoves her phone back into her apron pocket. 'What does this mean? Does she want to make a proper go of it again?'

My stomach was already in knots over the Christmas Cupid thing, but it tightens now as Eloise looks across the table at me, her eyes wide and child-like as she awaits my analysis. It'll make her so happy if I say that yes, I think Annie probably wants to try at their relationship again, but that would be lying and setting her up for a fall. But I also don't want to dash her spirits.

'I'm not sure. This is Annie we're talking about. She plays her cards very close to her chest.'

Eloise nods. 'That's true. But do you think I should meet up with her?'

'What about Isla? It sounds like you had a brilliant time with her the other night.'

Eloise pulls the sleeves of her cardigan over her hands. 'I did, and I think she's great. It's just Annie and I have all this history.'

I glance up at the clock above the till. The shop will definitely be open by now, and I can only imagine the state Milo has got himself into. This is his first taste of Christmas in retail, so he isn't used to the chaotic nature of the job at this time of year.

'Can I have a think about it and talk to you in a bit?' I stand up, already heading for the counter. 'I'll come down for my tea break and we'll have a proper chat. It's just the shop is opening and we don't have any gingerbread people for the cottage.'

'Oh! Of course.' Eloise scurries in front of me, grabbing a box that's waiting behind the counter. 'I'll see you in a bit.'

'See you in a bit.' I'm already legging it across the café with the box of biscuits tucked under my arm as I call out to Eloise. The shop has only just opened, but there's already a queue up on the second floor as kids wait for the grotto to open, their grown-ups tutting and rolling their eyes at the tiny delay. Squeezing past them, I leg it through the maze of Christmas trees, stopping off at the cottage to drop off the gingerbread people before dashing through to the North Pole. The sounds of surprise and giggles travel through from the Christmas tree maze, and there's a few minutes of peace before the first lot of kids barrel their way into our little snowy paradise. The most eager head straight for Santa's workshop, lining up for their turn to see the Big Man, while others mill around to take in their surroundings. There are far more children during the days leading up to Christmas so the North Pole is crammed, with extra

221

elf helpers plus the circus entertainment crew, from the moment it opens until it closes for a brief break mid-morning.

'I need you to come with me.' Milo has barely had the chance to put his camera down at the start of our break before I'm dragging him out of the grotto by the arm.

'Okay, but where are we going?'

Instead of going back through the grotto and passing the queue by the ticket booth, we nip out past the photo gift shop.

'We're going to the bakery. I need cake after that morning, don't you? And we're only halfway through the morning! Afternoons are always worse, especially if the little ones have missed a nap.'

'Can't we go down to the café?' We step onto the escalator that takes us down to the first floor. 'We only have fifteen minutes and it'll take us nearly that long to get there and back.'

'It won't.' If we walk really, really fast. 'And Maureen bakes some really nice stuff, don't get me wrong, but it isn't at the same level as The Bake House.'

The panic inside me has been building up all morning and it's starting to boil over. Milo and Kelsey haven't even exchanged numbers yet, so I'm going to have to give them another shove. And other than forcing them to snog at gunpoint, dragging Milo to the bakery is my only option right now.

We power walk through the heaving town centre. Milo pauses to let an old couple pass so I have to grab his hand to tug him around them and we make it to the bakery four minutes into our allotted fifteen-minute break. That means we have eleven minutes to chat, rush back, and be ready with smiles in place at the North Pole. Luckily, there's only one customer in the shop when we step inside. But, unfortunately, that customer is Scott.

'Hey, you. What a surprise to see you here.' I didn't think I could talk and grit my teeth at the same time, but it turns out I totally can. My voice comes out all growly though, which takes Scott aback a bit.

'Coffee.' Scott grabs the takeaway mug from the counter and holds it up. 'Kettle's still broken. What are you doing here?'

'Duh. Cake.' I roll my eyes before turning to Kelsey. 'Can we get two snowman doughnuts, please?' We probably won't have time to eat them as we make a mad dash back to the toy shop but we can't leave empty-handed. 'Are you still coming to the quiz on Thursday?'

Kelsey beams at me as she shakes open a paper bag. 'Absolutely. Wouldn't miss it. It was a brilliant night last time, even if we didn't win.'

'Great.' I beam right back, because this is exactly what I wanted to hear. It hasn't made my watch ping, but it *has* reassured me that there'll be another opportunity for the pair to be in the same room without having a ridiculously short time limit.

'Elaine's still coming, isn't she?' Because that's another couple I need to focus on. I haven't managed to exchange more than a few sentences with Cliff during the frenzied morning at the grotto, but from what I can gather, the dinner date went well but they haven't arranged another meet-up yet.

'Dunno.' Scott lifts a shoulder and lets it drop back down. 'She hasn't said anything to me about it.'

'Can you . . .' I'm about to ask him if he'll remind her, but I know that it will never happen in a million years. He still hasn't asked his sister what her girls would like for Christmas so I sent her a text myself this morning. 'Never mind. I'll be back in thirty seconds.' I aim this vow at Milo, who I'm sure gives me a skeptical look, but he's nothing more than a blur as I leg it from the shop and across the road to the estate agents. Elaine is delighted I've made the trip over just to make sure she'll be coming ('I wasn't sure, and I didn't want to intrude . . .') so we're both happy as I leg it back out again.

'Sorry about that.' Milo's waiting outside the bakery with the bag of doughnuts. 'How much do I owe you?'

Milo shakes his head as he hands the bag over. 'It's on me. An early Christmas present. But you'll have to save it for later because we have to be back in the grotto in . . .' He checks the time on his phone. 'Six-and-a-half minutes.'

We meet each other's eye for a nanosecond before we pelt it back to the toy shop.

Chapter 34

21st December

I wake up with that icky, uncomfortable sense of foreboding again. Today was the day of the Terrible Row and I'm still terrified that it's going to happen all over again, as though it's out of my control and no matter what I do, however much I appease Scott or throw games consoles at him, he's going to end up leaving me anyway. A memory of this day pops into my head: I'm crouching in the bath, water from a too-hot shower raining down on me as I cry gut-wrenching tears. I can't be that girl again. I simply can't.

It's early when I wake, still dark outside without a hint of morning poking through the too-thin curtains, and my alarm isn't due to go off for another hour. Scott's snoring beside me, the bed almost vibrating with the noise of it, but I'm relieved that he's here. It was after midnight when he got home from work and although I was still awake, waiting for him to walk through the door, I pretended to be asleep so I wouldn't have to ask him where he'd been or why he hadn't let me know he'd be so late. He could have been hit by a double decker bus for all I knew. But I hadn't wanted to rock the boat this close to the day of the Terrible Row, so I'd let him slip into bed beside me, my eyes squeezed shut, and eventually I'd dropped off to sleep for a few hours.

I'm wide awake now though, and I ease the covers off gently, inching my body slowly off the bed and creeping across the room. I can still hear the snuffles of sleep from Scott as I tiptoe out of the room and close the door softly behind me. I don't bother to switch the TV or radio on in case it wakes Scott even at its lowest level and instead sit with the Agatha Christie book and a cup of coffee. I'm a good chunk into the book now and I know Milo is dying for me to finish it so we can discuss it.

Light is starting to creep into the darkness by the time I've finished my coffee, so I make myself another cup and some toast, daring to turn breakfast TV on but keeping the volume so low I have to strain to hear it. There's a feel-good story of a man who rescued a dog from the canal and, when its owner couldn't be traced, he adopted him. The camera lingers on the dog – now named Swampy because of the way he smelled after he was dragged from the murky water – snuggled up in a basket by the fire with his new favourite elephant toy. I missed this story the first-time round, and it makes me smile as I carry my empty plate and mug into the kitchen and load them into the dishwasher. There's a plate with toast crumbs left out beside Scott's Man U mug, which he must have used when he got home last night. I load them into the dishwasher and pluck the used teabag from the worktop, wiping down the pool of cold brown liquid it's left behind once I've chucked it in the bin. My advent calendar is propped up on the breakfast bar and I locate today's window and pop it open, pushing the chocolate into the palm of my hand. But I don't shove it in my mouth like I normally would. It's a little chocolate robin, which makes me think of Milo, and then my gran, which in turn makes me think of the mammoth task still ahead of me. If I can't match Milo with Kelsey, plus Cliff with Elaine, *plus* a whole new couple in the next three days, I'm toast.

Scott gets up and I make him toast and coffee while he's in the shower. He thanks me politely before sitting at the breakfast bar, eating his toast with slow, careful bites and catching the crumbs with the plate instead of making a mess on the sofa. We head for the bus together and sit side by side in silence. Scott doesn't take his phone out of his pocket and my Poirot book remains in my bag. There's a weird atmosphere between us, as though the slightest sound or sudden movement could shatter us into a million pieces. I know why I'm treading on eggshells, but what has spooked Scott into this strange behaviour?

Steffi-Jayne and Owain get on at the same stop, their heads close together as they giggle and chat and kiss. Their relationship seems so *easy*. There's no tiptoeing around to avoid rows, no papering over the cracks in an attempt to hide problems from themselves and the outside world. I know their relationship is new and shiny, but should a relationship really be this *hard*? Scott and I only moved in together a few months ago, and it was supposed to be exciting and romantic but, if I'm completely honest with myself, it feels frustrating, with all the responsibilities of paying the bills and keeping the place clean and tidy heaped on my shoulders. Scott grew up in a female-dominated household, with his mum and grandmother and his older sister all spoiling him rotten and it feels like I've picked up where they left off, picking up after him, nagging him to put his dirty clothes in the laundry basket instead of letting them languish on the bedroom floor until I eventually give in and scoop them up myself. I've tried so hard to ignore it, but sometimes it feels as though I lost a boyfriend and gained an overgrown child the day we moved into the flat. On paper, Scott is my perfect match – he's handsome and charming and we had such good times in the past, with holidays and day trips, and we enjoyed each other's company – but lately I can't help wishing he'd be a bit more thoughtful. Take a bit more responsibility for himself instead of leaving everything to me. I wish he would notice me more. See that I'm taking on the lion's share of the cooking and the cleaning and that even when he does do these things, it's after I've asked him to do it, so the job of getting things done still lies with me. And it may seem silly, but I wish it had been him choosing those Friday cupcakes for me. Him thinking about me and what I'd enjoy instead of simply handing over a bag on autopilot.

We say a courteous goodbye followed by an awkward peck on the cheek from Scott before we part ways at the bus station. I watch him stride towards the estate agents and feel a strange ache in my chest. Is it longing, or grief over what has become of us? Fear of what may yet come? Because we *were* happy once. Stupidly so. We laughed until our stomachs ached. We kissed until we were breathless. We couldn't bear to be apart, but I honestly think Scott wouldn't notice if I didn't come home again until he ran out of clean underwear.

With my head down, I make my way through the shuttered town centre. The Christmas market is being set up for the day but I refuse to look across because it'll only remind me of the Carols by Candlelight evening. Scott volunteered to come with me, even though he hates that sort of thing, and he made an effort with the karaoke and the escape room, so he must still care, deep down, which only adds to the confusion of the situation.

I try to muster a bit of cheer as I change into my elf ensemble, because no child wants to be greeted by a grouchy North Pole helper. The circus acts have been drafted in to keep the kids entertained again while they wait for their turn to see Santa and I vow to chat to Jez and the others to find out their relationship status whenever the opportunity arises. There are four acts – juggling Jez, plate-spinner Annette, acrobatic Eva and balloon-modelling clown Binky Boo – so surely at least one of them is single and desperate to mingle?

The first part of the morning passes in a blur of spinning plates, tantrums from restless toddlers, and the same handful of child-friendly festive songs on a loop. My morning tea break is more than welcome and my aching feet are overjoyed when I sink into one of the yellow chairs in the café. My eyes search the room as I sink my teeth into my mince pie. Eloise wasn't at the counter when I ordered my festive snack and the girl on the till said she wasn't in the kitchen either. The café is buzzing with hyped-up kids and frazzled parents but I eventually manage to spot my best friend across the room, carrying a tray piled up with dirty dishes towards the kitchen.

'Eloise!' I wince as I stand up on tender feet to try to catch her attention with a frantically waving hand, but Eloise doesn't see or hear me in the din and bustle of the place. My eyes follow her to the kitchen, flicking up at the clock above the till as she disappears through the swinging doors. Damn it! I spent so long in the queue, I don't have time to sit and enjoy my mince pie. Ramming two huge bites into my mouth, I hobble up to the grotto while chewing and brushing crumbs from my elf top. The queue at the ticket booth is snaking around the perimeter of the dolls and action toys section. The rest of the morning is going to be very busy indeed.

Chapter 35

The rest of the morning is horrendous, but I do manage to engage Binky Boo and Annette in short snatches of conversation and ascertain that neither is single (though Binky Boo is apparently up for a bit of mingling, the grubby clown). I still have the possibility of Jez and Eva being single, but first I need to sit down, drink at least three cups of tea and eat something soothing. I opt for fish fingers, chips and beans from the children's menu in the café, which makes me feel nostalgic and comforted. All I need is a glass of banana Nesquik and I may as well be sitting at Gran's kitchen table on a Saturday afternoon.

'Eloise!' My knife and fork clatter down on the plate as I wave my hands above my head. She's making her way towards my table, threading her way through unruly, unsupervised kids with a tray laden with dishes.

'Can't stop.' She doesn't meet my eye as she says this, but then she does have to watch where she's walking as a kid is sprawled across the floor like an upturned starfish, and another has broken free from the play area on one of the tricycles and is squeezing his way through the rows of tables and chairs, crunching the tyres over a spilled pot of crayons and squishing half a sausage into the ground.

I still have twenty minutes of my lunch hour left once I've finished eating so, after a futile search for Eloise, I head to the staffroom and check my emails. There's a message from Franziska with several photos attached. It looks like she's having a brilliant time, and I feel a warm glow as I scroll down to a photo of my neighbour and her old beau on a carousel, heads thrown back with laughter as they bob up and down on their brightly-painted horses.

Switching off my phone, I shove it back in my bag and pull out the Poirot book. I'm determined to finish it over the next few days, because if I do end up dead on the tarmac, I want to, at least, go knowing who killed the nasty old bastard.

'How's the book?'

I hold up a finger, finishing my sentence before I answer Milo. 'Gripping, so shush.'

Milo heads to his locker, fumbling around quietly inside before dragging out the chair opposite mine and plonking himself down. I'm trying to concentrate on the words in front of me but I feel distracted with him there, even though he isn't making a sound. I pretend to read for a bit longer before I slot the old bus ticket I'm using as a bookmark between the pages and put the book back in my bag.

'I've got something for you.' I unzip the pocket inside my bag and take out the little foil package I put in there earlier.

'You brought me weed?' Milo grins at me as I push the little parcel across the table towards him. He unfolds the tinfoil and tips the little chocolate robin into the palm of his hand. 'But robins are your thing. They remind you of your gran.'

I shrug. 'Now they're our thing. Eat it before it melts. It's been in my bag all morning.'

Milo hesitates for a moment before he pops the chocolate in his mouth.

'Advent calendar chocolate is the best.' He licks a tiny speck of melted chocolate from his thumb and I look away. 'I got a reindeer this morning. I'd like to think it was Rudolph, but it's hard to tell when the entire thing is brown. Could have been Dancer for all I know.'

'Or Cupid.'

'Or Donner.'

'We could be here all day going back and forth like this.'

Milo smirks and folds his arms across his chest. 'You can't remember the names of any of the other reindeer, can you?' He tsks and shakes his head. 'Call yourself an elf?'

'Can *you* name all the reindeer?' I mimic Milo's stance and fold my arms across my chest, cocking an eyebrow in challenge. Milo responds by rattling off the rest of Rudolph's pals. I respond by scrunching up the tinfoil into a tiny ball and flicking it at his head. It misses, but Milo still sees it as an act of war and dives at me with poised fingers, ready to tickle me into submission. He's chasing me around the table when Philippa comes to a standstill in the doorway, her eyebrows raised almost up to her hairline.

'This is like a *Benny Hill* sketch.' She crosses the room as we scuttle to a stop. 'Have any of you seen Jez from Binky Boo's Circus whatsit?' She waves her hand as she struggles to recall the actual name of the company. 'I need a word with him about the parade. Apparently, he has stilts skills that I think would go well with our contribution.'

'They won't.'

Philippa gives me a sharp look, and usually I'd shrivel under her glare and retract my statement, but not this time. It was due to those stupid stilts that I failed to dodge the snail-paced Santa Express.

'Does anybody even *like* stilts? I find them a bit creepy. People being so tall and everything.' I look up towards the ceiling and shake my head. 'Giant people are pretty scary, don't you think?'

'No.' Philippa crosses the room again. 'I don't think.' And then she's gone, leaving Milo and I alone. He takes a step towards me, but I put a hand up to stop him in his tracks.

'Don't you dare.'

Milo narrows his eyes. His hands come up to waist level, his fingers splayed and slightly bent. 'I dare.' And then he pounces.

But I'm too quick and I follow in Philippa's footsteps, dashing out of the staffroom and out onto the shop floor where there's no way Milo can attack me with his tickly fingers.

'Coward.' Milo nudges me with his shoulder as we make our way up to the grotto. 'But you'll keep.'

'Is that a threat?' I try to sound cocky, but it's quite difficult when you're on the verge of giggles. I'm somehow still in good humour as we pack up after an overwhelmingly frantic afternoon in the grotto that involved mopping up after a small child's accident, more meltdowns than you could shake a stick at (though why you'd want to is anyone's guess) and a full-on, hair-pulling fight between two of the mums. But Eloise's mood doesn't mirror mine as I catch up with her out in the yard at the back of the shop.

'Eloise, wait.' Snaking past a couple of colleagues, I slip my arm through Eloise's and giggle at the memory of running around the table in the staffroom with Milo in pursuit. I open my mouth to recount our silly antics to my friend but her stony expression tells me she isn't in the mood to hear it. 'Hey, what's up? Bad day in the café? You should have seen it in the grotto. Madness.'

Eloise wriggles her arm free from mine. 'The café was fine.'

'Then what's up?'

Eloise stops, standing aside to let our colleagues pass. She tucks her gloved hands under her armpits and thrusts her chin in the air.

'You were supposed to meet up with me yesterday, during your tea break. I assumed you'd been caught up in the grotto – which is fair enough, obviously – but then I saw you with Milo, coming back from that bakery Kelsey works at. You were carrying one of their paper bags.'

The snowman doughnuts. I ate mine on the bus on the way home yesterday, despite its origins.

And it was delicious.

'Sorry. I completely forgot I said we'd meet up.'

'Thanks. I'm glad I'm so important to you.' Eloise marches off across the rest of the yard but I catch up with her as she slips out of the gate.

'You *are* important to me.'

'But not as important as *cake* or Milo, clearly. What's going on with you two anyway?'

'We're friends.' I'm having to quicken my pace to keep up with Eloise's speedy stomp.

'*We're* friends, and we don't sneak off for cake during our breaks. *We* make do with Maureen's mince pies and a brew in the café. When you remember.'

'We didn't sneak off. We went to see Kelsey. I really think they'd make a good couple but they need a bit of encouragement.' I scuttle forward so I can grab my friend by the shoulders, causing her stomping to pause. 'And I'm sorry about not meeting up with you. I really am. You wanted to talk about Annie, so let's do that now. We can go and grab a warm drink from the market and have a proper chat with no fifteen-minute time limit.'

Eloise shrugs, but she's no longer stomping when she sets off again, and she turns right at the corner of the side street instead of heading left towards the tram stop. We grab a couple of sticky toffee pudding hot chocolates and head for the Christmas tree where there are tables and chairs set up on either side. The chairs are a bit damp, but I don't complain as it's my fault we're out here in the cold instead of chatting in the warmth of the café.

'So. Annie.' I blow on my hot chocolate, creating a crevice in the cream topping. 'Did you meet up with her last night?'

Eloise wraps her hands around her mug and nods. 'Of course I did. I can never say no when it comes to Annie.'

'What happened?' I scrunch up my nose. 'Did she stand you up again?'

'No, she was there.'

'Then why do you look so glum?' The corners of my friend's mouth are turned down and she's hunched over her mug. 'Shouldn't you be skipping around or something? Annie asked you out and *she turned up*. And not only that, she let you meet her workmates. Actual people she knows. That's progress, yes?'

Eloise shrugs. 'I guess. And we did have a fun night. Annie's workmates are really nice. But . . .' She shrugs again. 'Something didn't feel right. I can't put my finger on it, but something felt . . . off. When it was time to go, Annie assumed I'd be going back to her place, but I made up an excuse and said I had terrible period pain and wanted to go home with a hot water bottle. But then the weirdest thing happened this morning.' Eloise inches her chair closer to the table so she can lean in towards me. 'She texted me, saying she hoped I felt better. Which is weird, right?'

'For Annie?' I snort. 'That's downright bizarre. She never does anything nice. She didn't even visit you in hospital when your appendix nearly burst and you had to have it whipped out.'

'And we were in an actual relationship then. She just sent me a message: let me know when you're up and about. That was it. The entire text. No kisses or anything. But now . . .' She reaches into her pocket and pulls out her phone, tapping at the screen before thrusting it outwards to face me. 'She texted me again this afternoon. She wants us to meet up on Christmas Eve to watch the parade together. We can get hot chocolate afterwards, apparently.' She turns her phone back round so she can read directly from the message. '*It'll be romantic*. Annie doesn't *do* romantic. And she doesn't drink anything that isn't coffee and/or laced with alcohol. *Hot chocolate*? Has the girl hit her head or something?'

'Maybe she was visited by three ghosts?' I'm only half-kidding, having been visited by my own dead grandmother and sent back to repeat the month leading up to Christmas.

'The thing is, I *should* be skipping around, but I'm not. I don't feel elated. I don't even feel bad. I'm . . . confused.'

'That's understandable. Like you said, Annie doesn't usually act this way. It *is* odd that she suddenly wants to spend proper, quality time with you. And that's no reflection on you, you absolutely deserve the romance and the attention. But why now?' This didn't happen the first time I lived this December. Annie continued to blank Eloise. She didn't invite her out to meet her workmates and she certainly didn't arrange a romantic Christmas Eve date.

Eloise bites her lip and stares down at her hot chocolate. 'The other night, when I was supposed to be here for the carol concert.' She glances up at the Christmas tree. 'She texted me. It was her usual "want to hang out?" nonsense.' Still holding her mug by its handle, she performs the quotation marks with the two fingers of her free hand. 'But I was . . . busy . . . with Isla. And I ignored it, then totally forgot about it. I've never *not* replied to Annie – I'm usually banging out a response within seconds. So maybe she thinks I've finally had enough of her messing me around and thinks she needs to put more effort in because I'm not going to come running when she clicks her fingers.' She peeps up at me, briefly, before returning her gaze to her mug. 'Do you think that's it?'

'Probably. You know the saying: treat 'em mean, keep 'em keen.'

Eloise grimaces. 'It certainly worked on me.'

'But now the shoe is on the other foot. *You're* the one in control. Annie's making all the effort and it's up to *you* if you go along with it. The snowball's in your court.'

'Snowball?' Eloise looks up, and there's an actual smile twitching at her lips.

'What? It's Christmas.' I take a sip of my drink, making sure there's a thick, foamy moustache left behind. It sends Eloise over the edge, and she giggles while I feign ignorance. 'Seriously, though. You need to think about what *you* want.' Grabbing a tissue from my pocket, I wipe the cream away. 'Because this could be just another game to Annie. A way to reel you back in. This new leaf – this being nice and considerate and acting like an actual

236

human being with feelings – could be a fleeting phase just to get what *she* wants.'

'But what if she finally wants the kind of relationship I want?' Eloise's voice is small as she drops her gaze to her mug again. I think about my watch, about the three hearts still outstanding. It would be so easy to push Eloise towards Annie in the hope that it causes a match. But I don't trust Annie not to hurt my friend again. I can't encourage Eloise to go for it with Annie, no matter what the consequences for myself are.

'What about Isla? You two seemed to have hit it off.' It may not be a Christmas Cupid match, but I can't deny that being with Isla makes Eloise happy, and if it helps to wean her away from Annie's clutches, that's a win for me.

'Isla's great.' Eloise's mouth stretches out into a smile, but it dims almost immediately. 'But it's hard to let go of Annie.'

'Just be careful.' I reach across the table and place my hand over Eloise's. 'Really think about it before you make any decisions. Sometimes history and habit aren't enough to keep a couple together, and even if it does, it doesn't make a happy, healthy relationship.'

Eloise nods. 'You're right. It doesn't.' She smiles sadly at me. 'You're so good at seeing the way forward with other people's relationships, I just wish . . .' She presses her lips together and shakes her head.

'You wish what?'

'Nothing.' Eloise smiles tightly and takes a sip of her drink. 'Doesn't matter.'

'No, go on. Tell me.' I have an uneasy feeling in my stomach, but I push it anyway. I think I need to hear whatever Eloise has to say, even if I won't like it. 'What do you wish?'

'I wish . . .' Eloise meets my eye and sighs. 'I wish you could see how unhappy and unhealthy your own relationship is.'

Chapter 36

I knew, deep down, what was coming, but it's still a punch to the gut to hear it out loud, and I'm still shaken as I trundle home on the bus. We didn't stay much longer after Eloise's declaration that my relationship with Scott is 'unhappy and unhealthy', returning our mugs to the hot chocolate hut almost full, the marshmallows still sitting on top, gloopy and as miserable-looking as we both felt. Eloise had apologised, saying she hadn't meant it, but she couldn't meet my eye and she couldn't stop her hands fidgeting all over the place: in her coat pockets, tucked up into her sleeves, wrapped across her front, fiddling with her handbag.

'My relationship isn't unhappy or unhealthy.' An image had popped into my head as I said this, and I could see myself crying in the shower, face tilted up to the stream of water so it would wash away the tears. And it wasn't even the shower-scene of an alternate post-Terrible Row me. It was about six weeks ago, on 12th November. The three-year anniversary of the day we went on our first date. I'd booked half a day off work so I could cook a nice meal, and I'd set up the breakfast bar with a freshly-ironed table cloth and candles. Soft music was playing, the lights were dim, and the flat was filled with the delicious smell of roasted peppers and garlic while a bottle of wine chilled in the fridge by the time Scott arrived home from work.

But he'd turned up with Dan and a couple of their mates, not even noticing the effort I'd gone to as they slung their jackets over the back of the sofa and slumped in front of the telly to play a newly-released video game. The sound of buttons being hammered and harsh but somehow playful ribbing drowned out the music, and the food I'd spent hours preparing was divided into tiny portions and shovelled down with cans of lager from the mini fridge. A romantic dinner for two became dinner for five plus a row when the others had eventually sloped home. I'd cried tears of frustration in the shower that night, because Scott didn't get why I was annoyed at the intrusion and lack of thought, and the more he told me to 'chill out' the less chilled out I became. And then there was the jibe he'd made about why he'd bought me the fitness tracker for our anniversary, just to get a laugh out of his mates.

But that was one incident, and one row doesn't make a relationship unhappy *or* unhealthy, and Scott apologised profusely when he realised how much his comment about my weight had upset me. Our relationship isn't perfect – which relationship is? – but I've been given this chance to get us back on track and I'm determined to work through this blip.

Still, my stomach is unsettled with nerves as I creep up to the flat, my feet meeting each step with careful precision and my hand gripping the rail so hard my fingers ache. Scott's already home – I can hear the rumble of gunfire from his new games console from out in the hall – and I find myself hovering by the door instead of heading inside.

'Everything okay?' Isla steps out of her flat across the hall, closing her door behind her. 'Forgot your key?' She pulls a sympathetic face, her head tilting to one side. 'Do you want to wait at my place until your boyfriend gets home?' She's already reaching for her key, but I shake my head.

'It's okay. I've got my key.' I pull it out of my pocket and dangle it in the air. Isla's still standing by her lit-up potted Christmas tree so I slot the key into the lock and give it a twist.

'Have you heard from Eloise today?'

I turn, the key still lodged in the keyhole. Isla's fiddling with the loose tendril of hair by her temple and concentrating on an area of the wall to my left.

'It's just that I haven't heard from her. I called her at lunch-time and sent her a couple of messages but she didn't answer. It's nothing urgent, I just wondered . . .' She tails off, switching her weight from one stiletto heel to the next.

'It's been really busy at the shop. Christmas and everything.'

Isla nods, managing a small smile. 'I thought that could be why. Anyway, I'd better . . .' She points at the staircase and starts to move towards it while I turn back to the door. I give it a little push, hesitating before I open it fully. It's as I step over the threshold that I realise I don't want to go inside. I'm *fearful* of going inside. I want to back away, to follow Isla down the stairs and rush outside where I'll be safe from the rows and the atmosphere and the anxiety of putting a foot wrong. I don't know what's going to greet me once I'm in the flat: the attentive boyfriend I see less and less of these days, the grumpy boyfriend who can't seem to find joy in anything, not even Christmas, or the worst option of all – the boyfriend who doesn't seem to notice my presence. I've been trying to hide from the fact that my relationship with Scott *has* been unhappy for a while now, making excuses for our behaviour, brushing it all under the carpet so I can continue on in ignorant bliss because I'm afraid to confront our issues. Afraid of the consequences of lifting up the carpet and exposing the truth of what we've become: a messy, dysfunctional couple. Just like Eloise and Annie. We may not behave in the exact same ways, but our relationships are both broken in one way or another. The question is, can we be fixed?

I slide the door closed gently behind me, as though I'm not really here in the flat yet if I don't make a sound, and ease my coat off and hang it up with the slowest of movements. My feet move stealthily across the hallway carpet and pause in front of the living room door. From within the room, I can hear the increased sounds of gunfire, along with yelling as Scott converses angrily with someone over his headset. My hand is frozen on the door handle. I don't want to add any pressure, to give away my presence, but I can't stay out here in the hallway all night.

'Hey, you.' I breeze into the living room with well-practised good cheer. 'How was work?'

'What are you doing, you knobdonkey?' Scott batters his control pad with his thumbs, growling with frustration. He isn't talking to me. At least I hope he isn't.

'Are you having a brew?' I head into the kitchen, glancing at the oven on my way to the kettle. It's empty and switched off. Of course it is. 'What do you fancy for tea?'

'Er, no I didn't, you little arse-camel.' Scott tears his eyes from the TV screen for the briefest of seconds. 'What was that?'

'What do you fancy for tea?' I open the fridge, but there isn't much on offer in there. 'I think we've got some pies in the freezer. Steak and kidney. Probably some sausages.' I open the freezer to check the contents, but Scott has stopped listening and is back to abusing whoever's listening to him over his headset. Whoever it is on the other end is a 'scroting shitbag', a 'festering ballbag' and a classic 'bellend'. Leaving the kettle to boil, I shut myself in the bedroom and plonk myself on the edge of the bed with my face in my hands.

Is this really what I'm fighting for? A relationship with a man who spends his free time abusing strangers? A man who can't seem to function as an adult? His work clothes are strewn across the bedroom: his trousers are at the foot of the bed, one leg inside out, while his half-unbuttoned shirt is slung across the bed and his tie is snaking across the chest of drawers. I could leave them where they are for Scott to deal with, but what's the point in that? They'd still be there in a month's time if I left them, except they'd have a bunch of other outfits joining them. It's the same with the teabags dumped on the worktop, and the dirty dishes piling up, waiting for me to stack them in the dishwasher. I can't remember the last time Scott set it going and I'm pretty sure he doesn't even know how to work the washing machine.

Scooping up the trousers and shirt, I head back to the kitchen and shove them in the laundry basket to deal with later. I rub the back of my neck to try to relieve the tension while Scott continues to verbally battle with his online companion.

'What do you fancy for tea?' I repeat my earlier question as I grab a couple of mugs from the cupboard, but the only response is the battering of thumbs on the control pad. 'Scott? *Scott.*' When he still doesn't react, despite my increased volume, I march into the living room area, planting myself between him and the TV.

'For fuck's sake, Zo.' Scott leans his whole body across the sofa so he can see past me. 'Shift out of the fucking way! I'm about to die. *Move it.*'

I step aside as my stomach squirms, seemingly attempting to flip itself over. Scott rights himself, his eyes glued to the screen as his thumbs and fingers bash various buttons.

Is that how he usually speaks to me? Because he doesn't seem phased by what just happened. His tone, his language, all seems normal to him. How much have I been kidding myself for these past few weeks? For the past few months, years even?

Is *this* what I'm fighting for?

Snatches of words start to creep out at me, whispering and taunting.

You're a fucking joke, Zo.

Look at the state of you.

Embarrassed to be seen with you.

My fingers find my fringe, which has started to grow out again but is still far too short.

Bag lady. Frumpy. Fucking frigid.

I look across at Scott, who's still bashing away at the control pad. He said those words to me. All of them. It was on this day, 21st December, but before the accident that sent me back to the beginning of the month. The Terrible Row that started over nothing but ended our relationship.

It's no wonder I don't fancy you anymore, looking like that.

No, he fancied Kelsey, with her matching photoshoot-ready ensembles and honey-blonde waves. He must have run straight to her as soon as we broke up. Free at last to pursue the woman he really wanted. And I've wasted the past three weeks trying to please him. Keeping quiet. Being a pushover. Letting him walk all over me, just to keep him.

She's starting to get podgy with all the cake she keeps eating.

I flinch as I remember the words he'd said to his mates on our anniversary, the reason he'd given me the fitness tracker. His mates had roared with laughter while I'd wanted the ground to open up and swallow me whole.

I've been so stupid trying to cling on to him all this time, concentrating on a doomed relationship when I should have been focusing on the Christmas Cupid mission that would save my life. Because time is running out and I still have three couples to match before history repeats itself.

'For fuck's sake.' Scott tosses the control pad onto the sofa and rips off the headset. 'Did you say something about a brew?' He stretches up, his mouth widening grotesquely into a cavernous yawn. 'What's for tea? I'm starving.'

I glare down at him, anger and frustration sitting like a rock in my stomach.

'If you're so hungry, why didn't you put tea on?'

He frowns at me, and when he speaks, his words are slow and careful. 'Because I was finishing my game. Anyway.' He grins at me. 'You know you're a better cook than I am. I burn everything.'

'That's because you don't pay attention. It doesn't take much culinary skill to stick some sausages under the grill.'

Scott holds his hands up. 'All right, calm down. I was only saying.'

My hands are trembling by my sides and my knees feel as though they're made of playdough while the rock of anger and frustration is quickly growing into a boulder.

'I brought us some cakes home, by the way.' Scott nods towards the breakfast bar, where there's a white box with black and grey stripes. 'There's all sorts in there. Cupcakes, doughnuts, vanilla slices, mince pies. They were only going to get chucked, so Kels let me have the lot for a quid. Have a look.' He flips the lid of the box open and something inside *me* flips. *She's starting to get podgy with all the cake she keeps eating.* I don't even realise what I'm doing, but suddenly my hand is swiping at the box, sending it flying from the breakfast bar. A doughnut with chocolate fondant icing and red and green sprinkles tumbles from the box as it flies through the air, plopping down onto the laminate flooring. The box continues on, crashing against the back of the sofa and spilling the rest of its contents onto the floor.

'What are you doing, you mad bitch?' Scott looks down at the doughnut, icing side down near his feet.

'What are *you* doing? Why are you *still* going to that bakery when I've asked you not to?'

I know perfectly well why he's still going to The Bake House, and it has nothing to do with pork and cranberry sausage rolls or Friday treats. It's her. *Kelsey*. And it always has been, probably right from the start.

Chapter 37

It's as though this moment is fixed in time. That no matter what I did or said over the past three weeks, this moment, this row, was destined to happen, whether it was about the coat slung over the back of the sofa, the way Scott has just spoken to me, the cakes from The Bake House or something else. *Anything* else. I certainly don't feel in control as the Terrible Row version two occurs, and I may as well be a spectator, looking on as my mouth runs away with itself. Scott yells, spewing the words I've heard before.

Look at the state of you.

Dan says they'd have cast you in Dumb and Dumber *if Jim Carrey's character had a sister with your fringe like that.*

I'm embarrassed to be seen with you, to be honest. You look like a bag lady most of the time. Why can't you dress like a normal person? It's no wonder I don't fancy you anymore, looking like that.

But this time, instead of curling in on myself and crying as the words rain down on me, I give as good as I get. I rain down my own truths, telling Scott exactly what I think of him. Spilling the words I've kept locked up tight for fear of rocking the boat and capsizing it. I tell him that he's lazy and selfish, that he needs to grow up, and fast, because he isn't a teenager anymore. He's a *thirty-two-year-old man* who can't take care of himself. He can't cook if it doesn't involve a tin of beans and the toaster. He doesn't have a clue how to work the washing machine and I'm not sure he even knows where we keep the vacuum cleaner. It's pretty pathetic, to be honest with you, and there's nothing attractive about a man-child.

And suddenly, I'm no longer a spectator. With a heady rush of adrenaline, I feel like I'm finally *me* again. I'm not Scott's girl-friend. I'm not the girl who couldn't believe this gorgeous man was interested in her, who was so in awe of him she let him trample all over her and take her for granted. I'm Zoey Beake, with her silly fringe and mismatched clothes. She's cute and quirky and I rather like her, thank you very much.

When Scott storms out, I don't collapse into a feeble heap. I don't cry in the shower or dial his number over and over again. I don't leave message after message, hoping he'll get in touch, hoping he'll come home, and I don't feel sick with grief. I feel fired up. Incensed. *Relieved.* I didn't realise until now how small he'd made me feel, but I feel myself straightening, stretching, filling up space again. I bent over backwards to try to make Scott happy, but it wasn't enough. It was *never* going to be enough, and that recognition is liberating.

Fired up and determined to remain in control, I march into the bedroom and pull Scott's suitcase down from on top of the wardrobe. He's going to turn up here tomorrow and pack his things, but for the last time, I'm going to take on his responsi-bilities. Unzipping the case, I start to pile in shirts and trousers, jogging bottoms, hoodies and T-shirts. I dump the entire tie rack in there before piling on underwear and toiletries. Each item that reaches the suitcase makes me feel lighter, and I'm practically walking on air as I drag the games console box out of the bottom of the wardrobe. I could box it up and sell it on, but I find I don't want to. I'll be glad to see the back of it, and I don't want any part of it remaining, even if it's the resale value in cash.

Pulling out the polystyrene blocks, something catches my eye. It's an egg-blue box tied with a white satin ribbon that definitely doesn't belong in here. I shouldn't open it. I should leave it where it is. But obviously I don't.

Nestled in the box is a beautiful necklace with two hearts; one silver and one egg-blue enamel. I pick up the blue heart and turn it over. It has one word engraved on the back that takes my breath away.

Shopgirl.

It's like stepping back in time, to three years ago when we were falling in love. Meeting in the toy shop. Flirting as I helped him to pick out the gift for Sophia's sixth birthday. Meeting again in the bar and hitting it off. The swirling butterflies, the electricity whenever our hands accidentally touched.

You'll always be Shopgirl to me.

It's the final quiz night before Christmas at The Spindles, but I'm not there. I told Milo that I wouldn't be able to make it earlier, but that he and the others should go ahead and take part. *Especially Kelsey.* I was adamant about that part, because there are only a matter of days until my Christmas Cupid deadline and I need that match.

I rushed home as soon as the grotto closed so I could be as prepared as possible for Scott's return. The flat has been tidied, with all traces of last night's cake box fiasco scrubbed away and pushed to the bottom of the bin out the back. I hear the key in the lock at about eight o'clock, and I take deep, even breaths in a bid to remain calm and collected. I've been practicing what I want to say to Scott ever since I found the Shopgirl necklace, rehearsing it over and over in my head as I guided little ones around the North Pole and grotto, but the words are all jumbled up in my head now.

'Oh. You're here.' Scott frowns when he steps into the living room and sees me. 'I thought you'd be at the quiz.'

'I decided to give it a miss. So I could talk to you.'

Scott digs his hands into his pockets. 'I don't think there's much to say, is there? It's over, Zoey.'

I take a deep, shaky breath. This is going to be harder than I thought it was going to be, despite all the practice. 'You're right. I agree.'

'You do?'

I nod, because I don't want to be Shopgirl. She was weak. A pushover. She allowed herself to be treated like dirt. I am worth more than Scott has ever given me, including the necklace because as beautiful as it is, it's just a necklace, engraved with just a word. It won't change the way Scott treats me. The way he sees me. I'm sad that the relationship is over, sad to say goodbye to the happy memories, but it's time to stop looking back at the past and embrace the present. And I'm going to start taking control of my life instead of being a passenger.

'Our relationship isn't working. It hasn't been working for a while.'

Scott looks down at the floor. 'I think I should have left ages ago but I didn't know how to. It felt like a big mistake when we moved in together. It just highlighted how different we are. I thought I'd have more freedom moving out of mum's place, but it feels like I have less. You're always on at me. Do this, do that, pick that up. I just want to *relax* when I get home from work, not be nagged at.'

'I didn't *want* to nag, but we're supposed to be in a grown-up relationship. I shouldn't have to remind you to pick your clothes up and put them in the laundry basket. I shouldn't have to ask you – repeatedly – to fold your towel and put it on the radiator after your shower instead of dumping it on the floor. This isn't how adults function, Scott.'

He snatches his hands from his pockets and spreads them wide. 'Well, now you won't have to put up with my childish ways anymore.' He backs out of the room to head to the bedroom, where his belongings have already been packed into the suitcase and several plastic bags. When he brings the games console box into the living room and starts to pack it all up, I notice the egg blue box isn't nestled within the polystyrene. I briefly wonder what he's going to do with the necklace now, because he can't take it back and get a refund with such a personal engraving, but that isn't my problem to deal with.

'I think that's everything.' Scott's belongings are piled by the living room door. He hasn't taken any of our mementos – the framed photos on the walls or the special magnets from the fridge – but at least the mini fridge is on its way out. I won't miss having to tune out its constant hum while I'm watching TV. 'Dan's waiting downstairs in the car so I'd better go.'

'Is that where you stayed last night? With Dan?'

Scott nods as he hooks the straps of his gym bag over the pull-up handles of his suitcase and rests it on the top. 'I'm going to stay there for a bit, until I get myself sorted out.'

So he wasn't with Kelsey. Not yet.

'Do you need a hand?' I point at the array of carrier bags, but Scott shakes his head and manages to scoop them up into one hand, the bags collecting into one giant bulge.

'Bye then.'

'Goodbye, Scott.'

And then he's gone. Officially. Scott and I are no longer together. I feel sad about the breakdown of our relationship, but I'm okay until my watch buzzes. I'm reaching for a mug from the cupboard, noticing with hazy despondency that Scott has left his favourite Man U mug behind, when my watch notifies me that I've helped create a fourth couple.

Milo and Kelsey, at the quiz. Just as I planned it.

I should be euphoric, but it's been a long day and I can barely muster a smile. I feel a bit numb, to be honest. So much so that I don't even note that I now have just two days to match up the final two couples before it's game over.

Chapter 38

23rd December

Brenda Lee is rockin' around the Christmas tree as I trudge across the kitchen with a couple of slices of bread. I drop them in the toaster and push the lever down before marching towards the radio and jabbing the power button to shut her festive joy down. I'm used to the sounds of Scott getting ready for work – his music playing too loudly while he's in the shower, his grumblings about lost shoes and ties, the way he seemed to slam drawers and wardrobe doors shut – so the flat is too quiet without him and I jump a mile when the toast pops up. I'm not particularly interested in current affairs right now, but I turn the telly on and switch it over to breakfast TV just to have a bit of comforting background noise while I butter my toast. I'm hoping for a bit of bad news – nothing *too* bad, just something non-cheery that will show I'm not the only one feeling glum so close to Christmas. There's an MP being grilled over claims he was participating in an orgy while his third wife-to-be was giving birth to his seventh child (first with her) so that'll have to do. At least my disastrous love life isn't being splashed over the front pages of the newspapers in all its gory details.

I pick at my toast before giving up the notion of a proper breakfast and instead open the last couple of doors of my advent calendar and chomp them without bothering to look what shape it is. Santa, reindeer, elf – who cares?

The cute couple are snuggled up on the bus, his arm pulling her in close while she rests her head on his shoulder. Despite my grumpiness, I can't help hoping that they get their happily ever after. Because somebody ought to, and it isn't going to be me. I really thought I could control my destiny, that I could keep me and Scott together, but willpower isn't enough when both parties don't want the same thing. And with two more matches to make before tomorrow's parade, it looks as though I'm going to be mowed down by that bus as well. Ho, ho, bloody ho.

'Jeez, what have those candy canes done to you?' Milo places his hand over mine as I snatch up another handful of the sweets in the North Pole, ready to dump them in the bucket with satisfying force. 'Since when did we start making peppermint fairy dust to give out to the kids?' He plucks one of the candy canes from the bucket and gives it a wiggle. The only thing keeping it together is the cellophane wrapper, otherwise there'd be a boiled sugar jigsaw on the floor.

'Sorry.' I step away from the bucket of cracked candy canes and place a hand on my forehead as I take in a deep, supposedly calming breath.

'Bad morning?'

I snort. 'Bad life.' Milo raises his eyebrows and I find myself telling him about my break up with Scott. I haven't told anyone yet – not even Eloise.

'Shit, Zoey. Are you okay?' Milo places his hand on my arm. His face is full of concern, and while I've managed to keep it together so far, the display of worry for my well-being is almost enough to tip me over the edge. 'Do you want to go home? I'll tell Philippa I saw you throw up or something.'

'Thanks, but I'd rather be here. I'll only wallow at home.' I smile weakly. 'Just keep me away from the candy canes.'

'That explains why you weren't at the quiz last night. We lost again, by the way. *Last place.* But then we were down four members, so it was only me, Eloise, Isla and Kelsey. Not exactly a *Mastermind*-worthy team.'

'Isla was there?'

'Yeah. Eloise asked her to come.'

Interesting. 'Where was Shannon? And Cliff and Elaine?'

'Shannon couldn't be arsed because there was no chance of us winning the two hundred quid – and that's a direct quote. And Cliff and Elaine *were* at the pub, but they wandered off to the bar after the first round and didn't reappear again until after Eloise found them in the pool room. Speak of the devil.' Milo's hand shoots up and he gives it a wave as Cliff appears through the gap in the Christmas trees. 'Hello there, you dirty dog.'

Dirty dog? I look from Milo's beaming face to Cliff, who's looking down at his shiny black Santa boots.

'What's going on?'

'Nothing.' Cliff peeks up from his boots as he passes, but only to glare at Milo before he dashes into the workshop. I turn to Milo, my arms folding across my chest as I await a more informative answer. Milo can barely contain his glee as he pulls me further away from the workshop.

'Eloise found them.' He nods towards the workshop. 'Cliff and Elaine. In the pool room. *Going at it.*'

My eyes widen. 'They were having sex?'

'Not quite. Eloise says there was some definite heavy petting going on though.'

No wonder my watch pinged. I'm surprised it didn't vibrate itself off my wrist, given the action taking place to activate the match.

But if my watch *did* ping for Cliff and Elaine, making them my fourth match, does that mean nothing happened between Milo and Kelsey?

'You said Kelsey was there last night.' I venture back towards the workshop and take a careful handful of candy canes. 'Did anything happen between the two of you? Not heavy petting – or if that did happen, please keep it to yourself. I'm just about coping with the image of Cliff and Elaine. In fact, no, coping is too strong a word.' I place the candy canes *ever so gently* into the bucket and pluck out the more badly damaged ones from earlier. 'But did you at least kiss?'

'Why would we kiss?' Milo grabs another handful of candy canes to replace the many I'm having to remove due to my mishandling of them.

'I thought you liked her?'

'I do like her, but not like that.' He lifts a shoulder in a shrug. 'She's not my type.'

I give Milo a hard stare. 'Extremely pretty isn't your type?'

'Well, yes, obviously. But I'm more into extremely pretty girls who are more . . . unique. Pretty girls with pointy ears and rosy red cheeks, for example.'

'An elf, you mean?' I glance around the grotto and spot a floor-length red cloak with white trim over by the penguin enclosure. Shannon doesn't wear the traditional red and green get-up, but she does have the silicone ears. When she remembers to put them on. 'Like Shannon?'

'No, not like Shannon, you banana.' Milo smiles fondly at me and shakes his head. 'But speaking of our ill-prepared colleague . . .' He places the last few candy canes in the bucket. 'I'd better go and grab the gingerbread peeps. We're opening in ten.'

'Perhaps he was talking about an extremely pretty girl with pointy ears, rosy red cheeks and a still-a-bit-too-short fringe? I mean you don't get more unique than that.' Eloise smirks as her eyes flick up to my forehead. My elf hat is sitting on the empty seat beside me and I resist the urge to plonk it back on my head to hide the ghastly fringe.

'He wasn't talking about *me*.' I roll my eyes and take a huge bite of my mince pie. The grotto was so busy this morning, we didn't even close for a tea break, so I've just shovelled my lunch down my throat and I'm on my second mug of tea. My feet are throbbing almost as much as my head. The closer we get to Christmas, the louder the kids become. The circus crew are in again today to keep the queuing families entertained but even that's starting to wear thin.

'Of course he was talking about you. Who else is cute *and* quirky around here?'

'He didn't say quirky.'

'Unique, quirky, it's the same thing, and you two have been hanging out a lot lately.' Eloise holds up a hand so she can count the upcoming points on her fingers. 'Hot chocolate at the Christmas market – which is very romantic, by the way. Wreath making, the pub quiz, karaoke. *Sneaking off to the bakery during your breaks.*' She holds five fingers up right in front of my face until I bat them away. 'And weren't you playing kiss-chase up in the staffroom the other day?'

I swallow a big lump of mince pie so I can refute Eloise's claims. 'We weren't playing kiss-chase.' Eloise raises an eyebrow in a that's-not-what-Philippa's-been-saying kind of way. 'And most of those other activities were group things where I was trying to set him up with Kelsey.'

'Hmm.' Eloise lifts her mug of tea, holding eye contact with me for a couple of seconds before she takes a sip.

'You can *hmm* all you like.' I stick my tongue out at her. 'I've just split up with Scott. Now isn't the time to be kiss-chasing somebody else.'

'Isn't it?' Eloise shrugs. 'Seems like the perfect time to me. What better way to get over someone than getting under somebody else?'

The girl has a point, and it isn't as though Scott will be mourning our break up for more than a nanosecond. In two days, he'll be snuggled up with Kelsey.

'Tell me about your ideal man. What qualities does he need to have?'

I don't even need to think about it. I simply describe the opposite of Scott.

'So, you want someone kind and thoughtful, someone who's fun but mature, and somebody who can work a washing machine without supervision.' Eloise holds five fingers up, shoving her hand in my face again until I prod it with my teaspoon. 'That sounds like you're describing a certain elf photographer to me.'

'I have no idea if Milo can work a washing machine.' I stick my tongue out at Eloise. 'Is that what you're doing with Isla? Getting over Annie by getting it on with Isla?' If Eloise notices that I'm shifting the focus from myself onto her, she doesn't show it. She simply sighs and places her mug down on the table.

'No, I don't think it is. I really like Isla. We have fun together and she's *gorgeous*, but then there's still Annie. I don't want to string Isla along – that wouldn't be fair – but I'm not sure I'm ready to give up on Annie either. She still wants us to meet up for the parade, but Isla's asked me out tonight. What do I do?'

'You have to follow your heart.' I smile sadly as Eloise pulls a face at me across the table. 'I know that's a really rubbish, vague answer, but it's true.' I check my watch and yelp. 'Sorry, got to get back up to the grotto. There was already a massive queue when we closed up for lunch. The kids will be going out of their minds, not to mention the parents.' I kiss Eloise on the cheek before I dash across the café, sidestepping an obstacle course of toddlers, stray chicken nuggets and spilled crayons. My watch pings as I reach the doors, and when I check behind me, Eloise is looking down at her phone, her thumb pressed to the screen. She's just sent a message, making the decision that's triggered my matchmaking counter. I want to go and hug my friend but she's already wandering back to the kitchen and I really, really need to get back to the grotto. We'll celebrate later. Big style.

With five couples matched, that just leaves one more to go. This gives me a fresh burst of hope, but with less than twenty-four hours until the parade begins, can I really pull the mission off and survive Christmas?

Chapter 39

Buoyed by Eloise's match, I return to the grotto with renewed vigour; I *will* make that final pairing before the parade tomorrow and avoid death by Santa Express. One more teeny, tiny little couple can't be that hard, can it? And it isn't as though I have to get them snogging – a connection that has the potential to lead somewhere is clearly all that is required to trigger my watch, judging by some of my other successful matches: the couple on the bus only had to chat, the exchange of numbers between Xavier the barman and the wallet guy, and now the text message from Eloise. The queue outside the ticket booth was snaking along the entire perimeter of the dolls and action figures section when I passed on my way back to the grotto, winding its way past the bank of tills and blocking the entryway to the down escalator (which is causing a bit of a stir. Trouble is definitely brewing over there). Very soon, the North Pole will be crammed with kids – and their parents and carers. There has to be at least one potential match in there.

'Do you fancy playing a game?'

Milo is fiddling with the settings on his camera, but he looks up, a smile creeping up onto his face. 'What kind of game?'

'A Cupid kind of game.'

Milo laughs, his eyebrows lowering as he pulls his chin back. 'A what kind of game?'

'Cupid. You know, the dude in a nappy? Bow and arrow or something. Makes people fall in love.'

'I know *who* Cupid is.' Milo rolls his eyes. 'But there's no way I'm stripping down to my undies, even if I am wearing my favourite Squidward boxers.'

Now it's my turn to pull a perplexed face. 'Squidward boxers? What the hell is a squidward?'

'From *SpongeBob SquarePants*. You've watched *SpongeBob*, right?'

'Not avidly, because I'm twenty-five.'

Milo gives me the tucked-in chin look again. 'SpongeBob has been around *forever*. And we have a whole section of SpongeBob merchandise in the shop. It isn't as though I'm admitting to watching *Octonauts* while I eat my Coco Pops before work.' Milo clears his throat and scratches the back of his neck. 'Anyway, Squidward is SpongeBob's grumpy neighbour.'

'And you have him on your underwear?'

Milo grins. 'Yep. It was a Secret Santa gift last year. Squidward's got a Santa hat on and his face is . . .' He clocks the bemused look on my face and clears his throat again. 'Never mind. You were saying something about Cupid?'

'Yes!' My eyes light up at the reminder. 'So, it's Christmas, right? And everybody should be happy at Christmas. And what makes people happy? Apart from Squidward undies?' I nudge Milo, and I'm sure his cheeks start to get even redder under the painted-on rouge circles. 'Love! So let's play Christmas Cupid and try to match up as many couples as we can.'

Milo gives me a skeptical look, but he agrees to the game anyway.

'Hey, Milo?' He's about to disappear into the grotto with his camera when I grab his attention again. 'You can work a washing machine, can't you?'

'Of course. Why?' He looks down at his top. 'Have I spilled something down my front?'

'No, nothing like that. Just checking.'

Milo heads into the grotto and we throw ourselves into the Cupid challenge as soon as the North Pole fills up. It isn't easy – the kids are super hyped-up and the parents and carers are frazzled, plus Milo has to keep dashing off to do his actual job of taking photos in Santa's grotto – but we do our best to start conversations with the grown-ups, somehow ascertaining their relationship status without coming across as creepy predators. My latest singleton is Laura, who's here with her nephew, Joseph. Joseph wants to listen to the giant polar bear sing 'Jingle Bell Rock' but I've just seen Milo subtly giving me the thumbs up from the workshop door, so I guide them towards the cabin and bundle them inside.

'I love this song, don't you?' Milo closes his eyes to appreciate Johnny Mathis urging us to spread the word about Jesus' birth as Laura, Joseph and I approach the end of the queue to see Santa. Usually, the kids can have a wander around the workshop but it's too crammed in here to do anything other than sardine your-self in. 'My favourite Christmas song is Shakin' Stevens' "Merry Christmas Everyone". You can't help but sing along, can you? Hey, Michael.' He claps the bloke next to him on the back. 'What's your favourite Christmas song?'

Michael shrugs. He seemingly couldn't care less, especially as he's sweltering in the seemingly never-ending queue right now, and he's probably praying for the end of everything to do with Christmas.

'Come on, you must have a favourite. What about a favourite Christmas film?'

Michael shrugs again. '*Die Hard*?'

Milo meets my eye for a second, his smile faltering before he brightens again and turns to Laura. 'What about you? What's your favourite Christmas film? Any chance it's *Die Hard* as well?'

'I like *Elf*. *Elf* is funny.' Laura's nephew frowns up at Milo. 'You don't look like Buddy. Buddy has curly hair.' He twirls his index fingers above his head. 'And he has yellow legs. Your legs are red and white.'

Milo looks down at his stripy leggings. Covering his mouth to muffle a gasp, he takes a couple of tiny steps back. 'So they are!'

'I much prefer the stripy look.' Laura lowers her gaze before looking up at Milo coyly.

'But how do you feel about *Die Hard*?' I take a step to the side, so I'm blocking Laura's view of Milo's stripy legs. 'It's Michael's favourite Christmas film.'

Michael had tuned out of the conversation and has been watching the mechanical elves hammering and painting new toys, but the mention of his name focuses his attention again. Not that Laura seems to care.

'It's okay, I guess, but I'm with Joseph on this one.' She tilts her head so she can see past my body-block. 'I'm more into *Elf*. There's something very appealing about a man with pointy ears.'

She's brazen! Here I am trying to set her up with Michael (who, to be fair to Laura, is now gazing up at the tinsel draped across the ceiling and couldn't be less interested in the conversation if he tried) and she's hitting on one of Santa's helpers.

'But what about Bruce Willis in that dirty vest, eh?' I place my hands on my hips, to make my body-block a little bit wider.

'Nah.' Laura scrunches up her nose. 'I'm more into the clean-cut look. Bad boys don't do anything for me.'

'Michael doesn't look like a bad boy to me. No offence.' I put my hands up as Michael tears his eyes away from the tinsel. 'I'm not saying you look weedy or anything. Far from it. You look strong. Have a flex.' I lift up my own arm and bend it to demonstrate. 'Go on, Laura wants to see your guns.'

Michael, quite rightly, turns his back on me. Not that Laura notices. She's too busy salivating over Milo and his pointy ears.

'Aunty Laura?' Joseph tugs on her hand and reaches up on his tiptoes. 'I need a poo.'

I try not to look smug as Laura leads her nephew out of the workshop, looking back for one more glance at Milo's pointy ears before the door closes behind her. Better luck next time, hussy.

'*Milo.*' The grotto's door has opened across the cabin, and Cliff is sticking his head through the gap. 'Can you get back in here and take the photo some time before New Year's Eve?'

Milo flashes me an apologetic look before he heads off to the grotto.

We have a lot of fun attempting to match up singletons in the grotto, but we fail to make any meaningful connections. Mainly because our targets were disgruntled, exhausted and very much at the end of their festive tethers. So I'm feeling down as we tidy up the carnage at the North Pole, sweeping up cellophane wrappers, sticky shards of candy cane, clumps of gingerbread and scattered bits of fake snow. One of the penguins is face down in the enclosure, the giant polar bear is missing his scarf, and the light box welcome sign has been rearranged and now welcomes the children to GATAR'S SNOTTO. I don't know who Gatar is, but the word 'snotto' is hilarious to six-year-olds.

'Cheer up, Zoey. It's Christmas Eve tomorrow.' Jez is packing his balls away (of the juggling variety) but he looks up to offer his calendar update. 'And now it's home time. You should be smiling from pointy ear to pointy ear.'

Acrobat Eva leans down and hisses something at her circus entertainer pal, probably something along the lines of '*she's just been dumped, you idiot*' and Jez pulls the corners of his mouth down in an 'oops, my bad' sort of way.

'You should come out with me tonight.' He zips up his ball bag (again, of the juggling variety) and throws it over his shoulder. 'My mate's invited me to this party with a *free bar*. Come and get rat-arsed. Take your mind off what's-his-face.'

Eva glares at him, but I'm not bothered about the Scott reference. I'm rattled by something else entirely.

'You're going out tonight?'

'Yup.' Jez claps his hands together and rubs them with glee. 'And I'm getting so drunk on free booze, I won't remember my own name in the morning.'

A stomach bug, my arse. The little git! I ended up wobbling around on stilts because of a free bar and Jez's inability to control himself?

'I'd be careful if I were you.'

Jez is already making his way across the North Pole and he turns, walking backwards towards the Gatar's Snotto sign now. 'Don't worry. I have a rape alarm and pepper spray.'

'No, I mean about Philippa.'

This stops him in his tracks and the grin he's been wearing while thinking about the unlimited free booze he's going to throw down his neck starts to fade. 'What do you mean?'

'She's been on the warpath. Says she's sick of people taking advantage of her.'

'In what way?'

I wrestle a Happy Meal box from the branches of one of the Christmas trees and dump it in the rubbish bag at my feet. 'She says she's had enough of people ringing in sick when they've really been out on the lash. She's stamping down on it. Disciplinary action. Sacking people if she has to.'

Jez shrugs. 'She can't sack me. I'm booked through the agency, and tomorrow's my last day anyway.'

'I'm sure I heard her say something about withholding payment for agency staff.'

Eva's eyes widen. 'Can she do that?'

I shrug. 'I wouldn't put it to the test. Would you?'

Eva shakes her head and while Jez doesn't say as much, he looks a bit unnerved.

'See you in the morning.' I turn back to the tree and grab hold of the paper cup wedged between the branches. 'If you can still remember where you work by then.'

Jez smiles, but it isn't the cocksure grin of a couple of minutes ago. He lifts his hand in farewell and turns to slope away through the Christmas trees.

'*We* could go out and get blind drunk if you want?' Milo hefts the bin liner he's just tied over his shoulder like a dirty Santa. Eva and the other circus entertainers have left, along with Shannon, Cliff and the other elves so there's only the two of us in the North Pole. 'A raging hangover would make dealing with a million screaming kids extra fun in the morning.'

'Thanks for the offer, but I'm going to go and see my mum.' I grab my own full bin liner and we start to head towards the Christmas trees.

'No worries. Another time?'

I smile sadly at Milo, because there won't be another time. This time tomorrow, I'll be in the morgue. It's strange, but I'm oddly calm about the prospect of tomorrow's events. I was given another chance and I failed, but I'm going to make the most of the time I have left. I'm going to see my mum for the last time and curl up on her sofa with a hot chocolate while we watch *Love Actually*, just like we've always done on Christmas Eve. Only this time, I won't just be crying for Emma Thompson when she discovers the necklace wasn't meant for her. I'll be crying for myself, and for Mum who'll have to deal with the fallout of the accident tomorrow, and I'll be crying for a life I won't get to experience. I won't get to see my best friend possibly live happily ever after with whoever she texted earlier, or see if the cute couple on the bus continue their shared commute into the New Year, or know whether Franziska and Klaus' relationship will work out this time. And I won't get the chance to get blind drunk with Milo, which sounds like a lot of fun.

Strangely, of all the things I'm going to miss, Scott doesn't appear to be on the list.

Chapter 40

Christmas Eve

I'm up early on Christmas Eve, mainly because my impending death-by-double-decker-bus makes it quite difficult to drop off into blissful slumber, but also because I want to decorate Franziska's tree before I head off to work. It's very important to my neighbour and I don't want to let her down by dying before I've decked out the tree as promised.

The tree arrived yesterday, and Pete's kindly dragged it into the hall and freed it from its netting. It's a beautiful tree; tall and plump with a gorgeous Christmassy scent, and there's just enough room for it to stand in front of the frosted window beside the main door. Franziska's decorations are wrapped in layers of tissue paper in the cardboard box, and I take great care as I unwrap them. There are vintage glass baubles, hand painted figurines and little hearts and snowflakes carved out of wood.

'Since when has your mother had a nut allergy? Because I swear she wolfed down the entire bowl of peanut M&Ms I put out last year. What are we going to feed her tomorrow?'

Miranda is barking into her phone as she pulls her front door shut behind her. She meets my eye for a second before she shoots her gaze up to the ceiling and shakes her head.

'I don't have time to pop into Tesco – you'll have to grab her something before they shut . . . I have to work too! And *she's your mother* . . . I don't know – a bag of mixed leaf salad? What the hell do vegans eat at Christmas other than nut roasts?' She sighs. 'The one I bought is going to go to waste now. Nobody else will eat it, not even Uncle Bernie and he's like a garbage disposal unit. Anyway, I have to go now, but make sure you get her something. I will not have the same kind of drama we had last year with her.' Miranda rolls her eyes as she ends the call and tuts. 'Men. Bloody useless, the lot of them. Oh, God. I'm *so sorry.*' Her eyes widen and she bites her lip as she shoves her phone into her handbag. 'I wasn't thinking. I mean, I was. I was going to ask how you are, and then I go and put my foot in it like the big idiot Pete's always telling me I am.' She tilts her head to one side. 'How *are* you, my darling? Coping okay? Because Pete and I are always here for you. You know that, right? All you have to do is pop down here and we'll crack open a bottle of wine and have a good natter. You're not on your own, okay?'

'Thanks, Miranda.' I carefully hook a delicate angel ornament onto one of the lower branches. 'That's really kind of you.'

'What are you doing for Christmas?' Miranda wrinkles her nose. 'You're not spending it on your own, are you? Because you are *more* than welcome to join us. Lord knows, everyone else is – we've got my mum and dad, Pete's mother, his sister and her brood, and an uncle who can't keep his hands to himself.' She wrinkles her nose again. 'I'm not selling Christmas at the Wolfenden's, am I? It'll be fun, I promise. Once you get used to Bernie's wandering hands and the headache from Kath's four kids running riot has subsided. I'm looking forward to having a full house, really I am, and there's definitely room for one more.'

'That sounds lovely, but I'll be spending the day with my parents.'

This is a great, fat lie. I haven't even told Mum about the break up. We had a lovely evening together last night, and I didn't even cry at the Emma Thompson bit (but only because my bladder chose that moment to insist I vacate the room, and I told Mum not to bother pausing the film). I didn't want to ruin our last few hours together by dropping in the news about Scott moving out of the flat.

'Well, you just let us know if there's anything we can do.' Miranda smiles as she reaches down to give my shoulder a pat. 'See you later.'

'Yeah, see you later.' I smile weakly at my neighbour as she heads out of the building, trying to push out of my mind the thought that this is probably going to be the last time I see her. I may only have a few hours left on Earth, but it's Christmas Eve and I'm going to do my best to squeeze as much out of them as I can.

'Sorry to have to dash like this, but I'll see you tonight, okay?' Isla patters down the stairs, her body twisted so she can call back up towards her flat. She flies across the hallway in her usual whirlwind-like manner, raising her travel mug in greeting as she calls out a merry Christmas to me before sailing through the door. Eloise follows her down the stairs at a much more leisurely pace, smiling fondly at the space Isla occupied a moment ago.

'So you chose Isla then?'

'Yeah, I did.' Eloise's smile widens into a full-on beam as she crouches next to me in front of the tree and gently lifts one of the tissue-wrapped decorations from the box. 'I decided it was time to let go of the past and move on.'

So Eloise and Isla *are* a true love match after all. She just needed to move on from Annie first for it to work out.

'Good decision.' I wish I'd come to that conclusion myself when I found myself transported back to the beginning of the month. I'd have saved myself a lot of wasted effort if I'd realised that what Scott and I had wasn't worth clinging on to. 'I'm glad you're giving things a go with Isla. She seems really nice and you look really, really happy.' If it works out with Eloise and Isla, or even if it simply puts enough distance between Eloise and Annie to allow my best friend to finally move on, then this whole do-over thing will be worth it. I may not have kept hold of who I thought was my own true love but I've connected my best friend with hers. Plus, I've helped to reconnect Franziska and Klaus, found a girlfriend for Santa (surely that should count for double?) and this extra time has given me the chance to find out how wonderful Milo is. He's been a good friend and I'm going to miss him. I'll miss everyone.

'I feel really, really happy.' Eloise beams again, but her joy quickly dims. 'But what about you? How are you after . . . everything?'

By 'everything' she means 'being dumped days before Christmas'.

'I'm okay.' And I am. I'm not doing cartwheels, but I feel a calming acceptance that what's happened with Scott was always supposed to happen. It's time for Scott to move on and for me to . . . well, move on in a whole different way, I guess.

I don't even bother to have a last-minute attempt at playing Cupid in the grotto; anyone who has left taking their kid to see Santa with only a few hours to go until the grotto closes for the season will be far too harassed and panicked to even think about romance, and simply making it through the day in one piece will be their focus.

The grotto is fully equipped staff-wise, with Jez looking a bit worse for wear after his night out but present nonetheless after my little threat of non-payment for no-shows. We close up just before lunch, to give everyone who's taking part in the parade the chance to get ready. Philippa doesn't approach me to take over stilt-walking duties, so Jez must be steadier on his feet than he looks, so I wander down to the café to say goodbye to Eloise.

'Have a great Christmas.' I mentally change 'Christmas' to 'life' as I pull her into a hug.

'I'll see you later. I'm going to Isla's, so we'll pop over for a bit. She said you'd invited her round for Christmas drinks or something?' I had invited her round for drinks but it had never happened, and it never will now. 'I'll even bring cake.'

I smile tightly at my friend, trying my best to force some happiness into my features. Because I won't see Eloise later.

'And I'll give you a wave during the parade. I'll try and get a spot near Boots.'

I hug Eloise once more before I head back upstairs in search of Milo. I'll see him during the parade, but I'd like to say my goodbyes now, in a semi-private setting. I search all over Santa's village, from the Christmas tree maze through to the grotto, up in the staffroom and out in the yard (where Cliff is having a sneaky e-cig break) but there's no sign of him. I return to the North Pole, where Shannon is stuffing the pocket of her cloak with leftover candy canes from the bucket.

'He's gone out.' Shannon helps herself to another handful of candy canes. 'I think he went taking photos or something.'

I turn at the sound of heels clicking on the floor behind the curtain of Christmas trees. Philippa pauses by the light-box welcome sign (which no longer contains the word 'snotto') and beckons us with her hand.

'Come along. We're all about to head off to the parade and the guys need to make a start on dismantling this place.' She's already turning around again before she's finished speaking, her words fading as she disappears behind the Christmas trees. Shannon and I follow and she pulls a face as we pass the gingerbread cottage.

'I'm so glad I'll never have to read those bloody books again.'

'You're not going to come back to the grotto next year?' It has its faults, but I've really enjoyed working in the North Pole, especially this second time around.

'Duh. I won't be working *here* this time next year. I'm going back into construction and outdoor toys on Boxing Day, but then I'm moving on to bigger and better things. There's no way I'm wasting my life working in a toy shop.'

I can't help smiling at that, because although I have little time left, I don't feel as though I've wasted my life working in the toy shop. Quite the opposite, because some of the most important points in my life have happened under this roof: I met Scott here, and although the relationship didn't work out, it formed a significant chunk of my adult life, and C&L's Toys also cemented my friendship with Eloise when I 'rescued' her from the grotty indoor market café.

'What about you? You going back into your old section on Boxing Day?'

I nod, even though I won't be going anywhere on Boxing Day.

'Cliff's going back on security. It'll be weird not seeing him in his red suit and beard. I'm thinking of asking Philippa if I can keep the cape.' Shannon performs a twirl between the Christmas trees. 'What's Milo doing after Christmas?'

Milo's a seasonal worker at C&L's, only contracted to work in the grotto and take part in the parade. 'He's got some admin temp work set up in the new year.' So I wouldn't be seeing Milo every day whether I completed my mission or not, which makes me feel glum. Spotting the robin on the bird Christmas tree, I reach out and unclip it, slipping it into my pocket, my fingers folding gently around its soft feathers. We emerge from Santa's village and join the others outside C&L's. Dominic's operating his giant ringmaster puppet and Jez is hopping about on his stilts, which I think is showing off a bit, while Eva's stretching to warm up in preparation for her acrobatics along the parade route. I take one last look at the toy shop; it looks magnificent with its opulent window displays and sparkly garlands. I'm really going to miss this place.

'Right then.' Philippa claps her hands together. 'Let's go.'

The managing director leads the way to the back of the town hall, and my stomach lurches as we pass the Santa Express. I'm not wearing the stilts this time, but I have a niggly feeling that I wouldn't be able to outrun the Santa Express even if I had Usain Bolt's legs attached to my body. My fate, I know, has been sealed.

Craning my neck, I try to spot Milo but I can't see him anywhere. I need to find him. There are only a few minutes until the parade begins. *He should be here.* Panic is making my breaths come out in rapid little bursts, creating a chain of wispy clouds chugging from my mouth in the cold, like a cartoon steam train. Where is he? I need to say goodbye. To say thank you, because he brought back the fun and the magic of Christmas. I need to tell him how much I enjoyed the Agatha Christie novel, which is waiting in my locker for him to take home, and to tell him that after careful consideration, I've changed my mind about the sticky toffee pudding hot chocolate being my favourite. It's still a close second, but the raspberry ripple has edged its way into pole position. And I wanted to give him the little robin decoration, as a memento of our time in the grotto. A memento of me.

Where is he?

Jez is juggling with five balls while somehow staying upright on the stilts, Shannon's flirting with a bloke in a penguin costume, and Eva looks as though she's trying to transform her body into a pretzel, but where is Milo? Somewhere far ahead, the rumble of drums starts up. The parade is starting without Milo. I need to find him *now* because I can't meet my demise without saying goodbye.

Chapter 41

I take off. I don't even think about it. The parade, the Santa Express, Philippa's face if she saw me running in the opposite direction . . . none of it matters. I need to see Milo one last time. To look at his lovely face and see his eyes light up as he smiles at me. I need to take his hand in mine, to thread my fingers through his and pretend that this isn't our final moment together because I can't actually bear the thought of not being around him anymore. To never hear his laugh again. To never walk through the magical Christmas market with hot chocolates in hand. To never kiss him, because I've never wanted anything more than I want to kiss Milo right now.

I've been such a fool. I was given a second chance at life, and I didn't take it with both hands. I hankered after an old, battered life, one that should have been left behind, and wasted the opportunity to be truly happy. Just like Scott and Kelsey look right now.

I stop in my tracks, watching as the pair wander towards the crush of the parade crowd. They're so interested in each other they haven't even noticed me gawping at them. Scott's shaved off his afro and while he no longer looks like my Scott, the close-cropped look suits him. As always, Kelsey looks as though she's stepped out of the pages of a fashion magazine in her winter wonderland get-up of white puffy jacket, baby-pink bobble hat with matching mittens and super-thick scarf. She's wearing black leggings with a Bake House apron just visible beneath the jacket, and she's playing with something sitting on top of the super-thick scarf. It's when I see a flash of egg blue that I realise what it is.

The necklace.

It wasn't even meant for me. I am Emma Thompson in *Love Actually*, except I don't want to cry. I want to throw my head back and laugh and laugh until my stomach aches. *Shopgirl*. But C&L's Toys is the wrong shop and I'm the wrong girl. Hope blooms as I realise this could count as my sixth and final, and more importantly, *life-saving* couple. I check my watch. Nothing. But then it dawns on me that this isn't a new relationship. That necklace was always meant for Kelsey, even when we were together. I have no idea how long it's been going on – months, I should imagine – and it's now clear Scott wasn't spending time with *me* this December. He was spending time with *her*. The karaoke, the escape room, the Carols by Candlelight – Kelsey was at them all. Was it damage control, perhaps, making sure she didn't spill the beans about them? Or was he jealous about my matchmaking efforts and was making sure I had the wrong end of the stick about her and Milo? Who knows? What I do know is that I'm *thankful* that the necklace isn't for me and I feel a bit sorry for Kelsey. She thinks she's the luckiest woman in the world right now, but does she realise her boyfriend couldn't even be bothered to come up with an original nickname for her? And who knows how many Shopgirls there were before me? I could warn her about what a terrible boyfriend he is, but nah. *Tag, you're it*. She wanted him when he was mine – she's welcome to him.

They disappear into the crowds, heading towards the McDonalds, and I feel a peacefulness wash over me. A little part of me still believed that I could have done more, that I could have worked harder to put our relationship back on track, but I'm *relieved* that my determination wasn't enough, that I'm no longer shackled to an idealised version of Scott, even if I am only free for a few more minutes before I have to leave.

I turn and sprint, my head too full of joy and Milo to realise my feet are pounding on the road rather than the pavement, that I'm slap-bang in the middle of the metal grooves that are bringing a tram my way. When I do see the tram, the momentum of my feet propels me closer, and even when I manage to control my feet, they simply stop, freezing on the spot. It seems to take forever for the tram to approach, as though time has slowed down to a trickle, forcing me to stand there and think about what is about to happen. I know it's going to hit me but I can't seem to do anything to prevent it. My feet are too heavy, as though they've been concreted to the ground, and my mouth is glued shut so I can't even scream in terror as the yellow and silver vehicle advances. The screen is displaying the tram's destination but with a flicker, 'Piccadilly' disappears and is replaced with three words that make my stomach lurch.

The Santa Express.

Different mode of transport, same gruesome outcome.

I close my eyes, because I don't want to see the moment of impact as well as feel it, but an image flashes into my mind that makes my stomach lurch again. I'm a little girl, clutching hold of Mum's hand, my little legs trying to keep up with her longer strides. We're Christmas shopping in the city centre, making our way from The Arndale to the bus stop, and there's a crowd ahead. A woman has been hit by a tram, people are murmuring, and as we pass the densest part of the gathering, I spot a woman's legs on the ground. One shoe is still on her foot while the other is missing, the slip-on shoe presumably knocked off during the collision. Mum drags me away ('You don't want to look over there, sweetie') but all I can see now, as I squeeze my eyes shut, is that poor woman's legs. I open my eyes and look down at my own legs, clad in stripy red-and-white leggings. If I end up underneath the tram, I'll resemble the Wicked Witch of the East, except I'll have green, curly-toed shoes instead of magical ruby-red slippers on my feet.

The tram is still looming towards me. If the driver's seen me, he won't have time to stop. I'm a goner. I close my eyes again, because even the image of the woman's legs and the lost shoe is better than watching the insanely slow approach of death. I reach into my pocket and feel the comfort of the little robin's soft feathers. I hope Gran will be there to greet me again, because I don't want to do this alone.

There's a long, stomach-churning screech. At first I think it's coming from me, a scream of terror building from the very depths of my soul, but my mouth still won't open even a crack. The screech must be the sound of brakes applied far too late to save me. I can feel the vibration of the tram's approach in my concreted-down feet, its rumble travelling up my legs and into my stomach, making me feel queasy and unbalanced. There's a *whoosh*! of air as I'm knocked off my feet, but I don't feel any pain until I hit the ground, landing on my right hip with a thud. I hear an *oof*! that can't have come from me because my mouth is still clamped shut, but I'm too dazed to really give it much thought. The ground shifts beneath me as the still-screeching tram sails past, and I remember the sand-like floor after the first Santa Express accident.

'Ow. I think I broke an arse cheek.'

The ground shifts again, except it isn't the ground at all. It's another body, which I'm half-sprawled across.

'Are you okay?'

I twist my body. The movement hurts, but it's worth it when I see Milo trying to prop himself up with one hand while checking his arse cheek for damage with the other.

'I think so.' My mouth opened! I can speak again! 'Are you?'

'I think so.' Milo shuffles so he's in a sitting position, helping me to sit up too. 'What were you doing, standing there in front of that tram?'

'I don't know.' I reach for the back of my head, but it's perfectly fine. There was no impact with the tarmac this time. 'I just froze.'

'Shock, probably.' Milo pushes himself up to his feet and reaches out a hand to help me up. 'Are you sure you're okay?'

I nod as I watch the tram, now travelling at normal speed, disappear around the bend of the road.

'I was looking for you. I wanted to give you this before the parade.' I pull the little robin out of my pocket and hand it to a bemused-looking Milo.

'You nicked it?'

I shrug. 'I like to think I liberated it.'

I look at Milo. He looks back at me. I'm totally confused about what happened just now. I was supposed to end up under that tram. I failed my mission to match up six couples. Is a Santa-driven double decker bus about to come roaring around the corner and pick me off?

Milo runs his thumb over the little bird's soft feathers and smiles at me, his eyes lighting up. 'Thank you.'

'No. Thank *you*. For saving me.' I take a step towards Milo, reaching for his hand and threading my fingers through his. There's a pause in time, just like when the tram was heading my way, except this time it's filled with anticipation rather than dread. And then Milo stoops down, his head tilting so his lips can meet mine, and I reach up on tiptoe, too eager to wait a millisecond longer. It all makes sense now. Milo. The tram. Me still being alive and kicking. My watch pings as we kiss but I don't need to look at the display to know that I'm being notified of match number six. It was here all along, right under my nose, but I was too wrapped up in trying to mend my shattered relationship with Scott to see it. But I see it now, clear as day. It's time to forget about the past and move on. And now, thanks to that last-minute match, I can do just that.

Chapter 42

Christmas Day

Franziska's tree looks glorious as I let myself into the building, the multicoloured lights bright and cheery as they bounce off the glass surfaces of the baubles and figurines. I turn to wave at the taxi driver as he pulls away before closing the door against the biting cold of the night air. He was a nice bloke, the taxi driver. Jolly, you might describe him as, with his Santa hat and festive music, and his stream of increasingly bad cracker jokes. And the more terrible the gag, the more he chortled, which was infectious and I found myself belly laughing at the worst jokes ever created.

Surprisingly, it's turned out to be a good Christmas. Great, in fact. Magnificent if you think about the fact I should be in the morgue right now. I spent the day with Mum and Dad, and I worked my way through a giant tub of Quality Street until I felt like puking while watching Christmas telly on the sofa. I told Mum about Scott, and about Milo, and how much I was looking forward to seeing what the future held. Mum squeezed me tight and told me I was the bravest person she knew.

I take a photo of the tree to send to Franziska. I sent her one yesterday, once Eloise and I had finished decorating it, but it wasn't

276

lit up in all its splendour then. I send the photo as I head up the stairs to the flat. It feels odd as I step over the threshold, but it isn't a bad sensation. Perhaps it's the missing knot of apprehension as I hang up my coat that feels strange. The lack of dread of not knowing what is about to happen when I step into the living room. Another argument? An evening of feeling alone despite my boyfriend sitting there on the sofa, talking to strangers through his headpiece but not to me? I don't have that anxiety anymore. It's just me, in my own space, and it feels freeing rather than scary.

After switching on the lamps in the living room and putting on some festive music (the taxi driver has really put me in the mood) I light some spiced apple and cinnamon candles to really up the Christmassy atmosphere. I don't have much in the way of nibbles, but I pour some crisps and nuts into bowls and set them out on the breakfast bar. It isn't sophisticated, but it will have to do. My phone rings while I'm searching the cupboard for the box of Ritz crackers I'm sure I bought during the last big shop.

'Hey, you.' I close the cupboard I've just ransacked and move on to the next. 'How's your first Christmas in Germany for fifty years going?'

'Hectic, but so lovely. Klaus' children and their families spent the day over here – even Beatrice, who's over from Switzerland for a few days. I miss my lot, obviously, but it's been so nice being looked after. Klaus won't let me lift a finger, and Beatrice is even worse! She wouldn't even let me wash the dishes after lunch. I thought they might find my visit intrusive, but they've all been very welcoming.'

'And how is everything going with Klaus?' I ask the question delicately, even though I'm after all the goss.

'Good, I think.' There's a hint of bashfulness in my neighbour's voice, which is at odds with her usual forthright manner. 'He's thinking about coming over to England for a little holiday in a few weeks. I've told him there are far better places to holiday than England in winter, but he insists.'

'I think he's more interested in seeing you than sitting by a pool.'

'Do you think?'

I shake my head as I laugh to myself. 'Of course. What else would attract him to rainy Manchester in January?'

There's a pause, and I take the opportunity to have a good rummage in the cupboard. 'I guess you're right.'

'I'm definitely right.' A-ha! I *knew* I'd bought some crackers. They've already been opened, but I take a bite of one and it's still crunchy enough.

'How's your Christmas going? Did Scott get you the bracelet you were dropping massive hints about?'

'No, but then we broke up a few days ago.'

'You did? Oh, my poor girl. Are you okay?'

Grabbing a small plate, I set it down on the breakfast bar and shake the crackers out onto it. 'I'm fine. Better than fine. Happy.'

'Good.' Franziska tuts. 'I never did like that boy.'

I pause my box-shaking. 'Didn't you?'

'Not one bit. Reminded me of my useless son-in-law. How can you respect a man who cannot wash his own underpants? Working a washing machine is hardly rocket science, yet these un-house-trained fools act as though doing the laundry is beyond them.'

'You never said anything.' I shake out the last of the crackers and push the plate so it's sitting next to the bowl of crisps.

'It wasn't my place. Just like it isn't my place to tell my Aggie she married an idiot.'

'You don't mince your words, do you?'

'Sorry.' Franziska giggles girlishly. 'I think I've overdone it on the gluhwein. Klaus' son Arnold made it and it's lethal.' She giggles again. 'Anyway, I'd better get going. Beatrice is about to leave and I want to say goodnight. Thank you so much for taking care of the tree. Merry Christmas, my dear.'

'Merry Christmas, Franziska. Enjoy the rest of your trip.'

The doorbell rings as I end the call, and I can hear Miranda and Pete bickering as I make my way down the hallway.

'I'm not saying she *pretended* to be vegan just to be a pain in the arse, but I am miffed that I went out of my way to make that god-awful looking cranberry and lentil bake, only to find her with her head in the fridge afterwards, stuffing leftover turkey into her gob!'

'You're right. She *is* a pain in the arse. But thank God I have you here with me to help me get through the day with her. I love you.'

'I love you too, you great big dope.'

Miranda and Pete have gone from sniping to snogging on the doorstep by the time I open the door.

'Merry Christmas, my darling!' Miranda has torn her lips away from her husband's and is thrusting a bottle of wine at me. 'Thanks for having us over. We've managed to survive the day – just about – and shoved everybody in a taxi home. Let the festivities begin!' She heads into the living room, turning up Jona Lewie and singing along while Pete hands me another bottle of wine and a platter filled with aubergine and chickpea bites, pecan-stuffed dates, cauliflower fritters and a curried cashew dip.

'All the vegan stuff my mother-in-law didn't touch.' Miranda rolls her eyes as I place the platter down alongside the other snacks on the breakfast bar. 'Not that I can blame her. Feel free to chuck it in the bin.'

The doorbell rings again, and this time it's Eloise and Isla, bringing with them a bottle of fizz and a box of Ferrero Rocher.

'The Ferrero Rocher are from Rosemary.' Eloise kisses me on the cheek as she passes. 'She insisted I bring them over. She's got a house full of chocolate, apparently, and if she's left unattended with it all, she'll eat the lot and have to be hoisted out through a window.'

'You're lucky. The only thing I came home with after spending the day with my family is a headache.' Isla rolls her eyes, but she's smiling fondly.

'Wiz zees Ferrero Rocher you are veally spoiling us.' Pete adopts a horrendously bad French accent as he spies the chocolates, which earns him a jab in the ribs from his wife.

279

'Help yourself.' I hand the box over while I take care of the drinks, making sure everyone has a glass in hand. With the chocolates and the platter of vegan canapés, the breakfast bar offerings don't look quite so meagre (and the cauliflower fritters dunked in the curried cashew dip are delicious). With drinks in hand, we start to share Christmas Day horror stories:

'My stepsister brought her new boyfriend round and he hit on my other sister while she was checking on the veg. He nearly ended up with a pan-full of sprouts crashing down on his head. Danielle was *mortified* and dumped him then and there. She'd have decked him if Rosemary hadn't bundled him out of the house before she got to him.'

'My twelve-year-old nephew sneaked off for a root around our bedroom and found a pair of fluffy handcuffs and a leather whip in the bedside drawer.' Miranda slaps her thigh with laughter while Pete looks as though he'd quite like to jump out of the window. 'He was mortified – and probably scarred for life – but it serves him right, the nosy little bugger.'

Isla's recounting a story of how drunk her grandfather had got, resulting in a slanging match between him and Isla's uncle, when the doorbell rings again. I can't help grinning when I see Milo on the doorstep, even if he is wearing the most hideous festive jumper under the coat he's just unzipped. Now, I like an ugly sweater at Christmas, but this is next level ugly, with tinsel, pompoms, jingly bells *and* sticky-out carrot snowmen noses that resemble an eighties Madonna get-up.

'What the . . .' I shake my head as I take it all in. 'Let me guess: you and your housemates have a competition to see who can find the tackiest Christmas jumper.'

Milo spreads his arms wide. 'I won, third year in a row.'

'What did your mum think when you turned up looking like that for Christmas dinner?'

Milo pulls his chin back and scoffs. 'She thought I looked adorable, obviously.'

'She was right.' I reach up on tiptoe to kiss him on the cheek. 'I guess.' I try to jump out of the way of Milo's wriggling fingers, but I'm not quick enough and I'm squealing for mercy as we stumble into the living room. He already knows Eloise and Isla, but I introduce Milo to Miranda, who offers him the vegan canapé platter, and Pete, who holds out the box of Ferrero Rocher on the palm of his hand and adopts the cheesy French accent again.

'I am veally spoiling you wiz these Ferrero Rocher.'

The chocolates almost topple off his hand after he receives a poke and death glare from Miranda, and he promises not to do it again.

'We were sharing Christmas dinner war stories.' Eloise pats the space beside her on the sofa. 'Come and tell us yours.'

So we sit and share some more tales, laughing and cringing in equal measure. I see Isla's gaze following Eloise as she gets up for a top-up, and it makes me feel all fuzzy inside. I helped to create this brand new, hopefully happy-ever-after, relationship, and I can't help wondering about how the others are getting on: Steffi-Jayne and Owain from the bus, barman Xavier and the wallet guy, Cliff and Elaine. I hope they're as happy as Eloise and Isla look right now, as happy as Franziska sounds with Klaus. As happy as I feel as Milo slips his hand into mine and presses my fingers to his lips as we listen to Miranda's tales of Uncle Bernie's wandering hands.

'I have a little gift for you.'

It's after midnight and the others have stumbled back to their flats, leaving Milo and I with the dying candles and the almost mute Christmas songs. I reach under the Christmas tree and slide out the wrapped parcel.

'I've got a little gift for you too.' Milo heads out into the hallway, returning with a tiny parcel in the palm of his hand. We exchange the gifts and tear at the paper.

'It's a book.' Milo meets my eyes and laughs as he holds up the copy of *Hercule Poirot's Christmas*. 'It's *my* book.'

'I know, but it's all I had to give you.' After I almost collided with the tram yesterday, we brushed ourselves off and joined the parade. By the time it had finished, the shops were crammed with desperate last-second shoppers and my hip was throbbing where I'd landed on the road. Home was the only place I wanted to be.

'Sorry.'

'Don't be.' Milo nods at the half-unwrapped gift in my hand. 'It makes me feel less guilty about yours.'

Guilty? I pull the rest of the paper away, leaving me with the robin ornament from the Christmas tree at the grotto.

'I thought it should go on your tree. To remind you of your gran.' Milo takes the little robin from where it's sitting on the palm of my hand and clips it onto one of the branches of my Christmas tree. 'Sorry it isn't a real Christmas present.'

'Are you kidding?' I join Milo at the Christmas tree and slide my fingers through his, pulling him close. 'It's the most thoughtful gift anybody has ever given me.'

I thought this Christmas was going to be terrible and lonely at best, but it's turned out to be the most wonderful Christmastime, full of joy and laughter and love, and I'm looking forward to what the future will bring.

A Letter from Jennifer Joyce

Thank you so much for choosing to read *The Christmas Cupid*. I hope you enjoyed it! If you did and would like to be the first to know about my new releases, you can follow me on Twitter, Facebook and Instagram, visit my blog or subscribe to my newsletter below.

I have a child-like connection to Christmas, so I wanted to write a book that was jam-packed with festive joy and a sprinkling of magic, so what better setting than a Santa's grotto? The town where I live has an annual reindeer parade, which was the starting point of the book (though to my knowledge, nobody has ever been run over by a Santa-driven double decker bus) and I wanted to capture the enchantment as families gather to watch the characters and performers. I hope I've managed to deliver the delight and wonder of the season.

I hope you loved *The Christmas Cupid* and if you did, I would be so grateful if you would leave a review. I always love to hear what readers thought, and it helps new readers discover my books too.

Thanks,
Jennifer

Blog: www.jenniferjoycewrites.co.uk
Twitter: www.twitter.com/writer_jenn
Facebook: www.facebook.com/jenniferjoycewrites
Instagram: www.instagram.com/writer_jenn
Newsletter: https://mailchi.mp/310b4ee4365f/jenniferjoycenews-letter

The Accidental Life Swap

Sometimes one moment can change your life forever . . .

Rebecca Riley has always been a bit of a pushover.
When her glamorous boss, Vanessa, asks her to jump,
she doesn't just ask how high . . . she asks if her boss
would like her to grab a coffee on the way back down!

So whilst overseeing the renovation of Vanessa's
beautiful countryside home, the last thing Rebecca
ever expected was to be mistaken for her boss – or that
she would even consider going along with it! Far away from
the bustling city and her boss's demanding ways, could she
pretend to be Vanessa and swap lives, just for a little while?

The Single Mums' Picnic Club

Katie thought she had the perfect family life by the sea – until her husband left her for another woman, abandoning her and their two children! She knows it's finally time to move on but she's unsure where to begin . . .

Frankie is shocked when gorgeous dog-walker Alex asks her on a date! As a single mum with her own business, she struggles to put herself first, but maybe she's ready to follow her heart?

George is used to raising her son on her own – but now he's at nursery, her life feels empty. So when she meets Katie and Frankie at the beach, she realises that her talent for rustling up delicious picnics could be the perfect distraction!

But of course, life isn't always a beach and as secrets begin to surface the three women's lives are about to be turned upside-down . . .

A cosy and charming romance set at the English seaside, perfect for fans of Trisha Ashley and Caroline Roberts.

The Wedding That Changed Everything

Love happens when you least expect it . . .

Emily Atkinson stopped believing in fairy tales a long time ago! She's fed up of dating frogs in order to find her very own Prince Charming and is giving up on men entirely . . .

But then she's invited to the wedding of the year at the enchanting Durban Castle and realises that perhaps bumping into a real-life knight in shining armour isn't quite as far away as she thought!

Will Emily survive the wedding and walk away an unscathed singleton – or finally find her own happily-ever-after?

A cosy and charming romance, perfect for fans of Trisha Ashley and Caroline Roberts.

Acknowledgements

A massive thank you to my editor, Abi Fenton and the team at HQ. I loved writing Zoey's story and I'm so happy it's going to be an actual book that people can read. This is my thirteenth book to be published but it feels as magical as the first.

Thank you to the Oldham Nanowrimo group, especially Jacqueline Ward for organising all our meetings and write-ins. I wrote most of *The Christmas Cupid* during Nanowrimo 2020, when we couldn't meet up in person, so I really appreciated every single Zoom call we had. The encouragement and inspiration was brilliant, as was seeing real people, mask-free, even if it was on a screen.

Thank you to my family, for all your support. Special thanks to my mum and, as always, to my daughters Rianne and Isobel who have listened – without much complaint – to Christmas music when it was not Christmas. Not even close. Another special thank you to Luna, my writing companion pup.

When I was plotting *The Christmas Cupid*, I gave my newsletter subscribers the chance to have their name used in the book, so an extra-special thanks to Stephanie-Jayne for lending her name.

Finally, thank you to you, the reader. For choosing *The Christmas Cupid*. I hope you enjoy Zoey's story.

Dear Reader,

We hope you enjoyed reading this book. If you did, we'd be so appreciative if you left a review. It really helps us and the author to bring more books like this to you.

Here at HQ Digital, we are dedicated to publishing fiction that will keep you turning the pages into the early hours. Don't want to miss a thing? To find out more about our books, promotions, discover exclusive content and enter competitions you can keep in touch in the following ways:

JOIN OUR COMMUNITY:

Sign up to our new email newsletter:
http://smarturl.it/SignUpHQ

Read our new blog: www.hqstories.co.uk

https://twitter.com/HQStories

www.facebook.com/HQStories

BUDDING WRITER?

We're also looking for authors to join the HQ Digital family!
Find out more here:

https://www.hqstories.co.uk/want-to-write-for-us/

Thanks for reading, from the HQ Digital team